Extraordinary

Rendition

Salman Shami

To Nazir, my father, a humble man of high principles. His gentle manner and good humour endeared him to all whose lives he touched. He taught me to think critically and search for the truth.

I would like to thank everyone who gave so much of their time and love to make this book possible. A special thanks to,

> Aliya, my wife and best friend who put up with my late nights and cantankerous moods and whose meticulous and painstaking editing turned a sow's ear into something resembling a silk purse.

> My good friends Graeme Cameron and Gilly Pogson who, in going over and above the call of duty as beta readers, pushed me to a higher standard of writing.

> My good friend Jamil Khalid Khateeb for his inspirational cover design.

> My mentor and fellow writer Kerry Hall whose critique and seal of approval gave me the confidence to push the publish button.

Above all I want to thank my readers whose love and enthusiastic support inspired me to burn the midnight oil and to write and rewrite till my fingers were sore.

For more information:
http:/salmanshami.com
https://www.facebook.com/SalmanShamiBooks

Please check out the glossary at the end of the book for an explanation of the Urdu, Malay and Afghani words.

7

October

2001

26 days after

The September 11 attacks on the NYC Trade
Centre

THE WAR WIDOW

Kandahar, Afghanistan, 10:04 pm

The smell of burning chemicals and concrete dust assailed her sinuses. Wafaa tried to swallow but couldn't. Her mouth was dry. Her tongue was a sandpaper balloon at the back of her throat. Every breath was harder than the last.

A strong foreboding of disaster roiled her stomach. She and Faysal were going to die. Somewhere close, an explosion convulsed the night, resonating her chest cavity. Her heart fluttered like a bird caught in a net as the accompanying shock wave rained debris on their vehicles.

Kandahar was under attack. The US Airforce were systematically pulverising the city into submission. The Taliban were on the run. The aerial bombardment mimicked the sheet lightning and rolling thunder of a dry storm that drew closer every minute. Every flash silhouetted the surrounding buildings in sharp relief and cascaded shadows along the narrow street.

Why were they not moving? Wafaa moved her veil and peered into the dark. The street lights were off. Black cloth covered all windows. Apart from the bombing the only illumination came from the thin crescent moon. Groups of men stood around the vehicles talking in muted tones. Like her, they were waiting for the order to move out.

A commotion near the entrance of a large house caught her eye. A cluster of men emerged, surrounding a tall man in a white turban. As they rushed towards the convoy, engines sprang into life. Thank Allah, they were finally leaving.

The tall man in the turban climbed into a Pajero two cars in front. 'That is the *Amir-ul-Momineen*,' Faysal whispered in awestruck tones. The *Amir-ul-Momineen* was the supreme leader of the Taliban, the reclusive Mullah Omar.

Wafaa was pressed back into her seat as they took off. An

audible breath of relief escaped her lips as she leaned against Faysal in the dark. Apart from the driver they were alone in their Landcruiser. Wafaa's relief was short lived. After only twenty metres the convoy came to a halt. What was it now?

Ahead, Mullah Omar and his bodyguards alighted from his brown Mitsubishi Pajero. They rushed back into the house they had come from, followed by a posse of men.

'Faysal, why have we stopped?' Wafaa whispered from behind her niqab. She was frantic with worry.

Faysal said nothing. He lowered the window and looked out.

'Wait here, I shall check.' His voice was calm as always.

'Do not leave me long.' Her words caught in her throat. Sometimes her husband was too calm.

Faysal opened the door and stepped into the night. 'You must not worry wife, we are always in the hands of Allah.'

The open door let in a gust of frigid air and the burning smell that aggravated her upset stomach. While the sun shone it was almost balmy, but at night the cold was vicious. She was glad she had packed a warm jacket. They had left hot Jeddah two weeks ago and she hadn't yet acclimatised to the Afghani winter.

Faysal closed the door with care and sauntered over to Mullah Omar's Pajero. Wafaa's veil made it harder for her to see. Not wanting to lose sight of him, she moved the flap sideways.

Mullah Omar's driver had stayed behind. The smoke from the brown Pajero's tailpipe meant the engine was still running. Allah willing, the Mullah would return soon. The driver extended both his arms out of his window and shook Faysal's hands. It was a gesture of camaraderie and an example of the warmth shown to all who had answered Bin Laden's call for jihad in Afghanistan. Faysal said something to the driver. His response made Faysal put his head back and laugh.

In the distance a motorcycle engine revved. It took Wafaa several moments to realise why it sounded wrong. It was above them, in the sky. She dropped her head to look out of the windscreen. Ice-cold fingers of fear stabbed her. Her mind was a huge ball of cotton; her thoughts were distant and disconnected. The sound's true significance overwhelmed her with a forlorn horror.

She still saw nothing as the revving motorcycle engine became the hum of a crazed sewing machine. The humming ended in freakish clicks like someone had stuck a screwdriver into the sewing machine wheel.

A rent of metal tore the night apart as something dark and long struck the brown Pajero. It rocked her vehicle and threw her back in her seat. The flash seared her eyes as the impossible thump almost made her stop breathing.

Up became down, everything became nothing, the world rocked back and forth and then spun in impossible directions. She was in a tunnel; her ears rang like a fire alarm. Flashes of light blocked her vision.

In a daze, she beat her hands against her head. Slowly, her sight returned. The intense white light had burned-in her retina and made the night even darker. She could make out the outlines of the burning four-wheel-drive. It was a mangled pile of glowing metal and burning plastic. Faysal was nowhere.

The ringing subsided, replaced by a loud hiss. An unpleasant tingle ran through her benumbed limbs as she opened the door to get a better look. Where was her husband, her only love?

A body was on fire atop a pile of bricks that used to be a boundary wall. She couldn't look, but she had to. Her stomach twisted, her breath stopped. All her strength left her. The flames were licking at hiking boots that looked sickeningly familiar. Faysal and she had gone shopping for them the day before their flight.

Wafaa's niqab and the ringing in her ears muffled her scream. Her legs felt like giving way. With an iron will she used the door to steady herself. She had to get to Faysal and help him. If she was quick enough, it wouldn't be too bad. He might hurt for a while, but he'd recover. She wanted to scream at him. 'Move, put out the flames before you get too burnt.' But the words caught in her throat. And Faysal continued lying there, horribly still.

Wafaa was now outside, her legs threatening to collapse. As she got closer, hope left her. Faysal's head was at an impossible angle. Reality punched her hard. She fell to her knees. A soundless scream rose from deep inside. She wanted to sink into the ground but a painful, gasping, throaty moan made her turn her head.

A second man, his clothes and skin blackened, lay on the pile of bricks to her left. Someone ran by with a torch. Its weaving light fell on a raw red face devoid of any skin, teeth highlighting a rictus smile, eyes black, staring, unseeing. Blood spurted from a gash in the man's throat. She crawled to the injured man. The smell of blood overpowered the stench of burning flesh. With trembling hands she pressed on the open wound to stem the flow, but it wasn't even a trickle. She was too late.

A commotion made her glance up. Mullah Omar and his staff came rushing back. A man shouted. 'Everyone, move out…' The demonic wail of jets streaking through the sky drowned out the rest of his words and jolted Wafaa out of her paralysis. There would be more bombs.

She turned to look at Faysal. Someone had smothered the flames with a heavy blanket that hid everything but his charred head and his boots.

Her stomach spasmed, and she heaved its contents onto the ground as more jets screamed overhead. A primordial instinct kicked in. She got to her feet and ran towards her vehicle. She climbed in and was about to close the door behind when someone grabbed it. She turned to see Mullah Omar climb in beside her. As she moved aside to avoid contact, she felt cold wet cloth against her skin. The smell of urine became overpowering. She had wet herself.

The mullah turned to face her. His single good eye reflected the lights on the car's dashboard. 'Do not worry my daughter. Most of my men have done piss or shit in their pants at least once. Many were not so brave as you.'

She didn't reply. She couldn't even think. Grief and fear

had overwhelmed her.

* *

Wafaa kept her head down as great sobs wracked her body. Her tears flowed unabated, her eyes were unseeing as they raced through the streets of Kandahar.

This should never have happened. Faysal had promised her they would be safe. 'Why would anyone harm a doctor?' he had said. They had both come to Afghanistan after seeing news footage of people horribly maimed in American air raids. The Afghan people had suffered for years. First the Soviets had brutalised them and now the Americans were doing it.

The Taliban government had welcomed them with open arms. Afghanistan was desperately short of doctors. Faysal had been given a job in Kandahar General Hospital and a small house in the adjoining doctor's colony. She had seen photos. The houses were small but neat and set in nicely cared for gardens.

But now, alone and homeless, she had become the victim. She could never return to her family in Lebanon. They had disowned her when she had donned the niqab. Faysal's family in Saudi Arabia had been more accepting, even though they had blamed her for their son's radicalisation. His death would be her fault too.

She had turned to Allah and now he was testing her as he tested his most beloved. But oh, what a cruel test it was?

Grief and loss altered her sense of time. The car stopped; the engine turned off. The men climbed out; someone opened her door.

A woman dressed in black with black gloves reached in and gave her a quick hug. 'Sister Wafaa, I'm Amal. I am here to help you. Come with me, quick. These cars need to leave.'

Legs shaking, Wafaa stepped out, 'I have made a mess of myself, please don't come too close.'

'Worry not sister. We are all Allah's creation. Come with me and I will arrange a warm bath for you.' Amal led her through an empty courtyard lit only by the faint moonlight. The house, fronted by a verandah, was at the back, its windows covered by shutters.

Amal opened the door and picked up a gas lantern from the floor inside. The flickering light illuminated the spacious but sparsely furnished interior. Even though she saw no one, Wafaa felt self-conscious as she followed Amal to a large bathroom lit by a candle. Mosaics of varying shades of grey covered its floors and walls. Plastic buckets full of steaming water sat in an enclave behind a plastic curtain.

Wafaa bathed in silence, letting the pungent soap and scalding water wash away the shock. As she towelled herself dry, the tears began to flow again, till her face was as wet as her hair.

'We are in the female quarters. You will not need your niqab.' Amal's voice was gentle as she reached in and handed her a folded thawb, still warm from being ironed. 'I will wait for you outside.'

'One moment please, sister...' Wafaa sniffed. 'Where am I?'

She almost slipped on the wet floor when she heard the answer.

The Present

THE PRECURSOR

New York City, Sunday 31 December, 11:59 pm

Spread around Times Square, the ten shadows held their collective breath in dreadful anticipation as they intermingled with throngs of excited people, high on the moment.

The revellers were like lambs to the slaughter. Fifteen seconds remained to midnight. Unaware of the danger, the crowd began the countdown to their oblivion. Nine, eight, seven, six, five, four. The woman dressed in black sat in front of her laptop screen watching the live feed on CBS. At two she pressed a button.

In milliseconds the signal travelled halfway around the world. Milliseconds later ten identical Apple iPhone received a call from a number in Melbourne, Australia. It triggered a chain reaction.

Hellish waves of searing flame propelled shards of razor-sharp metal that sliced through soft tissue, severing arteries, mincing organs, extinguishing life. Time ended for three hundred and sixty-four souls, their last moment blindingly bright and excruciatingly painful.

The world changed for everyone else. The newsfeed went black.

The woman-in-black opened the Kik Messenger app on her smartphone and typed, 'Now you hold up your end of the bargain, brother.' Her finger hovered over the send button. She was breaking her own rule to be incommunicado for seventy-two hours after every event.

But he would find out in a few hours anyway and he needed the head-start and had made her promise. He had sworn Kik was tough to break even with a supercomputer. In his line of work, he ought to know. She would have enough time for the next part of the plan.

Saying a little prayer, she pressed send. Outside in the distance the sounds of sirens reverberating through the steel and concrete canyons of New York City sounded like the baying of wolves.

Smiling, she closed Kik and opened the Uber app. The car to take her to the airport was one minute away.

MIKE HOUND

Islamabad, Monday 1 January, 4:00 pm

Mike Hound shivered as he looked out of the window. Fog and rain bands shrouded the peaks of the nearby Margala Hills. It had been raining non-stop for three days, unusual for this time of the year.

Shit weather in a shit country full of shit people and his career was going down the toilet. To top it off he was spending another fucking Christmas away from his family, and for what?

He'd been overlooked for promotion again. Instead of replacing the outgoing station chief, Samantha Wilson, he was the caretaker for another rising young star out of Langley.

If he couldn't even make station chief of this shit-hole country, he'd never make it to deputy director. Time had caught up with him. He was now too old, too set in his ways. His glory days were well behind him. They'd assign him a miserable role supervising a bunch of pencil pushers and at the end send him packing with a fucking gold watch.

He began reading his forty open emails. Most concerned the Times Square bombing; one was a memo cancelling all leave for foreign operatives. There were meeting notices, assessment requests, urgent attention reviews, minutes of meetings, budget reports and requests for approvals. His inbox was out of control.

The phone rang. It was the Secret Service guard at the front gate. 'There's a Major Amjad to see you, sir.'

'Huh, OK, escort him in please.' He hated the major more than most other Pakistanis he knew. He was as slippery as a toad dipped in butter. But today if he gave him even a tenth of what he'd promised on the phone he would adopt him as a son.

'Major Amjad's here,' Vanessa, his secretary put her head around the door. She didn't smile at him. No one did. Not that he gave a shit. He didn't smile at the fuckers either.

'Let him in,' Mike said with a wave. This had better not be a joke, or he'd ask the ISI, the Inter-Services Intelligence - Pakistan's military intelligence organisation, for another liaison officer.

The door opened almost as soon as it closed.

'Hello Mr Hound. Good Afternoon!' A short stocky man marched into his office beaming like a cat who'd just swallowed a mouse. His pockmarked rotund face sported a thick cropped beard showing streaks of white. Major Amjad managed to combine an affected friendliness with an air of exaggerated pomposity that had always irked him. Pakistan wouldn't be solvent as a country if it wasn't for American government aid. This fool worked indirectly for the American taxpayer, but he strutted around as if this office belonged to him.

'Please have a seat Major,' Mike held out his hand. 'Can I get you some tea or coffee?'

'I'll have coffee please, half milk and four spoons of sugar.'

Hiding his impatience, Mike pressed a buzzer. A man dressed in white entered. This was the only perk in this job, a personal servant.

'Hameed, get us two cafe lattes with lots of sugar. Also some cake,' Mike said as he arranged the scattered papers on his desk in a neat pile.

While they waited for the coffee, they made small talk. The rain was always a good topic for banal conversation.

Hameed came in with a tray and left without saying a word.

Mike pressed the secret recording button as Hameed closed the door behind him. 'Well Major,' he began as he handed his visitor the coffee mug. 'What's this treasure trove you've brought me?'

The ISI liaison said nothing as he tore sugar sachets and measured out four spoons of sugar with exaggerated concentration. He stirred the coffee and took a noisy sip. 'Aahhh.' The exaggerated expulsion of air irked Mike. 'That is very good coffee. Better than we have in our office.' Major Amjad set the coffee cup down on the table.

Mike was ready to throttle him. If the major stalled another moment, he'd stuff his cup down his throat.

'I have for you... the identity of the person who masterminded the Times Square bombings.'

'What?' Mike spat a mouthful of coffee back into the cup as he put it down with shaking hands. He interlocked his fingers above his head and took a deep breath. 'Repeat what you just—'

'We have the identity and location of the mastermind behind the Times Square bombings.'

'Who? How...?' He knew he was babbling, but the news was too incredible. The major couldn't possibly know. The Pakistanis were good, but not this good.

Major Amjad leaned forward and handed him a napkin as he pointed to his chin. Mike took the tissue and absentmindedly wiped the coffee dribble. His shirt had copped a fair bit as well.

'We have been monitoring Internet chatter now for over two years, but we have only now pieced together her identity,' Major Amjad said. The smug smile was now ear to ear.

'Her, it's a she? A woman?' Mike knew almost immediately who the major referred to. There could be no one else. Only one female terrorist could have pulled it off, a woman so deep in the shadows no one knew what she looked like. The CIA had only created her file a few years ago.

If the myth was to be believed, she led an offshoot of Al-Qaeda that made the original look like a stamp collectors' club. The burning sensation from the coffee was somewhere in the recesses of his mind. Unpleasant but not commanding any priority from his overworked brain cells. Fuck this smug Paki bastard! He hated him.

'Yes, here is what we know about her.' Amjad took a manila folder from his briefcase, opened it, placed it on his desk and turned it to face him.

THE TRANSGRESSION

Melbourne, Wednesday 3 January, 5:00 am

Sergei's Garmin smartwatch buzzed on his wrist; he always set his alarms to silent. Outside day was breaking. Razane and Jane were both fast asleep, their breathing deep and slow. Jane's cheek rested on his bare shoulder, her arm draped over his chest. His skin was damp where they touched. Moving ever so slowly, he peeled away and rolled over. Jane stirred and turned around, snuggling up to Razane who opened her arms.

Sergei lay on his side and watched them, deep asleep. They looked so peaceful together. Jane's long blonde hair had gotten lighter over the last few years and was a sharp contrast to Razane's silky raven black hair.

Waking up next to them never grew old. The only problem, tearing himself away. He watched as they snuggled together, their chests rising and falling in sync. Lovely. With a smile, he crept out of bed taking care not to disturb them.

In the background the chilled air whispered as it left the cooling ducts in the ceiling. It was gym time. He needed to stay sharp and look sharp. Physical fitness was one thing the three of them competed on. Jane had even gone several steps further; she was doing two different martial arts along with weight training and cardio. It had become hard just to keep up.

He tiptoed to the bathroom. A quick shower and he was wide awake.

Once he'd overcome the urge to snuggle up to them and go back to sleep, he enjoyed waking early, before them. Mornings were all about freshness and renewal and gathering his thoughts in solitude.

The kitchen light came on as he entered. He took the glass jug out of the fridge and placed it on the blender.

Outside, Melbourne was waking from its slumber. A tram

trundled along, picking up early passengers. Groups of joggers, each engrossed in what played on their headphones, mingled with cyclists and early birds going to work. A road sweeping machine turned off into a side street.

In another hour the street would fill with cars. People would rush. Stress levels would rise with the sun.

The blender clicked off. His smoothie was ready but something below had caught his attention. Three dark vans approached their building. It was an unusual sight. They looked like the armoured trucks banks used to transport money, but they were unmarked, and there was no bank or even ATM in their building. His smoothie forgotten, he looked on. Moments later uniformed men with rifles and bullet-proof vests piled out. While two men set up barricades, the rest disappeared into the building.

Maybe someone in the building was a drug dealer or an arms smuggler. Whoever it was would get a rude awakening. Hopefully, it wouldn't prevent him accessing the gym in the basement.

Sergei finished the smoothie and stretched. He felt a bit dizzy. The effects from New Year's Eve hadn't quite worn off and then the terrible news about the bomb blasts in New York had kept them glued to the news till late at night.

It was five fifteen; he walked to the front door. Today he'd do a shorter session, no cardio, just weights. They were sailing later in the afternoon; it would give him all the cardio he needed for the day. He opened the door.

Hands grabbed him and flung Sergei face forward to the floor. He tried to get up but someone's boot was between his shoulder blades. Furious and in pain, he rolled onto his back. A man dropped knee first on his stomach, knocking his breath out. Something hard, cold, metallic pressed against the bridge of his nose. He looked into the muzzle of a rifle, inches from his left eye.

The hand holding the rifle wore a black glove; it belonged to a tall burly man with a black balaclava over his face.

The fuckers. Why had they burst in here? The dumb incompetent bastards had chosen the wrong apartment.

'What the fuck...? Who the—?' His mouth was full of the barrel. It had jarred his front teeth. He tasted salt from the blood on his cut lip, or was it his tongue?

Sergei tried looking around, moving only his eyes. Six men entered the bedroom. He heard muffled screams as Jane and Razane woke. It was too much. Something clicked in his brain; rage took over. He pivoted as he moved his head back. The barrel chipped a tooth on the way out, but Sergei didn't notice.

He kicked the man with the rifle, making contact with his shin. Not stopping, he extended his right leg with all his might. His assailant doubled up in pain as the ball of Sergei's foot found his crotch.

Pulling his legs free, Sergei rolled out from under him. In the same motion he swept with his legs and caught another man below the knee, catapulting him onto a coffee table.

Sergei tried standing but two men jumped onto him, pushing him back down. A third man cable-tied his hands behind his back.

Moments later Jane lay next to him, hands tied, duct-tape over her mouth; silent tears of rage pooled on the floor.

They marched Razane out of the bedroom and out of the front door, her head covered in a hood and her hands tied behind her back.

'What the fuck are you doing to her?' Sergei shouted.

'Stay silent.'

'Fuck you! We have rights. Untie my hands now—'

'I said stay silent,' a man barked at him, waving a roll of duct tape.

'Leave her alone,' Sergei growled. 'Razane we'll get you... these fucks will—'

Duct tape muffled the rest of his words.

Razane mumbled something as they led her out.

Helpless, all Sergei could do was seethe in fury, his thoughts going haywire. He fought the insanity with ferocity and brought his mind back on an even keel. Raging wouldn't help. He had to think and observe. Who were they?

** *

The men stayed another ten minutes, searching their apartment, gathering their laptops and smartphones. Before they left, they ripped off the duct tape and cut the cable ties.

'Who the fuck are you?' Sergei said through gritted teeth as he ignored the rifle pointed at him and stood upright. His head was pounding, and he was aware he wasn't thinking straight. He looked around for an opportunity to gain the upper hand, but Jane and he were unarmed and outnumbered.

'Counter terrorism.' Their leader pressed the rifle barrel hard against Sergei's sternum.

'Where did you take Razane? Why?' Sergei put an arm around Jane who was shaking uncontrollably, her face red, her eyes crazed.

'Can't say, but I advise you to sit the fuck down.' He handed Sergei a document. 'It's a control order prohibiting you from discussing this with anyone. Not the media, your local police station or a lawyer. If you follow us we shoot you. No questions...' With that he pivoted on his heel and walked out. The remaining two men joined him, slamming the door behind them.

Sergei looked at the document as he ran to the window. Two vans had already driven off. They were too far for him to read the number plate. He looked at the paper. He had never seen that insignia before; if it was a control order, what was it for?

How could anyone connect Razane with terrorism? She'd been a soldier in the Kurdish Peshmerga units and had fought against terrorists for most of her adult life.

ASIO, The Australian Security Intelligence Organisation, had done an extensive background check and countless interviews with them all when Razane applied for a residence visa. Their tick of approval meant she was no threat to the country.

What had changed?

Thoughts kept ricocheting in Sergei's mind as they sat

together reeling from shock. The only sound was Jane sniffling.

He put his arm around her as she leaned on him. 'Don't cry, sweetheart, we'll get her out,' He took her hand and caressed it. He felt very much like crying too.

'Why is this happening?' Jane's voice choked in a sob.

'I can't even begin to think of a reason.'

'Sergei, I'm so scared they'll hurt her. What're we going to do?'

'First, I'll wipe our devices. How dare they take them?' Sergei walked over to the large TV. The men had missed their tiny media PC in the shape of an ice hockey puck. It sat, hidden, behind an old amplifier. Sergei sat on the floor as he logged in.

'I'm calling Daniel,' Jane said in a hollow voice. Daniel was their lawyer. 'We need to know where they're taking her.'

'Go for it. Tell him about the control order.' Sergei pressed a button to send a remote wipe command to his phone. Next he logged into Razane's account. The fuckers wouldn't get their private data.

RELUCTANCE

Melbourne, Wednesday 3 January, 2:30 pm

Sergei drove in benumbed silence down the narrow country lane. Jane, her face drawn and pale, rested her head against the side glass and gazed forward with unseeing eyes. She was no longer crying, but in a way her silence was worse. Her anguish mixed with his, the shame of letting them both down and the paralysing fear of what would happen to Razane crippled him. Flashes of almost uncontrollable anger had given him a headache that felt like a maniac with a jackhammer running amok inside his skull. The pain sapped his strength and further diminished his capacity for reasoning. An angry man could never control his destiny. He had to calm himself. He couldn't help sadness, but he could manage his anger. He took a deep breath and held it before exhaling.

Leaf mulch and gravel camouflaged the access road to the house. No letter-box or street number betrayed its presence. Sergei slowed to a crawl and turned left, taking care not to scrape the bodywork on the two nondescript boulders that marked the entrance. Ferns growing on both sides made it feel even narrower.

The bitumen ended in a gravel track that continued up the densely wooded hill before it levelled off near the summit. Sergei drove carefully, slowing around the bends as the tyres fought for traction on the loose gravel. The track ended in a flagstone driveway as the wild grown wattles and tree-ferns gave way to a double row of erect conifers. The house stood in a cutting halfway up the hill surrounded by an orchard of fruit trees.

Sergei switched off the engine and took Jane's damp hand in his. He wanted to comfort her, but he was close to hyperventilating, his stomach a knot.

Jane managed a wan smile. 'Let's hope Dennis can help

us.'

Dennis Tillerson was a former intelligence agent and had helped Sergei's father defect from the KGB. They became good friends. As a young boy, Sergei used to enjoy visiting Uncle Dennis, in large part because he had a crush on his daughter, Chelsea. Together they would spend hours playing in the overgrown gardens.

As he grew older, his visits became less frequent until in adulthood they stopped altogether. When his father died, Sergei got back in touch with Dennis. They would meet at least four times a year including Christmas and his birthday. Today they were arriving unannounced and desperate.

Jane shivered as she breathed in the fresh air. Dennis wasn't there to greet them even though his property bristled with surveillance equipment alerting him to visitors.

Sergei put his arm around Jane as they walked towards the house. 'I hope the old man is OK.'

Dennis stood in a grove of trees, his back to them, pruning a sapling almost as tall and thin as he was. His ruddy complexion that contrasted with his mop of white hair spoke of his love of the outdoors. He was unaware they had arrived.

'Hey Dennis,' Jane called out as they got within a few metres.

Dennis jumped. 'Oh, Sergei and Jane, what a nice surprise!' He put his secateurs away and shuffled over. His smile added even more wrinkles to the hundreds already present.

'Where is...?' He hugged Jane. His voice trailed off as he noticed their worried expressions.

'Razane,' Jane said.

'Yes, yes, Razane?' His expression mirrored theirs. 'Where is she? Is, is something wrong?'

'That's why we're here.' Sergei took a deep breath. 'We need your help, we're desperate.'

'They arrested her.' Jane's face was dark with rage.

'Who? What for?' Dennis moved closer and patted Jane on the shoulder.

'No idea... That's what's so frustrating and worrying. There couldn't be a reason,' Sergei said.

'Who was it?'

'Men with assault rifles and masks, like a SWAT unit in the movies,' Jane said.

'With strange uniforms,' Sergei said, 'like black battle fatigues.'

'How awful for you,' Dennis said, looking concerned. 'You better come inside.'

Dennis led them through the front door to a sun-filled lounge. The usually warm and welcoming interior was a mess. Empty dishes, books and papers littered the room. Dust coated the furniture, and the carpet was dirty.

He pointed to a leather lounge suite covered in a stack of newspapers and dirty plates. 'Please sit. I can't think standing up.'

'Here's what they gave us,' Jane handed him the paper as she cleared a space to sit.

'Something's not right,' Dennis shook his head and muttered under his breath as he looked at the document. 'I don't recognise this logo.' He was still speaking to himself. 'Besides, there's no law to stop people contacting a lawyer.'

Sergei and Jane exchanged glances. 'You don't think this is legit?' Jane said.

Dennis appeared not to have heard. 'They wouldn't be careless about something like this.' Dennis continued his distracted muttering. 'They'd need solid intelligence to act.'

'Uncle,' Jane spoke a little louder, 'could the laws have changed since you left the agency?'

'What...? Oh, I haven't left,' he said coming out of his thought bubble. 'Spooks like me don't... retire,' he winked. 'It's the skeletons in my many closets.'

'So you still go to work?' Jane looked incredulous. He was at least eighty-five and from his distracted manner he appeared unfit to even drive.

'Well, my work comes here. I sit in on a few policy

meetings and am called on for the history I have. But enough about me. Tell me about Razane. Has she done anything out of the… ordinary?'

'What? Why would you ask that? What are you implying?' Sergei said.

'I'm just being me,' Dennis said in a lighthearted tone. 'But seriously, one's gotta ask these questions--'

'We both know Razane,' Jane said, 'I'd suspect the Prime Minister of Australia before her.'

'The new one is a terror, if not a terrorist...' Dennis chuckled to himself.

'Razane can't watch the news without being affected by all the shit that goes on,' Sergei said.

'Well, terrorists are human, I'm sure they cry,' Dennis said. 'The reasons they do the terrible things are seldom straightforward.' He examined his left hand and scraped mud off his thumb. 'But I'm just playing devil's advocate, you know…'

'Yes, but Razane's all about love and peace.'

'But she was also in Syria and is Muslim and has been a combatant in a war zone fighting. So can you see how her risk profile is already sky high,' he said.

'That's a bit Islamophobic and Razane left the Peshmerga before we met,' Jane said, 'and she was fighting against the bad guys, not for them.'

Dennis nodded as she spoke, alternating between being alert and distracted.

'So what're we supposed to do?' Sergei said, 'the lawyer's been calling police stations and remand centres but nothing.'

Dennis gave a start. 'So you talked to a lawyer?'

'We called him straight away, I don't give a shit about a piece of paper,' Sergei said.

'Razane's still in a very fragile state. This could send her over the edge,' Jane said, 'we need her back right away.'

'You know if this operation is legal and this document legit, contacting the lawyer and coming here can get you arrested too,' Dennis looked grave. 'I hope no one followed you.'

'No, I am certain we weren't…' Sergei said.

Dennis looked at him and shook his head. 'How would you know? They no longer follow people like that. It's all done by remote…' he muttered.

'They have all our phones so they haven't been tracking us and I hired a rental. My car's being repaired.' Sergei said.

'Oh, OK, that's good but they've other means.'

Sergei didn't think so but held his tongue. He needed Dennis's help. 'So… can you please help us?'

'I can't do anything illegal or improper.' Dennis folded his arms.

'Arresting Razane without us able to defend her, or know the charges, is bloody improper,' Jane said. She wanted to shake Dennis.

'Can you at least check if it was a legitimate government agency,' Sergei said.

'Just give us something. Who do we approach?' Jane said, 'Or, or tell us why they arrested her?'

'Yeah, maybe they mixed Razane with someone else of the same name,' Sergei said.

Dennis rubbed the bristle on his chin. 'OK, let me do a search. I'll see what pops up. I can't promise to share anything.' He got up. 'Hey, you two look like you're starving. Go find some food in the kitchen.'

THE DELIVERY

Melbourne, Wednesday 3 January, 4:30 pm

It was the rudest awakening. Even worse than the night-time ambush in Syria when she'd woken to a barrage of bullets. But this was so much more personal. Bundling her out of bed, snapping handcuffs on her and covering her head like cattle being led to slaughter. But that was nothing compared to the agony hearing Jane's painful sobs.

Within minutes they had frog-marched her out of the apartment. The cold air hit her briefly before they bundled her into the cold hard interior of a van. They locked her handcuffs to another chain and then slammed the doors shut.

Razane tried removing the hood, but her shackles prevented her. The bench was freezing cold, and she was barefoot. She couldn't stop shivering.

'Ouch,' she cried as the van lurched forward, jerking her handcuffs and chafing her wrists. She had to relax and figure out where they were taking her and why? Who were they?

She willed her breathing slower and focused. The van was in heavy traffic. It crossed a tram line. Its tyres bumped over reflectors as it changed lanes. Several times it turned, first right and twice left. Traffic thinned, and the speed increased. They rounded a hair-pin bend, a freeway ramp. She tried but couldn't judge which direction they were travelling in. After a while she lost count and gave up.

It seemed so easy in the movies. Fictional characters had limitless attention spans and never needed to pee.

After an interminable journey the van stopped. Its doors opened, and they marched her out.

After several minutes, they walked through a door that opened with a creak. The place smelled of cleaning products. They walked through another door that creaked open and latched shut behind them with a metallic clang. They pushed her into a chair and chained her handcuffs to its arms before removing her hood.

The sudden shock as the light hit her made her screw her eyes shut. She looked around.

Four tube lights, one flickering, illuminated the windowless room. Silver insulation on the high ceiling suggested they were in a commercial building.

A burly woman in a black military style uniform stood over her as a man in a white coat and a stethoscope took her blood pressure.

'I badly need to go to the toilet,' Razane said in a hoarse voice, trying to sound as dignified as possible. She wouldn't show them how afraid she was.

The burly female guard spoke into a small shoulder mic. A broad-shouldered male guard came to the door. The woman unshackled Razane's chain and led her out into a passageway just wide enough for a single person. Could she try to overpower her guards? She might get lucky with the woman, but the man behind her was three times her weight and all muscle.

The toilet was a tiny affair with thick bars on the skylight. The guard stood outside while she went.

'Why am I here?' Razane said as she dried her hands on a paper towel.

'Be quiet!' the guard said in an uneducated drawl.

'Why?'

Her captor pursed her lips and shoved her back towards the room. They retied her to the chair.

'Why are you doing this?' Razane said as the doctor continued the examination, checking her eyes and ears and feeling the glands in her throat. Then he took out a syringe and waited for the female guard to wrap Razane in a bear hug from behind.

Razane struggled in vain as the doctor lowered her pyjama pants, swabbed her hip with disinfectant and jabbed her with the needle. 'This will make your flight easier,' he said.

Razane's chest fluttered in panic. 'What flight? Where are you taking me?'

The burly woman glared at the doctor. 'You know you don't talk to prisoners.' She spat out her words.

From his sheepish expression she knew it was true. They were taking her somewhere. Before Razane could ask, her mind fogged up. Drowsiness overcame her.

She was barely conscious when two more men entered, one pushing a wheelchair. While they held her, the burly woman stripped her and dressed her in an orange jumpsuit.

The last thing Razane felt was someone putting a pair of shoes on her feet.

Awareness returned some time later. A voice spoke over the roar of a jet engine. 'I'm Carl Briggs. We spoke earlier.'

'Hey, I'm Mike Hound and this is my associate Sebastian Corder, nice to make your acquaintance.' Came the reply.

'Likewise. I need you to sign these delivery documents.' Briggs crinkled a piece of paper.

She saw the top of a man's head as he bent down and signed the paper against his leg.

'Thanks mate. She's all yours. She'll sleep for around six hours.'

'Thanks buddy. Good job. I'm sure we'll do business again.'

As they pushed her up a ramp, she fell asleep again.

ALARMING NEWS

Melbourne, Wednesday 3 January, 4:45 pm

Sergei and Jane made sandwiches, poured themselves apple juice and ate in the front lounge.

'Dennis looks unwell,' Jane said. 'He was awfully distracted and out of breath.'

'Yeah, true, and he's aged since we last met. I don't think retirement agrees with him, poor fellow.'

'When I hugged him, he was all skin and bones.'

'Hmmm,' Sergei said, 'it must be tough being alone at his age.'

* *

'Bloody system,' Dennis muttered as he re-entered his password. He'd forgotten he'd changed it a week ago. 'Damn!' This time he pressed one wrong key. His fingertips were too big and his hands shook more than usual. If he got it wrong a third time, the system would lock him out. He'd have to call IT who'd require approval from his former boss.

What he was doing was wrong on so many levels. Access to the database was on a need to know basis. Arguably, he needed to know, but Sergei and Jane didn't.

Dennis tried the password again, pressing each key slowly. At the fifth character, he stopped. What came next? He had entered five characters so far. One, two, three, four, five. He entered the rest. Droplets of sweat appeared on his forehead as he pressed "Enter".

With a beep he was in. The screen came alive. He exhaled slowly. Thank God! Logging on to work never used to be hard. 'Razane, Razane, what have you been up to?' he muttered as he entered her name in a search bar. A bird flapped its wings in the garden. It was a rosella drinking from the bird-bath he'd hung from his favourite cherry tree last week. It had such beautiful colours. He looked back at the laptop, lost in thought. What was he there for? The screen went blank. Damn! He entered the password again and resumed the search. He liked Razane. She was quiet and refined and always polite.

After a twenty-second pause he got the data he was after. As he began to read, concern turned to unease and then alarm. This was bad. His hands shook even more. His chest constricted. A painful twinge in his sternum forced him to sit upright and take several deep breaths. He needed a drink. A sense of loneliness and malaise descended.

Keeping secrets from family and friends had always been the hardest part of the job. What he had found would devastate Sergei and Jane. If he was found out, it would destroy him.

Could he keep it from them? They had to know. Some of it would come out, eventually. The press would get wind of it. There would be leaks from other sources. They had already arrested Razane, so it mattered less. Damn these internal conflicts. Damn, damn, damn!

* *

Sergei's stomach churned when he saw Dennis's expression. 'What's wrong, Dennis?'

'It's bad. Extremely bad.'

'What do you mean, extremely bad?' Jane stood, her eyes wide with fear.

'I really shouldn't be telling you this,' Dennis's eyes became cloudier, his hands shook, his face reddened and a vein on his forehead throbbed. He looked close to having a stroke. His nose whistled as he took a deep breath. 'It seems Razane is a… a terrorist.'

'What…?' Jane put down her plate and took several steps towards him.

'That's not possible, how?' Sergei stood as well.

'It seems... Razane is Wafaa Aal Zubeidi.'

'What?' Sergei said. 'That's bull--'

'Who's Wafaa?' Jane said.

'That's a long story,' Dennis said, 'A lot of it is now on public record.' Dennis rubbed his chin as he contemplated what to tell them. He shook his head and went on. 'Ever since 2002 we heard rumours of a female high up in Al Qaeda's hierarchy. She had an almost mythical status among jihadi groups. Apparently, Ayman al-Zawahiri referred to her as *Al-ukht-ul-akbari* which means elder sister... But her existence was proven only four years ago.

'Since then we've learnt more. We know she masterminded many of the worst atrocities of the last fifteen years including commanding Jabhat-al-Nusra squads in Syria. And...' he paused for breath. 'You both need to sit down.'

Sergei and Jane stared at him dumbfounded. There was worse to come?

'She masterminded the Times Square bombings.'

There was silence as Sergei and Jane grappled with the revelation.

Jane was first to speak. 'What's it to do with Razane?' Her voice was several decibels higher.

'Like I said, Wafaa has always been a shadowy figure. Till a few days ago no one even had her photograph. Then we got lucky. A friendly intelligence agency interrogated a captured Islamic State militant and discovered that Razane and Wafaa were the same person. Apparently, he picked her photo out of hundreds of images.'

'Razane's not a terrorist. I'd bet my life on it,' Jane said fiercely. 'Also she's Iraqi Kurd. They are enemies of both Al-Qaeda and Islamic State.'

'You told me she came to you looking for a job. Maybe she fabricated her story of being with the Kurds.' Dennis rubbed the back of his head. He was developing quite a headache from all of this.

'I'd bet everything in the world she's innocent,' Sergei

said, 'without the slightest hesitation.'

'Hang on a second,' Jane put up her hand. 'Razane needed special security clearance because she had been a foreign combatant.'

'I thought so too, but her file doesn't mention that,' Dennis said. 'Which is surprising because I thought... Anyway, those checks aren't that reliable. In a war-torn region we often use intermediaries who could be corrupted.'

'I don't care what you say, it's a mistake or a setup. There's no way Wafaa is our Razane,' Jane stood again, 'I can't hear any more of this. It's too bloody annoying and... hurtful.'

'They have connected Wafaa to Razane,' Dennis's voice took on a faraway character.

'What do you mean?'

'A call from Australia triggered the bombs in Times Square. They believe it was from Razane's phone.'

The floor dropped beneath Jane's feet and she fell. Luckily a soft settee was in her way. Sergei rushed over. His legs were jelly as well; his insides were dissolving.

'Jane, sweetheart. It's not true. It can't be.' He whispered as he held her close.

'Jane dear,' Dennis's voice had grown softer, 'In my career, I've learnt you can only be sure of yourself.'

Sergei looked up at him and shook his head. 'Razane's part of our lives. We'd know if she was faking it.'

'I'm sorry you two. I know this must be bloody hard. It was highly illegal and improper for me to disclose this. But I also couldn't keep it from you.' His voice shook as he spoke. 'If Razane's mixed up in all this, you need to know. Your lives might be in danger.' He stood there looking miserable.

'Well, thank you for doing so,' Sergei said, his tone devoid of gratitude. His voice shook as he spoke. 'We'll tell no one about this conversation.'

'Do nothing and talk to no one. Just let the authorities deal with it,' Dennis said.

Sergei shook his head noncommittally.

'I think you need to leave now,' Dennis said after a moment's pause. He looked distracted again.

'Alright,' Sergei said. 'We'll go but… can you please tell us one more thing?'

'Probably not!' Dennis sounded exasperated. 'What's it?' He snapped.

'That friendly intelligence agency… Who are they?'

Dennis shook his head. 'Oh, the Pakistani ISI.'

Sergei and Jane stood with mouths agape. Two years ago they had encountered the ISI. They were ruthless and methodical. Why would they fabricate lies about Razane?

'Thanks Dennis,' Sergei recovered his composure. 'It might help.'

'I'm sorry, I wish for your sakes this information wasn't true but…'

'We're sure it's wrong.' Sergei said.

'I've violated the official secrets act and probably committed treason,' Dennis muttered. 'So just keep it to yourselves, OK.'

'We have to tell the lawyer' Jane whispered to Sergei as they walked to the car. Dennis followed behind, shaking his head and muttering to himself.

'We'll have her out by this evening,' Jane said, turning to Dennis.

'I… somehow don't think so.' Dennis looked dejected. 'I'm sorry guys but she'd have been extradited by now.'

Sergei turned to the old man, a frown on his face. 'Why do you say that?' Just the thought made his head spin. 'Extradited to where?'

'You told me their trucks had no police symbols. And your lawyer can't locate her. The men were probably private contractors. Which means the CIA took Razane.'

'But that's illegal,' Sergei nearly screamed. He felt Jane go limp again.

'Yeah,' Dennis said, 'and so is terrorism. The CIA doesn't care about laws. They don't even follow their own country's and in times like these people look the other way.'

Sergei helped Jane into her seat and buckled her belt, grateful he hadn't gone to water himself though he badly wanted to punch someone.

He turned around to say bye. Dennis had walked off and was pruning a rosebush, whistling a tune.

'Fucking crazy nutter,' Sergei growled as he started the engine.

DESPERATE TIMES

Melbourne, Wednesday 3 January, 6:30 pm

'Careful babe,' Jane shifted in her seat. Sergei was driving erratically. His breathing was ragged, his knuckles white, his brow furrowed. He had almost dropped a wheel over the edge as they descended the hill.

'I'm sorry,' he sighed as he backed off the accelerator. It took a conscious effort to lessen his grip on the steering wheel.

'Pull over a second, darling.' Jane said in a quiet voice.

Sergei pulled over and switched off the engine. Jane turned to him. 'I'm sorry I melted on you like that.' She touched his cheek as she gazed in his eyes. 'We can't let Razane down by being weak and... I don't care... whatever your uncle or the fucking CIA or ISI say... Razane's not a terrorist.'

'I know that,' Sergei said, taking a deep breath. 'OK, no more self-indulgent misery. We'll find a way out of this.'

'The question is, how can they get it so wrong? It kinda shakes my belief in the system.'

Jane leaned over and kissed Sergei on the lips. 'I love you.'

'Hmmm, I love you too,' he said absently. 'Where did that come from?'

'I love your loyalty, your strength and your kindness. You wouldn't for a moment desert the people you love.'

'How can I? You're my soulmates, I'd be lost without you.'

'And you're ours,' Jane moved the hair from his forehead. 'You're my rock, our rock. I love you.'

'I love you too, sweetheart. We're gonna get Razane back, no matter what... I just... don't know where to begin.'

'One more thing... Don't get silly and male on me,' her voice had lost its softness.

'What?' Sergei looked at her with a perplexed look.

'What happened isn't your fault and not only your

responsibility to fix. We're both in this together. You did what you could. OK!'

Sergei nodded. Jane kissed him, then she picked up her phone and dialled. 'I'm calling the lawyer.'

A man answered, 'Daniel here.'

'Daniel it's us, Jane and Sergei, have you found —?'

'No nothing yet, and trust me I've tried... Almost everything. Victoria Police don't have her, not that I expected them to. So I can't even get a visitation order or apply for bail. I'm waiting on my Federal Police contact.' He sounded tired.

'Daniel, mate, what are we supposed to do?' Sergei's voice had an edge of desperation.

'I wish I could advise you. It's most unusual. Look, I've got a free half hour first thing tomorrow morning. Hopefully by then the AFP's gotten back to me.'

'OK.' They hung up.

'I'm just thinking,' Sergei said in an absent voice. 'If like Dennis said she's on some terror watch list, maybe even if they have her they're gonna keep it secret.'

SAIPAN

Saipan, Thursday 4 January, 7:30 am

Razane dozed through most of the flight. Either the sound of the landing gear or the change in cabin air pressure jolted her out of the fog of a dreamless sleep. Groggy from whatever they had injected her with, every movement felt unnatural and strained, like she was encased in a large and elastic block of jelly.

The empty pit in her stomach acted like a clock telling her she hadn't eaten for at least eight to ten hours. Her mouth and throat were so dry that swallowing was painful. She tried to rub her eyes but her hands were shackled to the seat frame.

'What... where am I?' she said to the man sitting to her left. He was young and blond, with a pleasant chiselled face. He glanced sideways but made no other move to respond.

Outside, opaque white replaced the deep blue sky as the airplane plunged into a cloud. Her ears popped as they adjusted to the pressure rise from their descent. The cloud cover disappeared. Below, waves on the bright blue water sparkled with myriad points of light as it caught a reflection of the sun. The water gave way to flat sand covered with sparse vegetation and then they were over water again. They had to be flying over islands, somewhere remote. They were close to touch down but so far there were no signs of human habitation. Where were they?

'Where are you taking me?' she said more forcefully.

From behind someone forced a black hood over her head. The suddenness caught her by surprise. She was too exhausted to get angry; it wouldn't serve her well, anyway. She did the only thing she could, breathe, in and out and in, just like she had practiced with Jane.

They had spent Tuesday and Thursday afternoons practising Systema, the martial art used by the Russian special forces, the Spetsnaz. Seeing her svelte and petite lover spar with tall heavyset men was eye-opening. Like most other martial arts, Systema relied on speed and a mastery of technique. Strength was important too, especially for beginners.

Somehow Jane had transcended that stage. In ten months she was the best student. At the one year mark she won a sparring match against their instructor.

Razane had learnt to control her breathing by doing Systema. In fact, breathing and stretching took up half of class time. She was glad Jane had talked her into doing it with her. Even though she didn't have Jane's natural ability, Systema helped her conquer her post-traumatic stress disorder. Now it would help her stay calm and in control.

She took another deep breath and focused on the air tickling her nostrils as it escaped. She was already calmer, her breathing shallower, her heartbeat slower. This terrible situation wouldn't last; she would endure. Sergei and Jane would get her out. Meanwhile, she would remain dignified and calm. She closed her eyes and within moments was fast asleep.

* *

Razane took a sip of orange juice as she stared out of the window at the lush green meadow that swept up into a wooded hill. She was at her desk in her little alcove in their home in the Yarra Ranges on the outskirts of Melbourne.

It had started out as their weekend retreat, but they were using it more than their city apartment.

Her laptop was in front of her. She was writing a children's book, her fourth. It was a welcome relief from her stressful job helping companies protect themselves against terrorism threats. Her book was a fairy tale about a heron called Hama. It was a story her mother used to tell her. She was adapting it for a global audience and adding colourful detail. She'd been lucky; her books had been snapped up by a publisher who loved her style. It came with a down-payment but also a deadline.

Sergei walked in with a cup of tea and a scone with jam

and cream. He placed it next to her laptop and stood there with his hand on her shoulder. She moved her head side to side to relieve the soreness in her neck. He immediately sensed what she wanted and began to gently massage her sore muscles. 'That feels good, my love, don't stop,' she purred as she felt the pain dissolve. His hands were strong but sensitive and they always found every little knot and sore spot.

She grabbed his right arm in both hands and kissed his palm. He bent down and kissed her on top of her head. Then his mouth found hers. She stroked the back of his head. Their kiss lingered till the ringing of a telephone interrupted them.

'I need to get this,' he mumbled as he stood up.

She blew him a kiss. 'And I need to finish this book, otherwise, my publisher will kill me.'

Outside in the distance, a paraglider soared over the hilltop. The day was warming up fast. It would still be cool enough to go for a forest walk for another few hours, enough time to finish writing.

* *

The plane touched down with a jolt. The pilot slammed on the brakes. Razane awoke as the seatbelt dug into her as they decelerated to a stop. The hood was yanked off her head.

'Stay silent, or this goes back on,' a voice behind her said. Its breathy venomous monotone made her skin crawl.

Silence descended as the engines spun down. Four US Marines boarded the plane and walked over.

'She's all yours,' the venomous voice said.

'Yes sir,' the Marine in the lead gave a signal.

There was no use struggling. She let the Marines lift her out of the seat and tried to keep up as they half carried and half dragged her down the steps.

Currents of hot air rose from the baking tarmac mixing with the cool sea-breeze. The smell of the ocean was strong. They were somewhere warm and tropical. It reminded Razane of their holiday in Hawaii three months ago, which seemed in another lifetime.

Where in the world was she? And why?

8
October
2001

27 days after

The September 11 attacks on the NYC Trade Centre

THE FUNERAL

Kandahar, 8 October 2001, 12:00 pm

Faysal's funeral was a rushed affair even by Islamic standards. It had to be. After the drone attack Mullah Omar had gone into hiding with his retinue. The Taliban were still in control of the city and its surrounds but they were preparing to leave, to fight on in the countryside.

To soften them up, the US and its allies maintained an around the clock aerial bombardment. Life in the city had become next to impossible. It was already perilous to be out on the streets. A funeral procession would soon be out of the question.

Osama Bin Laden's house was in Tarnak Farms outside the city in an area that had so far escaped destruction, but the war was drawing ever closer.

Every detail of the funeral followed strict Islamic customs. Faysal's body was washed, enshrouded in a white cotton sheet, and placed in the largest room in the house. Over a hundred armed men attended the ceremony.

The room was full of smoke from burning incense as a *maulana* read from the Quran and then led the prayers.

Amal and Osama's other two wives, Khairiah and Siham, comforted her as they sat on the other side of a hastily erected cloth partition that separated them from the men.

Wafaa had to screw up her eyes to make out Faysal's enshrouded form through the fabric. Her strong and brave husband looked small and weak, wrapped in the white cloth and covered in rose petals.

Soon his physical form would be no more, as his body returned to the soil whence he came. She would never see him again. He was the only man she had ever known apart from her father and brothers. He was everything she had ever wanted in a husband ever since, as a young girl, she had started dreaming of marriage. After her liberal family disowned her for marrying a jihadi, Faysal became the only person in her life. Now she was all alone except for Allah.

As she sat there listening to the Quranic verses, surrounded by men and women who had forsaken all to wage holy war, she suddenly felt at peace. She realised it wasn't right to be mournful. Faysal was *shaheed*. If this is what Allah wanted for him, then he had achieved what he had come to Afghanistan for. If Allah willed it, she would soon attain that high place herself.

In the meantime, she needed to make herself worthy of her late husband and of the great man in whose home she sheltered.

After prayers the men formed a funeral procession and took Faysal's body to the nearby graveyard.

Wafaa fought the urge to embrace Faysal one last time; it would be most unseemly. Instead, she put her arms around Amal.

'Next time you meet in *Jannah*,' Khairiah said softly as they led her, sobbing, back to the women's quarters.

**

The next week in the Bin Laden household was surreal. The women had a separate house to themselves. It comprised six large rooms, a kitchen and a laundry that all opened onto a large family room where they spent most of their time doing chores.

The front door opened into an enclosed courtyard. The women had to be covered to venture there. Bin Laden lived in a small house to the left of the women's quarters that he shared with his most trusted lieutenants.

Their compound was surrounded by tall boundary walls that blocked the view to their surrounds. All she knew was that they were somewhere near Kandahar.

Khairiah and Siham were as warm and welcoming as Amal. Their many children ran around and filled the house with noise and laughter whenever their father wasn't around. When he was the whole house was nearly silent; the only sounds were from the children sitting on rice mats reading the Quran by rote.

When she wasn't helping with chores, Wafaa spent her time reading the Quran and studying the pamphlets and books in the small library. The ideas were radical and bold and spoke of the need to wage war in all forms against crusaders, Zionists, and apostates.

They spoke of violence and brutality but justified the need. Muslims had been enslaved and humiliated. Without waging a bloody jihad, they couldn't regain their former glory.

Wafaa still hadn't seen Bin Laden. He would always announce his intention to enter the women's section which would give her a chance to cover herself in the niqab and retire to an empty room.

She wondered how much longer she would be allowed to stay and where she would go afterwards. Her family had made it clear they never wanted to see her again. Where could she go?

* *

On the morning of the eighth day after the funeral, Wafaa had just finished breakfast and was helping Khairiah with the dishes when Amal came rushing in. 'Wafaa, he has summoned you to his office. He has two visitors.'

'Who?' she blurted out without thinking. 'Oh, but why would he wish to speak to m-me?'

'He has Al-Zawahiri with him.' Amal ignored her questions in her excitement.

Wafaa had heard of Ayman Al-Zawahiri. He was the second most powerful man in Al-Qaeda. Knots formed in her stomach. What did they want with her?

She donned her niqab and with nervous steps walked to Bin Laden's quarters. Not knowing what to expect, she approached the door and knocked softly.

Bin Laden opened the door. He was taller than in the photographs, '*Asalam aleikum.*' His tone was respectful. It appeared that his reputation as a humble man was warranted. 'Come in honourable sister.' He motioned her to sit in an armchair separated from a three-seater settee by a walnut coffee table carved with Quranic *ayats* and covered in a sheet of glass.

The two men with him rose as she entered. '*Asalam aleikum.*' They greeted her in unison, their eyes lowered in respect. She recognised Al-Qaeda's number two, Ayman Al-Zawahiri from his photographs in newspapers. She would realise only later that the other person was Abu Musab al-Suri, Al-Qaeda's principal strategist and the man who had invented modern jihad.

Wafaa nodded in reply and mumbled, '*Wa aleikum asalam!*' Her heart fluttered in trepidation as she sat. What did the leaders of Al-Qaeda want from a widow?

She didn't have to wait long to find out.

'We wish to ask about the attack that killed brother Faysal,' Bin Laden spoke in a solemn voice as he smoothed his beard with his right hand.

'The attack was like no other we have ever experienced before,' Aymen al-Zawahiri said leaning forward. His eyes, magnified by coke bottle lenses unnerved her.

Wafaa looked at the two men, her mind still blank, not comprehending, 'I-I...' she stammered.

'Sister, the missile came from the sky but no one had heard any aircraft, Bin Laden spoke in a gentler tone. 'It was only two minutes after... *Amreeki* jets flew overhead.'

'I hear you have a Master's degree in aeronautical engineering,' Al-Zawahiri chimed in.

Wafaa nodded. Where was her tongue? Why was she behaving like a little child? 'Y-yes,' she finally managed to stammer. Were they asking about the missile? Her mind cast back to the attack that ended Faysal's life. It was odd how the missile had appeared out of nowhere. But the strangest thing were the loud clicks that preceded the sickening explosion.

'Do you have any idea how the *Amreekis* did it?' Bin Laden was now growing impatient. He looked at Al-Zawahiri as if to say, 'Bad idea to ask a woman.'

'In university, we studied a new type of aircraft known as UAVs,' her mind was kicking into gear. 'UAVs are unmanned aerial vehicles. The common word is drone... Many universities in America, England and Israel are researching them.' She waited for a reaction. They stared, mouths agape. Was it interest or were they surprised by an intelligent woman?

'Brothers, as you both undoubtedly know, drones with cameras were used in the wars in Bosnia and Somalia to spy on the enemy. Much of the evidence of war crimes against Muslims came from photographs taken by drones. Later the Americans used them to point lasers at targets to help improve the accuracy of long-range missiles. It wouldn't be too difficult to make the drones carry and fire their own missiles.'

'I knew she would be a useful person to talk to,' Zawahiri said in a triumphant tone as he clapped his thigh.

Wafaa continued. 'When I think back to the attack, I can remember the sound of a small engine in the distance. At the time I thought it was a motorcycle engine with a damaged piston. But now that I reflect on it, I am certain it was a lightweight propeller aircraft.' The three men exchanged glances and nodded as she spoke. 'The missile that hit Mullah Omar's Pajero was small. It did very little damage to anything else, so it had to come from above.'

'That is very useful to know,' Bin Laden said. 'I thank you for your help. May brother Faysal achieve the highest place in *Jannah*.'

'Sister, your knowledge is most impressive, for a woman.' Al-Suri spoke for the first time.

THE CONVOY

Kandahar, 26 October 2001, 9:00 am

The sound of screeching tyres jerked Wafaa awake. A loud banging startled her into an upright position. She looked around in a daze. The grey wall clock decorated with Quranic inscriptions showed the time was one minute after nine.

The children ran to the front door and looked out. The commotion continued. It was at the main gate of the compound.

Wafaa hadn't meant to fall asleep after breakfast, but the last few days had been physically and emotionally exhausting. Never having worked a day in her life, domestic chores like cleaning, cutting vegetables and ironing clothes wore her out.

Khairiah's son Hamza came running in barefoot and out of breath. 'The Taliban have brought a letter from Mullah Omar,' he said. 'We have to leave; it is no longer safe here.'

'Where do we go? How?' Khairiah was panicking.

'Father says you must all pack your belongings. You have one hour. The Taliban will move everything else.'

'Is Wafaa to come as well?' Amal asked.

'Yes, father asked that she does.'

Wafaa heaved a sigh of relief. She had nowhere else to go and now not much else to live for. Something told her she had met Bin Laden for a reason. Even though the great man walked with a target on his back, she did not want to be anywhere else.

Khairiah smiled at Wafaa. 'You can see how impressed he is with you.'

Wafaa had told the three women about her conversation with Bin Laden and Al-Zawahiri.

She had come away with a warm inner glow. Now that the leaders knew about drones, they would be better able to protect themselves against the American Satan. She had contributed to the Jihad.

* *

Wafaa joined the wives and daughters in the back of a mustard yellow Mitsubishi Pajero that Bin Laden drove. His sons and his Taliban bodyguards followed in two black SUVs, each ten car lengths behind. A Taliban scout, in constant radio contact, drove a kilometre ahead to warn of hazards.

Wafaa sat diagonally behind Bin Laden. In contrast with his calm demeanour in public he was a distracted and impatient driver, constantly on the horn and oblivious to his passengers' discomfort as he crashed into every pothole on the road.

She said a silent prayer to keep them safe on their journey. Surely, Allah saw how important Bin Laden was and would keep him and his passengers safe.

Bin Laden frowned on what he termed idle talk so no one spoke, except occasionally and then only in whispers.

An hour later the two-way radio on the dashboard crackled to life. Wafaa couldn't hear what was said, but Bin Laden looked back. His passengers did too. A wall of dark grey smoke billowed into the sky. The Americans had resumed the aerial bombardment of Kandahar.

Wafaa would only learn later how close they had come to being killed or captured. A bomb flattened Tarnak Farms an hour after they departed. The Americans took Kandahar by afternoon prayers.

The ill-maintained roads, rough ride and Bin Laden's nerve-wracking lack of skill soon took a toll on his passengers. Wafaa had bumped her head so many times on the overhead handle that her scalp was aflame with pain. No one dared ask for a break, even to answer the call of nature.

They turned off the main highway after Ghazni. The hard-packed dirt road threw up clouds of dust that soon coated all but the lead vehicle. Two hours later the road started climbing. Green terraced fields and tiny villages replaced the dun countryside.

The grand and majestic mountains were mostly

uncultivable rock, leaving little space for crops. The fields were green but tiny and irregularly shaped. At a distance, it appeared idyllic but the ramshackle dwellings, tattered clothes and absence of modern farming implements spoke of grinding poverty.

As they climbed ever higher into the high country, the road became a series of treacherous switchbacks and off camber bends. Mountain peaks, covered in snow and ice, towered into the sky. The air was freezing.

It was midnight when their convoy stopped in the tiny village outside Gulghundai-Kalai. The Taliban commandeered the largest hut and built a fire to ward off the cold. Wafaa spent the night wrapped in a woollen blanket, still in her day clothes. The cold made sleep impossible.

Next morning, they ate a simple breakfast of flatbread and hot milk. After the meal, they discovered the engines had frozen solid. The Taliban rustled up a pack of mules and helped them tie their luggage onto their new conveyances. The women rode while the men walked.

The scenery stayed the same for hours as they traversed a rock-strewn plateau. Wafaa asked a few times where they were going but Khairiah told her to stay quiet. It wasn't her place to ask questions.

The road ended in a mountain pass overlooking a tree-covered valley.

Khairiah tapped Wafaa on the shoulder and pointed. 'Those are the White Mountains. The rocks are white, even when not covered in snow.'

'Allah's wonders never cease,' Wafaa said. 'It is beautiful.'

'You'll like where we are going,' Khairiah said as they dismounted the mules at the crest of a sharp rise. 'Allah decorated it most beautifully.'

'Have you been here before?' Wafaa said.

Khairiah looked around for Bin Laden before replying in conspiratorial tones. 'Yes, it was our home for many years. It is a hard life but you always feel Allah's hand on your shoulder.'

Wafaa could feel Allah's hand on her shoulder as she

admired the rugged mountainscape dotted with groves of pine trees.

After their guides tightened the mules' harnesses, they descended a narrow track covered in loose shale. Wafaa was glad for the rope tied to her surefooted mule.

'We are now passing through Pakistan for a while,' Siham said. 'It is the more direct but also the more difficult route.'

The path was strewn with rocks and boulders and covered with tussock grass which made progress glacially slow; they covered only five kilometres in twelve hours. Just when Wafaa could no longer feel her legs they stopped for prayers and a quick meal. Ten minutes later their trek resumed. Wafaa could no longer feel her feet in her shoes. Her heart wanted to pound its way out of her chest cavity. It seemed she was the only one so affected. The Bin Laden family and the Taliban soldiers showed no sign of tiredness. She decided to say nothing and press on.

Their next stop for *Maghreb* prayers was equally brief. Darkness descended as they set off down a narrow ravine. Heavy cloud cover made it almost pitch black. They were about to stop when the clouds parted to reveal the full moon that illuminated the final leg of their journey, an ascent up the side of a mountain to the caves.

Wafaa was so fatigued she was certain she would fall asleep while walking so she tied the rope around her wrist in case she let go. It would at least prevent the mule trampling her if she fell.

She was close to giving up when a dark figure appeared out of nowhere. He waved a shaded kerosene lantern as he ran towards them. It was Osama's son, Hamza. He had left Tarnak Farms a few days before to prepare the caves for their arrival.

'*Asalam Aleikum,*' he said as he took the rope from Bin Laden's hand.

Bin Laden clapped the young man on the back.

'Come dear,' Khairiah took Wafaa by the hand. She led her down hand-hewn steps between two giant boulders.

* *

Wafaa woke next morning aching all over; painful blisters covered her feet and hands. After breakfast, Khairiah took her on a tour of the caves.

Later, when they were alone, Khairiah led her out into the weak sunshine. 'There is something of great importance we must discuss.' Khairiah looked around to ensure their conversation was private. 'Come walk with me.'

Wafaa followed her towards a frozen lake at the base of a towering cliff. The ice reflected patches of blue sky above.

'Are we now in Afghanistan again?' Wafaa looked around, awestruck.

'Yes, my dear, and now we are with our own army. They and the Taliban brothers have returned from raiding the enemy.'

Wafaa glanced around. 'Where? I cannot see anyone.'

'Al-Qaeda soldiers are all around us. Above and below. You cannot see them but sometimes you might smell their cooking if the wind blows in the right direction.'

'That is good to know.' Wafaa said. It was like being in their own small country and she was with the king. It was a good, safe feeling.

'As you know, we are in the middle of a terrible war. You have felt its effects first hand,' Khairiah said as she glanced at Wafaa. 'There is no knowing how much longer the war will go on or where we go from here. We might stay here for many years or we might leave tomorrow.'

Wafaa nodded, wondering where Khairiah was going with the conversation.

Khairiah put a hand on her shoulder, 'I would like to propose that Osama takes you as his wife.'

THE LEGACY

Tora Bora Caves, 28 October 2001, 12:00 pm

An Imam performed the marriage ceremony at noon. A modest celebration followed it. The men sacrificed a goat and sat around a fire to eat *pulao*. Khairiah, Siham and Amal prepared Wafaa for the wedding night as best as they could by telling her Bin Laden's quirks.

'You must not speak,' Amal said, 'unless he asks you a direct question.'

'Do not show many emotions,' Siham added. 'He thinks feelings are a sign of a weak and impious person.'

'Aww, do not scare her!' Khairiah exclaimed. 'He is not a monster to be feared. Yes, he is stern, but he has never been cruel to us.'

Wafaa took it all in. Bin Laden was almost old enough to be her father. She would have to shift her thinking or nighttime would be unbearable.

* *

Wafaa remembered nothing of their nuptial encounter that night except that Osama had visited her in the dark and that neither of them had uttered a sound. He had left after it was over.

Next morning, he ate breakfast with them all sitting on a cloth spread over the floor.

'Wafaa, it would please me if you accompany me for a walk after we finish,' he said as he downed his stainless-steel beaker of goat's milk. 'I shall be outside.'

Wafaa looked around the room wondering whether she should finish her meal. Khairiah smiled and signalled for her to follow.

Bin Laden, his Kalashnikov was slung over his left

shoulder, stood fifty metres from the cave entrance at the edge of a drop. He was surveying the valley below with a pair of binoculars. He glanced back at the sound of her footsteps and put the binoculars back in their case.

She walked as fast as her blistered feet and the loose shale allowed. She shivered as she struggled with the zipper on her jacket as the wind cut at her exposed cheeks like a knife; even breathing was painful. By the time she had finished zipping up her jacket, her body felt like a block of ice.

'Walk with me.' He turned around as she drew near, his breath fogging as he spoke. 'We need to talk.'

Wafaa had to run to keep up with his long-legged gait. His face was blue from the cold but he didn't shiver or show any other signs of discomfort. 'It was the only honourable thing to do.' He didn't look at her.

'Y-yes, I understand.' She lied. She didn't understand. Islamic tradition encouraged believers to marry women widowed in battle after the period of mourning. In their case, it was too early. 'You are an honourable man. I believe it.'

'I know you have not served the waiting period after Faysal's death but Allah has made provisions for extreme circumstances.'

She nodded, breathing deeper with the exertion of keeping up.

'There is a reason God joined our paths.' He stopped on a rocky outcrop next to a stunted fir tree. A cloud had drifted in below them, cloaking the valley in tufts of white. A light mist surrounded them. Fresh snow covered the peaks. It explained the freezing conditions.

Bin Laden leaned against the tree trunk and poked its exposed roots with his cane. 'Jihad is not just about killing infidels. It is also not about dying a glorious death to enter paradise.' His voice was low. Wafaa was about to say something when she stopped herself. He wanted her to listen, not speak. She nodded quietly as he continued.

'A modern jihad is about strategy. When two unequal

sides battle, strategy and patience can even out the odds.'

Wafaa kept nodding as Bin Laden, the person she saw as the greatest Islamic warrior in modern history expounded on his jihadist philosophy. This was important. He was planning the future. How was it possible that he considered her worthy?

The Present

DEAD ENDS

Melbourne, Thursday 4 January, 8:30 am

'I'm sorry, I don't understand,' Daniel Wax spoke into his phone. He swivelled in his chair; his brow furrowed in concentration as he listened to the agitated voice. His frown grew deeper. Jane and Sergei exchanged glances as they waited for him to finish.

If Dennis's information was correct, Daniel might be unable to help. They still had to try. There was always hope.

Daniel slammed the phone down. 'Fucking hell. How can she be nowhere?' His keyboard rattled as he wiped off flecks of spittle. 'The police have no record of an arrest, nor any warrant. They assured me they wouldn't hold someone in secrecy.'

'Could it be the AFP or ASIO?' Jane said. 'What about... extradition... to another country?'

'ASIO don't normally arrest people, and definitely not without a warrant. The AFP have the power but can't extradite without a court order and besides, they told me they don't have her. The VicPol officer suggested you attend the nearest police station and report it as a kidnapping.'

'Could they be lying?' Sergei said.

'Not without committing an offence. Australian law prohibits secret detention or preventing access to a lawyer.'

'The people who took Razane were professionals. Could they be...' Sergei paused and looked at Jane before continuing, 'CIA or something?'

'If the US were hell-bent on getting someone, I reckon they'd find a way. You know them and us belong to the Five Eyes Alliance. There's probably underhanded stuff going on that no one admits to. I mean the CIA have operatives here for sure.' He paused his monologue and fixed them in a stare. 'Is there any reason they'd want to get hold of her?'

'Not a legitimate one,' Jane said.

* *

'I'm going to Pakistan.' Sergei waited for the lift doors to close. 'We can't do anything from here.'

'You mean, we're going to Pakistan,' Jane said looking at him.

'It could be risky for you, sweetheart. It's only been two years since they charged you with blasphemy. You know how fanatics are. It doesn't matter that the authorities have dropped the charges.'

Jane knew Sergei was right. After they had escaped from Pakistan, their attorney general's office had dropped the charges. For weeks after, Pakistan was aflame with demonstrations. Religious fanatics had issued fatwas and called for her death.

'Two years is a long time. They'll have moved on. I could dye my hair or cut it, but you're not going by yourself.'

'There are still fatwas on you,' Sergei said. He knew he couldn't stop her. A part of him was glad she'd accompany him. She lacked Razane's combat experience, but she was fearless. Once she got over the shock of a situation, she was cool under pressure and what she lacked in experience, she made up for in determination.

Her mastering Systema in two years was an example of that.

'I want to be able to fight for you two, the way you did for me,' Jane had said when he had asked her how she kept up her punishing training routine.

He hadn't argued. Being locked up in a Pakistani jail had been hell on Jane. He was happy she'd found a way to heal. None of them ever imagined that she'd ever use her newfound abilities.

'Why are you thinking Pakistan?' Jane said as they exited the lift.

Sergei waited till they were outside. King Street bustled with pedestrian and vehicular traffic. He looked around. No one was within earshot.

'It's where the false intelligence about Razane came from,' Sergei said. 'I'm hoping Major Hamdani can help with that.' The major worked for Pakistani Intelligence and had been instrumental in their escape.

'That's a seriously long shot,' Jane shook her head and sighed. 'But honestly, I can't think of what else we could do... You think he'd help?'

Sergei shrugged.

THE INTERVIEW

Saipan, Thursday 4 January, 11:30 am

Sebastian Corder's hands shook as he entered the name into the search bar. In the background the air-conditioner fan's squeaky bearing chirped loudly. Hopefully Maintenance would get to it before it failed. In the meantime, the office Mike had commandeered was a super cool oasis in the island's clammy humidity.

For the whole journey from Islamabad to Melbourne and on to Saipan Mike had stayed quiet about who they were transporting. Sebastian had sat next to Wafaa Aal Zubeidi for eight hours without realising. What a strange twist of fate!

Four years ago no one had heard of her. He had just joined the CIA as a young graduate. His first assignment was to transcribe an Al-Shabaab operative's confession. He ran all names mentioned through the database and created new files for those who didn't exist.

Wafaa was one of them. Her file remained empty until he had requested an NSA pattern search. The National Security Agency was responsible for monitoring global communications and gathering intelligence for use by the CIA. He had to jump through hoops to convince them to invest the resources for an unknown woman. The myth of the subjugated Islamic women was so deeply ingrained that no one believed a woman could rise high enough in the ranks of Islamic terrorists. His NSA contact gave in just to stop him sending daily reminders.

The data file, when it arrived, was massive and took forever to sort through. The effort proved worthwhile.

It turned out that Wafaa was one of Al-Qaeda's most dangerous leaders. According to rumours she had been Osama Bin Laden's sixth wife and close confidant. She had been involved in the most damaging terror attacks of the last fifteen years, including the assassination of a former Pakistani prime minister and several terror incidents in Europe.

The only problem was a complete absence of any personally identifiable information. No photograph, description, bank details, passport or police record existed. They had a garbled voice grab in Arabic which was only good enough to confirm she was a native speaker.

With no photograph she remained only a storied name, a composite of many data points.

Now as he opened her file, he could see it had grown to include a new tab, marked TBC.

'Someone's added to her file.' Sebastian found it hard to contain his enthusiasm.

Mike nodded. 'I did. We had a breakthrough two days ago.'

Excitement growing, Sebastian read on. She had an alias, Razane Silan and an address in Melbourne, Australia. Even better, they finally had a photograph. It was grainy and showed her holding a rifle and she was the main suspect in the Times Square bombing. Forensics was working on proving her phone had triggered the bombs. Until they did, the evidence linking her to the bombing was circumstantial. It sufficed to make her a person of interest but not to arrest or extradite her. It explained why Mike hadn't gone to his superiors. The reckless bastard was relying on extracting a confession.

Sebastian finished reading the file and looked up, 'Wow. What a break! But I don't understand. Why did we snatch her?'

Mike sat across the table drumming his fingers on the dark wooden table top. 'Are you finished?' He snarled, ignoring the question.

The air-conditioning had no effect on Mike. His clothes were soaked in sweat. His pale skin was covered in red blotches that looked like someone had taken a scrubbing brush to his face. The top two buttons on his once white shirt were undone and exposed tufts of grey chest hair. A crumpled mouse-brown tie, in need of a pattern to hide the food stains, hung limp around his collar. His oily, grey, slicked back hair reinforced the perception he hadn't showered in many days.

Sebastian had heard others describe Mike as old school, but antediluvian was a better descriptor.

He could forgive Mike his appearance and his disdain for protocol if he didn't behave like an asshole. He was a rude sociopath, a nasty, bitter and twisted man who didn't belong in the Agency. A good intelligence officer was an unbiased, equanimous machine. Mike was the complete opposite.

Skirting rules in the name of efficiency was one thing, but going solo on interrogating the CIA's highest value prisoner ever was quite another.

Sebastian was on the horns of a dilemma. Mike was his superior officer, so by rights he had to obey and interrogating Wafaa was a career defining opportunity. But it was also a potential career-ending cluster fuck. 'Mike, are you sure we can handle this on our own?'

'We need to break her... fast. We'll get the team to set up in parallel. But we can't wait. You know any intelligence has a use by date...'

'But the protocol—?'

'Fuck protocol.' Mike almost spat at him.

What the fuck! Mike was behaving like a child refusing to surrender candy. Sebastian rubbed his temples to ease a hammering headache. 'How long till the teams are in place?'

Mike picked at his fingernails and shook his head but said nothing.

'OK, at least tell me who at Langley knows...? Tell me they know.'

'You've seen. Everything's logged in her file.' Mike leaned forward as if daring Sebastian to challenge him any further.

'So you told no one, like personally?' Sebastian groaned as he held his head. Hiding something, even in plain sight, was deceptive.

The team investigating Times Square was analysing DNA samples, bomb fragments and tracing the mobile phone signal.

By the time they connected it to Razane, Mike would have either extracted a confession or killed her trying. Interrogations were hard on prisoners. To ensure their safety, the team always included doctors and psychologists.

'Look man, there's so much politics and I ain't flavour of the month,' Mike said after a while. 'They'll waste time and insist on safeguards and protocols. They'll poke holes in the evidence because of the source--'

'Safeguards are for a reason but why... would they poke holes?'

'Because... the source is a Paki and the fuckers have a history of screwing us.'

'Yeah, well... And what if they're screwing us... again?'

'To what end?' Mike said.

'OK, so let's say their info is legit.... It's even more important we follow the process.'

'Fuck process,' Mike spat again.

Sebastian was getting nowhere. 'So how did they suddenly get intel on someone as shadowy as Wafaa?'

Mike exhaled loudly and stretched his arms over his head. 'They tortured an Islamic State fighter. He told them her alias and from there it was easy.'

'Hmmm,' Sebastian said deep in thought.

'Also the flash memory chip of one of the bombers' phone, the call that triggered the explosion, came from Australia. It was an unlisted SIM card bought at a service station in Melbourne without identity. The police are looking through the service station's security camera feed and the phone company are tracking the user's location. It's only a matter of time.'

'Australia has twenty-five million people. We don't yet know it belongs to our prisoner,' Sebastian said.

'Forensics will have the results soon. Even now the evidence is compelling. Besides, remotely triggering suicide bombers is a classic Wafaa signature.'

'And so is extreme caution. Why would she use her own phone...?' Sebastian said.

'She thought she'd bought it anonymously.' Mike shrugged.

'Isn't it... a bit too convenient?'

'Nonsense. All big criminals are undone by a small mistake. It adds up. And there's more. I asked a buddy at the NSA to cross reference Wafaa and Razane Silan. Guess what? There are heaps of mentions. I don't know how we missed it before. And the devices we seized in the raid to capture her... they were remote wiped before we could analyse them. Innocent people don't do that.'

'Well, OK,' Sebastian said in a resigned tone. Mike was as loathsome as a toad with warts, but he was probably right. He'd play along but have a chat with his old supervisor. 'It sounds plausible...' Sebastian raised his hands to signal capitulation. 'So what's our strategy...?' Hopefully, the grease ball had one.

'We go hard on her. Make her feel like there ain't nothin' we won't do.' Mike replied with a dour expression. 'You ready sonny boy?' Mike stretched out his arms again and yawned, exposing yellow teeth, his coffee breath wafting across the room.

Sebastian ignored the rudeness as he forced a smile. 'You're the boss.'

'Never forget that,' Mike shook a finger at him.

Sebastian's line of questions annoyed Mike. For once in his life he'd gotten the jump on everyone else. And this upstart go-by-the-book, paper-pushing, still-wet-behind-the-ears, ass-licking prick was rocking the boat. He yawned again. Lack of sleep and the shit climate made him restless. He was sweating through all his pores.

'Then tell me what to do,' Sebastian said.

'I'll do the talking, I'm the nasty cop and you're the soft cop. But at all times show confidence... that'll scare the shit out of her.'

'And if she's the wrong person?'

Sebastian could be a persistent bugger. 'She ain't!' He spoke through clenched teeth as he stood. 'You coming or do I go it alone?'

**

Their hooded prisoner sat unmoving under a powerful lamp. Her hands were manacled together with a heavy chain tied to an eyelet on the steel table. Mike and Sebastian pulled up a chair each and sat across from her. Neither of them spoke. The longer they waited, the more pliable she would be.

Mike looked at his watch. Fifteen minutes should do.

**

Razane heard them enter. Hunger and the drugs made her dizzy. The shock made her feel detached from reality. Any hope this was just a bad dream had faded many hours ago. She had two choices, either curl into a ball and go to water or face it with dignity.

The hood was hot and stuffy. Her face and scalp itched from the accumulated perspiration. The discomfort made it hard to dig deep and find the strength she knew she had. She needed every ounce to calm herself and maintain control.

Where was she? Who were her captors? Why had they kidnapped her? The flying time, the humidity and the Marines suggested she was in a US army base. They had a few in the Pacific. The army didn't kidnap, but the CIA did, which was an unsettling thought. The CIA had a terrible history of masking its incompetence with money and indiscriminate brutality.

Despite the awful realisation, Razane felt more in control. She had a task she could focus on, to find out why the CIA had taken her prisoner.

She closed her eyes and worked on slowing her breathing. The suffocating feeling began to recede. She could hear every separate sound. The room had gone quiet. Except for a… footfall. Someone was taking pains to walk undetected. She opened her eyes. A hand yanked her hood off. The bright light stabbed her corneas. The cold air stopped her breath. She closed her eyes but couldn't shut out the stabbing brightness completely. An orange red orb, an image of the sun like bulb lingered.

Her eyes teared. Breathe! She had to stay centred and in control. She opened her eyes gradually, to give her pupils time to adjust. Two men glared at her. She recognised one from the plane. He'd been sitting beside her.

'Can I have some water?' The words stuck in her parched throat.

The younger man placed a bottle of spring water on the table, just out of her grasp. From the build-up of condensation, it looked chilled and enticing. Her every fibre longed for it, but she couldn't reach. They were torturing her.

'Why am I here?' she whispered.

'Do you think…' the older man leaned forward in his chair, 'you're in any position to ask questions?' He had a mean, repulsive look about him, like he hadn't showered in a month. She remembered his voice. He'd been sitting behind her in the aeroplane.

'W-why…' she struggled to speak, 'did you kidnap me?'

The younger man unscrewed the cap and, stretching forward, put it to her lips. The water rushed down her throat, faster than she could swallow. She coughed. Some dripped down the front of her body. The uncomfortable cold on her warm skin made her wince, but it was what she needed. She fought back her gag reflex and relaxed her throat. The water poured down faster. A current of life ran through her. The older man leapt forward and snatched it away causing more water to spill out and drenching the front of her jumpsuit. She shivered.

'Why am I here?' she said with more force. Her throat was still painfully dry. She was still insanely thirsty.

'The longer you pretend the more you'll suffer,' the grubby man said.

'You're completely mad.' Razane shook her head.

'Ms Razane, or should I say, Ms Wafaa. You're mad if you think you can attack the USA and get away with it.' The vile man's voice rose in volume and pitch as he spoke, flecks of spittle forming on the sides of his mouth.

Razane looked at the ugly American. The man was insane. She tried to recall what he'd called her. 'What are you talking about?' she raised her voice in anger. 'I demand to be released, immediately—'

'Your jihad is over. As an enemy combatant you have no rights. But if you talk, we'll make it easier for you.' The younger man spoke.

Razane fought through the haze. They seemed certain she was someone else. But why? Based on what information? They had to be guessing or they wouldn't be interrogating her. Even though she was in chains, they didn't have complete control.

'So how did I attack the US?' Razane's voice was ice cold. She had found the reserves she needed.

'Ms Razane, er Wafaa. Stop the pretence. It's over—'

'We'll get the truth out of you.' The older man interrupted. He wanted to show he was the boss. It meant he was insecure. Insecure men were dangerous.

The younger leaned forward. 'Trust me, my colleague isn't a nice man. He can make a brick confess.'

The conversation was going nowhere. 'Humour me. What am I supposed to have done?' Razane tried looking defeated, which was easy under the circumstances.

The younger man looked at his companion as if to seek permission. 'We know you masterminded the Times Square attack.'

'What?' Razane screamed, not believing her ears. The chilled air couldn't prevent her breaking out in a sweat. Beads of perspiration dripped between her shoulder blades and her breasts. The top of her lip was salty. Fear gripped her insides. She shivered. Her self-control was slipping. This wouldn't end well. But it couldn't end. She had to fight.

Breathe in, hold, breathe out. She focused on the sound of the air-conditioner and the feel of the air rushing into her nostrils. Breathe in, hold, breathe out. A flicker of strength returned.

'What makes you think I did it?' she said, shifting in the chair. Its forward edge bit into her thigh, making her leg fall asleep.

'You're not here to ask questions, we are,' the older man slapped his hand on the steel table hard enough to make her jump.

The effort to stay calm was draining her again. 'I didn't do it. I can't for the—'

'Stop lying!' the older man slapped the table again, hard enough for it to ring.

'That has to hurt,' she smiled at him. She had centred again. Ironically, his loss of temper helped her keep hers. 'I'm completely innocent.'

'Ms Wafaa—' the younger man leaned forward.

'Who's Wafaa?' They were after someone else. That was the glimmer of hope. If they investigated her, they'd discover their mistake. She smiled.

Infuriated, the older man lunged at her but the young man grabbed him by the elbow.

'I can't control my partner forever. And... you are Wafaa.' the younger man said.

Razane looked at him. Unlike his older partner, his voice was absent of hate or anger. Could she reason with him? 'How can I convince you I'm not Wafaa?'

'We have enough evidence. Our analysts are working on your smartphone and laptop. We know your phone triggered the bombs.' He was watching her intently.

'For God's sake, you've the wrong... what did you say? What phone?'

'You really think... we've never come across lying scumbags before,' the older man said. His rising anger made his face look like an over-ripe plum.

'You've the wrong person.' The chains had become a dead-weight and the lack of food made her light-headed. Moving her head made the room spin. 'The real Ms Wafaa must be out there somewhere, you incompetent fools. You idiots are supposed to—'

The blow reverberated inside her skull. Her ears filled with a loud hiss. The side of her face went numb, the pain taking its time before it overwhelmed her. Her head throbbed like a water hammer in a pipe. She had clearly pushed the older man over the brink.

'So you think I...?' her voice sounded distant, like at the end of a tunnel. She tried lifting her hands, but the chain around her wrist stopped her. 'You are incompetent fools... you can't see how wrong you are.' She was crying. The older man lunged again, but his companion held him back.

Razane wanted to speak more, but words failed her. Her head throbbed mercilessly, making her want to throw up. Hunger, nausea, and pain overwhelmed her.

THE LIEUTENANT

Kuala Lumpur, Thursday 4 January, 10:30 am

Najib ground his teeth as he stood on the balcony and watched the world go by. It was hotter than was usual for January, even for KL. At least the breeze was doing a good job keeping the worst of the humidity at bay.

As he walked back inside, he caught his reflection in the mirror. He had always hated his own face for the perpetual smile it wore. It made everyone who met him for the first time, smile back at him. They always started on the wrong foot. Usually they made the mistake of not taking him seriously, sometimes with fatal outcomes. Only when people noticed the arctic winter in his deep-set hawk-like eyes did most smiles freeze.

'They are the windows to your deep jihadi soul,' his Al Qaeda recruiter and mentor Ramzi Moizuddin had once said. Ramzi, may Allah grant him the highest level of paradise, might have been trying to flatter him. But it was true in a way. He did have a single-minded desire for jihad and ultimately martyrdom.

An air-horn nearby shook him out of his thought bubble. If he lacked for anything, it was patience. The strain of waiting made his fingers itch, his arms tingle, and his legs twitch.

Any junkie would recognise the withdrawal symptoms. They might, however, not recognise his addiction, which was anything but normal. He yearned for the touch and oily smell of a freshly cleaned rifle, the grit of sand between his teeth after shelling, the early morning prayers knowing they could lead to a martyr's death that day. But above all, he missed the mind-numbing, butt-clenching fear of charging into battle and the adrenaline rush that followed.

Najib resisted the urge to open the Kik app on his smartphone to check his messages. He would hear a beep when one came. This app made him nervous. It was commercially available and most likely was being monitored by the NSA and CIA. But he didn't dare question their commander's orders. Few people had the fortitude to question *Al-ukht-ul-akbari* Wafaa Aal Zubeidi. He certainly did not.

They used to use their own private network and a clunky app on a blue background. It had been designed and was maintained by Abu Kaseem, one of Al Qaeda's top computer gurus. It wasn't user friendly but was secure and had worked fine until Russian GRU agents kidnapped the man, tortured him, and dumped his body in a ditch on the outskirts of Damascus.

Checking his phone constantly was a sign of a creeping malaise, a breakdown of self-control that didn't behove *mujahideen*. It meant he needed more time in prayer and reflection.

He wasn't the only one feeling uneasy since returning from Syria. All his men were feeling the strain. If it hadn't been for their project, more than one of them would have taken a machine gun to a shopping mall and ended it all in a bloody massacre.

Allah willing, he would resist touching his phone until it beeped to alert him. He worried needlessly. Wafaa had always been a cautious leader.

One of her unbreakable rules was to maintain complete communication blackout for a minimum of three days after any attack. Post-operation Internet chatter had been the undoing of countless jihadi groups. The NSA would use its massive supercomputers to search for and analyse patterns. Their success rate was growing exponentially. A few days later a drone strike would martyr an unsuspecting brother.

Wafaa's strategy appeared to work and probably explained why she was still only a shadow, a whisper even in jihadi circles.

Three days were not yet up. There were still two hours to go. By Allah's grace, she wouldn't make him wait longer than that.

He had bought all the newspapers he could find, Malay

and English. None of the extensive coverage of the Times Square bombing mentioned any arrests.

Allah willing, that was a good sign. The capture of someone as important and well known as Wafaa Aal-Zubeidi would be big news.

A walk would do him good and could relieve his restlessness. He changed out of his *baju seluar* into a pair of jeans and a red T-shirt and checked himself in the mirror. His black beard and cap identified him as a devout Muslim. He removed his cap and brushed his hair. Now he could blend into the crowd.

Feeling calmer, Najib walked down the stairs. Zikri, his landlord, was pulling up the shutters of his homoeopathy store. He turned and waved, '*Selamat pagi.*'

'*Selamat pagi*, Zikri.' Najib waved back.

Zikri made his own medicine at the back of the store with the help of his two sons. Najib liked Zikri. He was a god-fearing man.

Najib set off on the narrow footpath, past the small shops and townhouses in his street. At the end, he turned right into an alleyway between two rows of houses. It was a useful shortcut to the main road.

As he emerged from the lane, he saw the giant golden statues guarding the entrance to Batu Caves. Despite living just a few streets from the world-famous tourist destination, he had never visited them. He decided to see what all the fuss was about. He might never get another chance. If he had understood Wafaa correctly, they could be going on a mission in a few days.

He followed the footpath as it passed under Jalan Lingkaran Tengah 2 Freeway, one of KL's ring roads.

The footpath ended in a public car park for the caves. With a look at his watch, Najib joined the milling crowds jostling to pass through the security screening at the entrance.

A plaque gave a brief history of the Batu Caves. Apparently, this was the second most important Hindu shrine in the world. Hindus were so stupid. They had made a shrine for worshipping idols out of a magnificent cave made by the one true

Allah.

Despite his derision, he did not hate them. Allah would judge them and deal with them. As Wafaa had taught him, his struggle was against the rich and powerful people of the West.

He bought a bunch of bananas from a hawker inside the gate and began to climb the stairs that seemed to go up without end. It smelled worse than a zoo. He couldn't put a finger on it until he saw people carrying containers of milk. Sour milk mixed with rotten banana peels and monkey shit was the worst smell in the world.

The monkeys were everywhere, on the steps, railings, even halfway up the rock. In some places they outnumbered their human visitors. Najib loved the monkeys. They were so naughty but innocent too. Humans were the only creatures that had taken the wrong path. He smiled as he threw them pieces of the fruit and marvelled at how they caught them.

His legs were on fire and he was panting by the time he reached the top. He thought of buying a cup of water, but the stench put him off. He looked at his watch. It was nearly one o'clock. He didn't want to spend prayer time in a Hindu shrine.

Walking down was almost as hard. The steps were worn smooth in places and covered in banana peels. The slightest misstep would end in disaster. By the time he reached the bottom he was drenched in sweat.

Najib used Google to find a nearby mosque. He reached it after a short five-minute walk and thanked Allah that it was air-conditioned.

By the time he had finished praying it was one thirty. Wafaa was now half an hour late. A knot formed in his stomach. Allah willing, there was a good explanation. Hopefully, it wasn't because she had been arrested. If so, he could be next.

Maybe he should move locations and change his phone again. No, that would make no sense. He had already changed it two days ago. It was another of Wafaa's precautions so their MAC addresses were never the same. It was understandable but tiresome.

He couldn't wait around any longer for Wafaa to call, he had work to do. He left the mosque at a brisk pace, stopping only to retrieve his slippers from the entrance.

A police siren howled nearby, startling him. What a jumpy old woman he had become. Clearly, civilian life did not agree with him.

Najib looked at his watch again; he had to hurry. Waiting around for Wafaa to call had made him late. His men would be waiting for him to make the final inspections.

They would also want to know what happened next. It was another reason he had hoped to hear from Wafaa. But it was not to be. He sighed as he flagged down a taxi.

* *

The driver, a small surly Sikh, dropped Najib in a deserted cul-de-sac in an industrial estate.

A rusted chain-link fence ran along one side of the road. The other side was an overgrown Meranti plantation.

Najib walked along the footpath littered with leaves past several closed gates. Signs showed they were shipyards. Apart from a few cars and the odd motorcycle, it looked deserted.

He stopped at a signboard on a post hammered into the ground. The lettering had faded over time but he could just make out "Dalam Baja Shipyards".

Invasive creepers had covered the fence and the rusty wrought-iron gate. To a casual observer, the property looked abandoned. A motorised surveillance camera painted green to fit into the surroundings tracked him as he unlocked a padlock at the end of a heavy chain.

He pushed the gate open on its well-oiled hinges and locked it behind him. A rusted bicycle leaned against a ramshackle security hut.

Najib rode it along the path that led towards a grove of plantain trees at the back of the property. As he drew closer, he saw steel clad buildings. They couldn't have chosen a better location for the important work they were doing.

Haziq stood outside an open door smoking a cigarette. He took a long puff and acknowledged Najib's presence with a nod of his head. Through the open door the bright blue light of arc welders mixed with the yellow spark showers from grinders. The men were busy.

'Selamat pagi, Haziq.' Najib had to raise his voice over the whine of the grinding wheels and the crackling of sparks.

Haziq grunted a response, glanced back inside the building, and walked towards him. Najib stopped. Something was wrong. Haziq wasn't easily flustered.

Najib waited till Haziq was closer. 'What is wrong, my friend?' Haziq was a devout Muslim, a ferocious fighter and a most trustworthy man which was why he had put him in charge of the shipyard.

Haziq steered him away from the door, out of earshot of the others. 'Aminuddin opened one package,' he looked at Najib as if trying to gauge his reaction. 'He asked me what those things were but... I think he knows and is only acting dumb.'

Najib cursed inwardly. It was unwelcome news. Aminuddin was a skilled fitter and machine operator and had been the only person able to understand Wafaa's technical instructions. He was also the only outsider. They had hired him to teach the men how to use their tools. They were behind schedule and Aminuddin could machine and weld twice as fast as the best. He was friendly and polite and was from a decent family but they couldn't risk him talking. 'I should not have hired him. We could have used YouTube.'

Haziq patted him on the back. 'Brother, did you not say Americans track YouTube?'

'Yes, I did.' Najib sighed. 'Where is he now?'

'I asked him to paint the racks. He has been there ever since.'

'Well done.' Najib looked at his watch. It was 3:32 in the afternoon. They still had a long work session ahead of them. Wafaa had already expressed her displeasure at the time they were taking.

'Oh, and we took away his phone.' Haziq added.

'You did well.' Najib nodded in appreciation. 'When did the men start work?'

'At six in the morning. They will work for another hour.'

'OK, you go back and supervise the men. I will check on Aminuddin. When they leave, come to the paint booth.'

Haziq nodded. He wore a sad expression. He understood what needed doing and why.

The paint booth was on the water's edge. Behind it, the turbid green slow-moving waters of the Langat river reflected the afternoon sunlight. A large expedition yacht was moored at the end of the jetty. It had been fitted with upgraded Caterpillar engines and long-range fuel tanks to allow it to circumnavigate the globe. They were kitting it out as a live-aboard dive boat. Tomorrow they would install the scuba tank frames and load the fake aluminium Catalina tanks containing their deadly cargo. They would stack real scuba tanks on top. No one would uncover the subterfuge.

Aminuddin was shrouded in black clouds of paint swirling in the small space. He didn't notice Najib approach.

Najib winced as he pulled his T-shirt over his nose to ward off the strong smell of solvents. He was glad the paint booth was separated from the workshop or the whole place would go up in flames.

Aminuddin would be busy for a while. 'Allah forgive me for what I have to do,' Najib muttered as he returned to the large noisy shed, entering through the open rear door. Large wheeled frames covered in green semi-opaque acrylic sheets divided the space into two.

The sound of grinders and welders was deafening. Two men were cutting the bottom of large scuba tanks. Another two were placing packages wrapped in oilskin into the open tanks. The packages were in three sizes. Each tagged with red, blue or green tape. They contained disassembled Browning M2 machine guns and 50 calibre ammunition belts, something only Haziq and he were supposed to know.

Najib watched as two more men closed and welded the tank shut, taking care not to heat the contents. To ensure the repair was invisible, they ground the weld smooth and wire brushed it to restore its finish.

A solitary operator was attaching a rubber base ring to painted tanks and filling them with 150psi of enriched air nitrox, enough pressure to pass a casual inspection.

A team of four men were fabricating scuba tank frames beyond the green divider. Sparks flew into the steel rafters and globs of molten aluminium plopped onto the sand that covered the concrete floor.

As he watched his men work, Najib said a little prayer that Wafaa would ask them to wield the machine guns.

THE LONG WAIT

Peter took a deep breath as he exited the escalator into the blue marble foyer. The top floor of the Black Diamond Tower, Melbourne's fourth tallest building was empty. He wasn't surprised. He had seen no one on previous visits either. The eleven penthouse apartments on the top floor were among the most exclusive real estate in Melbourne. It was unlikely any were the sole residence of their owners.

The cool dry air made him shiver. It was a sharp contrast to the mugginess outside. The mercury had climbed to a stinking hot thirty-eight degrees after an overnight thunderstorm. It had made normally mild Melbourne feel more like Singapore.

Something irritated Peter's throat. Without slowing, he hawked and spat into a potted plant. As he neared the entrance to penthouse eight, a face-recognition camera scanned his features. Bolts slid sideways with a well-oiled click that reminded him of his Lee Enfield rifle. As the double doors opened noiselessly inwards, the lights inside came on to illuminate a wide entrance hall with a highly polished brown marble floor.

Tall ceilings, ornate architraves and recessed floodlighting made the cavernous apartment look expensive and reminiscent of a hotel lobby. As his feet sunk into the deep pile of the taupe carpet that formed an island in the centre of the lounge, he felt almost guilty for not having removed his shoes.

He walked over to the floor-to-ceiling window that looked out onto Melbourne. The floor here was marble. A welded steel frame stood against the glass looking out of place in the refined apartment. He had brought it up in pieces and had assembled it a week ago.

Outside on the street below, the cars looked toy-like. People looked like ants. The Black Diamond Tower was on

Melbourne's south-west corner. In the distance, he could see two other buildings, one on Melbourne's northern edge and the other in Collins Street near Parliament. He owned the penthouse apartments in those buildings as well. The three apartments formed an equal-sided triangle. It had taken him nine years to buy all three. Wafaa Aal Zubeidi had paid for them as well as for two of his three farms that exported beef and butter to the Middle East.

She had transferred the money by allowing him to overcharge for his produce. It had been remarkably easy. He had always paid his taxes, and no one had ever questioned his profits.

The money also funded a growing army of fighters. Each handpicked by Wafaa, they slipped into the country illegally.

He hid them in clever ways. Two of his properties were in woodland in Melbourne's north east. One was in the remote outback near Alice Springs.

Wafaa had chosen the men well. Not one had ever been caught, and they were all perfectly content staying on his farms.

Like him, they all knew they had been chosen for a higher purpose that would one day be revealed.

In the meantime, they worked hard, trained harder, prayed, and waited.

Till the battle-hardened fighters had shown up, Peter had no idea what Wafaa's plans were. He had been curious but dared not ask. Now he knew it involved violence in Australia.

Six months ago, she'd asked him to buy four large Mercedes vans and install armour plating and movable turrets on the roof. She had also asked for three steel frames, one for each penthouse.

True to form, she sent him detailed engineering drawings but no information on their purpose. But he knew. The turrets on the vans and the steel frames in the apartments were machine gun mounts. Wafaa was planning an assault on Melbourne.

Something told him he wouldn't have to wait long for the machine guns. The thought of mass murder energised him. Man was made to fight and spill blood. Why else had God made it red?

THE BREAK

Saipan, Thursday 4 January, 2:30 pm

'That didn't go so well,' Sebastian sighed as he flopped onto the vinyl settee. They were back in the cool confines of Mike's office.

Mike stood in front of the corkboard, sucking on the end of a highlighter. 'They always start out saying the same thing.' He turned to Sebastian. 'But not to worry; we'll make her squeal.'

'You'll accomplish that how…' Sebastian pursed his lips, 'by hitting her?'

'Whatever it takes…' Mike was back to studying the corkboard again. Lost in thought, the sarcasm had washed over him.

'I'm getting something to eat.' Sebastian got up and walked to the door, glad Mike didn't follow.

The mess was almost empty and so were the food cabinets. A bucket of limp and lukewarm chips and two unappetising prepackaged sandwiches were all that remained of the lunch service. Sebastian chose a salami on rye with alfalfa sprouts and a bottle of Perrier and sat in front of a TV screen. The commercials ended and a CNN feature on the New York bombings resumed. Footage of people laying floral tributes in the square was interspersed with short clips of relatives crying, the mayor visiting the injured, and police with guard dogs rounding up suspects. It ended with the president saying they would hunt the perpetrators to the ends of the earth

It was ironic how media coverage amplified a terrorist's effectiveness a hundredfold by instilling fear and prolonging panic.

It was scandalous but understandable that no one did anything about it. Terrorist attacks were the media's bread and butter. Governments benefited too.

After 9/11 Al-Qaeda's capabilities were significantly

degraded till they no longer posed a significant public threat. The same applied to Islamic State.

Most terrorism incidents were lone-wolf attacks by mad losers on the fringes of society. Their attacks were limited to driving trucks into a crowd or running amok with a knife.

The solution for governments would have been simple; invest in mental health and promote social harmony and integration. But that didn't serve their political interests, which was to keep the public fearful.

Instead, they took a populist approach, spending money on more surveillance, strengthening anti-terror laws and curtailing human rights.

Whenever terror suspects were captured, they claimed allegiance to the terror network most recently in the news. The named terrorist organisation usually gleefully accepted responsibility. After all, a press release sent to Al-Jazeera was less work than organising a real attack.

In most cases, no such links existed.

By 2019, starved of money and hounded by the major intelligence agencies, most terror groups had been rendered impotent.

Wafaa Aal Zubeidi's organisation was a notable exception. That's why they had to destroy it.

Carrying the half bottle of Perrier, Sebastian returned to his desk. Was there a file on Razane Silan? He typed her name in the search bar.

After a brief search he found that ASIO had a file on her. He settled back in his chair and read it with interest. It mentioned her Internet history and use of the Darkweb to access information on weaponry and explosives. Ostensibly it was for her business that conducted terrorist risk assessments for companies.

In light of everything Mike had told him, this was incriminating as hell. As much as he hated it, Mike was probably right. Razane was Wafaa Aal Zubeidi. Still, a good intelligence officer always kept an open mind.

Mike had closed his a while ago. Nothing, not even perfect

evidence to the contrary would shake his belief that their prisoner had masterminded the Times Square atrocity.

Morally Sebastian had no problem with Mike torturing their prisoner, if she was the real Wafaa. The real issue was that while it was easy to make a prisoner confess under torture, it was hard to get reliable information. He had seen it before. Under extreme pain and deprivation prisoners made things up.

Mike was a sadistic bastard. There was a risk he'd go too hard and either kill Wafaa or drive her insane.

Sebastian took the last sip and sent the empty bottle sailing into the recycling bin. Somehow, he'd have to keep Wafaa alive till Langley could send the proper interrogation team.

BETRAYAL

Ghazni, Thursday 4 January, 2:30 pm

Major Hamdani put down the mug of milky tea and cupped his eyes. The heat and pressure from his palms gave him instant relief as tears lubricated his raw cornea. He opened his eyes and blinked away the wetness. The dark shadows at the back of the teahouse were soothing. He needed all the relief he could get. He still had a long drive and then a hike to the Pakistani border.

After three weeks in tense negotiations between local Taliban factions, he was exhausted and there was not much to look forward to when he got home. He was sick of the constant intrigue and political infighting in the ISI. If there hadn't been important work to still do, he'd be tempted to march into the colonel's office when he got back and hand in his resignation. An ISI major would always find a job in Pakistan's private sector.

But he couldn't leave just yet. The geopolitical situation had become more complicated than it needed to be. Everyone was meddling in Afghanistan. India, Pakistan, Iran, Russia, and the USA had turned it into a zero-sum game with no end. Even though they all realised there was no chance of winning, none of them could afford to pull out. It had become a Mexican standoff without Mexicans.

Pakistan, Iran, and Russia all needed a buffer zone in Afghanistan to keep religious extremists from their borders so they all supported various Afghan militia groups.

Pakistan supported the Afghani Taliban, a group they had set up with the CIA's help to harangue the Afghan Government. Some of the men and weaponry leaked to the militia groups fighting India in Kashmir. Even though Pakistan had little control over this, India retaliated and supported the Pakistani Taliban.

The madness had become the status quo. The only solution

was for all parties to end hostilities at the same time.

After many hopeless years, a paradigm shift was in the offing. After a lot of international pressure and spurred on by empty coffers, the Pakistani Government had decided peace was cheaper and easier to manage.

Islamic extremists were uncontrollable, mainly because they rarely recognised national borders. Over time, the groups sponsored by Pakistan had splintered. Hardened fighters moved from group to group and region to region till enough found their way to Pakistan, fighting the government that had initially supported them.

The doorbell tinkled as more patrons entered the establishment, their shadows falling on the far wall. The waiter, not yet old enough for facial hair, scurried out of the kitchen wiping his hands on the tea towel draped over his left shoulder. He was like so many Afghani children, slaving away at a young and tender age to feed desperately poor families and in the process dooming themselves to the same fate as their parents.

The young boy's exasperated expression turned to fear as he eyed the new arrivals. An unpleasant tingling sensation ran down the major's spine. Afghans feared only two things, the Taliban and the police. The polished tile wall reflected the drab steel blue of the Afghani Police uniform.

The major fought the temptation to turn around. Maybe they wouldn't notice him and leave. He stole a sideways glance at the surrounding diners. Their sudden silence belied their pretended nonchalance.

The footsteps became louder. He was out of luck. They had come for him. He turned just as a voice boomed out.

'Major Hamdani, you are under arrest on charges of espionage.' They knew his name. There was no point presenting fake papers.

He turned to see an Afghani police officer, his gun drawn, flanked by two burly constables. One held handcuffs.

Someone had betrayed him. Who had the most to gain by getting rid of him? He could think of several people. But this time they had gone too far. Factional infighting in the ISI was almost part of the culture. Moderates fought conservatives, but no one had ever betrayed anyone to the enemy. That was tantamount to treason. He put his wrists out and sighed. There was a first time for everything.

The bright light assaulted his eyes as they led him out of the teahouse to a waiting police Ford Ranger pickup.

This would not end well. Pakistani spies were routinely tortured and held indefinitely until the next prisoner swap.

What irony to be caught when he was trying to get the Taliban to agree to peace talks.

Of course, it was a secret until the deal was signed, sealed and delivered by all parties. Till then the Pakistani Government wouldn't risk the political backlash from extremist right-wing groups. So they would keep this quiet. Back at his office, on hearing the news of his capture, they would have a prayer session, everyone would shake their heads and praise him sky-high. The higher-ups would authorise a stipend for his children and maybe someone would name a conference room after him. Then they would send another agent in his place and forget all about him.

RETRIBUTION MACHINATION

Lahore, Friday 5 January, 9:30 am

Major Amjad scanned his inbox. There was still nothing from Mike Hound, the *haram-khor* bastard. With unsteady hands he picked up his teacup and took a sip. The burning liquid scalded his lips and his chin as it dribbled into his beard and down the front of his shirt. Amjad used the back of his hand to wipe his face and reached for a tissue. He had hoped for a conciliatory note telling him Mike had changed his mind or would at least consider bringing Razane to Pakistan. But there was nothing. It proved what he had known all along; Mike was just another arrogant American.

The major snatched a few more tissues to wipe his hand and blot the tea from his dark grey shirt.

Mike had proved more intransigent than he'd expected. Surely, the ingrate owed him.

The CIA had used Pakistan for what they termed extraordinary rendition. Recently, however, relations had cooled and the two governments no longer pretended to be allies.

Not that the US was ever Pakistan's friend. The Yanks always demanded more than Pakistan could give and they never reciprocated.

This case was an example. He had given them the world's most wanted terrorist. It was only reasonable that he be allowed to participate in her interrogation. He would have to come up with a way to force Mike to bring Razane to Pakistan, but how?

Major Amjad dipped a tissue in a glass of water and used it to wipe the stickiness off his hand. He had a sudden urge to smash the glass at the far wall of his office, but that wouldn't help him regain control.

He was so close to snapping the trap shut on the woman he hated the most in the world. The woman who had killed Fazal, his baby brother.

Ever since they had lost their parents at a young age he had been more like a father to Fazal, helping him through school, cadet college and then into the army. Fazal's death had been a hammer blow. The circumstances of his death were hard to accept. He had been shot from behind by Razane Silane, a Kurdish Australian. Razane was an accomplice of a fugitive escaping a blasphemy charge. Fazal had been part of Major Hamdani's team. They had tracked the fugitives to Karachi where Major Hamdani had inexplicably allowed them to escape. Fazal was martyred as he had tried to stop them.

Major Hamdani was a colleague and a stickler for the law. It beggared belief why he had allowed events to unfold the way they did and none of his subsequent reports had provided a satisfactory explanation.

After Fazal's death, he went through severe bouts of depression relieved only by violent fantasies in which he would torture Razane endlessly by cutting off bits of her body.

Revenge was the only way he would ever be at peace. But getting to her would not be easy. At first, he had toyed with the idea of paying for a professional hitman. He soon gave up on that. Australia was a rich country with an excellent police force. Too many things could go wrong and even if it succeeded, it was too easy an end for his brother's killer. Razane needed to suffer.

The solution came to him one day while watching the news about President Obama's decision to keep the infamous prison at Guantanamo Bay open. The news showed footage of manacled prisoners in orange jumpsuits, shuffling along a chain-link-fence corridor. Devoid of expression and a future, they looked like the walking dead. It was the worst fate for a human being. It was something he wouldn't wish on his worst enemy, except one.

Over the next week, a plan slowly crystallised in his mind.

The US Justice Department maintained a list of the most wanted fugitives. Shared with Interpol and the world's top spy agencies, it included paedophiles, terrorists and financial fraudsters. Carlos the Jackal, Bin Laden, Kim Dotcom, and the IS leader Baghdadi were all former listees. Through the 2000s the list was dominated by terrorists but nowadays it was mostly occupied by financial criminals. The notable exception was the third position held by Wafaa Aal Zubeidi, wanted for masterminding countless terrorist attacks against western targets.

Wafaa was a shadowy figure never seen in public. No spy agency had her photographs or her fingerprints.

He had first met Wafaa in November 2001. The US had just attacked Afghanistan and Bin Laden was on the run.

As luck would have it, he had been a part of the team that extracted Bin Laden and his household from the Tora Bora caves, in Afghanistan, and brought them to Abbottabad, a hillside town north of Islamabad.

Apparently, Wafaa and Bin Laden had married while at Tora Bora. Five days later in Abbottabad, Bin Laden divorced her and asked his ISI contacts to arrange her safe passage to Syria.

Major Amjad had arranged Wafaa's passport and personally saw her past airport security at Islamabad Airport.

They had stayed in touch. Over the years, he watched in admiration as she built up a formidable terrorist network. Every so often he would pass on intelligence to help her stay off the radar. It was his small contribution to the Global Jihad.

He had managed to keep his liaison secret for many years till one day Major Hamdani mistakenly picked up his phone and discovered his secret messages. By then the two majors were good friends. Hamdani was a pragmatist and had agreed to keep it secret as long as Wafaa stayed far away from Pakistan.

Wafaa's reputation in jihadi circles grew as she stepped up her attacks. But as her confidence grew, so did her mistakes. In the meantime, the NSA steadily improved their ability to monitor and decrypt communications. It seemed it was only a matter of time before they captured or killed her.

During their last conversation, Wafaa had told him of her plans to retire after one last attack, her pièce de résistance. She had refused to divulge any details but had promised it would make anything that had happened in recent history seem trivial.

The thought of Wafaa pulling off such an attack thrilled him. But he also worried that she would be caught. A large attack would necessitate lot of communication with many people.

Something about their conversation bothered him. Wafaa did not sound her usual cold and emotionless self. Instead, she sounded excited, almost like a breathless schoolgirl.

Wafaa was losing her edge at the worst possible time. She risked being caught by the relentless NSA.

If he could swap Wafaa and Razane's identities, it might give her the breathing space she needed and Razane would get what she deserved.

Swapping identities was easier than he had imagined. He began by setting up fake accounts on jihadi social media platforms. Over the following two years he regularly posted comments and engaged in chats where he mentioned Wafaa and Razane in the same context. Occasionally, he dropped hints that they were the same person. He knew the NSA would eventually pick it up.

The second part of the plan was harder. He had to erase Razane's real history.

Normally, only the Turks, Iraqis and Syrians gathered detailed intelligence on Kurdish fighting units in Syria and Iraq. However, since Razane had applied for Australian citizenship, the authorities there would have an intelligence file on her.

Pakistan had some of the world's best hackers. It took Arif, the ISI's nerdish computer genius, just four hours to access her Australian Immigration records and erase her background checks. Breaking into the other countries' systems was easier. Razane was mentioned in only one record held by the Turkish National Intelligence Organisation. It was easy to erase. When he was done, Razane had almost ceased to exist.

The only way to prove her Kurdish links was to contact the Peshmerga Command directly. The Peshmerga were engaged in a messy existential struggle in Syria. With the solid evidence he'd given Mike Hound, no one would bother to contact them.

Mike had lapped up the information about Wafaa like a starving puppy presented with a saucer of milk. He had acted fast and had taken Razane into custody. No doubt she was being interrogated by the CIA at that very moment.

The plan was close to fruition. The last step was to get Mike to bring Razane to Pakistan.

His phone beeped. He read the text message. "Jackals captured a lion in Ghazni."

He smiled. The jackals were the Afghan police. They had reacted to his secret tip off with alacrity. Major Hamdani's capture would get someone a promotion.

Hamdani had been a loose end. He knew everything about Wafaa, including where she lived. Even though he had agreed to keep the secret, the death toll in New York's Times Square massacre might prick his conscience. It was just a matter of a phone call to one of his many CIA contacts and the plan would unravel. Besides, the major deserved to be punished for his role in Fazal's death.

Major Amjad stood up and walked outside. A stroll through the manicured gardens was always refreshing. They weren't as large as the ones in the ISI complex in Islamabad, but they still had tall shade trees and well-tended flower beds. He glanced up and said a silent prayer. 'Ya Allah, help your servant avenge his martyred brother.'

THE WHITE ROOM

Saipan, 4 January, 4:00 pm

Razane woke with a start and stared, unbelieving. Everything, the walls, her bed, her clothes were a flat, featureless uniform bright white. She blinked. Nothing changed. She looked around. White lights shone down from the ceiling and the four walls. The almost total absence of any shadows or highlights made the white even more pervasive. It was like the inverse of what she imagined it felt like being blind and seeing only dark.

She examined her hands as she moved them. They had dressed her in a white one-piece coverall that encased her hands and feet.

A total lack of sound accompanied the total absence of colour. The space she was in was silent, not a whisper nor a rustle anywhere. Even her breathing was silent. It was so utterly soundless that the blood rushing through her brain was the loudest thing she could hear. But even that faded away. She tried shouting and then singing but the sound came out strange and disjointed as if it was being absorbed into the walls. Still uncertain she was awake, she got up off the floor and staggered to the nearest wall. It was closer than she'd expected; the absence of colour had interfered with her spatial sense.

Razane touched the wall. It felt soft and springy with a fabric layer that reminded her of the acoustic material that covered loudspeakers, but it was white.

Dizziness overcame her, and she sat back on the bed. 'What are you doing to me?' she shouted as loudly as she could. 'You can't do this to me. You can't...' Her voice trailed off.

Was she in a demented dream? Had she lost her mind? Perhaps it was a combination of both.

Razane returned to the bed and sat. Drawing her knees to her chest, she whimpered. 'Why?'

She must have drifted asleep because she lost all awareness. When she woke again, she was lying on her side. Her breathing had steadied.

She had to hold on to her sanity at all costs. She had spent the last two years recovering from severe PTSD from her life as a Kurdish soldier. Almost every night her screams had woken the two people she loved most in the world. Without so much as a frown, Sergei and Jane would gently hug her and stroke her till she'd fall asleep again. Because of them, Razane had become whole again. After all that, she could not let herself regress.

Besides, if she went mad, she wouldn't be able to convince her captors she was innocent. She might even confess, which was what they wanted.

Razane had read about white rooms. The CIA used them to disorient and break down a prisoner's defences and turn them into babbling idiots.

Her only means to fight was to relax and meditate. Sleep would delay its effects. She closed her eyes and began to focus on her breathing.

The next time she woke a white food tray lay next to her. Taking a deep breath to calm herself, Razane ate the boiled white rice from the white melamine bowl and drank the milk from the white beaker. She would not let them break her.

WAFAA

Wafaa rose from the prayer mat and looked at the clock on the wall. It was two minutes after eight in the evening. A storm had been brewing for the last hour. Thunder rumbled, making the pressed metal clock tizz. She walked to the window and looked outside. Trees were shaking in the wind. It was drizzling. People down below hurried for cover. A young woman opened her umbrella only to have it invert onto itself. She too ran as the rain pelted down. Beading water and the night-time colours from the traffic and the neon signs turned her window into a kaleidoscope.

Rain was Allah's gift, but it brought the cold with it. Wafaa shivered as she flipped open her laptop and looked at the sixteen public webcams. All had an NY prefix followed by a three-digit number. They showed roads, intersections, and shopping precincts in and around New York City. NY168 was Times Square, where, three days ago, she had given the Americans a taste of what was to come.

The news channels were still showing the bloodied bodies and the devastation but apart from the green debris nets covering many of the buildings, it all was back to normal. Traffic flowed freely, footpaths and road crossings were a crush of people. The city hummed, busily making money, something New York City was famous for.

New York City was big and resilient. Three hundred and sixty-four people out of eight and a half million were a drop in the ocean, a rounding error. The public had become desensitised to bombings. They rationalised their fears away, convincing themselves it could never happen to them.

It didn't matter. The bombing had served its purpose and had drawn her enemies away just like Major Amjad had promised.

By Allah's grace, her next attack would be the real thing. It would happen soon and no one would recover from it so easily. The blow would shake the West to its core and finally bring victory.

Sighing, she settled into her chair and let the raindrops lull her into a deep sleep

* *

Her breath fogged as she ran to keep up with Osama's long strides. For a moment, the only sounds were the crunching of their footsteps in the snow and her heavy breathing. In the distance, a machine gun opened fire. The Americans were close.

'Wafaa, have you heard of non-symmetrical warfare?' Osama said.

The question surprised her. She hadn't heard of the term but guessed what it meant. 'Is it when a weak side fights a strong side?'

Osama laughed heartily. She had never heard him laugh before. 'You are surprisingly correct, my young wife. It also involves the weaker side using strategies to enhance their strengths and mitigate their weaknesses.'

'You mean like our jihad?'

'Yes. It is an excellent example. Tell me who is the weaker side?'

She thought for a moment. It was a loaded question. She was tempted to tell him what she thought he wanted to hear but thought the better of it.

'It depends on how you count strengths and weaknesses. They have airplanes and missiles and money… but we have our faith and the truth of our cause. So they are stronger than us, militarily.'

Osama abruptly stopped and looked at her. His face was in shadow but something told her he wanted to hear more.

'But they are also weaker than us.' She finished rapidly.

'Tell me more, young wife.'

'We have nothing to lose. They have everything to lose. They live in a bubble of self-belief. All we have to do is to prick that bubble and prove they cannot be secure regardless of their riches and technology.'

Osama had sucked in his breath. He was smiling. '*Ma'shallah*, I knew Allah sent you to me for a reason.'

She would later learn that she had verbalised Al-Qaeda's key doctrine. They would never defeat their enemy in the conventional sense. The mighty US Army would never lay down its weapons and sign an armistice. Victory instead would take on another shape. It would come when western governments disbanded their much-vaunted freedoms and dismantled their so-called democracies. It would happen when the average person realised what they had lost in the war against Islam.

* *

A staccato sound jolted Wafaa out of her sleep. Large hail was bouncing off her window. She shivered as she walked over to draw the curtains closed. She saw that dream often because it was when she had started on her jihad. She was now so close to the end. It would be the greatest honour to bring the West to its knees and complete the mission Osama had entrusted her with.

It was time to begin the final phase and call the three commanders who would lead it. They would go down in Islamic history as the finest *mujahideen* the world had known.

She dialled a number and waited as it rang on the other end.

'*Pujian kepada Allah kamu baik dan sihat.* Oh, *Al-ukht-ul-akbari* praise be to Allah you are well.' Najib gushed.

The relief in Najib's voice was cloying, almost embarrassing. She had always found his obsequious nature unsettling. As if his feelings were more than just platonic.

'I am well, Najib. I hope you are well too.' She responded in a kind voice. If Najib was in love with her, now wasn't the time to quash his romantic aspirations.

'I am well. Even better now that I hear your voice.'

'How are the preparations going?'

'Very well, very well. We will be ready to sail in two days.'

'Allah be praised. You have proven yourself a fine soldier. I am honoured to serve as your commander.'

'The honour is all mine, *Al-ukht-ul-akbari*.' There was a brief but awkward pause. 'What do we do after we sail?'

'You and your squad sail to Singapore. When you reach there, I will give you more instructions.'

'Yes, *Al-ukht-ul-Akbari*.'

'Make sure you fill your long-range tanks. I do not want you to stop to refuel. Also, keep enough real scuba tanks to last two weeks. And also make sure you have an onboard compressor. I want no one to become suspicious.'

'Yes, of course.' His voice quavered.

'Put your trust in Allah!' she placed the receiver back on the cradle, deep in thought. Najib was fortunate he was one of the best snipers she had known. He had nerves of steel and had proven himself countless times in the heat of battle. But he was late in his preparations. Her other two commanders in Birmingham and Chicago were already in place, waiting for her final command.

It wouldn't be much longer now.

BACK TO LAHORE

Lahore, Friday 5 January, 4:30 pm

Drops of rain reflecting the runway markers cascaded down the acrylic window panes as the Airbus A320 touched down on Runway One of Lahore's Allama Iqbal International Airport with a bounce. It jolted Sergei out of his reverie.

Poor visibility because of an extra low cloud cover had forced the runway lights on an hour early. In the distance, a Pakistan International Airlines Boeing 777 jet in its white and green livery stood docked to its terminal. Smog shrouded the tip of its tail like it did the top of every light pole.

A weight pressed on Sergei's chest as he recalled their last visit. His old friend, Mack, had picked them up in his shiny Range Rover. Sergei opened his mouth to ward off the drowning sensation. He took a deep breath, but the feeling didn't subside. The pain was still raw.

'What's it darling?' Jane squeezed his hand.

'Just remembering Mack. The last time he...' Sergei bit his lower lip. 'came to meet us.'

Jane put her head on his shoulder. 'Poor dear Mack,' she sighed. Mack had died when a truck bomb struck the police station where she was a prisoner. Mack, Sergei and Razane were in the building looking for a way to rescue her. The bomb was meant to kill her, but by a strange twist of fate, it caused the police station walls to collapse, allowing her to escape.

She still found it hard to shake the guilt. Sometimes she couldn't sleep because of it. The chain of terrible events began with her losing her temper.

If only she'd kept her cool, Mack would still be alive. He was part of the reason she worked so hard on her Systema. All the sprains and bruises and fatigue helped assuage the guilt.

A terrible thought occurred to her. What if Razane's

kidnapping was somehow connected?

The plane came to a stop with a gentle jolt. Seat belt buckles clicked open all around them as the giant turbines wound down. Passengers sprung up and removed their luggage from the overhead lockers. Smartphones pinged and beeped as over two hundred and fifty devices connected to their mobile networks. The seat belt signs came off, the doors opened and the exodus began.

Sergei and Jane waited to let the mad rush subside before they got up. It made little sense after having spent fifteen hours on a journey to worry about being ten seconds earlier out of the terminal.

Two rows behind, a muscular man with short cropped dark hair and heavy stubble watched them over his sunglasses. He folded a newspaper and stowed it in the map pocket as he waited for them to leave. Sergei had noticed him before and assumed he was an air marshal.

Jane sensed his presence and moved sideways to let him pass. The man hesitated, nodded a silent thank you and walked ahead. With a final scan of their seats, Sergei and Jane followed him off the aircraft.

Immigration was uneventful. The officer scanned their passports, took their photographs and with a flourish placed a stamp on the visa page. 'Welcome to Pakistan,' he said as he returned their documents and waved them on.

'What a relief! That was so easy,' Jane said as they waited at the luggage carousel.

'They dropped the charges… so they'd no reason to stop us.' Sergei loaded the suitcases onto their trolley. He ignored the mob of porters clamouring to push their trolley as they walked to the taxi ranks.

'I'd prefer a rental, what do you think?' Sergei pointed to a hire-car company sign.

'Yeah, I agree.'

As if by magic several of the porters became representatives for car-hire companies. Sergei shook his head as he spotted an international brand, he was familiar with.

The car, a black Toyota Corolla, came with the choice of GPS or a driver. Sergei chose the former.

As they were leaving the car park, they became mired in standstill traffic. They remained in the same spot for several minutes till Sergei remembered what Mack had told him about driving in Pakistan. Polite people went nowhere.

It took a while for Sergei to psych himself up, but even at his most aggressive, it took them fifteen minutes to exit the airport.

* *

Shah Jahan, the immigration clerk, looked at the clock on the wall. It had been a quiet day. Ten minutes remained until the end of his shift. He had completed all of his tasks for the day and was about to log off when Naila, his supervisor, sauntered over.

'These are E category… Make sure they go out today.' She dropped two pieces of paper in his in-tray.

'OK, madam.' His voice was dour. She was the boss, but would it kill her to be more polite?

Category E were persons of interest, allowed to enter unhindered. However, their arrival had to be registered on the same day with several government departments.

Shah Jahan looked at the clock again and typed as fast as he was able. The passengers were Sergei Markoff and Ian Mearns. He attached their photos from the Immigration data stream, pressed send and waited for the status bar to confirm. Naila was watching him. She nodded as he gave her the thumbs up.

With a sigh of relief, he logged out. The reports were on their way to a distribution list that included officers of the ISI.

THE HOTEL

Lahore, Friday 5 January, 5:30 pm

Ian Mearns sunk into a plush leather armchair and dialled a number. Two rings later, someone picked up. 'Hi Ian, did you have a good flight?'

'Thanks Angela... Yeah, it was OK. I can't complain when it's Business Class... I'm at the Pearl Continental on Mall Road. Our targets have just checked in...' He shifted in the chair, trying to ease his cramped leg. 'I'll check in myself. It seems like a decent place.' He tried unsuccessfully to suppress a yawn,

'Thanks Ian. Your local contacts are on the way. They'll watch while you rest. Expect them in about half an hour.'

'Thanks Ange. I need a lie down bad... and then a beer.'

'Just show them your passport, they serve beer to foreigners. I recommend the local brand, it's really quite good. And once again... thanks for going.'

'No worries.' He hung up. On reflection, it was his fault. He'd opened his mouth at the meeting and had argued in favour of letting Sergei and Jane leave the country. Of course, it made sense. They would learn so much more by following them. The bosses had enthusiastically agreed and here he was.

The whole thing was a debacle. A dangerous terrorist was hiding in one of their major cities. The Australian intelligence community had been caught with their pants down. Now they were scrambling to get back in the game.

When the grown-ups had complained via their chains-of-command, they had received abject apologies from the Americans. It turned out the operation hadn't been properly authorised, otherwise, of course, they'd have involved the Aussies. They were close allies, after all.

"Not properly authorised" was an oft-used excuse to justify all CIA fuck-ups. This time Ian could sympathise with them. The American public were up in arms and their idiot president was foaming at the mouth, Twitter-bombing the Iranians and the Pakistanis. Even the Europeans were blamed for being soft on terrorism.

'The world is mad,' Ian sighed as he walked to Reception to check in. The worst thing was his eight-year-old son's disappointment that he had to postpone their camping trip in Apollo Bay. A close second was his ex-wife having another example to disparage him with. If only his fellow Australians realised the sacrifices some people made to keep them safe.

'Sign here, please.' The lady behind the counter smiled as she handed him a pen.

He signed and accepted the keycard with a little bow. 'Thank you!' He smiled back at her. She was stunningly beautiful. In different circumstances he'd be tempted to ask her out.

He had just sat down again when his help arrived. They looked like the street toughs they probably were before they'd been recruited.

'I am Afzal, sir.' The tall skinny man with a pale complexion offered his hand.

'And I am Rizwan. We are at your service sir,' the short man with a ridiculous moustache said.

'Thanks fellows. It's great to have some backup.' Their English was pretty good. They must have taken up the offer of lessons. It showed keenness, always a good sign.

After they shook hands, he gave them his mobile number with instructions to call if their quarry appeared.

It had been nice to fly Business Class, but it hadn't helped him sleep. Now he was beginning to see double.

Almost too tired to lift his feet, he trudged out of the lift, yawning as he looked for number 213.

The room was small but modern and well-appointed and smelt clean. He threw his case on the floor, kicked off his shoes and fell into bed. Hopefully, Sergei and Jane would be as tired as he was and would let him sleep.

* *

'The major hasn't replied.' Sergei dropped onto the bed, letting out an exhausted sigh.

Sergei rang the mobile number Major Hamdani had given them two years ago. He'd been trying it since they'd spoken with Dennis, but once again it went straight to an answering service.

'Is the voicemail message the same?' Jane said.

'Uh-huh.'

'Why don't we just call all the numbers for their local office. Someone will know the man.'

They both began to dial. Two of the numbers seemed incomplete because they ended in no ring tone. One number rang without a response. The last went to voice mail. Sergei put it on loudspeaker. It was in Urdu.

'You get any of that?' he said as he hung up.

'My Urdu's real rusty but I think it said, they're closed and will open at nine tomorrow.'

'Not bad, sweetheart.' Sergei looked impressed.

'Well, I was here two months. I'd have to be really stupid not to pick up a few basic words.'

'You've proven you aren't stupid.' He managed a tired smile.

'Serge, what're we gonna do?' Jane said in a pained voice. 'Just the thought of Razane locked up, maybe being tortured… makes me want to throw up. I won't sleep till we find her.'

'I feel the same sweetheart.' Sergei pulled her close. 'But we can't help her if we can't think straight.'

'We don't even know where she is.'

'Yeah well, Major Hamdani can help… And he's here… so hopefully…'

'I still think it's sad we had to come halfway around the world to get help from a person we met only once, when Dennis could have told us more.'

'He really believed Razane's a terrorist. I'm amazed he gave us anything. He could've turned us in. Dad used to say he was a stickler for rules.'

'He wasn't himself anymore,' Jane said. 'The way he faded in and out. I suppose he technically committed treason.'

'Imagine if Razane was really Wafaa, then we'd be doing the same.' Sergei said.

'Yeah well, we know she's innocent,' Jane murmured as she began to change into a pair of dark blue pyjamas. 'Let's hope Major Hamdani's a bit more helpful.' Jane flopped on the bed, 'He's our only hope.'

'If that fails, we might have to kidnap the US President and hold him hostage.' Sergei turned to face her.

'Talking to the major will be somewhat easier,' Jane managed a smile. 'But you know… I actually believe you'd try that if it was the only way.'

'What's that?' Sergei was on his back and was drifting off to sleep.

'Kidnapping the US President.'

'There's nothing I wouldn't try for you, Razane or the boys,' Sergei muttered as he gently pulled her into his arms. 'Even kidnap that orange-haired bonehead.'

'I believe you,' she replied softly stroking his hair. His breathing had slowed. He was fast asleep. She smiled. He had always been a good sleeper. Unlike her, who had to calm herself and order her thoughts before sleep came.

She wondered how the villagers in Shakar Parian were doing. Her local team had rebuilt everything, and her company had finally been paid.

Allah Boota, the village headman, had invited her and offered her the old hut as long as she liked.

Maybe after Razane was free, they'd visit. They would free Razane. They had to. She couldn't contemplate any other outcome.

THE CAR PARK

Lahore, Saturday 6 January, 5:30 am

It was still dark when Sergei woke. For a brief disoriented moment, he stared at the ceiling then at the large curtained windows. Green and red light from a nearby neon sign leaked into the small gaps around the drapes. The sporadic traffic, muted by the double-glazing, sounded unfamiliar.

A sick feeling in the pit of his stomach snapped him back to the present. It reminded him their lives had been brutally upended. They were nowhere close to locating Razane, let alone freeing her.

He played the sequence of events back in his mind as he fingered his stubble. He hadn't shaved since that morning. It was best to let it grow for now. Facial hair would make it easier to blend in with the locals.

He sighed. Regret gnawed at him. It didn't matter what Jane said. He should have tried harder to stop them taking Razane. If they harmed her, he would never forgive himself.

He sat up; his head was heavy from sleep. He was still in his day clothes. Jane stirred beside him. Her warm smile turned to a frown as she too was drawn into the present. He could see the digits on her watch. It was 5:30 in the morning.

Jane groaned, 'I feel sick.' Her voice was hoarse.

'Can I make you a cup of tea?'

'No, I'll be OK. I'm taking a quick shower. Can you please try the Major again?'

'It's still too early for the landlines but I'll try his mobile.' Sergei twisted his head to relieve a painful knot in his neck. He retrieved his phone from under a magazine. The battery was down to five percent. Damn, he'd forgotten to charge it. He found the cable, plugged it in and rang the major. It went to voicemail. Not expecting anything, he tried the landlines. They were all still closed. It was too early. He put the kettle on for tea and joined Jane in the shower.

* *

'What if the major doesn't show?' Jane took a sip of orange juice. She had to raise her voice over the noise. The Marco Polo was jam-packed with diners. Queues were forming at the breakfast bar.

'I'm worried the switchboard operator won't put us through,' Sergei looked towards the kitchen. Their omelettes were taking too long.

'Let's go to each of the ISI office locations... and wait outside,' Jane said, nibbling at a pineapple slice. 'We'll spot him when he arrives.'

'I like that,' Sergei was searching on Google Maps. 'Let's start with their Lahore head office. It's close by on Queens Road.'

Jane checked the map on her phone. 'That's ten minutes away. What about we split up and do them separately?'

Sergei was about to respond when the waiter appeared with two plates of omelette on toast. 'Let's see how these compare to yours,' Sergei said as the waiter straightened their cutlery. For the last two years, Jane had been trying to perfect her Pakistani style omelettes, making them at least once a week, much to Sergei and Razane's delight.

Jane smiled but said nothing. She waited until they were alone. 'So, what do you think?'

'I don't like it. Too many things can go wrong. I say we stick together.'

Jane thought about it for a moment. 'I suppose you're right. I just wanted to speed things up. It's... You know, I've...' she paused to compose herself. 'I've never felt so helpless.'

Sergei squeezed her hand. 'Stay strong, sweetheart. We'll get Razane back.' Inside, he felt like Jane, maybe worse. Even eating was a chore.

'Or die trying,' Jane said with a mouthful.

'Or die trying.' He meant it.

They finished their breakfast in silence and walked towards the multi-storey car park at the rear of the hotel. They were lost in their thoughts and didn't notice three men following them, almost running to keep up. One of them nearly tripped over a rug in the rear lobby in his haste.

The car park lift was out of order. By the time they reached the fifth storey, they were out of breath from the pollution and lack of sleep.

They drove slowly out of the parking complex and down the long driveway to the front gate. The guard saluted and opened the heavy iron gate.

Western-style hotels were targets for terrorists and security seemed even tighter than the last time. A police armoured personnel carrier stood in the service lane. A constable leaning against its bonnet glanced at them then went back to texting on his phone.

'That cop would be a real help in an attack,' Sergei said as found a gap in traffic.

'Poor fellow probably gets paid peanuts to risk his life protecting rich people,' Jane said as she settled in her seat.

It was still early in the morning and traffic on Mall Road was light by Lahore standards. Five minutes later they turned left onto Queens Road. At the following set of lights they took a sharp left and came to a police check-post. A wheeled steel-mesh-barrier blocked the road.

Behind it, two menacing armoured personnel carriers complete with roof-mounted machine guns showed this was no ordinary part of town.

Sergei had done some research. A suicide bomber had attacked and destroyed the police station in that location ten years ago. Thirty-five people had died. It also damaged the ISI building next door. The extra security was understandable.

An armed constable approached the car as Sergei slowed to a halt. The constable said something in Urdu. Seeing Jane's blonde hair, he switched over to broken English. 'Where going you?'

'We need to visit someone in the ISI building,' Sergei said.

'You need permit... for go ISI building,' the constable said.

A police sergeant with a bulging stomach hitched up his pants as he approached. He looked at their number plate and spoke into a walkie talkie as he eyed them suspiciously.

'What now?' Sergei whispered.

'Show him this.' Jane handed him the major's business card. He had given it to her two years ago on the boat outside Karachi.

'Good thinking, sweetheart. I'm glad you kept it.' Sergei passed the card to the constable. 'We have to an appointment with Major Hamdani.'

The Sergeant snatched the card from the constable's outstretched hand and examined it. 'Do you have ID?' His English was better than the constable's.

Jane and Sergei handed him their passports. The sergeant used his phone to photograph them before handing them back. 'Check the boot,' he ordered the constable as he looked around the interior of the car. 'Open glove-box, Madam,' he said to Jane.

The constable lifted the carpet in the boot, checked the spare tire and signalled something to the sergeant.

The sergeant nodded, 'OK, you can go.' He motioned to the constable to push open the barrier.

The ISI car park was empty. Sergei parked in a spot that allowed them a view of the main entrance.

'Fingers crossed we'll find him,' Jane said as Sergei switched off the engine.

'I hope so.' Sergei yawned as he kneaded a knot in his neck. His expression became sad. 'You know something? I really wish I had come to Pakistan the few times Mack invited me. I'd have gotten to know the country and now I wouldn't feel so alien.'

'Oh babe!' Jane reached over and touched his cheek. 'There's no use beating yourself up over it.'

'Have I told you recently, I love you,' he murmured as he

took her hand in his and lifted it to his lips.

'Hmmm, not recently, no,' Jane said with a solemn face. She ran her fingers through his hair. 'But under the circumstances I'll forgive you.'

The phone rang. It was Daniel Wax. Sergei answered and put it on speakerphone. 'Hi Daniel, any news?'

'Sorry no. I spoke with the Attorney-General and he assured me Razane isn't in anyone's custody. Not ASIO, the AFP or the police. If your theory about the CIA's right, she's out of the country.'

'Thanks for keeping on trying,' Jane said. 'And if there's anything…?'

'Yes, of course.' He hung up.

'If Razane's no longer in Australia, then I'm glad we've come here,' Jane said after a moment of silence. Sergei nodded as he observed a group of office-workers trudging by. Slowly the number of people arriving on foot, bicycle and by car turned from a trickle to a stream. Jane and Sergei focused their attention on their task as the car park began filling up.

'The major struck me as an early riser,' Sergei said. His face wore a worried frown. 'Let's call the switchboard again.'

Jane had been trying every five minutes hoping they would get through. She tried again.

'*Asalam Aleikum*. ISI Lahore office.' The operator spoke in Urdu. Jane understood most of it. Relief swept through her at hearing a human voice. 'Who would you like to speak to?'

Jane replied in English. '*Wa Aleikum Asalam,* I'd like to speak with Major Hamdani.'

'Major Hamdani does not work in the city office. I can transfer the call.' The operator spoke perfect English.

'Oh,' Jane replied, looking at Sergei. 'Which office does he work in?'

'Model Town. Would you like me to connect you?'

'Yes please.'

'OK, hold the line, please.' A dial tone replaced her voice.

After several rings the operator came back online, 'Madam

there is no answer. Would you like to leave a message?'

Jane looked questioningly at Sergei. He shook his head and silently mouthed, 'no.'

'No, that's OK. We'll try again later. *Bahut shukria.*' Jane said and hung up.

'That's good news. At least he's still with the ISI,' Sergei said as he started the engine and they slowly drove out of the car park.

Jane searched Google. The address was K Block in Model Town. With no street name or house number they were looking for one house among two thousand.

As Sergei navigated the traffic, Jane continued her online search. She found a reference to a suicide attack on the Model Town ISI offices many years ago.

'Terrorists seem to target the ISI a lot,' Jane said as she zoomed into a grainy photo in a newspaper article about the bombing. Finding nothing in the image, she read the article. It mentioned damage to a nearby seminary. Feeling hopeful, Jane searched for religious schools in Model Town's K block.

* *

Rizwan inserted the card in the slot. The little LED turned green, and the lock clicked open. It was a better way of breaking in than using bent wire.

He pushed open the heavy hotel door and entered. The room was tidy and smelled of perfume and soap. The *goras* staying here kept themselves clean. It surprised him. He had met none personally but had heard they seldom showered.

He glanced at his watch as he appraised the room. Ian had given him ten minutes. The room had two wall-lamps above the bed, two table lamps and one large floor standing lamp in the corner near the windows. He would use that.

Reaching down, he switched off the power at the wall. Then he reached under the shade and twisted the bulb out of its socket. From his pocket, he removed a box containing a round device with a camera. It was designed to fit between the bulb and the socket. Making sure he had it the right way round, he twisted it into the empty socket and replaced the bulb on top.

He stood back and examined his handiwork. The lampshade obstructed the camera's view of the room. Using his pocket-knife, he pried the camera loose from its housing; a thin cable was now the only thing connecting the camera to the main housing. He used the hook behind the camera to attach it to the bottom edge of the shade and stepped back to check. Even though he knew it was there, it was hard to see the camera. He clicked an app on his smartphone. The room showed up crystal clear. What amazing technology the Chinese had! And so cheap. He clicked his fingers; the sound came through on the phone's tiny speakers. Ian would be pleased. With a quick glance around the room, he left. On the way out he sent Ian a text to confirm the job was complete.

Ian's reply buzzed in his pocket as the door slammed behind him.

MALACCA STRAIT

Malacca Strait, Saturday 6 January, 9:30 am

The stout immigration officer handed Najib his port clearance document and began thumbing through the stack of passports. Even though Najib had told him, they would stay in Malaysian waters, it was still a requirement to carry one whenever they left port. The officer scanned each passport briefly, comparing the photo with the crew members and passengers standing in front of him. Satisfied, he handed them back to Najib.

'Take care of the shipping lanes, will you?' he said as he wiped his sunglasses with a tissue.

'Yes we will, *Tuan*. Thank you, *Tuan*.' Najib smiled and shook his hand. He watched as the officer turned and climbed down the ladder into his boat. It was time to be off. Allah willing, they were going on a long and rewarding journey.

A strong westerly breeze blew a constant stream of cirrus clouds over the sun, making it flicker as if an agitated monkey was playing with a light switch. Closer to the surface the brisk warm breeze sliced the crests off the waves and sprayed them in a fine salt laden mist.

Najib licked the salt off his lips. It was the taste of the sea that would carry them to their destination and he rejoiced. He scanned the bay more out of curiosity than concern. The water was a dirty turquoise. A catamaran carrying foreign tourists sailed past, heading towards the mouth of the river. A water taxi chugged nearby trailing black exhaust fumes. Near the shoreline, a fishing trawler was being manoeuvred under a maintenance crane. A scoop of pelicans took turns diving into the water. The bay would teem with fish at this time of the year.

Allah willing, this was the last time he would see these sights. He had grown up nearby and used to fish with his friends.

They were among the few memories of his childhood he hadn't blocked out.

After school he had gotten a job as a ticket collector on a water taxi. The owner also owned a religious school. Najib had joined to find meaning in life. That is where he found the true Islam. He realised that his life until then was a lie. His parents were degenerates, not worthy of being called Muslims. They listened to music, indulged in western traditions, never fasted and rarely prayed. First, he tried to change them but when he failed, he left home in disgust and never saw them again.

As he watched a seagull skim the surface of the water, he wondered where they were now; maybe already in Hell.

Najib signalled Haziq, who pushed the throttle lever slowly forward. His men scurried to their positions as the propellers churned the water, sending tremors through the large boat. Their progress was deceptively glacial at first, but the strong vibrations soon became a gentle thrum as they reached cruising speed.

Najib closed his eyes and took a deep breath of the tangy wet ocean air. He had timed it badly. A fishing vessel to their starboard side purged its holding tanks at that precise moment and he had caught the full brunt of it. He wrinkled his nose in disgust, spat into the water, turned, and walked to the bridge. That had put him off seafood for at least a month, maybe forever.

Haziq was examining three large screens arrayed above the large wheel. He turned his head as Najib approached.

'Is everything fine?' Najib looked at the digital speedometer on the middle screen. They were cruising at ten knots, the speed limit in the bay. Their boat was capable of more than double that with a comfortable cruising speed somewhere in the middle.

'Yes brother. By Allah's grace.' Haziq looked happy to be out in the water. They were silent as they watched the seagulls. 'Do we know yet where to?'

'Hmmm?' Najib was lost in thought.

'You did not say where we are going.'

'Oh...! We head towards Banda Aceh. *Al-ukht-ul-Akbari* will then call and tell us more.' Najib said. Banda Aceh was at the mouth of the Malacca Strait on the tip of Indonesia. By Allah's grace, this wasn't just a trial run but what Wafaa had promised for so long. Why else would she ask him to fill his tanks and take all his men? With their long-range tanks, they could sail almost anywhere.

'Do you know if we will see action?' Haziq read his mind.

'Patience brother. We shall see.' Najib patted him on the shoulder. 'You have put on a bit of meat.' He smiled as he patted him again.

'Only pure muscle from all the work I do, brother.' Haziq smiled back, flashing black teeth. He had almost died from an infection as a young kid. The antibiotics that saved him had ruined his teeth.

'Hah,' Najib raised his eyebrows and smiled. He turned to look at his men. They would have the same questions as Haziq.

Before leaving their shipyard he told them that they were pretending to be a long-range diving expedition. He had split them into crew-members and clients.

They had practised their roles till he was satisfied they would pass any inspection at sea. Many of his men were experienced divers already, so he didn't expect any problems. Diving tourism was a big industry. Long-range tours had become popular of late. It was why the immigration officer hadn't batted an eyelid when he inspected the boat.

There was much mirth as the men inspected the fancy designer T-shirts and shorts those acting as clients would wear. They were hard men not used to fashion or frippery.

Najib was intensely proud of his men. They were all battle-hardened survivors of one of the bloodiest conflicts in history, the Syrian Civil War. Together they had fought countless skirmishes, survived bombings, snipers, land mines and had buried scores of brothers. They all had the mental and physical scars to show it.

Wafaa had been with them from the beginning. All the Jabhat-al-Nusra brigades were under her command. When it was over, she had organised to have them smuggled back to Malaysia.

His men initially enjoyed their stay at the shipyard. It was a place to recover and regain their strength. But war had a strange effect on some men. Once bloodied they were never the same. Many couldn't return to a peaceful existence. The adrenaline rush from being so close to death was as addictive as heroin. For a true mujahid it was even harder. Death in the name of Allah became something they craved more than the kiss of a beautiful woman.

Najib sighed as he looked skyward. 'Please Allah, let this be our final journey.'

DISAPPOINTMENT

Major Amjad woke in a foul mood. He had overslept again. His mobile phone wasn't on his bedside table. That explained why he hadn't heard the alarm. Groggy, he stumbled around trying to find it. It was nowhere. He went downstairs to the garage; maybe he had left it in his car.

After some searching, he found it between the seats. Using two fingers, he fished it out of the narrow gap. He had seven new messages, fifty emails and two missed calls. His battery was on two percent. Cursing himself, he opened his email application. The phone died.

'Sister fucker,' he said to no one as he went back inside, put the phone on charge and sat down for breakfast.

* *

'Turn left now,' Google Voice said. Sergei dutifully turned off the Lahore's outer circle road. Another right turn later they were in front of the seminary, a large building twice the size of its neighbours.

'The ISI office must be close,' Sergei said.

'The blast that destroyed the ISI building damaged the seminary, so they must be near,' Jane said. None of the other houses on the street looked like offices of the country's intelligence services.

'What about behind, in the next street?' Jane said.

'That makes sense,' Sergei said as he prodded the accelerator.

Jane was right. They found the imposing ISI building behind the seminary. A forest of antennae sprouted from the roof. Two uniformed soldiers guarded the gates.

'That's it,' Sergei said as they approached.

Jane looked up from her phone and studied the building. 'Yup, it has to be.'

Sergei turned into the driveway and stopped at the gate. The guards swung their rifles off their shoulders and held them at the ready. The first guard approached Sergei, who wound down his window. '*Asalam Aleikum,* we're here to see Major Hamdani.' Sergei tried keeping his voice steady as he handed over the major's card.

Meanwhile, the other guard rounded the car and tapped on Jane's window.

The first guard read the card and spoke into a shoulder-mounted mic. Sergei didn't hear the reply but guessed he was communicating with someone inside the building.

'OK sir,' the guard said into his mic. He turned to Sergei and handed him the card. 'Major Sahib is overseas. Give me your name and I will give it to him when he comes back.'

'Ask him about his subordinate.' Jane leaned over, ignoring the other guard who had reached in and was opening the glove box. 'Do you remember his name?'

A car pulled up alongside. The first guard saluted as his companion rushed to open the gate. The bearded driver studied them briefly before he drove in.

'I don't remember the name,' Sergei whispered to Jane. 'What am I supposed to say?'

The guard returned to Sergei's window. 'Show me your identification.'

* *

Major Amjad was late to work. He was hungry and had a headache. Hafza, his wife was still on strike because of an argument two weeks ago. She hadn't cooked since and to drive the point home had sent their chef back to his village.

There was nothing worse than cornflakes for breakfast and he couldn't countenance cooking himself. That job was for servants or women. Why did he put up with the bitch? Maybe he should divorce her. Or better still, humiliate her by taking a second wife. That would teach the querulous cow. One day Allah would have mercy on him and take her, but maybe Allah wouldn't want her company either.

His mood lifted as he pulled up to the ISI building. He would have at least eight hours of peace, away from the witch.

Amjad was too riled up to give much thought to the foreigners in the Toyota. They were probably lost and asking the guard for directions.

His batman unlocked his office for him. 'Shall I bring you some tea, Sahib?'

'Yes Jamal, and a samosa.' The major sighed as he settled in his chair. 'No, make that three.' He pulled up the keyboard and turned on his computer.

The system took ages to boot. Bloody budget cutbacks had put new machines on hold. While he waited, Jamal came in with a tray of food.

'Thank you, Jamal. You are most efficient today. Close the door on the way out.'

The computer beeped its readiness. He clicked on his emails and scanned through the new ones. Meetings, more meetings, and a new policy announcement that he would read later. The Indian High Commission surveillance report would need an hour to go through. The Afghan troop movements were less important, as was the week's schedule of US drone attacks. It was bogus anyway and showed the lack of mutual trust. Next was the Incoming Persons of Interest report. It was light reading. He clicked on it. It was the usual, embassy personnel, political activists, high-profile businessmen, a member of the opposition returning from Saudi Arabia. Two category E passengers. He froze as he recognised a photograph. It was Sergei Markoff, one of the foreigners at the gate. An explanation in the footnote caught his eye. Sergei was a category E visitor because his father was ex-KGB. But why was he here?

The name rang a bell from elsewhere. He did a search

through his files as he took another sip of tea. Then it hit him. Sergei Markoff was one of Razane Silan's accomplices.

'Sister fuckers!' he jerked upright, knocking his tea cup over, his mind racing. What were they doing here? Why come to the lion's den? Something strange was afoot. His hands shook as he punched the number for the security gate. The guard at the front gate picked up straightaway.

'Faheem, are those foreigners still with you?'

'No sir, they left five minutes ago.'

'What did they want?' Amjad's heart raced as he heard the guard's reply.

* *

'Our targets went to the Model Town ISI office and spoke with the guards at the gate. They also showed them their passports.' Ian said.

'Hmmm, I wonder why. What happened then?' Angela said as she opened an Instant Messenger window. She needed to inform Graham Anderson, her boss, straightaway. She typed, '*hi, got a minute?*'

'That's it,' Ian was saying, 'Then they left. Right now we're following them. We've turned onto… Main Boulevard. It heads back to the hotel.'

'OK, don't lose them. I'll get back to you if we need to pick 'em up.' Angela hung up, lost in thought. Ian was a good operator, but this was turning into a massive clusterfuck. If the ISI were complicit in the Times Square bombing, it could start another war. But she was getting ahead of herself.

She needed to stay calm, which was hard because everyone at work was on edge. Discovering the world's number one terrorist was in Melbourne was embarrassing. Everyone wanted an explanation.

Under the circumstances, she didn't blame the CIA for what they'd done. They'd be in full scale damage control themselves. Their public would never forgive the lapse in their promised hyper-vigilance.

Heads would roll, careers would be upended, on both sides of the Pacific. She pitied the poor sod who'd given Razane Silan her immigration clearance.

If the Australian Intelligence community could prove Sergei and Jane were Wafaa's accomplices and maybe uncover their further plans, it would go a long way to restoring credibility.

The Instant Messenger icon flashed. Graham had replied. *'Am in a meeting but can chat.'*

'Our targets tried to contact someone at the ISI.' She typed.

'Inter-Service-Intelligence?'

'Yes.'

'Strange!'

'But not surprising?'

'It doesn't implicate the whole organisation.'

Angela knew what Graham meant. The ISI was rife with factional infighting which made it harder to understand where they stood. To complicate matters, they fought some terrorist groups but supported others.

On the surface that wasn't unusual. The CIA hunted Al Qaeda but supported their offshoots, Jabhat-al-Nusra and the White Helmets in Syria. However, the CIA wasn't at war with itself. The ISI was engaged in an internecine battle like the rest of Pakistan was. It was why western intelligence agencies, much to their own detriment, had begun to distance themselves from the ISI.

'I wonder who they tried to contact?' she typed.

'In a way it matters not. But it proves their relationship with Razane/Wafaa isn't just domestic.'

'What do you advise?' Angela typed.

'We need to bring them in for questioning.'

'I don't think Ian alone can manage.'

'I wasn't thinking of Ian. Let me make some calls. The CIA has a far bigger presence in the country. Make sure Ian doesn't let them out of his sight.'

** **

Sibtain opened the door and stuck his head in. 'May I come in, sir?'

Major Amjad looked up from his screen. 'Yes, come.' He beckoned. A quick search had revealed where the foreigners were staying.

Sibtain ducked as he entered. He was one of the biggest men in the ISI, built like a grass-fed bull, yet he walked light, like a dancer. Shakeel followed in behind. He was only slightly smaller but appeared equally formidable. Together they looked like the products of a soldier breeding program. Both were army commandos seconded to the ISI.

In peacetime, Military Intelligence had more use for their talents. The war against Pakistan's enemies would not be won in the courts. Extra-judicial killing was easier, as long as it was done with sufficient finesse. In Pakistan's violence ridden city streets a few extra bodies hardly raised eyebrows. And Sibtain and Shakeel were masters of their craft. They also had another quality, unquestioning loyalty. Because he had selected and trained them, they were answerable only to him.

The major printed off Sergei and Jane's photos and gave it to them.

'They are at the Pearl Continental. Make them disappear. No drama... understand? I don't want their faces in any newspaper, ever.'

Sibtain's eyes lit up. 'Yes, sir.'

'Thank you, sir.' Shakeel said in a deep booming voice as he followed his partner out.

THE KEYCARD

Lahore, Saturday 6 January, 11:10 am

Sergei drove in silence, his mind in turmoil. The chaotic Lahore traffic was murderous, but at least it made him focus on the moment; driving always calmed him. Still, a vein throbbed mercilessly in his temple sending bolts of pain through his head. He forced himself to unclench his jaw and relax his neck muscles.

Jane looked unseeing out of the side window, her thoughts in a whirl. Shock and dismay benumbed her; the world felt cold and empty. Their desperate gambit had yielded nothing; they were no closer to Razane.

The CIA were acting as the judge, jury and executioner. They believed Razane was guilty of a heinous crime and would stop at nothing to make her confess. Razane's resilience only made it more frightening. She wouldn't break easily and they had an infinite capacity to break her.

The madness didn't stop with the CIA. Every news bulletin ran video footage of the US President proclaiming his willingness to wreak vengeance on anyone responsible for the Times Square Massacre.

In this environment, innocence mattered nought, the public wanted blood and the CIA would give it to them.

Jane knew that Razane could not possibly have had anything to do with it. She was kind and gentle. She had been a Kurdish soldier and had killed people, but she was incapable of hurting innocents. The accidental deaths of civilians caught in a crossfire between her Kurdish unit and Islamist rebels was the main cause of her traumatic stress disorder.

Traffic was light for Lahore and they made rapid progress. Remarkably, Sergei had mastered the chaotic traffic. He drove fast, predicting gaps like a stunt driver and avoiding even the most suicidal locals.

* *

'He drives well for a white monkey,' Rizwan growled as he drove the silver Toyota Corolla. The strain of keeping up was making him sweat.

In the front seat, Afzal frowned at him. 'Shut up,' he mouthed as he looked at Ian through the sunvisor mirror. 'You do not know what Sahib understands.'

Their employer had given no sign he understood. But they couldn't afford to risk it. The pay was too good. Afzal slid back the mirror in the sunvisor. 'Maybe you drive badly for a black fucker.'

'Next time you drive then,' Rizwan said as he turned onto Mall Road without slowing, their tyres squealing in protest.

'Easy does it,' Ian said as he reached out and grabbed Afzal's seat from behind. 'Let's not kill ourselves. The tracker you put on their car will show us where they're going.'

'Yes sir. Sorry!' Rizwan glanced back.

* *

'Any thoughts?' Jane said in a subdued voice as she inserted the keycard into the slot in the door.

Sergei hadn't spoken since Model Town. He sighed and shook his head as he turned the handle. He pushed the door halfway and stopped.

Jane had her hand on his shoulder and felt him stiffen. He had frozen and was staring at the master switch just inside the door. It held a keycard. The lights were on. She had taken the card out herself when they left. Someone was in their room.

* *

Ian felt the phone buzz in his pocket. It was Angela. 'You two wait in the lobby,' he said to Afzal and Rizwan as he answered.

'Hey Ian,' Angela sounded rushed. 'We now think Sergei and Jane are complicit and there's a risk they'll trigger another attack. So you have a few more hours to find their contact before we...'

'What, you wanna kill them?' Ian said.

'We have to stop them. If possible... we capture, but killing is better than them getting away. Do you have a problem with that?'

He did. They were supposed to be the good guys, defenders of freedoms and all that shit. 'Nope, no problem,' he lied. 'But aren't you jumping the gun a bit? What if there's an innocent explanation...?'

'Don't you go soft on me, mate.'

'Have I ever been?'

'A few times, yes. It's a common thread in your performance reviews. You find it hard to make life and, more so, death decisions.'

Angela was brutally honest, but she was right. His conscience had gotten in the way a few times.

'I'm trying to improve, boss.'

'I'll believe it when I see it. Hang on a sec.' Angela put the phone on mute. 'Sorry that was Graham,' she said after a brief pause. 'Where are the two now?'

'At the hotel.'

'They've not booked a return flight so they have something planned. Whatever happens, don't lose 'em.'

'Have I ever lost anyone?'

'That you haven't.'

'I gotta have some redeeming qualities... given I haven't mastered the art of butchery... yet.'

'Hmmm, OK... so?'

'Don't worry, I don't intend to start. We've put a tracker on their car and... my two local helpers are pretty good.'

RUN!

Lahore, Saturday 6 January, 11:30 am

Jane was about to speak but her sixth sense and Sergei's raised arm stopped her. He turned and glanced back. His lips moved soundlessly. 'What the fuck?'

All the brooding thoughts were sucked from her mind. There were intruders in their room. How many and who were they?

Sergei put his finger to his lips as he backed out. She did too.

'Mr Sergei, wait!' a voice whispered furiously as footsteps raced towards the door.

It was too late to run. Jane braced herself. The door swung open. It was Yousaf. She looked past him. The room was empty. He was alone.

'Come in,' Yousaf motioned as he frantically gazed into the hallway.

Jane tried to focus. Yousaf was Major Hamdani's subordinate. At least he was the last time they met. Razane had killed Fazal, his colleague. So, was he friend or foe?

'Please come in fast, no time.' Yousaf was pleading.

Sergei and Jane complied. The door clicked behind them. Yousaf had been busy. Their suitcases were packed and sitting on the bed.

'I pack luggage for you.' He had anticipated their question. 'You go now. Very danger.'

'Why, from what?' Sergei said, attempting to compose himself.

'You no come Pakistan. Now Major Amjad know.'

'Who's Major—?' Sergei said

'He brother of Fazal. You know Fazal? He man who Razane kill on boat.'

'Now, wait, wait, hang on just a second. 'Jane took a step towards Yousaf.

'No. You no understand.' Yousaf's pupils were dilated. His voiced trembled. 'Yes, you say Fazal do wrong… but… right wrong no important.'

'Sit down, Yousaf,' Jane motioned to the blue upholstered armchair in the corner. 'We're not going anywhere till you tell us… what's going on?'

'And where's Major Hamdani?' Sergei sat on the edge of the bed.

Yousaf stayed standing. 'Afghani police arrest Major Hamdani two day back. Very strange how they know.'

'Yousaf slow down, please,' Jane said, 'we don't understand.'

'Major Hamdani go Afghanistan many time and never caught. He very careful man.'

'So what happened?' Jane said.

'Major Amjad ask Colonel must send Major Hamdani.'

Sergei and Jane exchanged glances. 'You're saying he was betrayed?' Sergei said.

'I no sure. But today in office I see you at gate. Then two commando from Major Amjad follow you. I think Major Amjad he want revenge on you for Fazal. Maybe also Major Hamdani and me. So I think he tell Afghani police.'

'Yousaf, I still don't understand. Which men?' Jane shook her head as she walked over to the window.

'Careful!' Yousaf started after her. 'No move curtain.'

'Don't worry, I won't.' She looked through the lace. Nothing seemed out of the ordinary. The two men were nowhere to be seen.

Sergei walked over too. 'What are we looking at?'

'You no see men follow you?' Yousaf was wringing his hands, clearly distressed.

'No. But we weren't looking,' Sergei said.

'Two car follow. One is agent from Australia. Other car is two very dangerous ISI commando. They killers… very dangerous, very, very dangerous.'

'You saw them here?' Jane said, 'Show us.'

'See dark grey Suzuki Jeep, near flower shop?'

A vehicle matching Yousaf's description stood in the temporary car park near the main gate. A burly man in a light brown *shalwar kameez* and a puffy blue jacket leaned against the driver's door looking into every car going past.

Jane sat on the edge of the bed. She had gone white. 'Why would the ISI want—?'

'Yeah, I'd like to know too, it doesn't make sense.' Sergei said, his hands on his hips.

Yousaf glanced up at Sergei. 'Why you say?' He looked frustrated as he shook his head. 'Oh ho, not ISI. Only Major Amjad. He want revenge. He kill us all.'

'Do you think they'll come up?' Jane said.

Yousaf walked to the window and looked out. 'Oh, no. They no there. They come up.' A note of panic had entered his voice. 'You leave from service exit. Then go airport and go home. Go now *fatafat*.'

'We can't leave. We have to see Major Hamdani,' Jane said.

'Why?'

'Our friend, Razane was taken by the CIA. They think she was responsible for the Times Square bombing.'

'Oh. Newspaper say they capture Wafaa Aal Zubeidi,' Yousaf said with a puzzled look on his face. 'Is Wafaa Razane?'

'Razane isn't Wafaa but the CIA think so,' Jane said.

'Yousaf, maybe you can check who gave the information to the CIA about Razane,' Sergei said.

'Mr Sergei, I no have security clearance for check anything. I only junior man.' Yousaf glanced out of the window again. He looked back at them. 'The men they coming up. They have room number. You go now!'

* *

Sibtain waited for the lift door to close, then he took a silencer from his pocket and screwed it on the barrel of his Ruger before placing it back in the underarm holster inside his jacket.

Shakeel looked at him and smiled. 'Do you want to bet I will get them before you do?' he fingered the throwing knives in his jacket pocket.

'Brother, put those toys away. You may be good but a gun is always faster than a knife.'

The lift stopped at the first floor and a family with three young girls entered. The youngest looked up at Sibtain. He smiled down at her, exposing a mouth full of metal fillings. The girl gave a little yelp and scampered behind her mother.

'Stop scaring the little cutie with your camel face,' Shakeel said. 'Sorry for my partner,' he said to the parents who nodded politely.

The lift slowly began its upward journey.

* *

'Yousaf, we can't leave Pakistan till we find the major,' Jane said.

'I told you he in Afghanistan.'

'Then we must go there,' Sergei said. 'Please help us.'

'Sorry, Mr Sergei. Please forgive but you is mad.' Yousaf placed a hand on Sergei's shoulder.

'Yousaf, OK... maybe we are crazy. But we're not leaving... so please help us!'

'OK, OK, we talk after. First you run. You no can fighting these men.' He walked to the door. 'So please go from leave hotel then we talk. Now come, fast. Bring luggage.' Yousaf opened the door and looked out.

'No, leave the luggage,' Sergei said. 'Come sweetheart, we better do as he says.'

They followed Yousaf as he ran towards the opposite end of the hallway. Jane looked back. The guest elevator was ascending. They rounded the corner. Yousaf pressed the button for the large service elevator repeatedly as they watched its slow ascent from the basement.

'It won't go faster, mate.' Sergei was panting from the sprint.

On the other end of the hallway the main guest elevator pinged followed by the sound of young children and running feet. If Major Amjad's men were in that elevator, they were too close. The service elevator door creaked open. The trio rushed inside, their hearts thumping as the doors took their time to creak closed.

'Yousaf, you're an army man yourself and pretty strong,' Sergei said. 'Why do you fear them?'

Yousaf said something unintelligible that ended in a coughing fit.

The elevator bounced as it came to a rest. The doors opened. In sharp contrast to the glitz and glamour of the guest areas, the basement was dingy, uncarpeted, and lit with naked fluorescent tubes. Paint was peeling from the walls and, it appeared, the ceiling fans had never been cleaned.

A group of men were gathered at the loading dock unloading a refrigerated van. A forklift was lifting a pallet of soft drinks from the back of a flatbed truck. Seeing them, a uniformed employee got up from a chair. He rushed over and opened his mouth to speak but closed it when he saw Yousaf's badge.

'Take that passage,' Yousaf said to Sergei and Jane as he pocketed his wallet. 'It go to side garden. Jump over wall near small gate. That street go to Lawrence Gardens. It is big park with many trees. Go there and hide. I bring car. It is silver Corolla. Run!'

**

The side garden was nothing more than a patch of yellowed grass and two benches facing each other. A line of silver birches, bereft of leaves, surrounded it on three sides. On the fourth was a white-painted brick wall with a white steel gate, topped with wicked spikes and locked with a rusty padlock.

Sergei grabbed two spikes and pulled himself up. The

metal creaked and bent towards him. 'They look nasty.'

'Either you're super strong or that's super weak,' Jane said. 'Try a few more.'

Sergei strained as he pulled on the next spike. It was as rusty as its neighbour. A minute later he had bent four more into a flat position. They now had a safe gap above the gate, wide enough for them to clamber over. Using the hinge as a foothold, he hoisted himself onto the gate. On the other side, a quiet residential cul-de-sac ran between two rows of houses just as Yousaf had described. A maid was sweeping the driveway of a white-marble mansion. Otherwise, the street was empty. Sergei reached down towards Jane. 'Give me your hand.'

'I'll manage.'

Sergei lowered himself onto the other side. Seconds later Jane jumped down beside him.

'Damn, I think I rolled my ankle,' she grimaced as she hobbled a bit.

'You should have let me help, are you OK?'

'I'll be fine. Walking should fix it...'

* *

The cul-de-sac ended in an intersecting road as busy as the former was quiet. Cars, bicycles, and carts vied for space in the bumper to bumper traffic. A few elderly women strolled by on the footpath. One of them pushed a child in a pram. On the other side of the street near the park entrance, a hawker was selling mandarins and bananas from a large wicker basket attached to the back of a bicycle.

Yousaf had already arrived and was waiting in one of the parking bays, his eyes on the park entrance.

'There he is,' Jane said.

'Wait,' Sergei said as he put a hand on Jane's arm. 'Let's make sure no one's watching him,' He gently pulled her back into the shadow of a large Coca-Cola sign.

They looked for anything that could signal a threat but in

the end they gave up. There were too many people. A watcher could be anywhere.

'Let's just go,' Sergei said.

'Yeah, I think it's fine.'

Yousaf gave a start when Jane opened the rear door and climbed in. '*Ya-Allah*, you scare me.'

'Sorry Yousaf.' Sergei climbed into the front passenger seat beside him.

'We must go from here so we can talk.' Yousaf started the engine and checked his mirrors before he made a sharp U-turn.

They were heading away from Mall Road into an unfamiliar part of Lahore. Yousaf was the first to speak. 'You very crazy. Afghanistan very dangerous. Taliban very dangerous. Afghan police very dangerous. How you find Major Hamdani? What you do when find? You very mad… very mad.'

'Yousaf, mate, we can't think of another way,' Sergei said. 'The major is our only hope.'

'What major do?'

'We hope he can talk to the CIA to clear Razane's name,' Jane said. 'We know the information to implicate Razane came from Pakistan so…'

Yousaf sighed. 'Major Hamdani very clever man… and good man. He have many connections but many enemy. He CIA liaison no more… You must understand. In ISI there is war. One group want modern Pakistan like *Amreeka*. Other want Pakistan have Shariah Law like Saudi Arabia and Iran. They support jihad in Kashmir and in Afghanistan. They think Pakistan only safe if India and Afghanistan not safe.'

'I take it Hamdani's in the first group,' Sergei said.

'What you mean…? Yes, yes. He is good man who want modern moderate Pakistan.'

'Doesn't the government control the ISI?' Jane said.

Yousaf gave a humourless laugh. 'No. ISI control government. No, no, OK, army control government and ISI control army… so ISI control government.'

'You said Major Hamdani was sent to Afghanistan by

Major Amjad,' Sergei remembered their earlier conversation.

'Major Amjad tell bosses to send Major Hamdani. Then he tell Afghani police. I think.'

'Yousaf, we're grateful you came to warn us. But we can't leave without helping Razane. Can you help us get the major out?' Sergei said.

'ISI men no follow. We stop here and have cup of tea,' Yousaf pulled into the Lahore Teahouse carpark. 'Tea here very famous. We talk.'

* *

Sibtain sat on the bed as he looked at a tracking app on his smartphone while Shakeel rifled through the two suitcases. 'I see Yousaf. He has just turned into Lahore Teahouse.'

Shakeel took the phone from his hand and clicked on History. It showed a line on the map where Yousaf had been before. 'Yousaf was here... The *haramzada* was here with the foreigners.'

'Hey *gandu*, show me that,' Sibtain snatched the phone back. 'The filthy traitor warned them. Maybe they are with him.'

'We better go there and find them or Major Amjad will fuck us in the arse if we return empty-handed.' Shakeel said.

Sibtain burst out laughing. 'I just saw a vision of Major Amjad standing on a chair to fuck you in the arse.'

'Fuck Major Amjad. Maybe we kill him someday. I am sick of following orders from that bastard. Always giving us orders and expecting miracles. Then he humiliates us if we fail once.' Shakeel said.

'You can complain on the way,' Sibtain said as he walked out of the room.

'I say we also arrest Yousaf.' Shakeel said as they entered the lift.

'Are you so stupid you need to say the obvious?' Sibtain said.

'Do not call me stupid,' Shakeel growled as his hands

closed over the knives in his pocket.

'OK, relax, relax. I was only joking, *yaar*. Why do you take things so seriously? You are my brother,' Sibtain said.

Shakeel smiled. 'I know you were joking, *yaar*.'

As they approached their vehicle, the security guard saw them and rushed to open the gate.

'How far is Lahore teahouse?' Shakeel said.

'Ten minutes,' Sibtain started the engine.

* *

The Lahore Tea House was nothing more than a tea-stand and rickety chairs under a tent on an empty block of land. It made up for it with the taste of the tea and the speedy service, remarkable because of the rush. All the outdoor seating was taken, so they remained in the car while a boy, not older than eight, served them.

'This is nice,' Sergei said as he copied Yousaf and dipped a piece of sweetbread into the steaming tea.

Jane took a sip and put the cup down. Her nerves were too much on edge to drink tea. She listened as Yousaf gave Sergei the names and locations of contacts who could help. If only he would offer to join.

She was about to ask when, through the throng, she saw another a car pull up. The man in the back looked vaguely familiar.

'Hey Serge, there's a man in that silver Corolla three cars down?'

'Which man?' Sergei said looking back.

'Try not to be obvious, but… to your left near the tree. I've seen him somewhere.'

Sergei turned slowly. A waiter blocked his view.

Yousaf saw the car and stiffened. 'That is Australia agent.'

'Why are they after us?' Jane said as the waiter left.

'That's the man from the flight,' Sergei said. 'Let's not worry about him.'

'How they find us?' Yousaf was perspiring again.

'They must have followed us?' Sergei said.

'No need follow. They can put tracker on car, easy.' Yousaf said as he started the engine. 'We must go.'

'Why are you worried about them?' Jane said.

'No them. I worry more about Major Amjad men.' Yousaf was reversing through the crowd.

Jane looked around for the ISI men's grey Suzuki. 'Where are we going now?'

'I have old car. You borrow,' Yousaf said as he engaged first gear.

STEAK AND CHIPS

Hathala, Saturday 6 January, 6:45 pm

A light drizzle started just as darkness set in. Sergei turned on the wipers and grimaced as the perished rubber blades smeared the water across the glass, turning it opaque. The lights of oncoming traffic turned the windscreen into a kaleidoscope.

A large roadside neon sign with blinking lights around the border flashed by. It advertised "The Steakhouse - American style Steak and Chips - 1km".

'That steak place is endorsed by the Pakistan Tourism Development Corporation,' Sergei said as he looked for an exit.

Jane stretched in the passenger seat. 'I guess it means it's safe to eat there.' Her stomach grumbled loudly.

Sergei smiled. 'I heard that. We better stop. I can't see anything anyway.'

'Yeah well, I'm hungry. I couldn't eat at the Lahore Teahouse. Besides, my bum has fallen asleep.'

Sergei eased off the throttle and took the slip road off the highway. The restaurant was behind a Pakistan State Oil service station abuzz with vehicles.

The oily smell of spilt diesel filled the air as Sergei parked Yousaf's ancient Nissan Patrol in the dimly lit restaurant car park.

Yousaf had told them he was planning to restore it. Jane didn't think it was worth it but she had held her tongue. Everything on it rattled and almost nothing worked. The shock absorbers were well past their use-by date and the ride was both floaty and bone-jarring.

'A cement mixer would have been more comfortable,' Jane moved her neck to ease the tension.

'Yes,' Sergei suppressed a yawn as he pointed to an eatery next to the steakhouse. 'That's another alternative.' The traditional outdoor eatery was packed with locals. In the middle, a man astride a *tandoor* oven flipped a huge *roti* into the air before a waiter caught it in a weaved basket.

Jane's mouth watered at the sight. 'That was a nice-looking *roti*.'

'Yup, looks more appetising than the steak restaurant. Do you wanna risk it?'

Jane looked back at the steak restaurant. It was large but only four tables were occupied. 'I so want the traditional food,' Jane said in an impassioned voice. 'But we can't draw attention to ourselves. Regardless of what Yousaf said, the ISI goons may still be after us.'

Sergei caught the smells from the outdoor place as he opened the creaking door. The spicy aromas made his mouth water. He sighed as he climbed out. 'You're right. Steak it is.'

Inside, the steak restaurant was nice and warm with dim lighting and classical music. Crisp white linen and silver cutlery adorned the tables. Now that they were inside it began to appeal more. At least they'd have more privacy.

'Welcome, sir and madam,' the head waiter bowed and showed them to their table in an alcove.

'Do your steaks look as good as the ones on the board outside,' Jane said.

'Oh yes, madam. Our chef was trained in Chicago.'

They each ordered a large steak with chips. A few moments later two waiters brought out a large bowl of salad, a bread basket and a bottle of spring water. The head waiter returned with a set of large steak knives. 'We have special knives for honoured VIP guests.'

Sergei studied the Japanese inscription on the blade. 'Wow, aren't these like those folded steel blades that the Samurai use?' He showed them to Jane.

Jane examined it. 'Wow, the pattern's beautiful. Ooh and they're razor sharp. We're so getting a set when we get home.'

The waiter smiled. 'They are handmade in Japan. The owner is a knife collector. He only allows use by special guests.'

'Do thank him for us.'

'Yes, yes, but please sir, madam... take care. They are very sharp.'

When they were alone Jane studied the other diners. A couple in their thirties were paying their bill and leaving. The other three were families with young children, probably passing through like them.

'I need to go to the toilet.' Sergei got up. 'Don't cut yourself with the steak knives.'

'Take your phone with you.' Jane smiled as she watched Sergei approach a waiter who pointed to the back of the restaurant to a door framed by two tall potted philodendrons. Sergei smiled at Jane and shook his head as if in surprise, then he walked to the door at the rear. The toilets were outside in the courtyard.

* *

Shakeel and Sibtain sat in the dark car park. Inside, their quarry had just sat down to eat. Sibtain scratched his beard. 'Is it possible we could do it here?'

'Maybe when they come out if there are no witnesses. One of us could drive their car with them in it. The tribal region is only an hour away. It is hilly and deserted. We could easily make their bodies disappear... forever,' Shakeel said.

They were both familiar with the semi-autonomous tribal region on the western border between Pakistan and Afghanistan. It was known for its rough beauty and lawlessness. Ordinary Pakistanis knew never to venture off the main highway, but they weren't ordinary Pakistanis. Even the lawless tribesmen feared the ISI.

It was the perfect place to dispose of bodies. Even if their remains were found, which was unlikely, their deaths would be blamed on dacoits.

'I'll order us some food; you keep a watch. If they move call me straight away,' Shakeel said climbing out of the passenger's seat.

In a way, Yousaf had done them a favour by making the foreigners run. If they had killed them in the hotel, it would have been awkward to dispose of their bodies. He still had acid burn marks from doing something similar.

They had reached Lahore Tea House as their quarry was leaving. They followed them till Yousaf dropped the foreigners off outside a car repair shop.

They had watched as Sergei and Jane drove off in a beaten up old Nissan Patrol. They could deal with Yousaf later so they decided to follow the foreigners.

Sibtain stretched in his seat. He was stiff from driving for the last six hours and needed a walk. He would check out the fancy restaurant. Maybe they could kill them here. Compared to the Pakistani food place it was nearly deserted. He got out and walked toward the back of the restaurant. Through the windows he saw Sergei speaking with a waiter and walk to the back door.

Excitement building, Sibtain sent Shakeel a text message as he continued to examine the rear of the premises. The restaurant building ended in a solid brick wall almost as high as he was tall. He heard a door open and slam closed, then the sound of footsteps. Sergei was in the courtyard at the back of the restaurant. Sibtain hoisted himself up on the wall and saw Sergei enter the toilet at the rear of the property.

In one leap he was over the wall, his rubber soles cushioning the impact. His phone vibrated in his pocket. Shakeel had read his message.

* *

The TV, high on the wall, showed a young couple singing and frolicking in a field of sunflowers. The woman alternated between coyly rejecting the man's advances and encouraging him to continue. Jane was glad the volume was low. She wasn't in the mood for music. Yousaf had been downbeat about their plan to rescue Hamdani. They really were on a fool's errand and their chances of success were next to zero but doing nothing wasn't an option either.

The couple on the TV had changed their clothes and were now dancing suggestively in the rain. It was strange how the local movies were so different from how people really behaved. She had never seen Pakistani women dancing in public.

The song ended in an ad break, making her realise that two songs had passed since Sergei had gone. An unpleasant feeling grew in the pit of her stomach. He never took this long.

Jane glanced towards the front of the restaurant. Outside, in the car park, a dark coloured vehicle was parked in the shadows next to their four-wheel-drive. It wasn't there when they arrived and no one had entered the restaurant after them. Was it the ISI men's grey Suzuki?

The emptiness grew in the pit of her stomach. Hunger and worry made her hands shake. She picked up one of the knives and sliced the skin off a cherry tomato. The blade had the finest cutting edge she'd seen, and it ended in a wicked point. A waiter watched her briefly before another diner distracted him. Making sure no one was looking, Jane wrapped the two knives in a napkin. As she stood she slid them into the waistband of her jeans, under her long shirt. She walked up to the waiter. 'Where's the bathroom?'

'Madam, it is outside the building in the courtyard.' He pointed. 'Through there.'

'Thank you,' she said as she made sure her shirt covered the napkin.

Jane walked up to the back door. She took one last look back, in the forlorn hope Sergei was back at their table. He wasn't. Steeling herself, she opened the door. Light spilt out of the doorway and lit the ground at her feet. How had Sergei seen well enough to walk to the toilet?

She hesitated as she peered into the Stygian courtyard. 'Please be OK, babe,' she muttered to herself before she took a deep breath and stepped into the yard. Jane fought a rising panic as the door slammed shut. An almost insane fear gripped her. Why was it dark? Sergei had a flashlight on his phone.

As her eyes adjusted, she began to see a vague contrast between the purple sky and the dark grey below. She was in an enclosed courtyard. A narrow covered-walkway led to the back. Lights from the outdoor eatery next door illuminated the angle-iron structure that held up the roof.

She could now see a faint outline of the toilets at the back of the courtyard. Her heart skipped a beat when she realised both doors were ajar and the insides were dark.

'Serge, where the fuck are you?' Jane muttered almost soundlessly. Her teeth were chattering, her palms wet.

She forced herself to focus. She had to for Sergei and Razane. Nothing else mattered. Fear was all in the mind. She wasn't helpless. Her Systema training made her a force to be reckoned with. Focus, breathe. Her senses heightened. Sounds flooded in. Diners were talking and laughing and moving chairs around, bottles were clinking, trucks in the service station rumbled. The freshening breeze whistled through the steel structure above her. The smells became more acute, burnt *rotis*, grilled meat and diesel, and perfume. It was cloyingly sweet. It was not hers, nor Sergei's. The wearer was near.

Jane pulled out the napkin and unwrapped the knives. Holding one in each hand, she tiptoed towards the toilet block. Between the doors was a drum and beside it a shape on the ground. Her heart skipped again. Was it Sergei?

Fearing the worst, she rushed forward. A stitch formed in her side as her nerves stretched every sinew to near breaking point.

A violent shove propelled her into a steel post. She managed to get her hands up to cushion the shock, but one of her knives fell. A shadowy face loomed behind the post. It was one of the ISI men, the giant with a huge moustache. He was grinning at someone behind her; it had to be his companion. Two against a slender woman must have seemed funny to him.

She could see the shape on the ground more clearly. It was Sergei. He lay on his back, arms out to the side.

Anger erupted deep inside. She pushed it deep down as

she harnessed something from the core of her being. Love, a need to protect and something far stronger, a complete absence of fear, or rules, or consequences. The veneer of civilisation fell away as a demon awoke.

Jane pushed back from the pillar as she pivoted in a downward spiral. From the sound of his breath and his smell, her assailant was within an arm's length behind her. Her head was now at his waist level. From her semi-crouched position he appeared even taller and more imposing.

Her knife flashed as she sliced in an upward arc. An overpowering smell of blood coincided with a viscous warmth on her hand. The blade had opened his soft belly below his ribcage.

Jane pulled the knife back and rotated sideways out of his way as he collapsed.

'*Oye...*,' his companion's cry turned to an enraged shout. '*Bahin chodd.*' Grunting, he used the metal post as a support to swing himself towards her from the right.

Jane could hear the metal post ringing and his shoes scuffing as he lunged at her, his fist raised. His recovery and the speed of his attack was shocking. Instinctively she stepped back and slashed at her looming assailant. Her hand hit something solid, jarring her wrist. The knife flew from her grasp and landed with a clatter. Her attacker fell forward. He had tripped over his dead comrade. Jane backed away. The ground was slippery as hell. The dead man's blood squelched under her shoes. She scraped her soles on the concrete to get traction as she wiped the blood from her hand. Slipping would be fatal.

The man rebounded back onto his feet like he was on a spring. His eyes stared through the dark as he sized her up. He was stronger by many orders of magnitude and she was now empty-handed and without the advantage of surprise. He now knew not to underestimate her.

Jane took a deep breath, trying to stave off the fear and maintain her state of hyper-awareness. She ran through the Systema moves like flicking through a catalogue. Not in her wildest dreams had she ever thought she'd use them. She regularly beat Anatoly, her instructor, a former Spetsnaz commando. But that was sparring. This was life and death and her opponent was bigger and meaner than Anatoly.

The beast of a man came closer; his movements were deliberate, his breathing even. Like her, he had put aside emotions. There was no anger or regret for his companion. He was a professional.

Jane cast around for a weapon. The only hard object was the immovable steel frame of the walkway. The first knife she had dropped lay on the ground somewhere forward of the pillar. Her opponent lunged. She was faster, the little squeak he'd made gave her the advantage. She jumped, grabbed the beam overhead and kicked at an upward angle. Her heel connected with something hard, jarring the arch of her foot. In the same move she snapped her leg back, let go of the beam, landed on her feet, and dropped into a crouch. He was on the ground, on one knee, a hand to his face, the other fumbling in his pocket. There was no time.

Pivoting on one foot, Jane swept the other into the side of his head. With a curse, he ducked and rolled backwards. Jane brought her leg down hard. Her heel made contact. He grunted as his head cracked on the ground. Convulsing he snatched a pistol from his pocket. In desperation, she kicked and contacted it. The gun left his hand and landed somewhere to the left.

In a frenzy, she searched for something, anything. She saw the outline of an object, rolled sideways and closed her hand around it. To her surprise, it was her knife. He staggered to his feet searching for his gun. Using the last reserves of her strength, Jane arched her back and sprung into a standing position. The man, expecting a blow, shielded his face.

With a primal scream, Jane launched forward and thrust the steak knife into his throat. The blade scraped against bone and was stuck. Warm blood soaked her sleeve up to her elbow. Some dripped down into her armpit. With a gurgling sound, he fell to his knees forcing her to let go of the handle.

Her breathing had become ragged again. She was at the end of her endurance. She saw the handgun on the ground and picked it up. But it was no longer needed. Her assailant fell forward in slow motion.

The demon inside vanished as the deep primordial haze lifted and tiredness, pain and revulsion flooded in. The blood on her arm was cooling. Her hands hurt. How the fuck had she done that? She knew she had walked through a door and there was no going back.

The restaurant door opened and closed. Someone entered the courtyard.

Jane put the pistol in her pocket and stumbled over to Sergei, dreading her worst fears. 'Please, please be OK, my darling,' she whispered as she dropped beside him. Her hands were covered in blood so she pressed her face to his. It was warm. His breath cooled the sweat on her face. He was alive. A dam burst in her and she sobbed as she cradled his head in her lap.

A hand grabbed her shoulder as a torch shone in her face.

DISCLOSURE

Saipan, Sunday 7 January, 5:15 am

Sebastian regretted his words before he finished his sentence. The response from the other end was predictable.

'Holy Cow?' Chip Balawski, The director of Counter Terrorism shouted, 'What in God's name are you tellin' me?'

Sebastian winced as he fumbled for the volume on his headset. 'Just what I said; Mike believes Wafaa is the Times Square Bomber.'

'Why am I hearing this now?'

'Sir, I don't--' Sebastian suppressed a yawn. It was stupidly early in the morning. He hadn't even made himself a coffee.

'Give us a second,' Stella Katsis, the Middle Eastern Chief interrupted.

Sebastian sighed as the other end went quiet. This wouldn't play out well. Mike would go nuts on him for breaking rank.

It began as an innocent mistake. His old supervisor in Langley was in hospital, in labour. Not remembering Sebastian was in a different time zone, she'd texted him to attend daily the status review meeting in her place. Chip saw he was dialling in from Saipan and asked him why he was there instead of in Islamabad.

There was no way for him to avoid answering Chip's direct question truthfully.

Why the fuck had Mike involved him in his stupid scheme to keep Wafaa's true significance secret?

The other end was live again. 'Hey Sebastian, sorry about exploding on you...'

'The... that's... quite OK sir...' he stammered.

'It was a shock, that's all... We need to talk to Mike... but don't worry we understand your situation. We'll handle it. Now let's get back to the agenda.'

'Sir, what are you gonna do?'

'We're shutting this investigation down till we get a full team on the ground over there.'

The conversation changed topic. A full team meant a planeload of people, from psychiatrists to forensics to profilers. Every director would want to be part of it.

Sebastian didn't want to be anywhere near Mike when they broke the news to him.

THE ROPE BRIDGE

Waziristan, Sunday 7 January, 1:20 am

The din of gravel pummelling their wheel arches drowned out all other sound as they raced down the dark, deserted, dirt road leaving plumes of dust for half a kilometre.

Jane was soaked in perspiration as she struggled to control the bucking and bouncing SUV. Its worn suspension and feeble headlamps were no match for the unseen dips and potholes, impossibly sharp switchbacks and off-camber bends. Fatigue made her eyes water. Her temples throbbed with a dull, nauseating pain. She badly needed to rest.

Sergei lay asleep beside her, his head resting on her folded jacket. As they came to a relatively straight patch, Jane leaned over and felt his forehead. Thank God, he wasn't feverish.

The restaurateur had freaked out at the carnage. It hadn't taken much for Jane to convince him they had done it to each other. She had to admit it was a more plausible explanation than the truth. Even one of his precious knives embedded in one man's throat didn't make him think otherwise.

Unexpectedly the owner begged her not to involve the police, telling her it would destroy his business and he would be unable to support his family. He had thanked Jane profusely when she agreed.

After she had washed up, he helped Sergei into the Nissan and packed their dinner in takeaway containers. Presumably, he would dispose of the bodies.

Apart from the feel and smell of the blood and the memory of her heel contacting her assailant's face, everything else was hazy. Contradictory feelings and thoughts swam through Jane's mind. She felt a strange exuberance that she'd overcome the odds and prevailed over an enemy most men would quail at. Yet the elation made her feel guilty. Killing shouldn't be joyful.

She had killed before, with a gun, but that had been almost accidental, a reflex action. Killing with a knife and getting blood on her hands and clothes, was an entirely different matter. It made her feel unclean. Humans hadn't fought with bladed weapons in centuries. Squeamishness was now part of their DNA.

One thing she was certain of. She didn't regret what she'd done. The men had themselves to blame. First for attacking Sergei and then for not taking her seriously.

The trip odometer she'd reset as they turned off the main road ticked to twenty. Where was Yousaf's rope bridge?

Sergei groaned as he came to. He tried to sit up. 'Shit! My head. What happened?'

'How are you?' Jane dared not take her eyes off the road.

'Not good.' Sergei winced as he spoke.

'Poor baby. Did you see who attacked you?'

'I just heard a footstep and then… everything went black.'

'It was the men from the hotel.'

'Oh shit.' Sergei tried sitting up again.

'Don't worry, they're dead.'

'What the fuck? How?'

'I… umm… killed them.' Jane was aware how bizarre she sounded.

'You what? Fuck!' Sergei looked at her, not sure he'd heard right.

Jane nodded. 'Yeah.'

'Sweetheart, I don't understand. How? Are you… are you OK?' His voice was full of concern.

'I-I don't know…' A numb feeling crept over her as she spoke. 'It's like something switched in me and I became someone… something else.'

'Wow!'

'I honestly don't know what to feel. So please, let's leave it?'

'Of course, sweetheart.' He touched her face. Jane had been an accomplished gymnast before starting Systema and she'd practised like a monk but neither explained the unreal progress she made.

And she still found time for sharpshooting and running her company.

He reached out and touched her shoulder, 'I want you to know... I'm bloody proud of you.'

'Thank's babe but... I'm not. I can still smell the blood.' She put her wrist to her face and crinkled her nose.

The road dipped sharply. In a sudden bout of panic, Jane slammed on the brakes. It wasn't a moment too soon. The bridge loomed into view as the tyres scrabbled for traction on the loose surface. They were still travelling too fast. As their headlights illuminated more of the bridge, her panic grew into desperation. It was the narrowest and flimsiest structure she'd ever seen. Made of steel cable and wooden planks of uneven lengths, it looked scary to walk over. They were now skidding sideways. Jane lifted off the brake pedal slightly. The Nissan straightened, some steering feel returned, but they were out of road.

She did the only thing she could, aim towards the middle of the bridge and hope, all the while keeping the brake pedal lightly depressed.

'No,' she involuntarily gasped as the planks grated in protest. The steel cables pinged, and the bridge swayed under their weight. Rope bridges were only designed for walking pace and their speed was over ten.

'Don't stop; whatever you do.' Sergei took hold of the pillar handle.

Too scared to respond, Jane managed to keep the accelerator depressed and her eyes away from the side window. They had reached the middle of the span and had slowed to a walking pace. The bridge creaked alarmingly as it sagged.

'We're almost there.' Sergei's voice shook.

'I don't want to die. Not without Razane.' Jane shrieked as she eased off the accelerator.

'We won't die.' He wished he sounded more convincing. 'Just keep going the way you are.' All his muscles clenched as they began to climb out of the sagging bridge. By the time their front wheels touched solid ground they were both soaked in sweat. Jane resisted the urge to press the pedal harder before all the wheels were off the bridge.

'Phew, that was scary.' Sergei let go of the handle. His fingers white.

Jane opened the door, jumped out and knelt on the dirt road, unaware of the sharp stones pricking her knees. Her breath came in fast gasps. Ignoring the stabbing headache, Sergei climbed out after her. 'Fucking hell. You did well, sweetheart.' He put his arm around her.

Neither noticed the three armed men emerge from the shadows.

FATA

The blinding light and the rifle barrel hard against Sergei's skull made it feel like his head was about to explode. The man was pressing the cold hard steel exactly on the lump that had formed after the ISI goon had hit Sergei unconscious. The pain made him feel faint.

'What you name?' a man barked.

'I'm Sergei. This is my wife, Jane. We're looking for Captain Sherdil Khan. Yousaf sent us.' Hopefully it was the right answer.

The men whispered amongst themselves. One spoke into a walkie talkie.

The pressure from the rifle barrels eased. 'Up!' The man with the torch barked as he pointed at the Nissan. 'You sit in back.' It wasn't a suggestion.

Their leader, a burly man in civilian attire, climbed in beside Sergei. As he closed the door, he took out a revolver and held it with a loose grip.

Sergei exchanged glances with Jane. The handgun didn't portend well. They had only one weapon between them, the semi-automatic from the steakhouse courtyard and it was in Jane's jacket pocket.

The driver appeared familiar with the roads and drove at a suicidal speed while the rest maintained a stony silence.

'If anything happens, go for the dude in front,' Sergei whispered in Jane's ear. He wasn't sure he'd cope with the other man, but he'd have to do his best.

Jane nodded casually and moved her hand to her pocket. If the man sitting next to Sergei noticed, he said nothing.

The road straightened and levelled off. Tall pine trees replaced the rocky cliffs along the roadside. The trees ended in fields bordered by a continuous low mud wall punctuated by the occasional opening. A few houses flashed by followed by more fields.

Sergei was about to ask where they were going when the driver slowed and turned left into a gap in the mud wall. The four-wheel-drive bounced alarmingly as they followed a straight and narrow track. It ended in a large property surrounded by a brick wall topped with outward curving spikes. Two soldiers were warming their hands over a brazier. They grabbed their rifles and stood to attention as the Nissan came to a halt.

* *

Ian took out his night vision binoculars but couldn't see anything worthwhile. The vehicle, with Sergei and Jane inside, had disappeared inside behind a row of dense shrubs that concealed a building that looked like a large house.

'Does Sahib want me to go closer?'

'No Rizwan. Stay here. We don't want them to see us.' Ian took out his smartphone. There was no phone or Internet, but he had a GPS signal that allowed him to get his bearings using saved maps. This part of the country showed no road or place names. He looked for a board to identify the building, but there was nothing.

It was time to call home. He settled back in the seat and marked the spot on his map.

'OK, Rizwan. Take us back the way we came. I need to find someplace I can get a signal.'

WATER

Saipan, Sunday 7 January, 7:30 am

Jane and Sergei linked arms with her as they walked in silence along the forest track near their home. It was early in the morning in springtime and a light mist covered the forest floor. They clambered down an embankment, damp from rain, and made their way across a stream, taking care not to slip on the water-polished boulders.

The forest ended. The path continued through their neighbour's canola fields, resplendent in golden yellow blooms that stretched into the distance.

They had an agreement with all their neighbours that they could walk freely in each other's fields. This gave the members of the small community kilometres of walking tracks through the beautiful and serene countryside.

A small steel gate separated the two properties. Sergei was the last through. The gate clanged as he pulled it shut behind them.

* *

The clang sounded again. Razane opened her eyes with a start. Sergei and Jane and the field were gone, but she was still in the awful white room. She had been dreaming. She must have fallen asleep while trying to meditate.

So far it had worked. She felt no ill effects from her white environment.

The door opened and two guards burst in. Razane held out her mitten-covered hands as one of them handcuffed her. She had decided struggling wouldn't help.

Bright light and noise assaulted her senses as she stepped out of the room. She tried to breathe, but the air was thick and humid. The world spun, making it hard to walk. She felt like throwing up. Everything became a whirl. The ground rushed towards her. Acting on instinct, she bent her legs and pulled her hands back to cushion the fall. The guard holding the chain felt her pull and yanked the chain hard. Razane was unbalanced and fell forward, her knees hitting the concrete hard. She was momentarily dragged along and then fell face forward. Her teeth jarred painfully as her chin hit the concrete.

The guards turned around. Seeing her sprawled on the ground, they rushed to pick her up. Her face and knees burnt fiercely.

'Get me a medic,' the guard on the left spoke into his shoulder mic.

'I saw that on camera. You were too rough,' the voice said. 'Bring her to sick bay.'

* *

The sick bay smelled of disinfectant and bandages. Razane sat on a steel bench surrounded by the guards as the nurse tended to her.

'You're lucky, they're only grazes,' she said as she cleaned Razane's wounds and applied a disinfectant followed by waterproof plaster.

'Thanks, but excuse me for not feeling lucky.' Razane was still dizzy and her voice sounded distant.

'You make your own luck, dear.' The nurse said as she threw the cotton swabs into the bin. Turning to the guard, she said. 'You can take her. We're done.'

* *

They frog-marched Razane into what looked like an aircraft hangar. It was empty save for a wooden bench in the middle, surrounded by four Marines and her two interrogators. On the ground, a dark green garden hose with a trigger nozzle snaked its way to a tap. One Marine held a video camera.

Her heart pounded against her rib cage as she realised what they would do. If the guards hadn't been holding her, she would have fallen.

White Room Torture took at least a week to break a prisoner, but it had a nearly perfect success rate. What had made them speed up the interrogation?

Someone slammed a hood over her head from behind, blotting out the light. Hands picked her up and slammed her onto the board with a force that sent shock-waves through her body and knocked the breath from her.

Razane fought to overcome wild panic as the black fabric interrupted her breathing. She tried retreating inside her mind, back to the last dream, of them walking through the fields.

They came to her as she squeezed the outside world away. 'Jane and Sergei, my loves, please help me through this.' Jane had her arms around her, stroking her hair as her moist lips kissed the side of her neck. Sergei was on the other side, holding them both. Oh, what a secure feeling. She was relaxing now, her breathing had slowed. Someone slapped her hard. It was a trick to agitate her. She clasped Jane and Sergei. She wouldn't let the pain in. The stinging receded. She nuzzled against Jane's warm, soft breasts. Sergei moved her hair and kissed her on the nape of her neck as he unzipped her dress.

In the outside world, the Marines strapped her down. The bindings stung as they bit into her skin. The board was hard against her bony back and inclined so her head was lower than her feet.

'Shh, my darling. You're strong.' Jane whispered in her ear.

Razane owed it to their threesome to pull through this. With them beside her, inside her, she would try.

Waterboarding was so cruel because it triggered the primeval fear of drowning. The drowning sensation was immediate but asphyxiation was delayed so the prisoner was conscious long enough to feel terrible distress. It was also incredibly painful because the sinuses filled with water.

If done more than a few times, the prisoner's gag reflex would eventually suck water into their mouth and lungs. If not timed perfectly and monitored carefully, it was fatal. Many had died, more had gone mad.

Even before the US ban, the CIA strictly limited it to forty seconds. Could she resist that long?

She had trained herself to control her gag reflex to pleasure Sergei. Both she and Jane competed to see who could last longer while Sergei tried his hardest not to explode. Something she had learnt to do for love would help in this exercise of cruelty and hate. She relaxed her throat as the water hit her hood.

* *

'Man, this is fucking wrong,' Sebastian had seen videos of waterboarding. They were horrific. Mike had crossed a line he wasn't willing to.

'Yeah, well! You ratted me out, asshole.' Mike growled. 'I was OK with the white room.'

'I can't lie to a superior.'

'Fuck you! You didn't have to tell.'

'They'd have found out anyway.'

'Well, fuck you!'

'And we've been ordered to wait till the team gets here. So what's this?'

'They changed their mind.' Mike didn't look at him.

'What, why?'

'Got some new intel… last minute.'

'What?'

Mike gave the Marines the signal to begin, then he balled his fist as he turned to Sebastian. 'Her associates flew to Pakistan and to the Afghan border. We believe they're setting something in motion.'

'Fucking hell,' Sebastian whispered under his breath, looking for signs Mike was lying. This changed everything.

Wafaa was planning another attack.

Sebastian ignored the water splashing on his trousers as he watched with morbid fascination. A stream of water cascaded over their prisoner's hooded face while a Marine stood by with a stopwatch.

Mike had asked for twenty seconds to start off with. The Marine counted down with his fingers and put his hand up to stop.

Two Marines rotated the board upright while another pulled off the hood. Razane coughed water as she struggled to breathe.

'Listen, you can make this stop as soon as you—' Mike put his face near hers as he spoke.

'I'm not the person...' A coughing fit drowned Razane's words.

Mike waved his hand and made a plus and a five sign.

The hood was put back on; the board was rotated down; the hose was aimed at her face. After twenty-five seconds they let her up for air. She coughed and spluttered but otherwise showed no signs of breaking.

After thirty-five seconds Razane had gone grey. She took more time to cough up the water and her subsequent breaths weren't as deep.

Mike's face darkened as he signalled forty seconds. He knew he was at the limit. Beyond that, they risked losing the prisoner. The Marines replaced the hood, lowered the board and aimed the hose.

The prisoner struggled against her bindings. Her legs shook violently as they counted down to forty. When they removed the hood, her lips were blue and eyes bloodshot; she coughed and vomited.

'Anything to say?' Mike said.

In a movement that was almost imperceptible, Razane shook her head. 'Fifty seconds.' He grabbed the hood and forced it back on her head, cutting her off mid-breath. 'Bitch!'

* *

Razane was soaked through. Her wet jumpsuit enhanced the sensation of being underwater. At the start, she had been acting, making herself cough and struggle, hoping it would signal distress and make them stop. It was hard to do and remain in Jane and Sergei's enveloping embrace. At some point, her lovers faded and then they were gone. The water was filling her mouth and more went up her nose. She still kept her throat relaxed but was rapidly tiring.

At forty seconds, she caved in and swallowed. Water rushed into her mouth and nose and into her windpipe, blocking her breathing. Fear gripped her like a wild animal, her mind melted. She would die. She looked for and begged Jane and Sergei to return, but they didn't.

Her tormentors let her up. The man with bad skin said something. Before she could breathe, he slammed the hood back on.

* *

Sebastian found it increasingly hard to watch. She still wasn't speaking and Mike, being Mike, was losing patience. He ordered fifty seconds. The Marines began to pour. She was struggling less now. As they neared fifty seconds, the man with the stopwatch prepared to put up his hand.

'Wait. Go sixty.' Mike said. The Marines exchanged glances.

Sebastian looked sharply at Mike. This was dangerous. They risked losing everything. He couldn't go along with it. 'No. We stop.' He shouted loudly.

The Marine put down the hose and was about to help his comrades lift the plank when Mike stepped forward. 'Fuck you. We'll stop when I say.'

The Marines winced and looked at Sebastian.

'I said continue,' Mike bent down to pick up the hose.

'Lift her up,' Sebastian spoke fast. 'If she dies it won't matter that you were following orders.'

Sebastian's words jolted the Marines out of their indecision. They lifted the plank and removed the hood. The prisoner had gone limp.

Mike went red. A vein pulsed on his forehead as he pulled Sebastian away from the other Marines. 'You've seen how well she's coping?' he said between clenched teeth. A fleck of spit landed on Sebastian's cheek. 'We need to go harder to break her.'

'You call that coping? Another few seconds and we'd have lost her.' He was shaking with anger. He tried to calm himself. 'Look Mike, you were right all along... And... I should have supported you better... But man, we can't fucking kill her. Only she knows her plans.'

'Fuck.' Mike shook his fist but his face began to relax. He exhaled loudly. 'Fuck!'

'I can see she's been trained to resist,' Sebastian said, 'She calmed herself like a Buddhist monk. But... that makes her more likely to drown. Then... we lose everything, OK.'

He knew he was right. Mike knew it too. The prisoner the world most associated with water torture, Al Qaeda's Khalid Sheikh Mohammed, had to be resuscitated five times and suffered permanent brain damage as a result.

Unexpectedly, Mike smiled. 'You know, I think you're right.' He clapped Sebastian on the back. 'This can work for us.'

Sebastian shook his head, mystified, 'What...? How?' Mike had gone nuts.

'My young protege, watch and learn.' Mike placed a hand on his shoulder.

'Take her back to her cell and get her a change of clothes,' Mike said to the Marines as he grabbed the video camera. 'She's going on a little trip.'

SHERDIL

Waziristan, Sunday 7 January, 8:30 am

The high ceiling covered in flaking yellow paint was unfamiliar as were the smells and sounds. It was in sharp contrast to Jane's soft warmth as she snuggled up to him. It never grew old. She was snoring ever so slightly. They had fallen asleep in each other's arms. It was warm under the thick wool blanket but outside it was icy cold and smelled fresh compared to Lahore.

A sick feeling in the pit of his stomach was the first reminder their world was in disarray. Razane was a prisoner, and they were no closer to finding her.

Sergei felt the back of his head. It still throbbed from the blow. He turned and moved Jane's hair from her face and kissed her tenderly on her forehead. She stirred and stretched lazily. Her smile was cut short as she too went through the gut-wrenching realisation he had. It had been that way since Razane's kidnapping; waking was awful.

As they lay gathering their wits, they heard voices, in conversation, outside their room.

A knock on the door startled them.

'Come in.' Sergei sat up on the thin foam mattress. A stocky man with a huge handlebar moustache poked his head in.

'Salam Sahib.' He raised his hand in a half salute. 'Sherdil Sahib coming here soon. Cook prepare breakfast.'

'*Shukria*,' Sergei responded in a hoarse voice. He shook off the lethargy and struggled out of bed.

He had to remain positive. Two years ago, they were in a similarly hopeless situation. They had managed to free Jane. He had to believe they would also free Razane.

Breakfast was served in a large dining room that resembled an army mess. Apart from the cook who scurried over, it was empty. The traditional spicy omelette, toast and sweet tea tasted good, but the nausea hadn't fully receded and their minds were occupied elsewhere.

'I hope Sherdil shows soon, my nerves are killing me,' Jane said, a frown on her face.

Shouting drew Sergei's attention. He looked out of the window. An officer was conducting a drill in a field. As he stood there, a motorcycle approached. Its rider got off and approached the mess. He was a broad-chested man with a thick bushy beard who looked like he lived in a bodybuilder's gym. A guard saluted and rushed to open the door for him.

'Sergei Sahib. Asalam aleikum.' The newcomer held out his hand. 'Captain Sherdil Khan, at your service.' He shook Sergei's hand and nodded to Jane.

'It's good to meet you,' Sergei said. 'Yousaf told me you're like brothers.'

'Yes, a friend of Yousaf is my friend also.' Sherdil put his hand to his heart to emphasise. 'You were late yesterday, so we drove down the road to look for you.'

'Yes, sorry. We got held up at Hathala,' Sergei said, 'at a roadhouse.'

'Oh, Hathala. What happened?' Sherdil's eyes narrowed as he looked at them both. 'We had news of an incident there.'

'We were attacked,' Jane said.

'Wait,' Sherdil put his fingers to his lips. He asked the guard to wait outside and closed the door.

'Captain Yousaf told me to trust you. Two ISI men were killed in Hathala. Was that you?' He pulled up a chair and sat at the table.

'Yes... they followed us from Lahore,' Sergei said.

'Oh no.' The captain shook his head. 'What happened?'

Sergei looked at Jane. 'Well... they attacked us in the dark and we fought back.' Sergei said.

'They did? You... killed them?' Sherdil's incredulity turned to mirth. He laughed. 'Sergei Sahib you are joking?' He wagged his finger at him.

'Good heavens, no. I'd never joke about something like

that.'

Jane rolled her eyes. 'Sergei is making it sound easy, but it wasn't.'

'Sergei Sahib, you surprise me,' Sherdil made an exaggerated show of looking him up and down. 'You look like a gentleman. Not a street fighter.'

'It wasn't—' Sergei began, but Jane squeezed his arm.

Sherdil had a hard time accepting Sergei had bettered the men. He'd never believe Jane had done it. She didn't blame him. 'Everyone says that about Sergei.'

Sherdil looked at them both and pursed his lips. 'Very good. I am so happy I am not your enemy, Sergei Sahib.' He grinned.

Sergei smiled at their musclebound host. 'I don't think I'd last long against you, Sherdil.'

'Fortunately, no need to find out. But let us now be serious and make preparations for your journey... but first, you finish breakfast.'

'Will you take us to Ghazni?' Jane said.

'No, only to the border. After breakfast we make your ID papers and you madam must make your hair black and wear a burka, please.'

'All right. I understand,' Jane said.

'Thank you,' Sherdil looked up at her, his face serious. 'Afghanistan is very dangerous for locals. It is deadly for foreigners.'

* *

Major Amjad paced the gardens. He hated waiting. Somewhere, somehow, he had lost the ability to be patient. Maybe it was the sign of the times. Everyone demanded instant gratification, and he was no different.

A man had left the Dera Ismail Khan offices to check on Sibtain and Shakeel's last known location. That was an hour ago.

The major opened the ISI navigation app again. It was like

Google Maps but used their own satellites. Their position hadn't moved for the last fourteen hours. It made no sense. Either the app was broken or something was wrong. The ISI network covered the whole of Pakistan. There were no dead zones.

Both men could handle any situation; he wasn't concerned for their safety. So what in Allah's name were they doing?

The phone rang. He answered. 'Yes!'

'S-s-sir, this is... Bilal.'

'What is it for God's sake?'

'We found the two phones in the tribal area, in a ravine, by the roadside. It seems like... like someone threw them out of a moving car.'

'Hmmm, that is strange. Did you learn anything else?' He suddenly felt unwell and needed to sit.

'The phones are at the lab being tested, but we found caked blood in the USB and audio jacks and in the speaker grille.'

'Whose phone?'

'I do not understand, sir.'

'Whose phone had the blood?'

'Both, sir.'

'Oh... how very strange. See if you can find out whose blood it is. Run a DNA match with all databases we have.'

'Y-yes sir.'

'And Bilal... speed it up!'

'Yes sir. If you authorise it, we can fly it to Karachi. They have a rapid DNA machine.' It was a new technology that used a specialised computer chip to analyse a DNA sample in two hours instead of two days.

'OK, I authorise it. Get it done, *fatafat*.'

* *

With Sherdil in the lead, they set off on dirt bikes. Corporal Asad rode pillion behind Sherdil and Jane rode behind Sergei.

The countryside was as beautiful as anything they had encountered. Rugged snow-capped peaks soared high above green valleys, often bisected by sparkling rivers and streams. The road surface was poorly maintained and in many places not wide enough for two vehicles to pass. Bridges were simple steel cable and plank affairs that required a good dose of courage to cross.

Apart from army jeeps and trucks and the occasional reconnaissance aircraft, the road was deserted. Sherdil had told them it was still a war zone. The army had driven out Taliban insurgents and were attempting to clear the area of landmines and roadside bombs. Till they did, the locals couldn't return to their homes.

They stopped for lunch in a green meadow. To stretch her legs, Jane walked to an escarpment that overlooked the valley they had come from. The tall pines trees on the valley floor were mere dots on a carpet of green.

'Do you want me to take over?' Jane said as they prepared to set off.

'Let me do another hour then you can,' Sergei said.

'You're getting the hang of the bike,' Jane said as she tightened the straps on her helmet. 'You learn fast.'

'Nothing compared to you, sweetheart,' he said.

'Really, why?' she looked puzzled.

'Have you forgotten the steakhouse massacre?' Sergei donned his gloves

'Oh…' Her voice trailed away. 'That's so not funny.' The memory made her pulse race.

Sergei sensed something was wrong and removed his helmet. 'I'm sorry, sweetheart. That was insensitive of me.' He squeezed her hand.

Jane removed her helmet and adjusted her goggles. 'Babe, just thinking of it gives me goosebumps.' She reached out and stroked his cheek with her gloved hand. 'But… I'd do it again… to protect you or Razane.'

The sun went behind the clouds as they climbed above the snow line. They were both glad for their heavy snow jackets and gloves that Sherdil had lent them.

An hour later they turned off the main road onto a narrow

forest track. Sergei stopped and swapped places with Jane. 'Are you sure you can manage?' he said as he stretched his aching muscles.

Jane scanned the forest track. 'I rode lots as a kid, just on a smaller bike,' Jane said. 'Let me have a go. When I can no longer manage, you take over again.'

* *

Amjad propped his elbows on his desk as he stared at his screen. The DNA results were hard to fathom. The blood was Shakeel and Sibtain's. It could only mean they had met with foul play.

The two were the best underlings he had ever had. He enjoyed the terror their strength and brutality induced in others. Even the colonel was extra nice to him because of them. He would hate to lose them.

Sibtain had last rung to report he had knocked Sergei unconscious behind a restaurant in Hathala. They were waiting for Jane to check on her husband. So what happened?

There too many unanswered questions and loose ends. Why were Sergei and Jane in Pakistan? What were they doing in the country's west? Why were they trying to meet Major Hamdani?

A crazy thought occurred to him. What if they believed they could free Hamdani and then Razane? They had done something similar in the past. It did not matter that it was impossible, but the fact that they might try made them dangerous.

He had to assume the worst. They were still alive and his men were dead. This called for a KCB, a Kill-or-Capture Bulletin. It would go out to all law enforcement personnel and the army, authorising any means necessary to ensure their capture. With KCBs, the police usually took the easy way out and shot the fugitives.

He turned on his computer screen and began to fill out the online form.

EXTRAORDINARY RENDITION

Saipan, Sunday 7 January, 7:45 pm

The sun shone in Mike's eyes, momentarily blinding him as the Gulfstream turned and banked and then levelled off. The strong shaft of light was gone before he could close the blind. Outside the sky and ocean were both a bright blue, but the horizon was black. They were heading into the night.

The pilot turned the fasten seatbelt light off. Mike grabbed a coke from the galley fridge and settled back into the seat with a sigh. He looked over at Sebastian who was reading something on his iPad. He would not get any conversation out of him. It would be a long flight.

The flying time to Cairo was sixteen hours. Their destination, Azouli Military Prison, was another two hours out of Cairo by road.

He had been there before to witness interrogations and had been impressed by the ruthless efficiency of the Egyptians who had turned torture into an art-form. No wonder they had a nearly perfect success rate.

He looked over at their prisoner. She lay on the floor trussed up in plastic cling wrap like a cocoon, a breathing tube her only connection to the outside world. Huge noise cancelling headphones were duct-taped to her head to deprive her of any audible sensations. Under the wrapping, she wore an adult diaper.

He had twice gotten lucky. The first time was when the ASIS agent discovered that Wafaa's associates Sergei and Jane were heading to Afghanistan. That had allowed him to continue interrogating the prisoner. Otherwise there was a good chance he would have been summarily dismissed and prosecuted.

The second bit of good luck happened after he had gotten carried away with the water torture and had almost killed the prisoner.

Normally that could have seen him suspended indefinitely on unpaid leave. In an ironic twist, the video of how Wafaa had resisted the procedure was seen as incontrovertible evidence of her guilt. The top brass had green-lighted the extraordinary rendition.

All US Marines involved in covert operations in the Middle East underwent interrogation resistance training. Waterboarding was one of the few torture methods for which training was voluntary. No one ever lasted longer than twenty seconds before they spasmed violently. Wafaa had lasted close to a minute.

Chip Balawski had agreed with his assessment that she'd been trained in interrogation resistance. He'd agreed to involve the Egyptians and had promised to expedite the approval process. They couldn't waste any more time. Finally, the CIA high-ups and he were on the same wavelength. It was hardly a surprise; success had many fathers. And the assholes were lining up to take credit.

At least he was still leading the investigations. He slipped on the headphones and sighed a deep sigh as Ride of Valkyrie lifted his spirits. He loved Wagner.

THE BLOOD TRAIL

Dera Ismail Khan, Sunday 7 January, 4:00 pm

The dark viewing room always reminded Major Amjad of the vivarium in Lahore Zoo. Instead of snakes, the one-way glass looked into prison cells containing suspects. It was fitting. Many were often reptilian in character.

The cells were deliberately small, a metre square and deliberately filthy. The prisoners had neither the space to sit nor toilet facilities. They had to relieve themselves where they stood. Each cell had a water pipe attached to the wall. Once a day water would flow and carry most of the waste into a sewer. It was never enough to wash away the stench nor prevent the swarms of flies.

Major Amjad studied their two newest prisoners as he took a bite of cake and a sip of the piping hot tea. The owners of the restaurants at the Hathala truck stop were in adjacent cells opposite the bench he sat on. Both had been roughed up a bit but neither had divulged any useful information.

Meanwhile, his men were going through security footage from the service station. If the blood on the phones was any sign the crime scene would be easy to find.

He was desperate for some good news. The Americans had not yet responded to his request to bring their prisoner to Pakistan and now Sergei and Jane were making efforts to free her.

He wondered whether he should let Mike know that Wafaa's associates were in Pakistan.

The door opened. Captain Ayub walked over and saluted.

'At ease Captain, what is it?'

'Sir, we have found traces of blood all over the steakhouse courtyard. It was everywhere. Someone spent the time to hose it down and then used bleach to hide the traces.'

'OK, let the other man go. Tell him if he talks, we bring him back. Then soften the steak man more… Tenderise him well.' He smiled as he paused for effect, but the captain didn't get the joke. 'Use the garden hose. But I want him able to talk.'

'Yes, sir.' The Captain turned smartly and left.

The softening would take half an hour and turn the toughest man into a blubbering mess willing to sell his kids so they would stop.

It was unlikely the restaurateur had killed Sibtain and Shakeel himself. He had probably just covered it up, which made him an accomplice to murder.

Regardless of who killed their men, Sergei and Jane's behaviour supported his narrative that Razane was Wafaa. In that context, their actions appeared suspicious. For all intents and purposes, they were accomplices of a major terror suspect. He could use this as leverage to force the Americans to bring Razane to Pakistan. For that, it was important that they stayed alive. He would replace the KCB with a standard arrest warrant.

He took out his phone and dialled Rehan, his assistant.

'Rehan, what is the status of the kill order?'

'We only need Lieutenant General Akram's signature.'

'Stop the order. I don't need it anymore.'

He sat and contemplated what to write. Satisfied, he opened the messaging app, found Mike in his contacts list and began typing.

* *

'Dumb fucking, Arab, Egyptian fucking camel cock suckers.' Mike was beside himself as he shouted abuse into the phone.

'Sorry Mike. We tried our hardest,' Ron said, 'and the Egyptians are really apologetic but —'

'Someone will have to fuckin pay for this.' Mike ground his teeth. He knew Major Ron Perion, personally. He was the military attaché at the US embassy in Cairo and a good guy. He would have tried everything to make it happen, but Arabs were pig-headed at the best of times. No wonder they didn't eat the animals.

Mike hung up and called Chip Balawski. Chip had requested hourly status updates. He was now being micro-managed.

'Yup?' A muffled voice spoke over the sounds of dishes clinking in the background.

'Chip, it's Mike. The Egyptians are refusing to cooperate.'

'Whadda you mean. Ron promised he'd get it sorted.'

'Well, he didn't and now…'

'This bloody president of ours. The ass-wipe moved our embassy to Jerusalem. Now the fucking Arabs have a rod up their asses.'

Mike liked Donald Trump, but he kept quiet. He wasn't going to debate politics with Chip.

'Let me put pressure on the Egyptians. Hang tight there, we'll get back to you.'

'Sir, we might have another option. You ain't gonna like it but it keeps us moving.'

'What?'

'I just got a message from my contact in Pakistan. Wafaa's associates are in his custody. He suggested we use them to put pressure on Wafaa. He strongly recommended bringing her to Lahore.'

'No fucking way!' Mike could hear something breaking. 'Those cocksuckers have tricked us—'

'Sir… I see merit in it. The prisoner is tough but might crack if we use advanced interrogation methods against her associates.'

'Goddammit, ten years ago, we had so many options, the Syrians, the Egyptians, the Yemenis and the Pakis. Now… fuck!'

'Yes sir, you're right.'

'Fuck, fuck, fuck…' There was silence then a resigned groan. 'OK, do it! I don't see another option. Refuel and head to Pakistan. Do you need me to speak to someone?'

'No, sir. Leave it to me.'

**

Captain Ayub entered again. 'Sir, the prisoner is ready to talk.'

Amjad followed him to the brightly lit interrogation room. The restaurateur's legs were chained to the legs of a steel table. His wrists were manacled to steel rings on the far edge, forcing him to stoop forward. It exposed him to any further beatings if needed. It was rarely necessary. The man was moaning quietly, shuffling from one foot to the other.

Two ISI men stood either side of him. They were the ones who had administered the softening.

Major Amjad sat in a chair facing the prisoner who showed no signs of defiance, only abject misery. It was understandable, he would be unable to sit for a few days or wear tight clothing. The major steepled his hands and studied the man's face. The wait was always the most fear-inducing part of an interrogation.

'What happened in the yard?' Amjad leaned forward.

'I w-will tell you the t-t-truth...' the prisoner choked back a whimper. The ISI man to his left coughed, making the prisoner cower.

'Of course, you will, son.'

'Sahib, these two foreigners... they entered my restaurant. After they ordered food, the man went to the toilet outside in the yard. Then the lady went sometime later. My servant heard strange noises and told me. I went out to check.

'The foreign man was lying on the ground unconscious and the woman was checking him and crying. Her hands were covered in blood. Apparently, the men had tried to grab her but... then began fighting with each other over wh-who could have her f-first. The poor lady was crying and I have never seen so much b-b-blood...'

'Nonsense...' Major Amjad massaged a sore spot on his neck.

'N-n-no, it is true.' The man's legs gave way. He would have fallen to his knees had his wrists not been restrained. He was left dangling, the handcuffs biting into his wrists. Crying in pain, he pulled himself upright and tried to put his hands together in supplication. 'I b-b-beg you, sir. Believe me. I have small children and a wife and a mother. I am the only bread earner…'

Amjad exchanged glances with Captain Ayub. 'What happened then?'

'Sir, I got very scared. The men were dead. We tried to revive the foreign man but could not. So we placed him in the passenger seat of his four-wheel drive. Then I asked my men to put the bodies into sheets and dump them.'

'A likely story. How about another one? I think you tricked my men and killed them yourself. Maybe you first poisoned them.'

The prisoner's eyes opened wide in fear. 'Oh no, sir. I am a decent man. The men never came into the restaurant. They must have jumped the back fence. We thought they were dacoits, so we dumped the bodies. I, I was afraid of revenge attacks.'

The man's story was plausible, except the part about Sibtain and Shakeel killing each other. They were good friends. On the other hand, the surveillance footage didn't lie. Sibtain and Shakeel had jumped over the wall into the courtyard. No one else entered or left the restaurant until the restaurant staff carried Sergei to his vehicle.

But if Sibtain and Shakeel hadn't killed each other and Sergei was unconscious, that left Jane. The thought made him laugh. It was too preposterous.

THE ODD PACKAGE

Lahore, Monday 8 January, 12:05 am

Abdul Moeez hated working the night shift at the airport. It disrupted his sleep and made him constantly tired. He yawned as he walked out of the toilet and almost collided with a group of men wheeling a hospital trolley. An oddly shaped package wrapped in shiny plastic lay on the trolley; a pipe, the diameter of a garden hose stuck out of one end.

'Dumb Paki fucker,' a fat man with red blotches on a pasty white face growled at him in an American accent.

'Sorry,' Abdul Moeez mumbled. 'Damn,' he muttered to himself, almost immediately after. Why had he apologised? The arrogant fat American should take a dog's cock up his arse. He had a good mind to stop them and ask what they were doing, but this was the corridor that led from the VVIP Arrivals area. They would already have been priority cleared by customs and immigration.

He could at least ask them for their papers. It might rattle them. At least it would teach them a thing or two about manners.

With his jaw set in a determined frown, he set off after them. They had already rounded the corner and were out of sight. He reached the end of the corridor. Up ahead the men had stopped and were shaking hands with a uniformed Pakistani army major accompanied by two junior officers. Based on the obsequious nature of the underlings, he was important.

Abdul Moeez considered his options. Should he interfere with such a senior man? He was about to turn to go back to his office when the oddly shaped parcel convulsed. His heart beat faster. Allah, that was a human being. The Americans were smuggling a prisoner into the country in collusion with army officers. This was way above his pay-grade. His anger forgotten, he turned and walked back to his desk. He had a lot of work to finish before he went home.

What a strange sight that was… He sat at his desk and logged onto his computer. It was a bizarre way to transport a prisoner. The Americans pushing the trolley were in their military uniform; the other two were civilians. Could they be CIA? Perhaps the prisoner was someone from Al Qaeda or the Islamic State. How humiliating! This was even worse than the orange suits they made Muslim prisoners wear in Guantanamo Bay. If Muslims were stronger, and united, the Americans would never dare humiliate them like this. Even terrorists deserved dignity.

What should he do? It could be risky to mention this on an official report. But he would tell Burhan, his friend who was an immigration analyst at the Intelligence Bureau. He might find it useful. Abdul opened WhatsApp and began typing.

* *

Burhan sat up in bed. He blew his nose vigorously, but it didn't clear. The tissue was beginning to feel like sandpaper. The doctor had prescribed him antibiotics and a decongestant, but they weren't helping. With a groan, he rubbed the side of his forehead to relieve his blocked sinuses.

He had caught a cold from his drafty office. In five hours, he would have to wake up and go back to work. Without sleep, it would be a miserable day.

He was about to get up to go to the toilet when his smartphone beeped; a green light flashed.

He forgot about his stuffy nose as he read Abdul's message. In all his time at the Bureau, he had never heard of prisoners being transported that way. The army officers were most likely ISI, but what were they up to? What should he do? Information like that could land a junior officer in serious trouble. He could think of only one person he trusted. Major Hamdani had always been nice to him. He had appreciated every bit of information he had passed on. Often, he would take the time from his busy schedule and call him to thank him. He copied Abdul's text onto an email and pressed send.

YOUSAF

Lahore, Monday 8 January, 12:30 am

Yousaf turned off the TV. The cricket had become boring and would end in a draw. He also couldn't stop wondering what Sergei and Jane were doing.

He had helped them escape because they had wanted to free Major Hamdani. It mattered little they were on a fool's errand. He owed his boss and mentor at least that much.

By rights, he should have gone with them. At least they would have had a fighting chance. But the thought of crossing into Afghanistan without permission from a superior officer scared him.

The all too familiar self-hatred, and hopelessness, overwhelmed him. His chest tightened. His heart thumped sickeningly.

It was all coming back.

Time had muddied the point when it had all started, the beatings, the anger, the shouting. No one in their family had ever found out what had turned his mild-mannered father into a brutal tyrant.

Almost overnight their lives became a living hell. He and his mother would do everything to avoid being punched and thrown about, but it was the cruel taunts and verbal abuse that hurt even more. His father used to call him a loser who would never amount to anything. The only person immune to his father's tirades was his older brother Aslam, who could do no wrong.

When Yousaf was nineteen, he left home and joined the army. His father celebrated by changing the locks.

Free of fear and abuse, Yousaf thrived. The army became his family. He put his hand up for every tough assignment and pushed himself to the limit. His first two promotions happened faster than anyone else in the brigade.

His father died of a massive heart attack on the day before he was accepted in the Special Services Group, Pakistan's elite commando units. Yousaf had lost the chance to show his father he was not a loser.

While he didn't mourn his father's passing, his death left him with an emptiness. The burning ambition that had driven him dulled.

After a stint fighting terrorists in Pakistan's tribal belt, he was sent to the highest battleground in the world, the Siachen Glacier.

Even though it was strategically worthless, India and Pakistan fought over it as if their survival depended on it. Control over the years shifted back and forth at the cost of hundreds of lives; most were killed by the weather, not enemy bullets. In reality, the prestige gained was overshadowed by who won at cricket. Still, the two armies persisted.

Yousaf spent the next six months in the frigid altitudes, cheating death, avoiding frostbite, avalanches, and enemy fire. Two days before his tour ended, he fell in a crevasse and almost died from hypothermia. He had to be evacuated by helicopter.

As luck would have it, Major Hamdani was looking for assistants. He arranged Yousaf's transfer to the ISI while he was still recuperating.

Major Hamdani was more like a father than a boss. Under the mantle of a strict disciplinarian beat a kind heart. He encouraged Yousaf to go to night school and study criminology.

The pursuit of knowledge opened a floodgate. He read books at a rapid rate. His mind expanded. As his misery receded, he looked outward. As he understood his connection to the universe, he grew more confident. The major saw this and gave him more responsibility.

'You must aim higher than Captain,' he used to say.

And he had begun to. For the first time in his life, he believed in himself. The open wounds of self-hatred and doubt began to close and heal. His panic attacks subsided. He thought less and less of those terrible times, the beatings, the anger and the shouting.

And now he had failed his saviour.

The major's arrest in Ghazni made no sense. He was known as an honest and decent man and was liked by the Taliban.

He was there on a mission to help negotiate a truce. Someone had betrayed him. The military and the ISI were rife with factions of moderates and extremists. Peace did not suit everyone.

A thought struck Yousaf. Could they be after him as well? He had no political affiliations, but maybe his association with Major Hamdani was enough for him to be considered a threat.

If that was the case, his life was in danger. In the morning he would reach out to Major Amjad and tell him he was not in any faction. His only loyalty was to Pakistan. He would happily obey and serve whoever he worked for.

He switched off the light and walked over to the window. His room overlooked a dark courtyard separated from the street outside by a tall brick boundary wall. The steel gate would be locked. Aslam, his older brother, would have made sure of that.

A street light briefly shone on an elderly couple taking their dog for a walk. A cyclist rode by on his way home from work. An old car, its muffler rattling, drove slowly past, its wheels clunking into the many potholes in the road.

Relative silence descended again as the car's engine faded into the distance. Neighbours all around were talking, some were watching TV, someone played a flute, several dogs barked. A woman was scolding someone in shrill tones. In the distance, the hubbub of Lahore's dense traffic sounded like a river flowing. Everything seemed normal.

He closed the window. The outside receded. Apart from the TV downstairs, the house was quiet. Sameena and Qasim, his niece and nephew, were fast asleep. Their parents, Aslam and his wife Raheela, were watching a drama.

He was safe here in his brother's house and after tomorrow hopefully he would again be safe in his own little apartment.

Yousaf was about to go to bed when he remembered. He hadn't checked Major Hamdani's email account all day. He would do it one last time and then hand the laptop in to Major Amjad along with the password. That would be the peace offering.

He sat in the dark as he read the new emails. There was nothing out of the ordinary. Nothing that had to be read. What was he expecting, news that the major would be released? That was absurd.

He scanned them again. He had missed an email marked urgent. It was from Burhan at the Intelligence Bureau. He clicked on it and began to read.

It made no sense. Why would Americans bring a prisoner wrapped in plastic to Pakistan? What could it mean? But why should he care? He wasn't responsible for everything. He closed the email and turned the computer off. It was time for bed.

He drifted off to sleep dreaming of prisoners wrapped in FedEx boxes.

* *

The headlight from a faraway car swept across his ceiling. Yousaf realised he was awake. How long had he lain there? What had woken him? Was it a sound? Except for the overly loud tick-tock of the cheap Chinese made alarm-clock, the house was silent.

It was his overactive mind. He couldn't stop thinking of Burhan's description of the oddly wrapped prisoner. He had heard how terrorism suspects used to be brought to Pakistan to be tortured. It was called extraordinary rendition. Back then Pakistan had been pressured to cooperate. But that was a long time ago. The Pakistani government had since outlawed it. It was one of the reasons the American relationship had soured.

So why had they restarted? Who was the Pakistani officer mentioned in the report?

He had a crazy thought. What if the prisoner was Razane? Sergei and Jane had told him that the CIA had kidnapped her. If they believed she was Wafaa Aal Zubeidi, they would torture her in the most horrible way.

Yousaf sat up. He began to type a text message to Sherdil. Sergei and Jane needed to be told. A flash blinded him. The loud crump of a detonation followed. He dropped his phone. The door burst open. Men ran in and pounced on him. He was spun around onto his belly. His hands were stretched behind his back till he could feel his shoulder muscles tear. Cable ties cut into his wrists before the pressure on his arms and shoulders reduced. Despite the pain, his mind was occupied with one question. Had he pressed the send button?

Amjad strolled in. Yousaf couldn't see his face but he knew the walk, and he recognised the sickly-sweet perfume. 'Yousaf, Yousaf, Yousaf, do you know the punishment for treason?'

'Sir, what—?' Yousaf's reply was muffled as someone pushed his face into the pillow.

'More lies will only dig you into a deeper hole.' Amjad put his face close as he spoke. Yousaf could smell his rotting teeth over his cologne.

'Sir, I am just a humble…' again his face was smothered by the pillow.

'Sir, here is his phone,' Sadiq placed the large smartphone into Amjad's hand.

'Oh, a premium smartphone, young Yousaf. Is that not above your pay scale?' Amjad straightened up. 'Take him to our safe house. We will make him sing to us.'

'OK Sir. Do I also take his brother and family…? Perhaps they will make him cooperate…'

Amjad scowled at him. 'Damn fool. Do you think we touch innocents?' His men knew the answer. They did whatever they could get away with. He would have loved to take the whole family. There was something disturbingly satisfying about torturing a child. They had zero tolerance to pain and no understanding of why it was happening.

Unfortunately, he wasn't all powerful. If Yousaf's brother had been a poor man, it would have been no problem to stick chilli powder up his arse and cut his children's fingers off. But he was a manager at a large paper mill owned by the richest family in Pakistan. He knew people who knew people.

'Sir, please, I am a loyal man…' Yousaf's protests were muffled again as a pillowcase was placed over his head and tied at his neck with a large cable tie.

Amjad walked down the stairs and back to his car. Yousaf's phone was unlocked. As he read the text message Yousaf had been writing, he stopped in his tracks. Fear paralysed him from the belly up.

This was inconceivable. How did Yousaf know about the prisoner? The mother fucking traitor was about to send a message to alert Sergei and Jane.

How fortunate he had stopped him in the nick of time. His hands were still trembling as he fumbled to press the delete button.

A thought stopped him. He smiled as he modified the text message. He pressed send and rubbed his hands in glee. It wouldn't be long before he had them all in his torture rooms. It was working out better than he had hoped.

GHOST TOWN

Shawal, Monday 8 January, 7:00 am

The last rays of the sun were casting long shadows across the valley as they reached Shawal. Bomb craters and charred ruins marred what was otherwise a picturesque valley. But they barely took any notice. The long ride and constant tension had exhausted them to the point where Jane and Sergei could barely sit upright on the motorbike.

Sherdil led them to one of the few structurally sound buildings. Shawal had been the scene of bloody fighting between the Pakistan Army and militants from Al Qaeda and the Pakistani Taliban, and it showed. Only a few houses still had roofs. Most were burnt to the ground or were piles of bricks and stone.

The town was deserted. Until the army cleared the IEDs and landmines, civilians couldn't return. The only sound was the breeze rustling through the treetops. A fine mist hovered close to the ground, giving everything a ghostly appearance.

'It looks spooky.' Jane shivered as she put the large motorbike on its kickstand.

Sergei removed his helmet and gloves and looked around. The treetops swaying in the breeze and the occasional grey rabbit scurrying in the undergrowth were the only things moving. 'Yeah, I don't like it either.'

The abandoned army rest-house was large and solidly constructed with tall ceilings and a fireplace in every room.

Jane and Sergei chose a small west facing room near the back of the building. A faded carpet covered the floor. A woollen rug in an advanced state of decay was the only other furnishing.

The inside felt no warmer. A gap, large enough for Jane's hand, around their window frame showed why. Snow piled up on the windowsill had fallen inside, creating a wet, mouldy patch on the carpet.

Hungry and freezing and too tired to look for firewood, Jane and Sergei snuggled into a canvas sleeping bag. They covered it with both their jackets to ward off the bitter cold. Even wrapped in each other's arms they shivered for quite a while before they were comfortable enough to sleep.

Gnawing hunger and the sounds of men stirring outside their room woke them early. Someone had gotten a fire going. The smell of chai wafted into the room.

Jane shivered as she stared at a mouldy patch on the ceiling while her mind caught up. The knot in her stomach reminded her of their dire situation. They were running full tilt into the unknown, totally out of their depth. Their recklessness would likely get them killed, but what choice did they have? Life without Razane wasn't worth living. She was somewhere all alone, depending on them not to give up.

Jane wriggled out of the sleeping bag and slipped on her jacket. She was still covered in goosebumps as she zipped it up. Her hands hurt as she pulled on the snow pants over her jeans.

Sergei stirred. 'Oh, shit. It's cold.' Jane threw him his jacket and examined the attached bathroom.

The army rest-house had escaped the battles but not the ravages of the weather. The walls in the bathroom were all covered in thick green mould and most of the tiles in the shower had fallen off. She tried the tap, nothing. The pipes were most likely frozen solid. She would have to use snow to freshen up.

After the freezing night, it felt warmer outdoors. The mist had cleared, to reveal the extent of the tragedy that had turned Shawal into a ghost town. Beyond the settlement it was idyllic. Green grass and the dark green of pine trees punctuated a thin cover of snow.

To wake themselves up fully they rubbed snow on their faces before joining the men for a light breakfast of hot tea and sweet bread.

They set off again after breakfast, Jane's teeth still chattered as she sat pillion behind Sergei. It was about to become worse. A wind change brought a patchy fog, pea-soup thick in places, forcing them to ride at a walking pace.

The motorcycles had winter tyres with steel spikes, but Sergei still needed all his skill to avoid losing traction. After half an hour the fog turned into a blizzard that blew tiny icicles at them. Before long Sergei's face was raw and his lips were on fire.

They were about to stop when the fog cleared and they emerged into sunshine. They had descended into a valley with no snow.

At midday they climbed a ridge that represented the international border. Sherdil got off and spoke into his satellite phone as he waved at something that neither Sergei nor Jane could see.

'What did you do just then?' Sergei waited till Sherdil had pocketed his phone.

'Making sure we don't get shot.'

'Always a worthwhile thing to do.' Sergei nodded.

'Yes. See those towers? They have watchers that guard the border... With infrared for the nighttime and machine guns and sniper rifles. They can neutralise any threat.'

Jane strained to see but couldn't make them out. They were well camouflaged among the rocky outcrops of the mountain ridge.

'So what about on the Afghan side? Surely—'

'Nah. The Afghan army do not control this province.'

'So the Taliban do?'

'Yes, Taliban, Islamic State and many more. All rubbish we push out of Pakistan in the war.'

They followed Sherdil along the narrow, well-worn trail as it snaked its way down into the valley below. They had entered Afghanistan. If Sherdil hadn't told them, they wouldn't have known.

Their phones had been out of signal range ever since they left the base but amazingly the GPS still worked here so they could see themselves on the saved map. Google would maintain a trace of their journey. It would ease their return.

Sherdil slowed to a halt. 'This is as far as our snipers can protect us. So I go back now.' He handed them each a semi-automatic rifle. Sergei looked it over. It was the ubiquitous AK74 Kalashnikov.

'It is the good quality original one made in USSR,' Sherdil said. He also took a portable satellite navigation unit out of his pocket and handed it to Sergei. 'This has a long battery life and works anywhere with satellite coverage. You can see all the little towns.' He pointed at the small screen. 'Head to Barmal, which is here.'

Sergei had used something similar before. They were useful for hiking in remote areas. 'Thanks Sherdil. We'll bring everything back to you.'

'Yes, please and may Allah bring you success.' He saluted them.

'Thank you.' Jane said as she and Sergei saluted in return.

'Jane Madam and Sergei Sahib, you are most brave.'

'Thank you, brother.' Jane didn't feel brave.

'Thank you, my friend.' Sergei shook his hand.

Sherdil's phone rang, startling them. 'Yes.' He had to shout to make himself heard over the strong breeze. Worry creased his face as he listened.

IMPOSSIBLE DECISION

Afghanistan, Monday 8 January, 12:00 pm

Sherdil ended the call. 'My sergeant at the base relayed a text message from Captain Yousaf.' He paused, seemingly unsure how to proceed. 'Razane is in Lahore. He asked that you return immediately and meet him in room 218 at the Ambassador hotel.'

Sergei and Jane looked at him and then at each other, their expressions a mix of shock and relief. Jane didn't know whether to laugh or cry. What now? A weight lifted off her shoulders but a burning anxiety immediately replaced it. They had to get to Lahore, fast.

'Who is Razane?' Sherdil said.

'Razane's our companion,' Sergei said. 'She was kidnapped. That's why we're looking for Major Hamdani.'

'Oh, I understand.' Sherdil sounded unconvinced.

'So what do we do?' Sergei muttered, a frown creasing his forehead.

'What do you mean, darling? I don't see us having a choice. We need to go to Lahore.'

'But... what if the other way gets her out faster?' Sergei bit his lip, deep in thought. He put down his backpack and sat on the nearest boulder.

'They'll torture Razane...' Jane had gone silent. 'I'm sure... that's why they brought her here.'

'But we don't know how long it'll take to rescue Razane.' He didn't want to add, if we can at all.

'We know where she is. We have to get close. Somehow something will work out. We just have to go.' Jane's expression brooked no argument. 'If you won't...'

Sergei pulled her close. 'Hey, of course I'm coming with you.'

* *

Razane woke with a start. A hot and clammy wetness surrounded her. Her nostrils were blocked, she couldn't breathe. Something unyielding had been shoved in her mouth. Her skin itched all over. Her entire body was immobilised. She couldn't even move her toes. It was too bizarre to be real, yet felt too real to be a nightmare. Stabs of panic assailed her; she would die.

The mind-bending fear was mixed with terrible sadness and regret. She would never hold and love Jane and Sergei again. They would never know what happened to her. These monsters would make her disappear forever. If they had any plans to release her, they wouldn't be violating all UN human rights conventions so blatantly.

The thing in her mouth tasted of plastic. It was a respirator. She sucked and air filled her lungs. That is how she was alive. She took another breath. The air tasted dry and almost metallic, but at least it was air. Where was she? She was wrapped in something, and had been for a while. The surrounding wetness was sweat, and she had soiled herself. She recoiled at the thought. A part of her wanted the earth to open and swallow her.

SPLENDACIOUS NEWS

Lahore, Monday 8 January, 8:30 pm

The inside of the shop was warm and toasty, a relief from the bone-chilling cold on the street. Major Amjad fumbled for his wallet, extracted three five-thousand-rupee banknotes and handed it to the *degwalah*. 'This is for the poor.'

'Thank you, Sahib. May Allah bless your children and grant *Jannat-ul-firdous* to your elders.' The *degwalah* touched his chest in a sign of respect. The money would feed at least a hundred people.

Amjad accepted a steaming plate of rice and chickpeas from the *degwalah*'s helper and handed over another one hundred rupee note. He was feeling generous, and the smell was making his mouth water. All the food in the street next to Data Darbar, Lahore's largest sufi shrine was free for the poor. Everyone else donated whatever they could.

There was no shortage of poor people. As he stood there a man approached and held out an empty plastic bag. The *degwalah*'s helper gave him a generous portion.

The major took a bite. It was steaming hot and smelt delicious. The rice was fluffy and perfectly spiced, the chickpeas soft but not mushy. The *degwalah* was a master and came from a long line of *degwalahs* at the shrine. He would have learnt the trade from his father, and he from his.

Major Amjad hadn't eaten since Mike had called from Cairo saying he would accept his offer.

His heart bursting with happiness, the major drove from Dera Ismail Khan and reached Lahore Airport as Mike, his assistant Sebastian and two US Marines were deplaning.

The sight of Razane wrapped in plastic had made his heart lift with joy. It was a fitting way to treat his brother's murderess.

His prisoner was now in a holding cell under the Lahore

Fort, still wrapped in plastic. A doctor was running tests to document her condition. Meanwhile, Mike and his team were at the Hotel Avari freshening up.

It gave him the opportunity to come out to Data Darbar to show his gratitude to Allah, and what better way than to give alms to the poor.

He handed the plate and spoon to the helper and walked to the shrine. The guard manning the metal detectors saw his uniform and let him pass. The metal detectors were installed in 2010 when two suicide bombers killed forty-five people. It had been a bad year for bombings in Pakistan. Since then the security situation had improved immeasurably. It was a reminder of the need for a strong intelligence agency.

He removed his shoes and walked across the courtyard to the main hall. The central dome lit from below glowed a rich green in stark contrast to the white marble of the main buildings. Flood lights pierced through the thick fog and illuminated a throng of worshippers as they milled about for evening prayers. It was crowded for a Monday night. Times were bad. Too many people needed saintly solace.

He looked at his watch. He had just enough time for a quick prayer before his strategy meeting with Mike.

THE STORM

Indian Ocean, Tuesday 9 January, 5:00 pm AWST

Najib watched the fearsome burgeoning cumulonimbus clouds with trepidation. They had formed in the last half an hour, out of a clear blue sky cloud. Towering into the heavens, their bases were blacker than night. They glowed as jagged lightning forked through it to the water below in a continuous light show. Najib's chest cavity resonated to the rumble of the accompanying thunder. The balmy morning breeze had turned into a cold and frenzied gale that whipped up a spray that soaked all on deck within minutes.

'Allah's ferocious might,' he cried, looking skyward. A water drop the size of a large grape landed softly in his right eye. 'And his tender kiss.' He opened his mouth to catch more as oversized raindrops beat a syncopated rhythm on the yacht's steel surfaces. It was soon replaced by a band of torrential rain that deafened as it bucketed down.

On the bridge, Haziq was caught unawares by the speed of the storm. By the time he realised its severity, it was too late. At first, he tried to steer away but as the wind picked up and the waves became bigger he was forced to change tack. He was an experienced seaman and knew he had to keep as perpendicular to the waves as possible to avoid the risk of capsizing. Yet that led them the wrong way, towards what seemed like their impending doom. They would experience the full brunt of the storm.

Najib faintly heard Haziq shouting, 'Tell the men to secure themselves to the rails, close the hatches and doors and put on life jackets.'

The wind howled as it intensified further, making the deck treacherous as Najib ran around to pass on the message. He had to shout to make himself heard above the wind.

'Get your life jackets,' he upbraided a group pulling in a

fishing net. 'You two take over.'

Najib felt no fear. Allah loved to test his most beloved, but he wouldn't let them sink to the bottom of the Pacific; they were too precious.

It began to hail. Najib's cheek smarted as a fast-moving ice pellet hit him on the cheekbone. The hailstones falling on the deck were large, some as big as plums. Almost as soon as it began, the hail stopped. On the bridge, Haziq was a study of concentration as he aimed at each approaching wave. The weight of the boat worked against them. The old yacht shuddered repeatedly as it crashed through each wave only to meet the next and the one after that. Najib's heart skipped a beat as a hard drop elicited a loud bang from somewhere in the hull. Their boat was old, and the structure was rusting. The boat had needed more work, but Wafaa had run out of patience.

Najib muttered a prayer. 'Save us, O Allah, so we can do your work.'

'Go downstairs and check we are not taking in water,' Najib shouted at Saiq.

The next dip was gentler. The banging noise didn't repeat. Najib relaxed his tense muscles. Allah willing, it was nothing bad.

'Thank you, *Allah subhan it tala*,' he mouthed. As if in response, the wind speed dropped. The sound lost some of its intensity. The waves became gentler, no longer pounding the boat into submission. He was no longer being thrown about as hard. He relaxed his grip on the railing. He had been holding on so hard his knuckles hurt. Overhead the rain was slowing. Ahead the sky was clear.

'The boat is listing. We must have taken on water.' Haziq said. He still needed to shout.

'What should we do?' Najib said.

'We need to get the pumps working and check for leaks.'

Najib walked haltingly down the staircase that led to the lower deck. The pumps were in the engine room and worked off a belt feed from the main engine.

He opened the hatch to the engine room. The throbbing

sounds of the diesel engines grew louder as a blast of warm, humid, oily air hit him. He descended the winding stairs. Saleh and Nizhar stood in knee-deep water fixing the pump. Saiq was rummaging in the toolbox.

'What is wrong?'

'The clutch pack is not working,' Saleh pointed under water.

'The seals must be leaking.'

Wafaa had bought the forty-year-old French vessel cheaply. The diesel engines were the only thing in top condition.

'Can you fix it?'

'No, but we can bypass it so the pump works continuously.'

'Do it.'

'Just warning you, the pump can burn out.'

'Don't worry, just do it.'

'Yes, Najib.'

'How did the water get in?'

'It is seeping from below. We must have cracked something when we heard that loud bang.'

Najib looked around. The water was rising slowly and had reached just above their knees.

'How long will the fix take?'

'Twenty minutes. I just need to bypass the coupling.'

'Hurry.'

Najib left them and returned to the bridge. The storm had receded, and the seas had calmed. The pump repairs were taking too long. The boat was listing badly; they were close to capsizing.

'They said twenty minutes,' Najib said.

'It better be no longer or we sink.' Haziq said. 'We were supposed to pretend to be in trouble. There is no need to pretend now. Should I put out the Mayday call?'

'No, we must wait.' Najib said sharply. 'We are too far from our rendezvous. If the Australian Coast Guard reaches us before… then… all is lost. But let us prepare… and soak the boat in turpentine oil.'

THE RENDEZVOUZ

Timor Sea, Tuesday 9 January, 10:00 pm AWST

The Australian vessel approached slowly, its blue, red, and white flag making cracking sounds as it fluttered in the breeze. The wind had picked up again, and the waves had become choppy.

Docking in open waters was hard at the best of times, but at night it was downright dangerous. To cushion the impact, men on both boats were busy lowering fenders made of stacks of tyres.

Someone threw a coiled dock line across. Najib caught it and secured it to a cleat. He was about to signal for the second one when it came whistling through the dark. He ducked and caught it, a smile on his broad face.

The blow when it came was softer than he had expected and within minutes the boats were tied together, bobbing in the water. Najib let out a sigh. He had worried for no reason.

A tall man jumped from the Australian boat onto theirs. As he stepped into the light, Najib could see he had western features and blonde hair. Wafaa's description had been accurate.

Najib stepped forward with open arms. '*Asalam Aleikum* brother, I am Najib.'

'*Wa aleikum asalam*, brother Najib. I'm Peter.' They embraced warmly. 'I welcome you to the Fatah. Our boat is your boat. We must work quickly. The nearest coast guard is two hours away but a seaplane or helicopter could get here in half an hour.'

'*Wa'allah* you got here fast. I sent out the distress signal just twenty minutes ago.'

'We had you on radar for a while and were waiting for your signal.'

'Oh, ours must be faulty, because we tried looking for you. Thank goodness you found us. Our boat is really leaking.'

'Peter guffawed and clapped him on the back. Allah made

it so you don't have to tell a lie. He does this only for his most beloved. Now we must hurry.'

'Move it men,' Najib shouted, 'you know what to do.' They had discussed the plans endlessly after every evening prayer since they left Port Klang.

The arm of a boom crane swung from the Fatah over theirs. The scuba tanks were neatly arranged in bundles of three held together with snatch strapping. Working in pairs, the men hooked the crane's chain onto the strap holding the tanks. The crane arm then swung back. Another pair of men on the Fatah unloaded the crane and swung it back.

Some of his crew were already on board the Fatah, helping transfer the tanks into the hold.

'We need to go faster,' Peter shouted as he looked at his watch. 'Or we'll be caught.'

'Hurry men,' Najib shouted, reinforcing the message.

Half an hour later the last of the tanks was safely onboard the Fatah. Najib counted as the remaining men crossed on the rope gangway. Peter and Najib were the last to leave his boat.

As soon as he landed on the Fatah someone cut the ropes that tied the two boats together.

'Would you like to do it?' Peter handed Najib a flare gun. 'I hear you're a great shot.'

'We are all good shots, by Allah's grace. It is one reason Wafaa chose us for this mission.' Najib took the flare gun with a smile. He aimed it at the pile of broken crates on his boat and pressed the trigger.

Flames raced along the deck, fuelled by the turpentine oil. Within a minute the boat, that had carried them from Malaysia, was aflame; the heat rapidly became uncomfortable. 'I think we should get as far away as possible,' Najib said, a note of fear in his voice. 'It caught faster than I thought.'

Peter gave the command, and the Fatah moved smoothly away from the burning vessel.

The acrid smoke followed them as the wind changed direction. Overhead they could hear the faint sounds of a seaplane over the wind and the crackling and popping of the burning boat.

Najib looked skyward but saw no signs of an aircraft. 'Can you hear it?' he tapped Peter on the shoulder.

'You must have better ears… no wait. I can… just hear it,' Peter said, his voice taking on a serious note. 'All of you get down below deck. My men will show you where to hide… and be absolutely quiet. If anyone needs to go to the toilet, do it now or hold it in for the next eight hours.'

* *

Najib opened his eyes with a start; he must have fallen asleep. He tried unsuccessfully to move then remembered he was in the narrow cavity under the floor of the living quarters. It was pitch black. His neck was stiff from keeping his head turned sideways. He had crawled into it from the hold below. It had been easy sliding in but either he had grown bigger, or the cavity had shrunk. A weight pressed on his chest, making it hard to breathe. He was going to suffocate!

The vibrations from the engines reduced. They were slowing down. Footsteps sounded above him. In the distance, someone was hammering something. The smells of brewing tea made him hungry. His stomach grumbled. He hadn't eaten in a while and his bladder felt close to bursting.

The engines slowed to a rhythmic idle as their vessel bumped against something, sending a shock wave through his neck. They had docked. Allah willing, they had reached their destination.

He tried moving his neck again and realised he couldn't feel it. A mild panic set in. Was it broken? He had to calm down. Getting tense would only make the pain worse. Patience was the only way. Patience and remembering Allah. He recited a few *Quranic verses*. The words of God had an immediate calming effect. His discomfort diminished.

The engines started again. This wasn't their final

destination.

Wa'allah. Peter told him they would first need to dock at Immigration, which made sense. They were in international waters. If they were sailing off again, it was because no one had discovered them. That meant they had safely reached Australia.

THE AMBASSADOR

Lahore, Wednesday 10 January, 1:40 am

A heavy fog set in as they approached Lahore's outskirts, forcing them to slow. Sergei was beyond tired, his face, head and neck a sea of pain. Jane seemed no better; her face was drawn and grey from lack of sleep.

It wasn't surprising; they had been driving for eight hours stopping once to refuel, and a second time to swap places.

Their ancient four-wheel-drive buzzed, shook, clunked and rattled but what really kept them awake was knowing Razane was near.

Jane was keeping an eye on Sergei in case he fell asleep, but was finding it hard to keep awake herself. As day became night, and the traffic thinned, it became even harder to focus. They had tried every trick they knew to stay awake; they had frozen themselves by rolling down the windows, had deafened themselves with music and had kept up a conversation even after running out of things to say. At the end it was to no avail. Sergei was effectively running in autopilot mode. He could not remember the drive.

Following Google's direction, he swung off the M2 Motorway onto Bund Road. Here visibility was down to a metre. The fog obscured traffic lights and shrouded the road's edge. Lacking a reference, Sergei slowed to a walking pace. A car in front braked even harder, forcing Sergei to swerve sharply.

They turned left onto Mall Road and five minutes later left onto McLeod Road, narrowly missing a broken-down bus shrouded in the mist.

Jane tried calling Yousaf again but like the last few times it went straight to voicemail.

'He's still not answering,' Jane could hardly get the words out. Her jaw locked with exhaustion.

'I wonder where he is.' Sergei sighed as he shifted in his seat. He could no longer feel his bum.

'Yeah.' Jane was too tired to respond.

'Hey, you know when I was being flippant about the men you killed...?'

Jane looked at him. 'C'mon, that was hours ago. Do you think I'm still mad at you?' Her tone suggested she didn't want to talk about it.

'No, hopefully not... but... I know it's an awful feeling... taking a life. Even in self-defence... and I know I can be insensitive, sometimes.'

'Serge... Darling, I saw you on the ground and... something just kinda' snapped. I became someone else... I was like possessed by a demon or something. I can remember... there was no anger or fear or anything... just this crazy focus... and determination. And I... I just acted.'

'I saw the men. They were huge. I don't think I'd have had a chance against the two.'

'Well...' Jane yawned. 'They were arrogant.' She paused as she yawned and rubbed her eyes. 'They saw a weak and defenceless woman and they thought with their dicks. I'm sure the first man thought he'd have fun with me or something. And then after he went down the second man still wasn't taking me seriously. Honestly, I don't know what went through his mind... but it gave me the edge and I feel I've become decent at Systema.'

'Decent? You've gotta be kidding. You're phenomenal. You've beaten me now, how many times?' Sergei said yawning loudly. He rubbed the wet film from his eyes. It was true. Jane had become unbeatable as a sparring partner. Systema relied more on technique than physical strength and so was almost the ideal martial art for her. But he'd been in enough serious scraps to know that all the skill were useless without nerves of steel and a killer instinct. That part was so hard to fathom. How had their sweet, almost angelic, Jane become a dangerous killer?

* *

The Ambassador was smaller than the Pearl Continental and less flashy. The sleepy guards inspected their passports and opened the gate to let them in.

Sergei pulled in to a parking spot under an awning and killed the engine. 'We shouldn't both go in, just in case. You turn the car around and get ready to leave.'

'In case of what?' Jane was taken aback. 'Do you think it's a trap?'

'Look, sweetheart, I don't know. I'm just being cautious.'

Jane took Sergei's hand. 'Let's talk about this a second…'

'Sweetheart, it's probably nothing.' Sergei stroked her hand. 'I'll be really careful and give you a running commentary.'

They were at an impasse. Sleep had fogged Jane's mind. She couldn't think of a plan that involved Sergei not going by himself. 'Take care darling and keep the phone on.'

'Of course.' Sergei managed a wan smile. 'And, if something happens, a killer woman will rescue me. Ouch!' Sergei wasn't fast enough to avoid a playful jab in his ribs.

Thankfully, the brightly lit lobby, decorated in green marble, was empty. He was too tired to interact with anyone. He walked through the spacious lobby and looked for the elevators. A small sign pointed the way.

The lobby opened into a wide passage decorated with illuminated glass cases containing Pakistani handicrafts. He passed a darkened restaurant and followed the hallway left.

The two elevators were to the right of a carpeted staircase; they might be useful if he had to escape. He pressed the elevator button. The right door opened straightaway. He entered, pressed the button to the second floor and waited impatiently, as the door slowly creaked closed.

* *

Qaseem watched his laptop screen with a smile. He had patched into the hotel's security camera feed. The tall, broad-shouldered foreigner hesitated before entering the lift. 'Come to me, come to the lion, little goat,' he intoned as he checked the magazine in his Glock. Bugger, he had forgotten to tell Major Amjad. With fumbling hands, he dialled his number. He heard the major's voice after three rings.

'Yes Qaseem?'

'Major Sahib, they are here. The man is coming up, alone.' He closed the laptop screen and stood.

'OK. we're near the hotel. Make sure he does not escape. I want him alive.'

* *

Jane listened to Sergei's footsteps and his breathing over her smartphone speaker. She could hear the elevator begin its slow upward journey. The car's windows were fogging up. She rolled down her window to let in some fresh air. It wouldn't do if they needed to escape and couldn't see.

What if Sergei ran into trouble? How would sitting out here help? Stupidly, she had forgotten to give him the gun.

Why would Yousaf ask to meet them in a hotel? Surely there were better places, like a private residence.

Something was amiss. She could feel it.

Over the speaker she heard the elevator doors open. Sergei would find out in a minute. Her heart palpitated madly as she climbed out of the car and raced inside. Feeling light-headed, she ran as fast as her legs could carry her; the lack of sleep was catching up to her. She took several deep breaths to steady herself. She'd be no help to Sergei if she collapsed before she got to him.

She ran to the elevators, calculating; it had taken Sergei three minutes and forty seconds to get to the second floor. She had to hurry. Otherwise... She didn't want to think beyond otherwise.

If it was an ambush, she'd run into it too. She decided against the elevators. Her soft-soled shoes made almost no sound as she ran up the stairs, taking two steps at a time. Her breathing was under control now, her legs strong and steady; the gym time was paying off.

* *

Not knowing what to expect, senses fully alert, Sergei knocked on the door. A tall man answered the door. 'You Mr Sergei?' He asked as he craned his head to look into the hallway.

'Yes. Where's Yousaf?'

'I already call him on phone to say you here. You wait. Sit on chair.' He pointed into the room.

Sergei hesitated. He tried looking into the room. The man was unarmed and alone. Maybe he wasn't dangerous, but something made Sergei hesitate. Through the fog of his tiredness he tried to remember the man's exact words. Something he had said sounded wrong. The only way to have known they'd arrived was if he'd been watching them.

'I forgot something in my car. I'll be back.' Sergei backed away from the door, wanting to kick himself for how lame it sounded.

'What? No, no, you come inside and sit.' The man insisted, his voice hardening. He was giving an order.

'Listen.' Sergei clenched his fists as he growled at the man. 'I'll wait in my car.' He turned with clenched fists, ready to spring into action.

'Stop or I shoot you.' The man's voice betrayed no emotion. Sergei turned and looked into the barrel of a Glock. 'Come inside and sit.' The man motioned.

Sergei heard footsteps on the staircase but dared not look in case it was Jane. If it was, he needed to stall. 'OK, I'll come inside if you tell me where Yousaf is.'

'*Oye*, he come soon… You come inside and sit or I shoot you.'

'OK.' Sergei tried to smile, but it turned into a grimace. 'I will come inside. You call Yousaf *fatafat*…' He brushed past him with exaggerated slowness. The gunman kept his eyes and weapon trained on Sergei. With his free hand, he reached back to push the door closed. Sergei turned, keeping his face impassive as he saw Jane in the doorway.

'You'll be sorry,' Sergei stopped and locked eyes with his assailant.

The man hesitated, a look of annoyance on his face. He recovered and pushed against the door. It didn't budge. Jane had jammed her foot against it. The gunman swore as he turned, but Jane was quicker. Moving like a dancer, she jabbed the barrel of her pistol against his throat.

'Drop your gun.' Her voice was icy. The man didn't move.

Using both his hands, Sergei twisted their assailant's weapon out of his hand and turned it on him.

'Now sit,' Jane shoved him forward with a force that nearly made him fall. Sergei scrambled out of the way, just in time.

Seeing the tables turn, the man collapsed onto the chair, looking defeated. Jane closed the door as Sergei glanced around the room. He spied a smartphone on the coffee table and beckoned to the man.

'Your password?' Sergei pointed the Glock.

'Three one two one.' The response was immediate.

Sergei tried it. The phone unlocked.

'Mister Sergei, I call Yousaf. You making mistake. I am your fri—'

Sergei smashed the pistol butt into his head. He went limp. 'Friends don't point guns at each other.' Sergei grunted. 'Now let's get outta here,' he said to Jane.

Holding their weapons close, they ran down the stairs; like before they encountered no one. By the time they clambered into the Nissan, they were wheezing and out of breath. Trying to control a coughing fit, Sergei started the engine and drove towards the closed gate.

'Shit,' Sergei looked around for the guards. They were gone. A thick chain with a heavy brass padlock snaked through the bars.

Blinding headlights sliced through the dark. 'Put your hands where we can see them. You are under arrest.' A voice on a loudspeaker boomed. More lights came on. Armed men came out of the bushes. They were surrounded.

DEPREDATION

Lahore, Wednesday 10 January, 5:30 am

The agony had overwhelmed Razane's sense of time, place and self. She had no memory of before. Her skin itched like a million ants gone berserk and her joints burnt as if injected with sulphuric acid. Her own sweat and the forced immobility had turned into tools of torture.

The light hit her as the wrapping was torn off her face. She closed her eyes to relieve the pain. When she opened them she was on the floor. Four men wearing disposable respirator masks looked down on her.

Red-hot needles pierced her neck as she tried moving it. She was on a packed dirt floor. Two floodlights shone on her. She couldn't see the ceiling.

A similarly masked man crouched beside. He was cutting the plastic wrapping from her body with a pair of oversized scissors. As he did, a putrid stench bloomed out of nowhere, making her want to retch. The men recoiled in disgust. The stink was coming from her.

A blast of cold water from a fire-hose interrupted the mind-bending humiliation. It struck her naked body with the force of a sledgehammer, the water jet stinging like a thousand needles. The torrent shifted her along the rough ground, abrading her bare skin. In panic, she pulled up her knees and curled into a ball. The gush of water was relentless. Razane used her hands to cover her head so she could breathe.

The man with the hose shifted the jet to her nether regions. Razane used her feet to shield her most sensitive bits, but the torrent felt like a thousand needles blasting the softest, most tender parts of her body. She tried to shift her position but to no avail; the torture continued.

Two men leapt on her as the hose was turned off. Bolts of

pain shot through her limbs and the side of her face as they pressed her down. A third man forced her buttocks apart. Razane was powerless to move. The horror of the moment made her lose her self-control. Something warm flowed out onto her leg. The men turned their faces away in disgust.

She forgot her mortifying shame as the man shoved what felt like a finger inside, the burning sensation momentarily overshadowing the affront to her dignity.

They were doing this to break her, but why? She was already shattered.

The men holding her eased off the pressure. She could still not move her face, but the pain on her cheekbone and the twist on her neck reduced. The third man stopped moving his finger inside her.

Razane could hear footsteps through the ground. A pair of polished black leather brogues came into view. The man's khaki trousers were creased to perfection. He smelt sickly sweet.

Razane strained to look up. The new arrival was a short and stocky man in a military uniform with an ugly pockmarked face and a thick closely cropped beard. He surveyed the scene in silence. Razane's tormentor pulled out his finger.

The newcomer said something in Urdu, to which the men replied. The newcomer seemed pleased.

He turned as he heard more footsteps approach. Razane gasped as she recognised the Americans who had tortured her.

'Howdy major. Great to see you up bright and early.' The older one with the bad skin rubbed his hands together enthusiastically. 'So, we begin.'

'Yes, now that we have them all in our custody. Yes, we do.' The major signalled to his men who released Razane and stood to attention. Razane tried sitting up. One man pushed her back with his foot. Not having the strength to fight back, she curled into a foetal position.

'Take her to the empty room and hang her from the roof.' The major spoke in English and touched his wrists to illustrate.

'And be patient, you will all get your turn. With this prisoner, you'll have your fill.'

The American with the bad skin smirked. 'As long as she stays alive your boys can be as thorough as they wish to be.'

The major clapped his hands and shouted in Urdu. Two men picked Razane by the arms. One squeezed her left breast till she yelped. He put his face inches from hers and shouted in English. 'Walk fast!'

* *

The overpowering stench assaulted her nostrils as the door slammed shut. It took a while for Jane's eyes to adjust to the dark. She was in a space no bigger than a broom cupboard. She couldn't sit without squashing her legs against her chest.

The surrounding walls were oppressively close. The space was too small. Her throat constricted, her breathing became ragged. She wanted to scream at the top of her lungs but held back. If Sergei heard, it would only increase his torment. Jane shivered involuntarily as she fought for her sanity. Breathe in, breathe out, breathe in. It was hard with the revolting smell.

The memory of her previous incarceration came flooding back. It had taken months of therapy and all Sergei and Razane's love and support for her to recover. She had believed it could never happen again and her nightmares had slowly receded. Just thinking about that now made her breathing ragged. She tried once again to control it, focusing on how the rushing air felt cold on her nostrils. The stench of faeces and urine and unwashed bodies made it hard to concentrate.

She tried to focus on the sounds instead. Someone nearby, a woman, thankfully not Razane, was crying nonstop. Now and then a faint scream from deep inside the building shook her. It was too far away to make out who it was. Please let it not be Sergei. Where was he?

They'd taken her watch, her passport and wallet. Her feet and knees were hurting from standing on the hard floor. The breathing exercises weren't working. Her fighting spirit was ebbing away. It was hopeless. They were up against a force far stronger than them in a country where they had no rights.

Their only other family, their sons, Damon and Ben, didn't have a clue they were even in Pakistan.

Her tiredness was smothering her, but it wasn't the kind that brought sleep. An unbearable sadness made it hard to breathe. Razane, Sergei, and she had the sweetest thing possible. Maybe so much happiness wasn't natural and nature had found a way of re-balancing it.

SHIFTING ALLEGIANCES

Yousaf shifted his weight from one leg to the other as he tried to lessen the agony. His calves were covered in welts from the caning Major Amjad had supervised.

Yousaf was no stranger to interrogation rooms, but it was always from the other side of the one-way mirror plate-glass. Every safe-house had one in the basement. He had even been to Lahore's biggest one, in the dungeons of the Lahore Fort.

He guessed he was in the basement of Major Amjad's safe-house. Every ISI major had exclusive use of at least one safe house, the locations of which were a tightly controlled secret. Yousaf didn't know its location, but it would be somewhere on the outskirts of Lahore.

The secrecy allowed them to operate autonomously, unhindered by law and process. Witnesses could be hidden and prisoners interrogated without interference from the courts or the police.

ISI safe houses had an even more important purpose, to coordinate an underground resistance movement if the Indians invaded. As a result, each safe house was a veritable fortress. They bristled with communication devices and each contained a substantial armoury.

Major Amjad had enjoyed seeing him suffer. They had hung him upside down by his ankles. A huge man clad in only a loincloth had whipped him with a cane, soaked in oil. The few that struck his heels were tolerable, but when they had landed on his calves, made taut by his weight, he had nearly passed out. By the time the beating stopped his skin was covered in bleeding welts that would take weeks to heal.

After they were done, they placed him inside a tiny cell so narrow he couldn't sit. The floor soon became slippery and then sticky with his blood that continued to ooze from the deeper cuts.

It was just the beginning. He knew what came next. They would either sprinkle a mixture of salt and chilli powder or use electricity on his cuts. To stop him from fainting from the excruciating pain they would pump him full of adrenaline.

Through sobs, he had tried to tell Major Amjad he didn't need to torture him. He tried to convince him that people of his low station didn't take sides. He had followed Major Hamdani's orders and would be equally willing, and in fact honoured, to switch sides. His tormentors were unmoved by his entreaties. Maybe they didn't believe him. More likely, they were sadists who got off on administering pain.

It was so unfair that the senior officers played dirty political games, but juniors like him copped the punishment.

He hadn't been untruthful. The political infighting in the ISI made little sense to him. An intelligence organisation like theirs existed to serve and protect the country, not further anyone's personal beliefs. He had enjoyed working for Major Hamdani. He was a good boss, tough but fair, but he might never return. Hoping Sergei and Jane could rescue him was stupid; he should have tried to dissuade them instead of helping. Now they would die because of him.

Major Amjad was right to be angry with him. He deserved a beating for being so stupid. Who was he to take sides? He was just a lowly captain. Somehow, he had to convince Major Amjad to forgive him and let him go.

His foot squelched in the pool of congealing blood as he shifted his weight to his right leg. He winced as the pain shifted from his left leg to his right.

EXCRUCIATION

Lahore, Wednesday 10 January, 8:30 am

'Sir, thank you for giving me another chance.' Yousaf wondered if he should shake the major's hand. He was sitting opposite Major Amjad in an airy lounge, adjoining a formal dining area. The furniture was plush and expensive. Thick rugs lined the floor, ornate lamps and tapestries gave warmth and a sense of luxury. Large French windows overlooked a lush garden. It looked like a normal rich person's house with no signs of the horrors in the basement.

The major ignored Yousaf as he stared at the morning news on a large TV above a fireplace. It was old news, rehashed from the night before. India had accused Pakistan of supporting a terrorist attack on an army truck in Kashmir; the US president had announced he was scrapping a missile treaty with Russia; heavy rain was forecast for the weekend. He dunked a biscuit in a cup of tea and continued pretending he hadn't heard Yousaf.

'Major, sir, I was only following orders.' Yousaf was growing frantic. 'I have given you all the information you asked for and… and I told you everything truthfully. On my mother's life, sir…'

The major wiped his fingers on a napkin and studied the man before him. His face was covered in bruises. Both his legs were bandaged from the knee down. Maybe he could use Yousaf to break Sergei and Jane and then the two to break Razane. 'Yousaf, you have a good service record… I have been thinking about what you said. I… will consider your misdeeds an error of judgement. An error, in part, because of your youth. It is possible I may forgive you.'

'Oh, sir…'

'If I give you another chance, you better not let me down… or.' The major leaned forward, his face a mask of cold fury. 'My vengeance will be most severe.'

'Thank you, sir. You will not be sorry…'

'Not so fast. You must first pass a test.'

'Yes… yes anything, sir.' Yousaf sat upright. 'Anything…'

'OK, come with me.' The major scrunched the napkin and stuffed it into the empty cup as he stood.

Yousaf groaned with pain as he got up and followed the major down the stairs to the basement. Inside he was quaking but there was a glimmer of hope. Perhaps the major wasn't as bad as he had thought.

'Say nothing till I tell you to speak,' the major said as he opened a soundproof door to a well-lit room lined with polished concrete. It was larger than the last one. A row of chairs faced a raised stage, making the room resemble a small lecture room. Hooks were embedded into the walls, floor and ceiling to hold prisoners at all angles and in any position. Steel cables hung from the hooks on the ceiling. Two cross-racks and a wooden horse with a sharp wedge along its spine sat against the far wall alongside display cabinets that showed off an array of horrendous torture implements.

Yousaf swallowed when he saw the wooden horse. He had only seen it used once. It was one of the most brutal torture devices he had seen.

'Stay here,' the major pushed him into a chair and walked out, not bothering to close the door.

Yousaf swallowed in trepidation as he looked around the room. What test did the major have in mind? He would do anything to redeem himself. He noticed a video camera observing him. Had his test already begun?

The major was back moments later. 'I want you to sit over there.' He motioned to a director's chair on the stage.

'Thank you, sir. I am very relieved you are not asking me to sit on the rack.' He managed a weak smile as he pointed to the wooden horse.

The door opened with a clang. Two of the major's underlings, Sarfraz and Yasin half carried, half dragged Jane between them. The shackles on her wrists and ankles were joined with a heavy chain. On the major's signal they removed the connecting chain and attached the steel cables dangling from the roof to the shackles around her wrists, stretching her arms above her head to do so. From a steel cupboard, they removed a short length of steel cable with two loops and used it to tie her ankles to the floor.

Yousaf was still reeling from shock when the door opened again. This time two more of the major's men, Kareem and Tahir, led Sergei in. He was thrashing about as best as he could but getting nowhere. It took all four men to tie him to the hooks in the ceiling and floor.

'I'm sorry,' Sergei looked at Jane.

Jane shook her head. 'Don't be. Don't ever be…' Yasin slapped her face hard.

'You bastards…' Sergei thrashed about in frustration as Jane reeled from the shock.

'Don't just stand there. Gag the white dog,' the major said standing. His face suddenly a mask of fury. 'These prisoners are not yet afraid of us!' His voice rose in a crescendo.

Working fast, Tahir placed a ball gag over Sergei's mouth and tightened it behind his head. Then he used a length of cloth and wrapped it several times around his head to muffle any remaining sounds.

Yousaf's heart beat in trepidation. He was certain the major would want him to torture Jane. It was one thing to torture a low life criminal or an enemy spy. Quite another to hurt an innocent person. Jane and Sergei had always treated him with respect. Torturing them would be hard, but he had no choice. If he refused, the major would get one of his goons to do it, anyway.

'*Ya Allah* forgive me,' he whispered silently as he clenched and unclenched his fists.

Major Amjad walked over to Sergei and Jane. He smirked as he put his face close to Jane's. 'You will tell me what you are doing in Pakistan and what happened to my men in the truck stop.'

Yousaf gave a start. Who was the major referring to? Shakeel and Sibtain? What had Sergei and Jane done to them?

The major turned to Yousaf. 'Yousaf, son. Here is your chance.' He reached under his thick sweater, took a Glock from its holster and offered it to him. Yousaf swallowed noisily. His hands shook as he accepted the weapon. It was the standard issue automatic pistol all ISI personnel used. He could tell from the weight it was loaded; out of habit, he removed and checked the magazine.

'What do you want me do sir?' Yousaf steeled himself as he ignored Sergei's muffled grunts.

'Easy. Blow the white dog's kneecaps off and fuck the woman in both her holes.'

Yousaf's ears were ringing from shock. He did not hear the second half of the major's order. Disoriented, he cocked the pistol as he looked at the major. He would shoot Sergei. It was nothing personal. He moved closer to him. The correct way was from behind the knee; the bullet would blow off the kneecap and render it irreparable. He would prove to the major he could count on him.

He also barely registered Jane's screams. 'No, no, Yousaf, stop, please. Don't hurt him! Please, please, please…'

Through the haze he was aware the major had said something else 'Sir what was the second thing?' Yousaf positioned himself behind Sergei.

'I want you to rape the white bitch.' The major looked at him strangely. 'Are you deaf?' The rising pitch in his voice betrayed his rage.

Yousaf swallowed. He was a virgin. He had never even been near a woman. How could he do it? In any event it was sinful and wrong. The ultimate wrong. He could kill her, but raping her ran against every grain in his being. Women were supposed to be protected and honoured. His mother had taught him that. He would rather die than live with the shame of letting her down. But not following the major's order? How could he?

Yousaf's hands shook as he pressed the gun barrel against

the back of Sergei's left knee. If he maimed him but didn't follow through on the other order, what would the major do? He badly needed to go to the toilet. 'Oh Allah help me, forgive me.'

BROKEN

Lahore, Wednesday 10 January, 8:45 am

A dank and foul breeze swirled around Razane's bare skin, covering it in goosebumps. Naked and suspended from the ceiling by her wrists, she was too exhausted to shiver. The only sensation that remained was the intense burning in her wrists, forearms and shoulders. Soon she wouldn't feel that either.

The pain had caused tunnel vision. She was barely aware of her surroundings. Overhead an ancient, dust-covered bulb hung by its cable from a ceiling too high to see. It cast a feeble circle of light on the uneven brick floor below.

The bulb mirrored how she felt inside. Her light was extinguishing as darkness won its battle. She couldn't remember a worse predicament and she had no reserves of strength left to fight it with. She was broken.

Sergei and Jane wouldn't come. It was unreasonable to expect them to; they were only human. It was a nice fantasy that had helped her cope till now, but it was no longer possible to fool herself.

Her tormentor sat in the dark outside the circle of light on an old plastic chair that used to be white. He held a large flexible cane which he used to periodically poke and prod her to keep her swinging. Every now and again he would use it whip her all over. Her legs and belly were covered in welts. It had burnt earlier, but the pain had receded. Even her arms and wrists were no longer throbbing. She slipped into darkness.

* *

Mike yawned and rubbed the sleep from his eyes as he waited for his computer to boot up. Sebastian sat next to him, cradling his coffee. He had already logged in.

Lahore was cooler than Saipan, thank God, but the

humidity was replaced by pollution so thick he felt it in the back of his throat as an ever-present metallic tang.

But he wasn't here long enough to care. Only two outcomes were possible. Either they would break Wafaa today or he would be sidelined when the main team arrived from Langley. They were expected at midnight, so he had a whole day.

The Pakistanis could do things he never could have and it was already working. Wafaa was nearly broken. Just to make sure, Amjad had captured her associates and was softening them in another location. It wasn't necessary but it could help and the major appeared to enjoy torturing people.

Mike entered his login details and took a sip of coffee. On reflection, he should have listened to the major when he first suggested bringing Wafaa to Pakistan.

Few facilities in the world had such a track record of extracting confessions as the ISI Interrogation Centre at the Lahore Fort. He had done some research. It had been in continuous use as a torture centre since 1799. That made it the longest operating facility of its kind in the world. It had been a revolving door for political prisoners from Nehru to Bhutto. Countless people were tortured to death. It was said that alone the threat of being sent to the fort was often enough to loosen the tongues of even the most hardened men.

Mike had last visited in 2002 while Pakistan was part of the CIA's Extraordinary Rendition program. Back then the interrogation centre was an unobtrusive red brick building among a myriad of structures within the outer walls of the fort. To keep out tourists it was fenced off and guarded by armed soldiers. The ground floor was the administrative area and used for offices. The prisoners were kept one level below in the basement.

A public outcry saw the program scaled back. Pakistan eventually pulled out of the program altogether.

Domestic political pressure from human rights groups and the Lahore Heritage Society continued and literally drove the centre underground.

In a move to appease the public, the ISI pretended to close the centre. They moved the administrative area one floor below. To make way, the prison cells were moved down one level into the old dungeons first used by the Mughal Emperor Akbar in the sixteenth century.

Visitors to Lahore Fort no longer saw a torture centre. The soldiers were gone. The old administrative area was empty. The fence was replaced with a sophisticated electronic security system and a board that said "Hazardous material removal - Do not enter." Uniforms were forbidden. It was no longer used for political prisoners or anyone who could draw public attention.

In a literal sense it went out of sight and out of mind. Nowadays it was used for spies, terrorists and anyone who ran afoul of the ISI. Even though it had changed shape and modernised, its output remained the same, broken people and exposed secrets.

The new administrative area was bright and airy with glass doors on offices, light timber floors and down lights dotting the false ceiling. If he hadn't seen it before its transformation it would have been hard to imagine the dark dingy interior and the stench of fear, blood and urine that pervaded this space.

His laptop fully functional, Mike used the username and password the major had given him to login to several ISI video feeds. One was from the dungeon below. Chip had given strict instructions to keep the prisoner alive so she could be formally charged and stand trial.

The video camera in the dungeon was equipped with night vision. He saw Razane hanging by her wrists, just like he had left her, swinging in an arc as the guard prodded her with his stick. She had gone silent and was no longer struggling. It was time to untie her, revive her and interrogate her, hopefully for the last time.

'We need the fucking major to be here now. He can torture the other fuckers in his own time,' Mike said to Sebastian in a low voice. 'Can you check where he is?'

'Yeah, OK!' Sebastian clicked on a series of windows to

open the video feed Amjad had linked him to.

'The major's wasting time we don't have.' Mike looked at his watch.

'He said he'd begin before lunch,' Sebastian said as he scanned the feeds. 'Don't you think he's doing the right thing to soften her associates?'

'Maybe, maybe not...,' Mike's voice trailed off as the video feed popped up on Sebastian's screen. Sergei and Jane were suspended from the ceiling. Major Amjad and five other men were talking. One of them pointed a gun at the back of Sergei's knee.

'Holy shit!' Sebastian spat out his coffee. He put the cup down, 'What the fuck?'

EXPOSURE

Lahore, Wednesday 10 January, 8:45 am

A knot formed in the major's stomach as he stared aghast at Yousaf. Giving him the gun suddenly didn't seem like such a good idea. He had given Yousaf a simple order, something any ISI captain should be able to do without flinching, especially when moments ago they had begged for a chance to prove themselves. Yousaf was hesitating as if torn.

It was time to get tough. 'Remove her clothes.' He used his most authoritative voice as he pointed at his men. 'And you...' His eyes drilled holes into Yousaf. 'Either obey or give the gun back.'

Yousaf stared at him, not comprehending. The major softened his tone. 'Don't worry son, I will not be angry. Just hand me the gun.' He held out his hand.

Sarfraz gripped Jane's shirt by the collar and with one pull yanked it off her. The sound jolted Yousaf out of his daze. He looked at Jane and back at the major. Sarfraz had a smirk on his face as he used a scissor to cut her bra straps. Jane was naked from the waist up. The sight was too much for Yousaf. He turned his face away.

Seeing his opportunity, the major lunged at the gun. Yousaf saw him out of the corner of his eye and sidestepped.

'Sir stop.' Yousaf moved his gun arm out of the major's reach just in time. 'I tell you it is wrong... what you are doing.' The major tried to grab the pistol, but Yousaf was stronger. Sarfraz raised his scissors as he leapt to the major's aid. Yousaf turned and fired.

Time slowed as the sound reverberated around the room, decaying into absolute ear-ringing silence. The heavy scissors clanged as they struck the hard concrete floor.

Sarfraz fell against Sergei, then he slumped to the ground.

His head wound leaving a wide red streak down Sergei's jeans.

Startled, the major stepped back, knocking over two chairs. They struck the floor with a loud bang.

Yousaf couldn't believe what he had just done. Now he was really finished. He might as well put the gun into his own mouth and pull the trigger. He was about to when he realised they were all staring at him, mesmerised at the way he was waving the Glock around like a madman. It wasn't surprising because he felt like he had just lost his mind.

* *

'Yousaf, take a deep breath and calm yourself,' Jane was the first to recover. Her voice was urgent.

Yousaf was both soothed by her voice and unsettled by her nakedness.

'Oh, what have I done?' He wailed.

'Yousaf, son. It is OK. I forgive you. Just give me the gun. Sarfraz was wrong to treat the lady…'

'Yousaf,' Jane said. There was a steely edge to her voice, a combination of desperation and determination. 'Don't trust the major. He will shoot you the minute you hand him the gun.'

'Jane madam, I have no choice…' Yousaf looked at her and shook his head.

'You have a choice. Untie Sergei and me. Do the right thing.'

'Don't listen to the bitch. She is the devil who will lead you astray.' The major walked forward. He was now a short lunge from grabbing the gun. Yousaf turned and fired at the ground in front of him. 'Aaah,' The major jumped back as shards of concrete sprayed onto his legs, his face a mask of fury.

'Untie them both.' Yousaf pointed the gun at the major's men. 'Now!' His unhinged scream made them jump.

Startled, Major Amjad jumped back. He would make sure the disloyal dog died a painful death as soon as he regained control of the situation. He stole a glance at the camera mounted on the ceiling. A red and a blue LED showed it was recording and transmitting the signal.

THE VIDEOSTREAM

Lahore, Wednesday 10 January, 9:00 am

Mike watched with growing disbelief and alarm as the scene unfolded. Major Amjad had turned out to be the biggest fool he had ever seen. Who in their right mind handed a gun to someone they had recently tortured?

'Shit! What are we gonna do?' Sebastian was looking over his shoulder.

Mike said nothing as he stood transfixed by the videostream. He clenched his fists as the major's men freed the captives. He caught the major's furtive glance at the camera. He was hoping someone was watching. 'Hmmm. I think…,' Mike said, deep in thought. 'I think I'll have a word with the guy in charge here. Maybe we can organise a rescue party.'

'OK! That's one option…' Sebastian said.

'What you mean? What's the other.'

'Sergei and Jane have control of the situation. What do you think they'll do?'

'I think they'll beat the shit out of Amjad… serves the motherfucker right. They'll make him tell where Wafaa is.'

'You are thinking what I'm thinking,' Sebastian said with a smile.

'What I'm thinking is… I might have underestimated you.' Mike's face broke into a toothy smile. It wasn't something Sebastian had seen before and he preferred Mike scowling. When he smiled, he looked even more like a toad.

'People do,' Sebastian said breezily as he tried to get the image out of his head.

'It's definitely easier to let 'em come to us.'

'It's how a spider catches its prey,' Sebastian said.

'Yeah, I like it. Besides, by the time we'd have reached wherever this place is they'd have left, anyway.'

'You think the major was trying to tell us something when he looked at the camera?' Sebastian said.

'The man's an asshole with shit for brains, but still... maybe. I'm hoping he leads them to us.'

'We should plan for that,' Sebastian said.

'Keep an eye on the video while I organise a welcome party.' Mike got up. He glanced at the video stream. Sergei and Jane were tying up the major's men.

* *

Captain Usman gathered the printouts and walked up the steps. He swiped his card on the reader and pressed his thumb to a pad. With a well-oiled click, the steel-reinforced door unlocked and swung outwards. He was now on the ground floor, in what used to be the old admin area. It was an empty shell, abandoned except for a sparrow that must have made its way through a hole in the skylight. Seeing him, it flew around in panic, trying to escape.

The captain walked out into the weak sunshine. On the way he propped the door open with a wooden wedge. Hopefully, the sparrow would fly out. He lit a cigarette and took a puff as he scanned for the police vans.

He didn't have to wait long for the two troop carriers to arrive. A police sergeant alighted from one and approached him.

'Sir, are you Captain Usman? I am Sergeant Arsalan.' He held out his hand.

Captain Usman shook his hand and handed him a bundle of leaflets. 'Tell your men to spread out and look for these two. As soon as they are spotted, you are to call for reinforcements. On no account should anyone approach them on their own. Do you understand?'

'Yes, sir,' the Sergeant said in a clipped tone.

'They are dangerous and very clever. You need to understand it. How many men are you?'

'Sir, we are thirty here. We will keep a lookout inside the fort. Another thirty are on their way. They will position themselves on the approaches.'

'OK, I have printed enough leaflets. My number is printed on them. We have several teams on standby with a helicopter and cars if needed,' he said as he handed the Sergeant the leaflets. 'Remember, they are very dangerous. Oh, one more thing. Make sure all your men have plenty of ammunition. If the fugitives run before our men can reach them, you must shoot them. I don't care if passers-by are hit. You shoot.'

'Yes sir, don't worry, sir. If they come, they won't leave.'

TRANSFORMATION

Lahore, Wednesday 10 January, 9:30 am

Sergei clenched his jaw as he looked at Yousaf. He was lost somewhere inside his own head. 'Yousaf, my friend, we need you to focus.' Sergei shook him by the shoulder with his left hand as he kept the Glock trained on their captives who lay on their stomachs with their hands on their heads.

'Ya, yess. Oh...' Yousaf came out of his reverie. He massaged his temple with shaking hands.

'Is there anyone else here?' Sergei repeated himself.

'Oh, I not know. Every safe-house different. But... I think only them.' Yousaf pointed at their captives.

'Are you sure?'

'No.'

'Then check while we wait for you here.'

'Yousaf, I warn you again. I will kill you if you cooperate with them,' Major Amjad huffed. Yousaf seemed to hesitate.

Jane walked over and swung the steel cable she was holding across the back of the major's thighs. 'For the last time...'

The major let out a high-pitched yelp as the cable cracked fabric. A red line appeared on his trousers.

'Say one more word and the next time it'll be your head.' Jane said, her voice icy. She was on edge.

Sergei nodded approvingly. 'That's my girl.' His voice was a whisper.

'Did anyone check his pockets?' Jane said looking at the major writhing on the ground, moaning in pain.

'Oh shit, no.' Sergei said.

Jane dropped one knee onto the small of the major's back, eliciting another scream.

'Ayeee, my back, my back! You are killing me.' the major's breathing became laboured.

Jane ignored him as she extracted a smartphone and a wallet. She handed the phone to the major. 'Unlock it.'

The major's hands shook as he complied. Jane snatched it back from him and stood up, ignoring the major's pained cry. She handed Sergei the wallet as she looked through the phone.

Sergei turned to Yousaf. 'Please check this place is clear? We'll take care of these four. Hurry!'

'OK, I will see,' Yousaf said as he ran out.

'Darling, he needs a weapon,' Jane said as Yousaf slammed the door behind him.

Sergei furrowed his brow and shook his head. Jane understood. Sergei was reluctant to relinquish their only weapon. Yousaf was still torn. He might change his mind.

With one eye on their captives Sergei looked through the major's fat wallet. Two CIA business cards caught his eye. The names Michael Hound and Sebastian Corder meant nothing to him. 'Isn't it odd for the CIA to carry business cards?' he said as he showed them to Jane.

'They're probably for giving to the KGB...' she muttered as she scanned the phone.

'The KGB are no longer—'

'Hey, I've found a Mike Hound, in his contact list,' Jane said. 'In the notes it says CIA. But the other guy's not here.' Jane began looking through the emails.

Yousaf came running back. 'Nobody here.' He was panting loudly.

'Thank you,' Sergei nodded as he moved close to Yousaf. 'What do we do with these fuckers?' he whispered.

'Tie with rope and lock door.'

'What if someone comes?'

'This secret house for Major Amjad's. Nobody come.'

'OK then help me,' he nodded at the major's underlings. 'The major comes with us.'

Jane trained the gun on their prisoners as Sergei and Yousaf tied the men to the hooks in the floor and the ceiling.

They marched the major into the tiny cell Jane had been

held in and sat in the viewing area to plan their next move.

* *

'Do you know these CIA agents?' Sergei showed Yousaf the business cards.

'No.' Yousaf shook his head.

'Look at this,' Jane had gone white. She held up the phone. 'The major emailed Mike Hound offering to interrogate Wafaa in Pakistan.'

'Oh, fuck!' Sergei looked at Jane and then Yousaf. He had gone pale too. There was only one reason the CIA needed help with interrogation. 'Is Pakistan still torturing for the CIA?' He dreaded the answer.

'No.' Yousaf shook his head. 'It is illegal.'

'Then why…?'

Yousaf shrugged. 'The ISI mostly very good but ummm… few senior officer is very bad.'

'We need to move fast.' Sergei stood and paced the room.

'Do you have any idea… where Razane's being held?' Jane looked expectantly at Yousaf.

'Jane madam, I have… idea but no sure.'

'Where? Tell us!' Sergei stopped and took Jane's hand in his; she was tense, ready for violence.

'I find Razane being in country only by chance. She come with Americans. It was very ummm… surprising…'

'Why?' Sergei said.

'America and Pakistan, no friends. No making co-operations. So I thinking this is very uh… strange. Why American bring prisoner to Pakistan?'

'Isn't that what they used to call extraordinary rendition?' Sergei said.

'Yes, that is words I also was thinking. After Al Qaeda attack World Trade Centre, many prisoner tortured in Lahore Fort. I have friend. His brother was with ISI before he died. He did tortures for Americans.'

'Is that where Razane is?' Jane said.

'Yes… maybe. Government say to stop tortures at Lahore Fort so Police they stop. But ISI take the prison and make it their… head office. They put prisoner in cells in basement.'

Jane had visited Lahore's beautiful fort as a tourist the last time she was in Pakistan. 'It's a beautiful old historical monument. I can't believe they use it to torture people.'

Sergei was Googling the Lahore Fort and torture. 'Oh shit… you're wrong, there are heaps of references… and… it goes back more than two centuries. It's one of the world's most notorious prisons. We better move fast. Fuck knows what they're doing to Razane.'

'Many famous peoples is torture in fort,' Yousaf said.

'I'm gonna confirm with the major before we charge off,' Jane said. 'Give me thirty seconds.' She took the Glock from Sergei's hand and walked out of the viewing room.

'Yes, of course…' Sergei said. He watched her go. He was witnessing an amazing transformation. This wasn't the old Jane. She had probably died when they led Razane away with a hood over her head. The new one was born in courtyard of The Steakhouse.

Jane appeared moments later behind the thick plate glass. Without hesitating she punched the major under his jaw. It must have been with tremendous force because his head snapped back and struck the wall. She followed it with a sidekick to his abdomen that had the major doubling up.

'Jane Madam is very angry.' Yousaf observed.

* *

Major Amjad's head exploded in pain as it hit the wall. The kick to his midriff that followed stopped his breathing. The biggest blow was to his male pride. He felt emasculated. No woman had dared strike him before. The agony obliterated any anger.

He touched the source of the pain. His fingers came away wet with blood. The skin had broken and blood trickled down his neck. What would Mike and Sebastian do with the video-stream? He was sure they were watching. Would they rescue him or wait for Sergei and Jane? He knew what he would do.

He realised Jane had said something when he saw the barrel of the gun milliseconds before it tore across the bridge of his nose. Blood erupted from the open cut. A heavy dull throb emanated from the wound. The pain was less than he expected. The shock had delayed it.

Jane's face was a mask of fury. She pressed the barrel hard in the tender space above his kneecap. The woman was mad. He needed to focus before she killed him. She was mad and dangerous. What if she had killed his agents? He had seen no one move like her, let alone a woman.

'Where is Razane?' Jane enunciated slowly.

'W-w-w-w…'

'You have one chance,' Jane said through clenched teeth as she increased the pressure on the kneecap tenfold. 'You won't like standing in this cell with no kneecaps.'

'Don't sh-sh-shoot. At the f-for-fort. She is at the fort!' He blubbered, blowing bubbles of blood from his nose wound.

'The next time I see you. I'll finish what I started.' Jane said and was gone. The door slammed shut behind her.

* *

Jane entered the viewing room at a fast pace. 'We need to move. God knows what they're doing to Razane.' Her voice was grim.

'Of course, sweetheart. Yousaf, have you ever been there?'

'Yes. It is very, very bad place.'

'So how do we get Razane out?' Jane towered over Yousaf, arms akimbo.

'I think… no possible.' Yousaf shook his head. 'Fort in crowded part of Lahore. Very busy. Very slow traffic. If you enter how you run away? Where you go?'

Yousaf was right. As Wafaa, Razane was the most wanted person in the world. By rescuing her, they would be too. Even the

Russians wouldn't shelter them.

'One step at a time. Let's first get Razane out… and then we figure out how to rescue Major Hamdani. He's the only person who can help us… I hope.' Sergei ran his hands through his hair. He realised he sounded mad but the whole idea of coming to Pakistan had been unhinged from the beginning.

'Sergei and Jane, if I not see what you do last time you in Pakistan I say you big bluffer. But Sergei bro, last time you no escape from ISI. We watch you all times.'

Yousaf was referring to the last time they were in Pakistan. They had rescued Jane from a police lock-up and together they had fled Pakistan. Yousaf had a point. What he hadn't verbalised was how dumb luck had played a major part in the outcome even though they had spent quite a bit of time planning. This time around, they had no time to plan.

'Yousaf, trust me, I understand. It's next to impossible, but I truly believe there's always a way. And if you're with us, we have an advantage. So let's look at the situation.' Sergei zoomed into Lahore Fort on Google Maps. 'Show me the ISI offices.'

Yousaf pointed at a structure inside the walls of the fort.

'It says Royal Kitchens?' Sergei said.

'It is wrong. This broken building here was the royal kitchen. This small building is entrance to ISI offices.' Yousaf pointed to a tiny brick building.

'This looks like only a few rooms. How can they be ISI offices? And this whole area seems open to tourists.'

'This building have security door with camera. Office in the basement. Very big basement. Many many room.'

'I'm confused. You said the prison cells are in the basement.'

'That is basement below basement. How do you say English word dun-ge-on.'

'You mean a dungeon,' Jane said.

'Yes, dun-ge-on. It is very old. That is where prisoners be kept in time of Mughal Emperor.'

'So how do they bring in prisoners when it's a public area?'

'Prisoners only come at night when no publics.'

It looked hopeless. The only entrance they knew of was in the middle of a tourist attraction and crowded with hundreds of visitors and police. Even if they could get in, they couldn't leave. They wouldn't get fifty metres before being shot.

'Tell me, does the fort have tunnels?' Jane said.

Yousaf sat up, startled. 'Oh yes. Many, many tunnels. How you know?'

'Castles often have tunnels, so their owners could secretly escape.' Jane looked at Sergei. 'Are you thinking what I am?'

Yousaf caught her glance. 'No Jane madam, not work what you thinking. Tunnels all closed. Many collapse and closed for safety.'

'Oh,' Jane's face fell. 'Have you seen the tunnels?'

'Yes, but they closed. One tunnel in dungeon. But is blocked.'

Jane sighed as she sat back, deflated. 'If only…'

'It's still something we should explore,' Sergei said. 'What are the other options?'

'Could we try to enter at night?' Jane said, 'Maybe—'

'Jane madam. At night, double security. Forty police guard building and every gate in fort. Full spotlight everywhere makes bright like day.'

'Can you describe the security?' Sergei said.

'The ISI centre has many security layer. First is when you enter empty building. Plain clothes commandos ask for ID. If no ID you arrested. Minimum twenty commando on duty. They have Uzi in backpack.'

'Can you describe everything? What does it look like when you enter?' Sergei was examining Google Maps closely.

'Building on ground floor look empty with some broken furniture,' Yousaf said, 'But there is big black door in middle. Fingerprint and retina scan for open. Stair go down to office area. There security guard check bag and scan for weapon. In office there is six army commando. Every ISI officer also have gun. ISI officer are expert with gun. A lift goes from office area to dungeon. This dungeon very very big and very dark. Only one bulb near lift and in cells. So look very dark. This make prisoner very afraid and make confession easy.'

'How many prisoners would they have?' Sergei said.

'Not many. Now ISI only torture spy and terrorist. No more for government. Only part of dungeon near lift used. Only four or five cells have door. Rest empty with no door.' Yousaf took a breath before continuing. 'Other end of dungeon is steps to a lower dungeon. There is entry to tunnel. This is block with thick steel bar.' Yousaf showed the thickness with his hands.

'So you have been down there?' Sergei said.

'Yes, Sergei. The brother of my friend. The man who die show me dungeon when I join ISI. He try scare with ghost.'

'So where does the tunnel lead?' Jane said.

'Tunnels are collapse. No go there.'

'Yousaf, we need to make sure—'

'OK, OK, we look through bar with torch but no see end. But... it possible it go to here.' Yousaf pointed to a small structure on Google Maps called Lava Temple.

Sergei did a Google search for Lava Temple. All he could find were obscure references dating back to the twelfth century. It was next door to the royal kitchens. There was nothing to show it could lead to the tunnels.

Sergei searched for tunnels. There were lots of references but nothing that described their current state. No one had explored them. Maybe Yousaf was right. They were all blocked.

'Can one enter the Lava Temple?'

'No Sergei, bro. Lava Temple is very old building. Closed with brick. It very near to royal kitchen. Police and commando will arrest you or shoot you before you step inside.'

'Does anyone in Lahore know the tunnels?' Sergei said. Maybe someone had done research. Like a professor of history or archaeology.

'Serge darling, we don't have time. I think we should visit the fort and see the place Yousaf described. Maybe it'll help us figure out a plan,' Jane said. 'I can't continue sitting here knowing

Razane's in a dungeon being tortured. I'm dying inside...'

'I know sweetheart,' Sergei said in a gentle voice. 'I feel the same but... the way Yousaf describes the place we'll only end up killing ourselves.'

'I'm close to not giving a shit anymore,' Jane said, 'I'm not gonna live without her... So I might as well die.'

'No one's gonna die just yet. We'll find a way,' Sergei said a little too sharply as Jane teared up.

'Jane madam is correct. Razane is big danger. Torture very bad. Many people not walk or use hands after. Some have heart attack!'

Sergei glared at him. Such comments weren't helpful. It would only add to their desperation, and desperate people made mistakes.

'Oh...,' Yousaf stood up with a shout. 'Why I no remember... I know man is expert on walled city. He work for Lahore Heritage Society. Is possible... he know tunnel.'

THE ESTUARY

Scambridge Gulf, Wednesday 10 January, 2:30 pm AWST

The screech of nails being pulled out of wood awoke him. A board beside him was pulled back, allowing light to flood into the cavity he was in. With it came a gust of fresh air. He coughed involuntarily as he sucked it in and was startled by a shadowy head that popped up beside him. 'Brother, you can come out now,' the man said.

Najib tried to respond, but he had lost his voice; his throat was painfully parched. It felt like he had swallowed razor blades.

He swallowed to get the saliva flowing before speaking again. 'Thank you, brother. I thought I would be entombed here.' His voice was hoarse. He tried moving but his legs had fallen asleep. 'You might need to help me. I am too stiff.'

'Of course, brother. I will pull you. Tell me if you want me to stop.'

The man pulled on him without waiting for a response. Najib's neck jerked as he was dragged slowly sideways. He had to force himself to not scream in pain.

He braced himself for the inevitable drop but a second pair of hands grabbed him by his legs. Gently the two men lowered him to the floor below and sat him on a chair.

'Thank you. My legs have fallen asleep.' Najib rubbed them to restore circulation.

Peter smiled as he entered. 'I apologise for the long confinement.' He crouched down beside Najib. 'I had to be sure we were safe.'

'Brother Peter, don't apologise for doing the right thing.'

'When you're ready, you can come up on deck but I've asked your men to stay below. We don't want to draw attention to ourselves.'

'Where are we?' Najib replied, but Peter had already

bounded up the stairs.

It took another minute before the pins and needles abated. Najib stood unsteadily, testing his legs. They were wobbly, and he didn't have complete control of his left foot but he wouldn't appear weak in front of Peter's men.

'Allah is great,' Najib exclaimed as he alighted onto the deck. The scenery was truly breathtaking and like nothing he had seen before. They were in a wide estuary bounded on both sides by sheer ochre coloured cliffs. Dry shrubs covered every horizontal surface. In a few places lush green mangroves came to the water's edge, but they were the only green in a red brown landscape.

Najib scanned the waters in all directions. They were alone. Unfamiliar sea birds soared overhead. Now and then one would swoop onto the turquoise water and fly off with a struggling fish.

Peter stood at the bow scanning the water with a pair of binoculars.

'Are we in Australia?' Najib asked.

'Yes, finally,' Peter said. By the way in case you're wondering, I'm Muslim.'

'I was not wondering. I was sure. Wafaa would not have entrusted your job to a non-believer.'

Peter exhaled and smiled. 'I have a Muslim name. It's Zulfiqar.'

'That is a nice name,' Najib said.

'I prefer Peter. It seems more natural to me.'

'Names mean nothing,' Najib said. 'But I notice a slight Arab accent.'

'I'm Aussie born and bred but spent time in Lebanon learning about Islam. That's where I got the accent.'

'Oh, I see.' Najib nodded his head. 'How long have you been Muslim?'

Peter sighed, 'Not long enough. I spent too many wasted years. You know I was for a time a neo-Nazi.'

'Really.' Najib didn't know whether Peter was joking.

'Yes… I ain't proud of it. We burnt mosques and beat up many Muslims. I nearly killed a young man as he was leaving a mosque after Friday prayers.'

'W-what happened?'

'I punched him. He hit his head and ended in hospital. He needed a plate in his head and rehab for two years.'

'Ow… So how did you…?'

'I felt really bad for what I did. I ah… visited him in hospital to see how he was doing. When I saw his family, I couldn't take it anymore. I apologised and offered to hand myself in to the police. The man was so warm and friendly. He told me he forgave me the minute the ambos were putting him on a stretcher. When I heard that I started… crying. He reached out and grabbed my hand. He told me my redemption lay not with the police but with Allah and offered to help me. I was high as a kite on meth most days. I mean, I was a really lost cause. To feed my habit, I broke into houses, even beat up my girlfriend when she refused me money.

Anyway, something in me wanted to be found. And I took the opportunity he offered.'

'That is quite a story. Was your friend also…?' Najib stopped, unsure how much he should disclose. Maybe Peter hadn't been brought into Wafaa's inner circle.

Peter laughed. 'You mean was he a jihadi?'

'Y-y-yes…' Najib's face darkened.

'Nah. He believed in a peaceful struggle. As if that works.'

'Then how did you…?'

'I went to Afghanistan in '87 to fight the Russians and since then I fought in most jihads including Syria. I find it easy to go in and out of the country because I'm white. Obviously I don't fly directly to the war zone. Only the idiots do.'

'I fought in Syria too. Who did you fight with?'

'The Free Syrian Army, but then also Jabhat-al-Nusra. I was going to join Islamic State before I realised what they were.'

'Good you did. Islamic State was American created.'

'They all were. Al Qaeda too, which is where Jabhat-al-

Nusra came from…' Peter sighed.

'Yes well. The Americans start things they can never finish…'

'You are so right, brother. No deep thinking from those people.'

'So what made you come back?'

'I was only with Jabhat a short time when I joined Wafaa's brigade—'

'But I commanded the brigade. You were not there.' Najib tried to keep the accusation out of his tone.

'There were two. We were stationed near Aleppo. You must have been south of Damascus.'

'Y-y-yes. We spent most of our time fighting Assad's forces for control of outer Damascus.' Najib's mind was in turmoil. Peter knew more about Wafaa's brigades than he did. What did that mean?

'She told me her intention was to train men, not win battles,' Peter said. 'That's why she sent us back early. I returned to Australia in December of 2013.'

'We got trained all right!' Najib smiled. 'And have many scars to prove it.' He rolled back his sleeves and lifted his shirt to show Peter an ugly burn mark. 'This was a flamethrower.'

'Allah forged you in fire.' Peter placed his hand warmly on his back.

Najib smiled. It was hard not to like Peter. 'Yes I suppose so,' Najib said as he scanned the shoreline. 'So tell me brother, where in Australia are we?'

'In the Kimberleys, at the top end.'

'Is it near Melbourne?' Najib knew nothing about Australia.

Peter grinned. 'We're near nowhere. This is Australia. The emptiest country in the world.' Peter said.

Australia was one enemy Wafaa always spoke about as one that would be defeated in the coming jihad, *Insh'allah*.

The water became brown and turgid as the estuary narrowed. The seawater was mixing with the sediment from two rivers.

'How far to Melbourne?'

'About forty-eight hours.'

'*Ya Allah*!' Najib shook his head and looked at Peter. 'You are not joking?'

'No, brother.'

They followed the right fork of the estuary past sheer cliffs punctuated by sandy beaches. The murky water forced the captain to keep to the middle of the channel.

They rounded an archipelago of small islands. The channel halved in width as the sheer cliffs became rounded hills that gradually receded inland to be replaced by mangrove forests.

Many of the hills were cleaved down the middle by fast-moving creeks of all sizes. This was wet country.

As they followed the channel, the hills became taller and headed further inland. Here and there he could see waterfalls. The atmosphere became oppressively humid as the wind shifted.

Najib pointed at the shoreline. 'Are those alligators, brother?'

'No, they're crocs. Saltwater crocodiles.'

The boat turned to port-side and headed towards the shore. Najib could see the crocodiles close-up. The giant beasts lay still, seemingly unconcerned by their presence, except for their eyes that followed their movement.

'Are they dangerous?'

'Not as much as you, brother. You know I heard about you.' Peter was referring to Syria.

'Oh,' Najib found it unnerving that Peter knew more about him than he did about Peter. 'I hope good things. Anyway, let us pray we have more opportunities to be dangerous,' he smiled.

The boat entered a narrow bay through a gap in the mangroves. A lone jetty interrupted the smooth curve of a sandy beach as it disappeared into the dense greenery that lined the shoreline.

Najib watched as their yacht docked. The anchor chain sang out as it dropped to the bottom of the bay even before they had come to a full stop. In the blink of an eye, the deck was a hive of activity as the crew and his men emerged from below.

'It's time to go. We need to move the cylinders and your men off into the tree-line fast. We can't afford to be seen.' Peter said.

'There is no one here.'

'There's always someone somewhere at the wrong moment. Has Wafaa not taught you caution?'

'Ehhmm yes, of course, she has.' Najib was annoyed. 'I was just making conversation. I am alive because I am cautious.' Maybe he liked Peter a little less.

The jetty was old and rickety. The waterlogged boards sagged unnervingly underfoot as the line of men carried the cylinders to shore. After the bright sunlight, it felt like night under the dense tree cover. Najib stopped to let his eyes adjust. He marvelled at what he saw. The crystal-clear water surrounding the jetty teemed with life. Schools of brightly coloured fish darted in all directions. What looked like crabs scurried along the sandy bottom, seeking refuge among the myriad of aquatic plants along the seabed.

'Allah's bountiful treasures,' he mumbled 'but in the land of ungrateful and unthinking infidels.'

'Yes, that's why his warriors are here to bring them to their senses.' Peter responded.

The jetty became a wide boardwalk as it emerged from the tree-line. It traversed over what looked like sandy ground covered in tufts of short sharp bladed grass.

'This is important. Tell your men to stay on the boardwalk,' Peter said loudly. 'If anyone falls off, they'll sink into the sand before the crocs get them... if they're lucky.'

The walkway climbed in a series of steps. A large canvas, strung between four steel poles, covered two prime movers each with two trailers loaded with shipping containers.

'Drop the cylinders here and go back for the rest. We need to hurry. It'll get dark soon and we can't use lights. We are very close to Wyndham and don't want to attract attention.'

* *

An hour later all sixty cylinders were loaded on the trucks.

'It's your turn next,' Peter said. 'You're going into cavities I have built into the front of each shipping container.'

Najib had not noticed any hiding spots. 'I cannot see what you mean.'

'Don't worry, I'll show you. But let's first eat.'

They sat in a circle and had a quick meal of bread and dates followed by *Maghreb* prayers.

After Najib divided his men into four groups, Peter's men helped them climb onto the shipping containers and down small hatches into their hiding spots.

Najib marvelled at the cleverness. The shipping containers were over twelve metres long. From inside no one would spot that the last metre had been partitioned off.

Najib had joined Haziq, Mokhtar, Jasni and Razak in one of the hiding spaces. The cavity was lined in thick foam and had a large ventilation fan in the roof.

'It's a bit tight and will be noisy but you won't die. I've made sure of that,' Peter said as he looked down onto Najib.

'We will be fine,' Najib smiled and waved up to him.

With the hatches closed, the interior was plunged into darkness. Najib sat in the corner and recited a prayer. Allah would look after them. The truck engines sprang to life and with a crunch of gears they were off. He wondered how Melbourne compared to this place.

UNCLE

The taxi turned into a right-angled parking bay along Shahi Mohalla Street. Traffic noise from the nearby Fort Road assailed them as they alighted from the vehicle.

The outer rampart of the fort towered above them. A giant banyan tree growing out of a crevice in the ancient brick wall seemed tiny in comparison.

To their left, the ancient labyrinthine walled city of Lahore spread in a bewildering maze of buildings and laneways.

A knot formed in Sergei's stomach as he looked at the ancient fort. His heart thumped in his chest. Razane was somewhere inside those four walls, possibly in terrible agony. The feeling of runaway panic made him nauseous. A crushing weight threatened to suffocate him.

Movement kept them sane. They had to keep trying - something, anything - regardless of the chance of success.

Jane heard him sigh and squeezed his hand. 'Keep your spirits up, darling. We'll get her out.' Her voice broke.

He looked at her burka clad form. Yousaf had asked them to dress in local clothes to blend in. He himself wore a dun-coloured *shalwar kameez* under his jacket. 'Whatever it takes,' he sighed as he watched Yousaf pay the driver. 'Let's hope his uncle can help.'

Yousaf pocketed his wallet and joined them as the taxi turned around to leave. 'Please come fast,' he set off down a narrow street. The burka restricted Jane's vision and got under her feet as she tried keeping up with Sergei's long strides. To make matters worse, the footpath was a minefield of potholes and litter, from fruit peels to small stones and bits of wood.

The buildings were a mix of old and new and unlike any they had seen in other parts of Lahore. Most were heavily decorated with ornate plaster friezes or carved wood panelling on enclosed balconies and painted in bright colours. With a few exceptions the houses were of the same width, but their heights varied between three and six storeys. Some buildings had a different style facade on each floor. The effect was artistic chaos that nevertheless was unique and charming.

'Those balcony for dancing-girls.' Yousaf pointed. 'This place was very famous red-light district known as Heera Mandi.'

'What does that mean?' Jane tried looking through the veil. Most houses had ornate timber balconies on all except the lower two floors.

'Diamond market.'

'And the women were the diamonds?' Jane said with a grimace.

'Yes.'

'I was expecting it to be run down and poor,' Sergei said. 'Except for the footpath it's nicely looked after.'

'These houses are UN heritage listed. Lahore Heritage Society help to renovate.' Yousaf was panting as he spoke.

They came to a fork. 'Come, come… this way we go.' He turned right.

While in the taxi, Sergei had done another Internet search on the tunnels under the fort. The first network of tunnels were built during the Mughal era for servants to move between sections of the fort without being seen. Later the tunnel network was connected to the walled city. The king and his courtiers reputedly used them to visit the red-light district that made up a sizable portion of the walled city.

A far more ambitious expansion saw them connected to other towns and cities to allow the royal family and their generals to escape during wartime.

One led to Delhi in India and from there to Agra. Another connected to a Mughal residence at Hiran Minar near the town of Sheikhupura and a third to Hyderabad in Sindh.

Over time, they fell into disrepair and became a safety hazard. Not having the money for repairs, the city authorities blocked them off.

The laneway they were in became narrower and darker. Sergei looked up. The top floors of most buildings touched their counterparts across the street because of extensions that spread outwards and upwards.

Space was obviously at a premium. Wherever opposing buildings didn't touch, the intervening space was taken up with clothes hung out to dry on lines strung between the buildings.

'These buildings look ancient,' Jane caught Sergei's gaze.

'They never fall down.' Yousaf guessed what was on Jane's mind.

'They look like they will. Some of them seem to lean.' Sergei joined in.

'They build house strong,' Yousaf shook his head firmly.

The laneway opened into a market square. Cloth vendors mixed with greengrocers, hardware stores, handicraft makers, restaurants and musical instrument sellers. A chemist had a queue of people lining outside.

'I don't see any dancing girls,' Jane said from behind the burka.

'They sleep in day and dance in night,' Yousaf said.

'Yeah, of course. Silly me,' Jane muttered to herself.

'Most dancing girl gone away. Mens today not want dancing, only want one thing.'

The market square ended in a laneway. Five houses down, Yousaf stopped at a door and knocked.

Chains rattled, a bolt snicked, hinges creaked as the door opened. A plump grey-haired woman wearing thick horn-rimmed glasses stuck her head out. She smiled when she saw Yousaf.

'*Asalam aleikum*, aunty,' Yousaf said before turning to Sergei and Jane. 'This is Farhana Aunty, daughter of Uncle.'

Farhana brightened and moved forward to give Yousaf a hug. 'Yousaf *beita*, what a long time.' She looked at Sergei and Jane who had lifted her veil. 'Are they your friends? Welcome... come in,' she gestured as she gave Jane a hug.

They entered the dark and warm interior and waited as Farhana bolted and chained the doors. They were in a dark passage that ran along the front of the house. A small bulb hanging from the tall ceiling competed with daylight streaming through a row of narrow *roshandans* above head height. Neither did much to lessen the oppressive effect of the dark wood panelling that lined the walls and the ceiling.

Heat enveloped them as they followed Farhana through a doorway closed off with a bedsheet. The room was lit by a table lamp beside a couch. Its warm light fell on a wizened grey-haired man. His eyes were closed. A book with an Urdu title lay open on his chest that heaved rhythmically to the sounds of his gentle snoring.

Farhana muttered something and turned down the gas heater. She motioned them to sit on the chairs beside the man before rushing out.

'It's warm in here,' Sergei took off his jacket and sat beside Jane.

'This is Uncle,' Yousaf said in hushed tones. 'He very old.'

Farhana returned carrying a tray with three bottles of Pepsi. She offered them to the trio. 'I've put the kettle on for tea. You must stay for lunch?'

Jane knew it was impolite to refuse the drink. 'Shukria,' she nodded as she took a bottle and handed one to Sergei.

'Aunty, very sorry but we cannot stay for lunch,' Yousaf took a sip. 'We must to talk to Uncle urgently.'

'OK, at least have tea.' Farhana said as she gently shook the old man by the shoulder.

'I feel bad waking your uncle,' Sergei whispered. 'How old is he?'

'He no my uncle. He everybody uncle.' Yousaf said.

'Uncle is a respectful term for an elder,' Jane explained.

'I get that,' Sergei said.

'I think he over hundred,' Yousaf said.

The old man woke with a start. For a moment he stared at them with rheumy eyes. Noticing his visitors he mumbled something unintelligible in a thin, shaky voice as he leaned forward and offered Sergei his hand.

'He is saying *Asalam aleikum,*' Yousaf explained.

'*Wa aleikum asalam,*' Sergei and Jane both said in return.

The old man brightened considerably. 'May you live long, *beita,*' he muttered.

'Uncle, we need your help,' Yousaf said. 'These are my good friends. They search for tunnel under fort.'

The old man's eyes sparkled as he straightened in his chair. 'That is a surprise. Not many people ask me about tunnels. Only people my age still talk about them.' He paused to clear his throat. 'Tell me… why are you interested?'

Sergei looked at Jane and Yousaf. 'Uncle, we aah… find tunnels fascinating and… aah…'

'Oh, they are… Did you know? Many older houses are still connected to a tunnel,' He paused for effect, his voice had grown in strength. Apart from a strong accent, his English was excellent.

'Are any still usable?' Sergei said.

'Some tunnels collapsed, so the authorities closed them. Some with bricks and others with steel gates and heavy locks. While I was still with the Lahore Heritage Society, we had plans to open some for tourism. But orders from above stopped the work.'

'Oh, that's not good.' Sergei exhaled. The heat was suddenly unbearable. He struggled to breathe. A dark dread was seeping into his thoughts. It sounded hopeless.

'Every time the government changes, the Heritage Society tries once again. But someone powerful wants to keep them closed. I do not know why. It is sad. The older tunnels, built in the times of the Mughal dynasty, are mostly in good condition. They are lined with bricks and are mostly structurally sound. In a few places they caved in because the new tunnels undermined them.'

'Uncle, what you mean by new and old tunnels,' Sergei said.

'Son, the old tunnels are the ones built by the Mughals.

They allowed the king and his ministers to visit the city in secret. The new tunnels were built only forty years ago during the dictator General Zia's time. He wanted to turn Pakistan towards Islam so he banned alcohol and cracked down on dancing and prostitution.

'The tunnels were dug by owners of prostitution dens to smuggle alcohol and drugs and to allow patrons to enter and leave. They were built with little skill. Whenever the River Ravi flooded parts of the old town would be inundated. Some houses collapsed, and the town became infested with rats. So the city authorities forced people to close the tunnels.'

'Uncle, do you know if any Mughal era tunnels lead to the Lava Temple or the royal kitchens in the fort?'

The old man's face darkened. His hands shook violently. A glob of spittle dripped from the corner of his mouth, 'That is the one part of the tunnel that should stay blocked. Why do you want to know?'

'Why should it stay blocked?' Sergei said.

The old man hesitated before replying. 'There are stories that say ghosts haunt Lava Temple and the tunnels. When I was young, three local boys vanished. A search party went looking for them. They found no traces of the boys but near Lava Temple, they heard horrible screams and moaning. The men were so scared many soiled themselves. Next day armed police contingent continued the search. They found nothing. After that incident that branch of the tunnel was closed with a steel grate.'

'How do we find the tunnels?' Sergei said as he exchanged glances with Jane.

The old man didn't reply. He had dozed off again.

Yousaf shook him gently. 'Uncle, where is the nearest tunnel entrance.'

The old man woke with a start. 'The tunnel is sealed, my son.'

'But where is it?' Yousaf persisted.

'In the basement...' his words trailed off.

'Which basement?'

'Ahhh, hmmm, try at the new clinic.' Farhana said. She had returned wheeling a trolley with a teapot and a sponge cake. 'I think he means the new doctor on the corner near the market. The building used to belong to a famous family of dancing girls. They are now gone.' She sounded almost sad.

'Thank you Aunty,' Yousaf said as Farhana poured tea.

'*Bahut shukria*,' Jane sat down next to her to help. She poured a cup for the old man, but he had fallen asleep again. She placed it on the lamp table next to him.

'Can you get us into the clinic's basement?' Sergei asked Yousaf.

'I show ISI badge. Maybe it help.'

* *

Yousaf's badge proved as effective as he had predicted.

Brenda Chaudhuri, the clinic manager, seemed surprised by their request. She checked Yousaf's badge, shrugged her shoulders and led them down a narrow winding staircase, to the basement.

Jane struggled to hear what she said as she took up the rear.

'The tunnels have been a lot of trouble for us ever since we moved in. I know more about them than I want to. The house is slowly collapsing and making the walls crack. We have three levels of basements. The top level was the original basement built with the house. It has an entrance to the old tunnels. More recently, two more basements were dug, one below the other. The lowest… also has a tunnel. It is newer. I was told it was built maybe thirty years ago.'

'Where does that go?' Sergei said.

'Who knows?' Brenda threw her hands up.

'That's amazing,' Jane said as she looked around the basement. Brenda turned on a torch she had brought with her. It smelt musty and damp. Jane was sure she could hear creatures scurrying away.

'Do you have mice?'

'Mainly rats and snakes,' Brenda said.

Jane suppressed a shiver.

'I hate snakes. Are they poisonous?'

'Very poisonous. This is very near the River Ravi. We have found cobras and kraits in the clinic,' Brenda shivered at the memory.

'I guess they're after the rats,' Jane murmured.

The tunnel was on the furthest wall from the stairs. A pile of rubbish partially obscured the heavy metal gate across the entrance.

'Shit,' a whistle escaped Sergei's lips. He shook his head in disappointment. 'We'll need a locksmith to break into here or someone with an oxy-acetylene torch.

'We wanted to block the tunnel or at least brick it up, but the city authority would not give us permission. It is historic, they said... We blocked off the newer tunnel and filled in the lower basements but this one we cannot touch... but why are you interested in the tunnel?' Brenda asked.

'We looking for terrorist in tunnel,' Yousaf said as he and Sergei pulled on the bars. They wouldn't budge. The hinges were rusted solid. Sergei examined the padlock. It was the size of half a brick and coated with rust.

'I have an idea. Wait here please,' Yousaf said.

Before they could respond, he had bounded up the stairs.

'Is the terrorist dangerous?' Brenda looked afraid.

'Very. But we're keeping it secret,' Sergei was thinking fast. 'We can't risk the news getting out. Social media makes it hard, you know.'

Brenda opened her mouth to say something but then closed it again.

'Is something wrong?' Jane said.

'We were told the tunnels are impassable. I am surprised someone would hide down here.'

'Yes, we're too,' Jane said.

'OK. You can borrow my torch. Just drop it back with my

receptionist when you are done. Now please excuse me.' Brenda said. Jane lit the way for her as she returned upstairs.

A few minutes later Yousaf returned. He was accompanied by a young man wearing a scruffy *shalwar kameez* and sandals. Yousaf helped him lower a two-wheeled cart carrying two gas cylinders down the staircase. Sergei rushed to help.

'This man is Billa,' Yousaf said as he wiped his hands on his trousers. 'He will help.'

'Is this what I think?' Sergei pointed to the gas cylinders.

'Yes, oxy-acetylene to cut gate.

'Fantastic, but where did you find him… How did you convince him…' Jane said.

'I promise you pay ten thousand rupees. I also buy these from shop.' Yousaf showed them two anodised aluminium torches.

'It's amazing how things work in Pakistan,' Sergei said.

Yousaf said something to Billa who nodded at Sergei and Jane. He lit the torch with a cigarette lighter, turned a second wheel, focused the flame and began to cut; a pair of Raybans with one lens missing was his only safety equipment.

'Brave man,' Jane said as globs of molten metal cascaded to the floor, missing his exposed feet by millimetres.

'Brave and foolhardy,' Sergei said.

'Allah protects,' Yousaf said cheerily.

It took less than five minutes for Billa to cut through the rusted bars. As he cut the last bar, he pushed the gate forward. It fell into the tunnel in a cloud of dust.

Billa held his hand out for the payment.

'Tell him he gets double if he comes with us. There may be another gate inside,' Sergei fished in his pocket for two five-thousand-rupee notes.

Yousaf said something in Urdu.

'He says no coming. He scared from ghost.'

'Tell him it's just the wind whistling.' Sergei took out four five-thousand-rupee notes. 'I'll triple it if I hear no more complaints.'

Billa's eyes lit up. He hesitated for a moment. 'OK... I... go,' he said in broken English.

DEAD RECKONING

Lahore, Wednesday 10 January, 3:10 pm

Jane couldn't remember feeling such a combination of excitement, uncertainty and terror. She dared not hope the tunnel would lead to the ISI dungeon because even if it did, the ISI would surely have ensured it was impregnable.

Yet a glimmer of hope shone in the dark recesses of her mind. Pakistan had surprised them before. She had her fingers and toes crossed that it would again.

Yousaf handed Sergei a flashlight as he aimed his into the dark opening.

'Let me go first.' Sergei stepped over the fallen gate, his torch beam cleaving the dark.

Jane was next, followed by Yousaf and then Billa. After twenty paces the tunnel levelled off. Like a blanket had been thrown over the world, the sounds of the street vanished, replaced by their footsteps and the clang from the gas cylinders on Billa's cart.

The tunnel's brick lining was mostly in a good condition except for signs of rising damp. The air smelt dank and old. As they descended, the smell of mould grew.

'It smells wet,' Jane said.

'Damn,' Sergei's left shoe splashed into a deep puddle sending water up the inside of his trouser leg. 'There's standing water here.'

'I was just wondering how they kept it drained,' Jane said.

'They don't.' Sergei shone his torch all around. The walls were black and shiny with algae. They were under some water source seeping into the tunnel. After a short while the tunnel climbed, and the wetness receded.

'We very near Ravi River. Much flood when monsoon,' Yousaf said.

'Hey, look.' Jane pointed. The tunnel ended in a T.

Sergei pulled out his phone, 'Left or Right?' He clicked on Google Maps.

'You love asking and answering your own questions.' Jane playfully bumped into him. 'My guess is left.'

'You're spot on, babe.'

'See, I don't need technology. I have this thing… It's called a sense of direction.' Jane poked him in the ribs, her fingers bumping against the holstered Glock automatic pistol under his jacket. They had found a weapons cache in the major's safe house and had each taken a semi-automatic and a hunting knife. She felt for her own. They felt good under her jacket and made her feel powerful, like anything was possible.

'We can't afford to guess,' Sergei said as they turned left into the larger tunnel. 'I've turned on an electronic breadcrumb trail… so we don't get lost on the way back.'

'Good thinking,' Jane said, 'but… how are you getting a GPS signal down here?'

'I'm not. The phone uses dead reckoning. It records the direction I turn and the steps I take and makes an approximation. It's only slightly less accurate.'

'Sergei bro, *wah*, amazing technology,' Yousaf said.

'Does it show how far to the dungeons?' Jane's heart beat faster. She guessed they were less than a kilometre away. She was trying not to think too far forward. The thought of not finding Razane was too confronting. Having their hopes dashed now would be the cruelest blow.

'We're around two hundred metres to the fort… then it's another hundred to where Yousaf said the dungeons are.'

It was painfully close. She ached all over at the thought of holding Razane. What state would she be in? Her breath caught in her throat at the thought she could be hurt or worse.

She remembered her Garmin fitness watch. The step counter showed 5439 for the day. She recalled her stride length was slightly over half a metre. 'I'll count my steps so we've another way to measure.'

'OK, good. But… it mightn't take a direct route. Or… not even…' Sergei paused for breath, 'lead to the dungeon.'

What a horribly sobering thought. They were relying on a tunnel built hundreds of years ago; no amount of willing would make it change its course.

Jane said a little prayer in her mind. It was all she'd ever ask from God, or whoever controlled the universe. 'I'm just hoping those stories of ghosts screaming and moaning means the tunnels connect to the dungeon,' Jane said.

'You'd expect that's where the moaning came from. And hopefully, the connection's more than just an air vent. How frustrating would that be!' Sergei said.

'Absofuckinglutely… but you know I just realised something. If we're that close, we should be extra quiet…' Jane whispered as she bumped into Sergei.

He had stopped. She looked past him. A heavy grille blocked any further access. As she shone her torch on it, she was sure it looked newer than the one in the clinic's basement.

'Serge, how far have we come?' Her Garmin showed 5781 steps. That was roughly two hundred metres.

Sergei checked his phone. 'We're probably under the outer ramparts.' He looked at Yousaf. 'Could you ask Billa to cut? This time let's make sure the grille doesn't fall.'

It took ten minutes for Billa to cut through the last bar. As he did, Sergei and Yousaf lowered it carefully to the ground.

'Yousaf, can you ask Billa if he has any wire to weld it back again,' Jane said.

'Yes, he has wires but why?'

'It may be useful on the way back.'

'Good thinking, Jane madam. You are very clever,' Yousaf said as they set off again.

'I don't wanna take chances.'

Sergei had stopped again and was studying the ceiling and then the walls. 'These few meters look new.'

Jane flashed her torch. Sergei was right. This part of the tunnel had been recently repaired. The bricks were modern and uniform and the mortar was freshly pointed. 'Well observed, babe!'

'Why repair a tunnel then close it with grilles?' Sergei said as they veered left to follow the curve.

'No idea,' Jane said, a note of concern entering her voice. 'This is taking us northwest, away from the fort.' Her breath became shallow. Her chest constricted. 'We're supposed to head slightly east of north.'

'You're right but we've no choice but to follow it.' Sergei checked his phone. His voice was level.

His calm was infectious. Jane took a deep breath and held it before exhaling. She wouldn't lose her cool again.

The bricks changed to a rectangular grey stone as the tunnel widened. Sergei ducked to avoid the first of a row of rusty iron brackets embedded in the wall.

'I wonder what these were for.' Sergei touched one.

'Possibly for torches,' Jane said. 'Careful of the sharp edges.'

They trudged on. Ten minutes later they came to a fork.

'Unless we want to head outside the fort walls, let's take the right one,' Jane said.

No one argued. They walked on trying to tread as silently as possible. Within minutes, the tunnel forked again.

'What now?' Jane said.

Sergei looked at his tracker. 'The left one. It's heading towards Lava Temple. We can always retrace our steps.'

No one argued. Jane's heart beat faster as they walked on. The moment of truth was close. A few minutes later Sergei stopped abruptly and shone his torch on the ceiling. 'Look at that. More repairs.' The ceiling was lined with timber boards held up with steel scaffolding.

'Someone seems to have gone around fixing the cave-ins. But why?' Jane whispered.

'Maybe they want to open them to tourists,' Sergei whispered.

Jane froze as she heard something. She put her finger to

her lips. 'Ssshh. Turn off the torches and quiet.'

As their eyes slowly adjusted, they could see the tunnel ahead wasn't as pitch black as it was behind. In the near silence, they heard the thrum of a large group of people, among them children.

With slow measured steps they walked on a few paces to discover the source of the sound.

'Look up. There is light.' Yousaf whispered and pointed a shaft that had opened above them.

A faint beam of yellow light shone from above. It was just bright enough to illuminate a vertical shaft, as wide as the tunnel, leading up. The remnants of a helical staircase lay crumbled into piles of stones at their feet.

'That's about ten metres high, we'll never get up there.' Jane whispered.

Yousaf shone his torch at the grille that closed off the shaft. Some light escaped and illuminated a domed roof decorated with artwork.

'Yousaf, turn the light off buddy.' Sergei whispered sharply.

'So sorry. Yes, must be careful.' Yousaf said.

'That could be Lava Temple above us,' Jane said.

'That's also what the GPS says,' Sergei whispered. 'The people we can hear must be visitors… tourists.'

'That means… we're near the dungeons,' Jane whispered. Her anxiety was through the roof. There would be an impenetrable barrier right at the end, she knew it. 'Be very quiet!'

They all nodded and walked on slowly. The tunnel curved to the right before it straightened. Ahead of them, the path was blocked by another grille. According to Google Maps, they had reached the dungeon.

Sergei found Jane's hand and gave it a squeeze. 'I think this is it.' His beard tickled her ear.

Jane's heart was almost coming out of her chest. Beyond the grille was darkness. Did she dare believe Razane was somewhere behind there?

'Yousaf, can you ask Billa if it's possible to not make those popping noises with the cutter?'

Yousaf spoke to Billa. 'He will try,' Yousaf translated. 'He ask why?'

'Why what?'

'Why be quiet?'

'Tell him we don't want to wake the dead.'

'No no no, that scare him. He run off.'

'Just tell him to cut quietly,' Sergei's tone betrayed his frustration. The tension was getting too much.

Billa said something.

'He wants five thousand rupees more.'

'What an extortionist. Tell him OK, but then no more.'

Yousaf handed Billa the money, and he began to cut.

* *

Mike shifted in the plastic chair, his eyes fixed on his prisoner. The solitary light bulb illuminated the left side of her naked body as she hung, suspended by her wrists. The rest of the large room was in deep shadow.

He shivered involuntarily. The dungeon gave him the creeps in a big way. It was damp and cold but there was something more; a malign feeling had crept over him when he entered. He had never felt anything like it before. It was an inexplicable sadness coupled with an unreasonable fear and an inexorable urge to run. It threatened to grow into a mad panic unless he fought it.

His career had inured him to unpleasantness, but nothing had prepared him for this. If he'd been the slightest bit superstitious, he'd have blamed it on evil spirits. If ghosts were real, this place would be teeming with them.

When they arrived, Major Amjad had taken Sebastian and him on a tour. The ancient dungeon was built on three levels connected by steps hewn into rock.

The top level was divided into prison cells and four larger

torture rooms all connected by a central passageway that began at the elevators and ended in the steps down to the lower dungeons. The torture chambers were built in the middle of the top level so all the prisoners would hear the screams.

Each room specialised in a form of torture. One had a large gas furnace, another was a cold room. A third was a surgery to change a human into something else. He was in the stretching room. Hooks were embedded in almost every surface; a medieval rack stood in the corner.

The major had also shown them the two lower levels. They had apparently been abandoned for over a century; the intermediate level used to have rows of steel cages but was now empty. According to the major, a former director had sold the cages to a scrap merchant and pocketed the money.

It was on this level that the major had shown them the entrance to an abandoned tunnel that used to lead into the fort's nether regions. It used to be the prisoners' entrance during the time of the Mughal emperors. It was blocked off with a steel grille with bars as thick as his wrist.

When Mike had expressed his concern about how the tunnels could pose a security risk, the major had laughed. Apparently, the tunnels had collapsed, and the authorities had places similar steel grates at all entrances to the tunnel and at intermediate points along the way. He had assured Mike that there was no way anyone could access the tunnels let alone the dungeons.

One level down, the lowest dungeon was easily the biggest and contained scores of deep, narrow pits covered with steel bars. They were last used in the Mughal era to keep the most troublesome prisoners in solitary confinement. Sometimes they were dropped in headfirst. If the drop didn't kill them, their wounds would. Few prisoners were ever released from the pits.

Nowadays the dungeon was reserved only for special prisoners, mainly suspected terrorists who had no prospects of being released.

The day before their arrival the major had moved the

existing prisoners, an Indian spy and two Pakistani Taliban, to another location. So, they were alone.

Mike looked at his watch. Safdar, the old guard who had been watching Wafaa, had gone to relieve himself in some dark corner. He was taking his time. Maybe the creep had been aroused by their naked prisoner and was jerking himself off.

Mike looked at her with distaste. She was too lean, muscular and brown. He liked them whiter and with more meat on their bones.

He yawned and stretched his arms over his head. His neck was stiff and knotted. The tension headache that had started on the tarmac in Cairo still hammered away. He closed his burning eyes, took a deep breath and focused on the surrounding sounds. The dungeon was almost silent. He could hear his own heartbeat. Somewhere above, water sloshed in a pipe, a toilet flushing. Now it was too silent; his prisoner had stopped whimpering.

An alarming thought struck him. He got up and stood on tiptoes to feel behind her jaw for her pulse. He wrinkled his nose at her rancid smell. She hung silently, limp and lifeless. Her skin was clammy and cold.

Sweat broke out in rivulets as he frantically searched for the spot with his fingers. If she died, his own life wouldn't be worth living.

He laughed with relief as he found the pulse. It was irregular and he could barely feel it but it was there. She must have fainted from pain or dehydration.

As soon as Safdar returned, they would cut her down and revive her. He could ask Sebastian, but he was keeping an eye on the fort's camera network. It was a pity the Pakis didn't have face recognition technology, but the police contingent around the fort would make up for that.

An unfamiliar sound startled him as it echoed in the dark. He tried to make sense of the crackle and pop, followed by a dull ringing clang. He held on to its memory as he struggled to identify it. It reminded him of radio competitions where participants had to guess everyday sounds. He had never had a critical enough ear to be good at such games.

He walked out of the room and into the passageway and shone his torch first towards the elevator and then to the stairs to the lower dungeon. Maybe Safdar had tripped on something. He took his phone out of his pocket as he turned to go back to the torture room. Fuck, there was no signal.

* *

The grille was far heavier than they had expected. Sergei and Yousaf had braced themselves, but it still dropped out of their grasp. It fell the last few centimetres, striking the stone floor with a metallic thud that shattered the silence.

Sergei froze. Damn it. They were too close to be undone by carelessness. The echoes died down and once again there was silence. Slowly, he exhaled and looked at Jane and Yousaf. 'Let's go. Super quiet now.'

They stepped over the grille and found themselves in a cavernous space, empty except for bits of metal and piles of stones strewn about.

'Yousaf, is this...?' Sergei said as he flashed his torch around.

'This dungeon middle level. One level is up, one is down.'

'Where should we look first?'

'Only top level used. We go there.'

'OK, then ask Billa to go back to the last grille and wait for us. Tell him to stay there no matter what happens. He needs our help to get back,' Sergei said. He waited till Billa had walked off. 'So, how do we do this?'

'Let's first find Razane and see how many guards there are,' Jane whispered as she removed the burka and placed it next to the fallen grille. 'Then let's return here and work out what to do.'

'Sounds good. Yousaf, please show us the way.' Sergei switched off the torch as he stood.

* *

Safdar swallowed painfully and his heart skipped a beat, as he watched the three dark figures walk up the stairs to the top level.

Ya Allah, he had almost bumped into them. Where had they come from? Could they be ghosts? He had always scoffed at the stories, mainly because they were too scary. He could handle humans, but ghosts were another matter.

He breathed a sigh of relief as one of them took out a phone from his pocket. Ghosts didn't use phones. He let them go around a corner and turned on his small flashlight. Within minutes he found what he had been looking for, a solid steel pipe. He felt its weight. It was perfect for cracking skulls. The three figures were climbing the stairs. He followed noiselessly.

* *

A faint glow wicked through the dark as the trio reached the top of the stairs.

'Please let Razane be OK,' Jane prayed silently as she tried to see. A wide straight passage disappeared into the dark. The light source came from a door, left ajar, twenty metres away on the right. It cast a pallid glow onto the opposite wall that was punctuated with a row of open doorways, all of them dark.

'Let me go ahead,' Jane whispered in Sergei's ear. 'One person will make less noise than three.' Without waiting she crept towards the light, the rubber soles of her shoes making no sound.

That's when she saw the man. His movement separated him from the surrounding shadows. He had put something in his pocket and was walking towards the room with the light.

Jane followed on tiptoes. There was no one else around. How could it be? Ancient hinges groaned as the man pushed open the solid door, decorated with two vertical rows of rivets. Jane's breath caught in her throat as she saw into the room. Razane, stark naked, hung by her arms from the ceiling. She was motionless. The angle of her head suggested she wasn't conscious.

The cruel bastards had hung the love of her life by her delicate wrists, like a piece of meat. A sob escaped Jane's mouth.

Shoes scuffed against the floor as a piercing white light blinded her. The man ahead of her had turned around. 'Fuck... freeze... H-hands where I can see them.' His voice quavered from the shadows. She could tell from his accent, he was American. And he held a gun. She was trapped.

'You're a fucking wom... On the floor, bitch.' The voice thundered.

Jane dropped to a crouching position, her arms extended forward. She watched his legs as he approached. She glanced up; he was close enough for her to see the outline of his round face. He came closer; he was middle-aged with thinning hair and foul breath.

Behind her, Sergei cried out in pain. The beam flickered away. She pivoted and kicked the American's legs from under him. His gun went off as he landed heavily. His torch rolled away from his outstretched hand, briefly shining on his head. As he tried to get up, Jane thrust her heel hard under his chin but he blocked her with his forearms.

Still trying to sit up, he kicked blindly. Jane hopped sideways, out of range. Without pausing, she somersaulted forward. In the same movement, she removed her hunting knife from its sheath. He was no slouch either and rolled onto his feet. Jane let him straighten and sliced the tendons on the back of his knees. He screamed and fell into a praying position. With another pivot, she plunged the knife into his lower back. With a deafening bellow, he fell forward, writhing in agony. Jane leapt to a crouching position behind him. Reaching forward, she grabbed his sweat-soaked hair in her left hand. With a yell, she yanked his head back and sliced his throat open, cutting off his screams in a frothing burble.

'This is too good for what you deserve,' she growled in his ear as his lifeblood spurted out. It was the last thing he heard.

Jane shone the torch at Sergei and Yousaf. They were

struggling with a man holding a metal pipe. She aimed the light in the man's eyes. Sergei pushed forward but held on to the pipe. The man stumbled, but he too held on. Yousaf took out his knife and stretching forward plunged it into their assailant's chest. The man let go and crumpled in a heap. Yousaf stooped down and drew his knife across the man's throat. Within seconds he stopped twitching.

'I've found Razane, come quick,' Jane shouted.

The words had an electrifying effect on Sergei. Nervous energy coursed through him as he ran to where Jane pointed.

Sergei's heart leapt from his chest as his eyes fell on the woman they both loved. Her limp and lifeless form brought tears to his eyes.

Heart pounding, he ran to her and lifted her by the legs to take the weight off her wrists. Her skin was clammy and cold. He put his head to her bare chest, desperate to hear signs of life.

Her skin was so cold, and she didn't move a muscle. His terror grew. It couldn't be. Life couldn't be that cruel. His legs went weak. It took an effort to stay upright.

Jane climbed on the plastic chair, trying to balance as she cut the rope. 'She's free,' she sobbed as she climbed down. Removing her jacket, she placed it on the floor and helped Sergei lower Razane onto the ground.

'Check her pulse!' He wanted to cry like a child. He put his head to her chest again. 'Please be alive,' he screamed silently. His tears pooled on Razane's bare skin as he moved his head, hoping to hear something.

With trembling hands Jane felt the side of her temple as Sergei carefully removed the rope around her wrists, wincing at what he saw. The rope had chafed her skin in several places and left a deep swollen welt. Her hands had puffed up to almost twice their size.

'I think I feel something,' Jane was crying.

Sergei put his head to her chest again. A faint heartbeat made his own heart start again.

'Her pulse… I think I feel it. We need to get her core body

temperature up… Fast!' Jane said as she felt the deep rope marks on Razane's wrists, her voice breaking with emotion.

Sergei removed his sweater and put it on Razane, leaving her arms inside. Then he placed the jacket around her shoulders and zipped it up.

A rumbling sound echoed through the dark. Yousaf came running, out of breath. 'Someone coming down.' He had gone pale.

They heard the elevator groan as it descended. 'We go or they cut us off.' Yousaf said with fear in his voice. 'They are army commandos… with guns.'

'Take Razane and go as fast as you can,' Jane said. 'Wait for us at the grille. We'll follow. Yousaf, come with me.' She ran off before Sergei could protest.

Sergei grunted as he stood with Razane in his arms, grateful for the extra time he spent in the gym. 'Keep her safe,' he shouted after Yousaf.

Jane had killed two men back at the steakhouse. It still didn't prepare him for how efficiently Jane had disabled and killed the armed American. Her movements were graceful and efficient and lightning fast and she didn't hesitate.

But that mightn't work against whoever was descending in the elevator. They would come armed and in numbers. They'd have heard the gunshot and would be prepared to shoot first and ask questions later.

Jane's only armed combat training was from playing laser skirmish in the hills around their home. No amount of war games could equate to an encounter with live rounds. But he had no choice. Jane could never have carried Razane. In saving one he was risking the other.

A sense of dread threatened to overwhelm him as he walked as fast as he could manage. Razane was still limp and unresponsive in his arms. It made it harder to carry her as he slowly descended the stairs to the second level.

* *

Jane undid the safety lever on her Glock. Behind her, Yousaf did the same.

'How many ways are there to come down?' She said as she joined Yousaf behind a thick pillar opposite the elevator.

'Only this.'

'So what should we do?' Her jaw was set in grim determination as she fought to keep her voice steady and herself focused. Maybe she was in way over her head, but the men coming down in the lift had taken part in torturing Razane; they were about to encounter their worst nightmare.

'You shoot left men, I shoot right.' In the dark, she could see Yousaf gesturing as he spoke.

The elevator dinged as it came to a halt. Through the crack between the doors, she could see the inside was dark.

The doors opened slowly. Jane aimed left and low, her finger tense on the trigger.

THE MANHUNT

Lahore, Wednesday 10 January, 3:40 pm

The gunshot was faint but unmistakable. It came from the dungeons. Why would Mike discharge his weapon? Their prisoner was barely conscious; trying to scare her wouldn't work.

Sebastian looked for the dungeon's camera feed. Mike had asked for it to be set up to record the interrogation, mainly to protect himself if something went wrong. Now that the chiefs had given a reluctant go-ahead, Mike was off the hook, unless she died.

Sebastian would have preferred to have been in the dungeon ensuring that didn't happen. He also wanted to keep an eye on the major's men. They behaved like animals. Wafaa deserved everything she got, but rape was wrong. He couldn't let it happen on his watch. What was the point of winning against evil if one became evil oneself?

He clicked on the camera feed window. It took a second to register Razane wasn't there. Had the camera moved? No, that wasn't it. The light bulb was still there, so was the rope, now dangling from the roof. Razane had been cut down. Why? What was Mike playing at?

Sebastian rewound the recording to thirty seconds before the gunshot. Razane hung there, limp, lifeless and alone. Then the gun went off. What he saw fifty-seven seconds later, beggared belief.

Two strangers, a man and woman, ran up to Razane and cut her down. Their backs to the camera but he was sure they were Sergei and Jane. Jane had dyed her hair black. They must have entered through the tunnels and shot Mike, the tunnels Major Amjad had promised were secure.

Sebastian ran to Captain Usman's office. He was discussing the gunshot on the phone. The same video feed was on his laptop screen.

The captain hung up and called to his men. 'You four,' he singled them out. 'We are under attack. Put on full armour and go down, *fatafat*.'

'I'm going too,' Sebastian said. 'That's my partner down there.'

'No. This is our responsibility. We take care of it. You stay and watch.'

Sebastian knew better than to argue. He was in their territory. 'Will four people be enough?'

'Hah, not you worry. They are Pak Army commandos. But just to be sure, I request special forces brigade to seal Walled City. Terrorist no escape.'

* *

The shadows emerging from the lift were a blur. They didn't run; they rolled out, and faster than Jane had expected. She adjusted her aim and fired two rounds. One smacked into the elevator wall. The other appeared to hit an attacker, but he showed no ill effects. Along with his comrades, he dissolved into the shadows. Fear stabbed her in the stomach. She was hopelessly out of her depth.

'They have body armour.' Yousaf whispered from behind, making her jump. 'Shoot at head.'

It was easier said than done. She couldn't see them. Razane or Sergei would know how to handle this situation. What had Razane said about night combat? It was all about listening.

Jane tried, but the loudest sound was the blood pumping in her head. She would die and then they'd go after Sergei and Razane.

Hearing a shuffle behind, she looked for Yousaf. He'd taken cover inside a doorway to her right and was signalling something to her with his palm facing down.

'What?' Her mind was numb, her legs number. Through the fog of fear, she remembered Razane's words. "Always present the smallest target to the enemy." That was it. Yousaf wanted her to get down.

With shaking legs she dropped to the ground, bumping her elbows on the uneven dirt, packed hard over two centuries.

Their assailants were whispering. She fired towards the sound, a wild, desperate act. For the briefest moment the flash changed the darkness to daylight, and she was blind.

Something made her roll to the left. Razane had told her how she'd been caught on a hilltop at night, surrounded by enemy snipers whose fatal mistake had been to forget how brightly a muzzled glowed in the dark.

Bullets whizzed inches past Jane and smacked in the dirt. She'd be dead if she hadn't moved. Yousaf returned fire four times in rapid succession. A man cried out in pain.

On her left, an object clattered to the ground and rolled towards her. Was it a grenade? Not letting thoughts get in the way she leapt towards Yousaf in the doorway. More bullets whizzed past, missing her. She crawled behind the wall out of the line of fire. Now she had even less chance to see their assailants.

The rolling object burst and hissed like a manic snake. Gas poured out. Acting on instinct, Jane held her breath and covered her mouth and nose. What was it?

A light source flew in a low trajectory, landed on the ground and rolled away. It took a second to comprehend that Yousaf had rolled his flashlight. She watched mesmerised as it bounced on the rough ground, illuminating two attackers. Yousaf stood and fired. A hail of bullets whizzed in his direction.

Jane crawled to the edge of the wall. She was now beyond scared but she had to fight back. Three of their attackers lay still. The lone survivor, now desperate, lay on his stomach firing off round after round at Yousaf, forcing him to take cover. The torch came to rest; its light shone on the shooter's boot. Jane had one chance. Holding the pistol steady she estimated where his head was and squeezed the trigger three times in rapid succession, adjusting her aim in small steps. The first two bullets ricocheted off the floor, the third pinged off his helmet. In the intervening period, the shooter managed a return shot that dislodged a shower of mortar in her face. She fired at the flash. The man slumped where he lay, his foot convulsed, and then he was limp.

Not believing what she had done, Jane picked herself up off the ground. She remembered the gas and covered her face again.

'Only smoke,' Yousaf said as she walked towards the bodies. 'Be careful.'

'Help me with these rifles; we can use them.' She prodded each body with the toe of her boot before bending down and retrieving their weapons.

'You shot very well,' Yousaf said in a strained voice.

'Beginner's luck. I should thank you for saving me. That was a good trick with the torch.'

'I do many year commando training. Many trainings… but you good fighter. Brave woman.' He wheezed as if talking through clenched teeth.

'Are you hurt?' Jane looked at him. She picked up the fallen torch.

'Only hit head on wall. I OK.' Yousaf said.

The lift door squealed as it began to close. 'Oh shit.' Jane ran forward and wedged a rifle in the doorway. If the doors didn't close, the lift wouldn't return. It would buy them some time.

* *

'We've got a few minutes head start.' Jane was panting as she and Yousaf caught up to Sergei and Razane, who had reached the grille. The cart and cylinders were still there, Billa wasn't.

'Can't say I blame him for taking off,' Jane said.

'I suppose,' Sergei grunted as he adjusted Razane's weight in his arms.

'Anyway, Yousaf can you help me lift the grille?' Jane said.

'I no can weld,' Yousaf said.

'I can. I'm an engineer…' Jane was rummaging through a

dirty cloth bag tied to the cart. 'If I… aah great…' She brandished a welding rod. 'That'll do the trick…'

It took all their strength to lift the door back into place.

'Serge, you're the slowest,' Jane was breathing heavily from the effort. 'Keep walking to the next grille. We'll be right behind you.'

'Good thinking, babe. By the way, you're fucking amazing.'

'I know.' Jane lit the flame and focused it.

* *

The fading daylight blinded them as they staggered out of the clinic into a world gone mad. Sirens blared, people ran in all directions in a mad panic. Someone was shouting through a loudspeaker. Two helicopters circled overhead, throwing up clouds of dust and making the clothes on the lines above them dance like mad.

'Yousaf, what's happening?' Sergei shifted Razane's weight in his arms.

The look in Yousaf's face told them everything they needed to know. They were being hunted.

'Come, we go to Uncle house.' He set off at a fast pace.

'What are they announcing?' Jane asked as she ran behind.

'Curfew. Order resident indoor and all visitor to mosque or army shoot on sight.'

A helicopter made a rapid turn and corkscrewed downwards. Sergei ducked under an awning. Jane followed. Yousaf kept running.

The chopper hovered momentarily and then flew on.

'Are you OK with Razane?' Jane said.

'My arms are about to fall off, but I'll be OK,' Sergei said through gritted teeth as they set off again.

Yousaf was banging on the door. It opened. 'Come, come, come.' He beckoned.

The helicopter made another pass. The loudspeaker blared

again. The rat-a-tat of machine gun fire sounded.

Sergei strained to increase his pace. They had another forty metres to go. Jane ran beside him, doing her best to support some of Razane's weight.

* *

Farooq Bhatti, Lahore's Corp Commander, looked out the side of the helicopter as the setting sun cast an orange glow onto the tightly packed rooftops of the walled city. The operation was going as planned. The six army units had deployed in record time. The curfew was in place and they had begun a house to house search.

In normal times escaped terrorists wouldn't have caused such a kerfuffle, but these weren't normal times. A new government had come to power. Their major foreign affairs policy was to move Pakistan from being a Yankee vassal to an independent state that acted in its own interests. Talks were underway to allow the Russians and Chinese to invest, and diplomats were urgently mending fences with India and Afghanistan.

It was a delicate balancing act. If the country moved too aggressively, the US would impose sanctions, freeze aid and cut off military supplies. If they showed timidity their new friends would baulk.

If Pakistan was seen helping the CIA torture prisoners, it would bring the whole thing crashing down. An even more pressing problem was the idiot US president. He was unhinged at the best of times. How would he react to them letting the most wanted person since Osama Bin Laden escape?

It was why the Prime Minister and the Chief of Army Staff had given him full authority to bring the situation under control. One of his brigades was encircling Lahore in a ring of steel. He had no doubt that the terrorist and their accomplices would be captured before *Maghreb* prayers.

RING OF STEEL

Lahore, Wednesday 10 January, 4:10 pm

The sound of soldiers running in lockstep echoed in the narrow alleyways. Any moment they'd be spotted. Sergei's lungs were on fire and he had lost all feeling in his arms. He held Razane with grim determination but had it not been for Jane helping him he'd have dropped her for sure. They were now twenty metres from the open door.

Bedlam surrounded them. A motorcycle engine raced. Men were shouting and running. It was followed by a volley of gunfire. Sergei nearly stumbled.

They staggered through the doorway. Yousaf slammed the door. Darkness descended. Sergei dropped to one knee and pulled Razane close. His heart threatened to pound out of his heaving chest. His tongue was like sandpaper. He began to cough.

'He needs water,' Jane gasped.

Farhana thrust a bottle at Sergei. Jane snatched it and put it to Sergei's lips as she knelt beside him. He swallowed and immediately coughed most of it on to Razane, who was beginning to stir. He took a deep breath before taking another sip.

Uncle shuffled out of his room. 'What happened, *beita*?'

'Help me up,' Sergei stood with Jane and Yousaf's help.

'Uncle, outside is curfew,' Yousaf said. 'We need help.'

'What was that gunshot?' Sergei said.

'Man on motorcycle... he no stop. Army *jawan* shoot.'

'Shit, was he OK?' Jane said but Yousaf had walked off with Uncle.

'We need to revive Razane,' Sergei said.

'Yes, yes, come with me,' Farhana led them to a bedroom. Sergei placed Razane gently on the bed.

'What is wrong with lady?' Farhana said.

'She's hurt,' Jane said.

'Oh no… she no have pants!' Farhana noticed Razane's bare legs, her hand flying to her mouth in shock. 'Wait, I bring.' She disappeared.

Jane pulled a blanket over Razane and herself. Sergei helped to tuck it under them. Jane pulled Razane close, stroked her hair and kissed her on the forehead. Razane's eyelids fluttered. A moan escaped her lips.

'Pass me the water,' Jane said.

'Let me do it. You hold her,' Sergei said.

Jane helped Razane into a half sitting position as Sergei trickled water through her parted lips.

'Here is apple juice, and cloths for lady,' Farhana returned. She placed the items on the foot of the bed and stood there, arms akimbo. 'Juice better than water for lady. Have sugar.'

The liquid and their tender ministrations seemed to have an effect. Razane stirred weakly, her moaning became louder, her hands jerked.

'She's coming to.' Tears were streaming down Jane's face. A few drops fell on Razane's cheek. She opened her eyes and stared at Jane. A moment passed in silence.

'How can…? Tell me you're real,' Razane's voice was hoarse. She reached out and touched Jane's face, and then Sergei's.

'We're real, sweetie… We…' Jane began weeping uncontrollably.

Wincing in pain, Razane pulled Sergei and Jane close. Tears erupted and streaked down her face before she broke into a weak smile. 'I never stopped… you two… how…?'

'Tell you later, first let's patch you up,' Sergei kissed her purple, bruised wrists, taking care to avoid the abraded skin.

'Oooh, they hurt.' Razane flinched but didn't pull away.

'I'm sorry,' Sergei stopped.

'No… don't stop… rubbing will restore the circulation.'

'Wait, I bring….' Farhana ran off again.

'Poor Farhana,' Jane said. 'We're making her very

uncomfortable.'

'Jane my love, you've coloured your beautiful hair?' Razane touched Jane's black tresses.

Yousaf and Uncle walked in, 'Uncle says we need to leave fast. On mosque loudspeaker they announce house to house searching.'

'But where? And how?' Sergei stood. Farhana returned with a bowl of warm water and some bandages. She sat next to Razane and began to wash her wrists.

'How happen?'

'Bad man kidnapped her and tied her hands,' Jane said, watching as Farhana expertly tended to Razane's wounds. She picked up the *shalwar kameez* Farhana had brought and stood up. 'Guys, can you please leave the room while I help Razane dress?'

'Uncle, what we do now?' Yousaf sounded desperate as they walked out.

'We need to think through our options,' Sergei said, 'and not panic.'

'I face firing squad.' Yousaf's voice rose a few octaves. 'How to not panic.'

'We either stay or leave. If we—'

'You cannot leave with the army outside,' Uncle said. 'They will shoot on sight. No questions.'

'So either leave without them seeing us or hide so they can't find us.'

'Where to stay? Army will find. They have dogs,' Yousaf was sweating profusely.

'Does this house have a basement?' Sergei leaned against the wall. Exhaustion was catching up to him.

'No good. Army will check basement.'

'The lady in the clinic said something about newer tunnels,' Sergei said, 'they were used for smuggling alcohol.'

'Yes I remember,' Yousaf said.

'Yes, I know about the newer tunnels but...' Uncle ran his finger through his white hair. 'The authorities sealed them shut... and we do not have a basement.'

'The clinic lady said they had to block the new tunnel themselves...' Sergei said.

'Hmmm, that makes sense. You can never trust authorities. They are corrupt. Maybe they only blocked some and embezzled the rest of the money.'

'But why go to the trouble? Were they still being used by smugglers?' Sergei said.

'No, not being used. For many years no one understood why sandbags did not stop floodwaters from the Ravi. Eventually someone remembered the tunnel network and worked it out. Lahore's authorities got a grant from UNESCO to seal them. But... it seems they left a few...' He shook his head. 'It is very typical!'

'If only we could find an open tunnel,' Sergei scratched his scalp as he tried to think. He hadn't showered in a while and was itchy all over.

'Oh, oh, oh!' Uncle let out a shout, a faraway look in his eyes. 'I remember a story in the newspaper about a developer arrested for illegally demolishing an old house to build a shopping centre. They were digging the basement when the police arrested the developer and the site supervisor. They had discovered a tunnel opening while excavating and tried to escape through them but... they got stuck in the mud.'

'Oh, yes, I also remember news,' Yousaf said, grabbing his uncle by the arm in his excitement. 'That is near here.'

'The tunnel would still be there,' Uncle said.

'How can you be sure?' Sergei said, wondering if it was the break they needed.

'I have walked past the building site many times. It is sealed off with tape because of the court case.'

'So where is it?' Sergei said.

'Not far.' Uncle's face fell. '*Beita*, sorry I got you excited for nothing. It is too far with the army outside.' He shook his head. 'You will be caught.'

Sergei had a thought. 'Uncle, how long ago did you move into this house?'

'*Beita,* only fifteen years ago.'

'Was it also used for prostitution? I mean before…'

'*Beita,* they all were.'

'Then are you sure there's no tunnel under this house? Have you checked?'

'Oh-hoh *beita,* like I said. This house has no basement. How can it have a tunnel?'

Just then Jane walked in. She looked around at their faces. 'What's going on?'

Sergei turned to her, defeat writ large on his face. 'It's bloody hopeless… How's Razane?'

'She's weak and she can't use her hands. I tried massaging her wrists, but she's in extreme pain and couldn't tolerate it. I think her circulation got blocked; maybe there's nerve damage…' Jane shook her head. 'So what are we doing about getting out of here?'

'There's no basement under this house… so no tunnel.'

'Why a tunnel again?'

'We have no other options. The army has a curfew and are doing a house to house search.'

'Yeah, but how come the tunnels…? Won't they be crawling with soldiers by now?'

'I'm talking about the newer smuggler's tunnels. They are supposed to be separate.'

'But we know nothing about them. Where they go… if they go anywhere at all.'

'True, but it's our only chance. Even if they're blocked, at least we could hide there till the soldiers leave.'

'And what if they follow us down there?'

'Babe, can you think of a better plan?'

Jane clenched and unclenched her fists. 'I can't either… OK the tunnels then.'

Sergei exhaled slowly. 'That's the problem, this house hasn't any.'

'How do you know?'

'What?'

'That there's no tunnel here.'

'Uncle said so. He oughta know.'

'What if it's in the other half?'

'What... other half?'

'This house looks subdivided. Didn't you notice? It's twice the size from outside. In here it's tiny...'

'Yes, Jane *beiti* is right.' Uncle nodded. 'The other half belong to my neighbour. That is the partition wall to subdivide it.' The old man shuffled over and pointed.

'Do you know if he has basement?' Yousaf said.

'How would I know *beita*?' Uncle said. 'Subdivision was done before we bought.'

'We've no other options,' Sergei said. 'We have to check.'

'I cannot ask him. He is not living there.'

'How was the subdivision done?' Jane said. 'No, forget it. Let me have a look.' She ran off.

'I don't know these things.' The old man said. He looked pale. 'I have to sit down.'

Jane returned in a few minutes, all out of breath. 'I think I found a way into the neighbour's place. Come with me.'

Sergei and Yousaf followed her to an upstairs bedroom.

'On the ground floor they bricked up the doorways between the two halves. For some reason, in this room they locked the interconnecting door and built a wardrobe in front. Maybe to save bricks or who knows?'

Sergei parted the hanging clothes and examined the door at the back. Its handle had been removed. He pushed against it. It wouldn't budge.

Jane removed the clothes and placed them on the bed.

Sergei gave the door a few kicks before the lock gave way. The door opened into a similar wardrobe. This one was empty. Sergei pushed its doors open to reveal a dark room.

Sergei removed the torch from his pocket. 'Let's find ourselves a tunnel.'

Yousaf stepped forward. 'Wait Sergei, you and Jane bring Razane. I find tunnel.'

**

Razane was whimpering in pain, but her face lit up when Sergei and Jane entered. 'My loves, have you found a way?' Her voice was weak.

'Yousaf has gone down to the basement next door to check. We need to go after him.'

Razane sat up with difficulty and swung her legs over the side. Jane and Sergei rushed to help her.

'Please mind my wrists. They hurt really bad.'

'Of course,' Sergei kissed her on the cheek.

Farhana walked in carrying a tray with tea and sandwiches; Yousaf's uncle followed behind.

'I am so sorry we have to go,' Jane said.

'Go pack them, *beiti*,' Uncle said. 'They cannot wait.'

'Oh, yes, yes.' Farhana rushed off.

'Let me carry you,' Sergei said to Razane. 'It'll be quicker till we get to the tunnel, then you can try to walk.'

Razane was too weak to argue. She smiled at him. 'My knight in shining armour.'

Jane scooped up their rifles and followed Sergei and Razane up the stairs.

Farhana rushed to catch up. She thrust a thermos and a plastic bag at Jane, 'For you.'

'Thank you so much, Farhana *Baji*.' Jane gave her a hug. 'Thank Uncle for us.'

Farhana watched as they disappeared through the door in the back of the wardrobe.

Jane closed the door, and the room was plunged into darkness. She shone her torch around. The room was bare except for thick curtains that blocked the outside. Jane tried the light switch; there was no power.

'I'll try to light the way,' Jane said, 'just be careful not to trip over anything.'

'There's nothing to trip over, the house is empty.' Sergei

said as he followed Jane down the stairs. The house was silent and smelt musty and closed. Hopefully Yousaf had found the basement and a tunnel.

Like its neighbour, the ground floor had four large rooms in a line. Each opened into a passage that ran along the front of the house. Jane shone the torch into each one. They were empty with no signs of a basement.

'We haven't come across a kitchen yet. The clinic's basement was through the kitchen,' Jane said as she opened the last door.

* *

The second needle hurt far less than the first. Major Amjad's face was already going numb.

'Consider yourself fortunate I did not order them to stitch you up without a local anaesthetic. You deserved that. I have been too soft… But that can change.' The colonel droned on.

The colonel's rant gave him a headache that no painkiller could erase. That was the real problem with the ISI, bad leadership. The colonel was happy to give him autonomy and take credit when things went well. The minute the shit hit the fan all responsibility went straight back to him, the underling.

'Why the fuck did you agree to do the CIA's dirty work…? And now… all the jihadi groups will be on our backs… stepping up attacks, and, and… all because of what…? You damn idiot!' The vein on the colonel's forehead was pulsating furiously. 'Our leaders are questioning your soundness. They want you replaced. You know what that means? Most likely they doubt me too.'

'But sir. You said so many times. We need to get more CIA agents here… so that we can learn their secrets…' Amjad was trying to think on his feet. 'It was not for personal gain… trust me.'

'You gave our top brass reason to doubt me.' The colonel ignored him and droned on. 'A reason to fuck me in the arse. Well, I tell you this fucking will happen to you.' He walked around in a circle looking for something to punch. 'You better find the woman and get the CIA out of the country or... God cannot help you.'

The nurse began stitching the major's face, her expression impassive. The anaesthetic was working. He felt nothing except for a tightness.

'Sir, if you relax your face, it will be easier,' the nurse said sympathetically. He smiled at her. Maybe she understood how it felt to be fucked in the arse.

'I am going back to my office. When you are stitched up... come straight there with a plan to fix this.'

* *

The quiet was punctured by the sound of soldiers running outside in the street. Orders were being shouted. Jane's heart skipped a beat as the empty house reverberated to a loud knocking followed by a jiggling of the front door handle.

A loud booming voice shouted in Urdu. Jane only recognised one word, *kholo*. It meant open. All the while the banging continued nonstop.

'Hurry,' Jane whispered. 'They'll be inside in minutes.'

The kitchen was empty save for an ancient fridge in a corner. A door at the back gave them hope. Jane ran and opened it; a staircase led downwards. 'You go first,' she said. 'I'll shine the torch for you, but be careful.'

'My love, let me walk,' Razane said. 'Please.'

'OK,' Sergei grunted as he put her down.

Razane was unsteady but stayed upright. 'I'm just a little dizzy... that's all.' She attempted to smile.

Jane watched him as Sergei helped Razane down the stairs. She closed the door behind her and followed. The sounds of knocking had stopped. The silence lingered before it was shattered by a resounding thump, followed by two more. The soldiers were trying to break down the door.

Jane shone her torch around the cramped L shaped

basement. Bricks lined the floor and walls; concrete beams and slabs covered the ceiling. A few rusted bits of metal lay in a heap in a corner. Apart from the stairs, the only opening in the walls was a large fireplace. Yousaf was nowhere.

'Where is he?' Jane tried hard to quell her rising panic.

'What the...?' Sergei was on his knees examining the fireplace. He looked up. 'I can stand in here. He shone his torch into a hole a metre off the ground. 'There's like a narrow tunnel here large enough for a person to crawl through. That's where Yousaf must have gone.'

Jane looked. 'We've no choice. But how will Razane manage?'

'I'll go first and pull her,' Sergei said.

Fear coursed through them like an electric current as a crash, much louder than the others, shook the house.

'I think they're inside. Hurry!' Jane whispered.

Sergei crawled feet first into the space. Jane helped Razane up into the tunnel.

'I hope you're not claustrophobic, darling,' she said as Razane disappeared into the chimney.

Jane waited for Sergei to pull Razane in before she grabbed the rifles and followed. Above them the sounds of men running and shouting slowly receded as they crawled deeper.

* *

'Careful!' Yousaf's warning was too late. Sergei fell. It was a short drop, but the landing jarred his tail bone. The tunnel had ended in a small space barely tall enough for them to stand in. Yousaf helped Sergei up. 'Very sorry I no warn you. I looking way out.'

'That's fine.' Sergei helped Razane and then Jane out of the tunnel. Yousaf continued examining the brick walls. It seemed futile. They were in a space with no exit except for where they had come from.

Jane shone the torch on the floor and ceiling. They were both dirt. She carefully examined the brick walls as she shook her head in frustration.

Razane watched as she leaned against Sergei. 'It's a dead end.' Her voice was weak. 'I feel… faint.'

CAUGHT IN A VICE

The anaesthetic was wearing off at the worst time. Major Amjad almost passed out from the habitual head-check as he merged with the peak hour crawl. He opened his mouth to scream but his face felt like it was being ripped apart. His eyes watered in pain, turning the headlights of the approaching cars into a dazzling monotone kaleidoscope.

He wiped the tears with a tissue. Even his eye socket throbbed. He took the strip of codeine tablets from his top pocket and put four in his mouth. The maximum recommended dosage was two every four hours, but the pain was unbearable. He swallowed them dry and tried to compose himself.

The nurse had told him to wait in the hospital for at least an hour in case of a bad reaction. He couldn't think of a worse one than the sledgehammers and blowtorches that attacked his face. He also couldn't afford to wait that long. Otherwise, he would need more anaesthetic for what the colonel would do to him.

The bloody foreigners and Yousaf, the traitorous bastard, had turned out smarter than he had expected. Instead of walking into a trap, they had found a way in through the tunnels.

After the attack on the World Trade Centre, the ISI had been approached by the CIA to help in their extraordinary rendition program. They needed a small facility to keep the captives apart from the general prison population. The dungeons under Lahore's famous Mughal-era fort were considered ideal.

The ISI's top brass had wanted the tunnels filled with concrete, but the cost would have been prohibitive. They would not have been able to get the funds and keep the program secret.

Pragmatism won the day. The tunnels were inspected and found to have collapsed in many places. The civil authorities already had blocked the tunnels for safety reasons with iron grates.

The dungeons were for all intents and purposes impregnable. Just to be sure, the ISI got contractors to add a few more grilles near the dungeon. That was more to satisfy the CIA than for any real reason.

The fact that the foreigners had accessed the tunnels meant that tunnels had been repaired, and the grilles were not there or they had found a way to cut them.

The only organisation interested in, and capable of, unblocking the tunnels was the Lahore Heritage Society. Over the years it had become famous for restoring Lahore's walled city to its former glory. Flush with UNESCO money, it was constantly trying to access the Fort's dungeons and had even taken the ISI to court.

Now the worst had happened. The world's most wanted terrorist had escaped, and an American and five army commandos were dead. The ISI were a laughing-stock and he, the illustrious Major Amjad, was in the biggest shit hole he had ever been in.

He took a turn onto Lawrence Road. The colonel would be waiting and he had nothing new for him. The reaming would be most unpleasant. He sighed as he dialled a number.

'Sebastian.' The voice was curt.

'It's me, Amjad. Thanks for sending the cavalry and having me rescued.'

'Yup… Good you turned on the video feed…'

'I was hoping the Australians would let me lead them to you but—'

'You know Mike's dead?' Sebastian said.

'Yes. Ya… I am most terribly sorry.' He felt like kicking himself for not having opened with condolences. 'He was a good man.' He offered. There was no response. Maybe Sebastian didn't think so. Honestly, neither did he. Still, it was always polite to talk nice about the dead. 'I have set up a task force to catch them. I need all the help you can give me.'

'Sure, whaddya need?'

* *

'Meester Ian Mearns pleeess report to Airport Security,' the heavily accented voice said over the tinny sounding loudspeaker.

Ian groaned. Turning off his phone early had helped nothing. They'd still found him, the bastards.

He shouldered his carry-on bag and walked out of the lounge.

'Ian Mearns.' He showed the burly security chap his passport. 'Someone paged me.'

'Yes, Mr Mearns. A message from Mrs Angela to turn on your phone. She want to call you.' The man was extraordinarily courteous for someone in airport security.

'Thank you.'

Earlier, while checking in, he'd had an odd feeling; he wasn't leaving Pakistan that soon, even though he wanted to. Bugger! He waited for his phone to boot up.

* *

Major Amjad shivered as he walked like a zombie out into the ISI Lahore HQ car park. The wind's vicious bite was finding its way through every opening in his clothes. He was covered from head to toe in goosebumps. He wrapped his scarf around his throat and zipped up his leather jacket. He had forgotten where he had parked his car. All the white Toyota Corollas looked the same and the car park was full. On normal days most people left around six. Today everyone was on tenterhooks; no one in Pakistan's history had ever broken a high-profile prisoner out of an ISI interrogation centre. The consequences would shake the organisation to its core. Heads would roll and no one wanted to be out of the office when the bloodletting began.

He fumbled in his pocket for his keys. His hands shook as he repeatedly pressed the remote, his eyes scanning for a flash. He found his car towards the back near the gate and walked over to it.

The leather jacket wasn't helping the cold. His shivering became more uncontrollable and compounded his headache. His face hurt even more. All he wanted was to go home and go to bed but that wouldn't happen tonight.

The conversation with the colonel had been the most uncomfortable of his career. His head still rang from shouted insults hurled at him.

'Why the fuck did you take the Wafaa intelligence to the *Amreekis* before your own leadership? Who died and made you the mother-fucking General? This is not your fucking decision to make you *bahin chodd*.'

In response, his mind had frozen, and he had been unable to think of a plausible excuse.

'If the woman is not caught you get the firing squad. If the *Amreekis* get her first, you still get the firing squad. You find her or you get the fucking firing squad…' The colonel's voice had risen in a crescendo. 'Now get the fuck out of my fucking office you fucking monkey's son.'

How quickly he had gone from a favoured star to a pariah. The colonel had been his biggest supporter as he had moved against Hamdani and his men. All that was forgotten. Now the man was suddenly his fiercest critic. The only consolation, he was probably getting an even worse ass-fucking from his boss.

* *

The army had commandeered a four-storey restaurant on Food Street on the edge of the walled city. It overlooked the magnificent Badshahi Mosque, resplendent under floodlights.

Amjad showed the guard his security pass and waited for him to move the mobile barrier aside.

Sebastian waved from afar and came rushing over.

'You look terrible. What happened?'

For a second Amjad resisted telling him. The ignominy of having his face rearranged by a woman was almost more painful than the physical damage. 'The woman, Jane, caught me off guard.'

'We're not dealing with ordinary people here.' There was no judgement or gloating in Sebastian's tone. 'Mike had his throat cut and five ISI men were killed. Their weapons were taken.'

'Yes, I know... Again... sorry about Mike.'

'Yup,' Sebastian shook his head. 'But you know... this will have consequences.'

'What do you mean consequences?' Amjad was beginning to colour, his tone sharp. It was one thing for his boss to threaten him, another for an American.

'There's gonna be ummm... Questions will be asked. I saw a Tweet from our president. He's accusing Pakistan of orchestrating Wafaa's escape.'

'What?' Amjad's voice was shrill. He clenched his fists. 'Your president is a fucking dog with no brains. I gave you —'

'Don't get all twisted about it. We know our president's a loose cannon. But it's about politics and he's gonna find a scapegoat and it's not gonna be the US.'

Amjad shook his head. Had the colonel known about the Tweet? It might have explained his severe reaction.

'Look Amjad, we'll all come out of this if we work together and catch them fast.'

A car beeped its horn. Sebastian waved at someone. Amjad turned to look. 'That's Ian Mearns, ASIS,' Sebastian said to Amjad. 'He's working with us too.'

Amjad waved to the guard to let him in.

This was turning into an even bigger disaster. It was bad enough to have an American looking over his shoulder. He did not need an Australian as well. Did the colonel know? Should he text the colonel to ask his advice? Some contrition and arse kissing might serve him well. Just then his phone beeped; it was the colonel. 'Allow Ian Mearns and Sebastian Cole to assist. But stay in control.'

SOUTHBOUND

Wyndham, WA, Wednesday 10 January, 10:00 pm

Najib had been on difficult journeys before. Being confined in that tiny cavity on Peter's boat was hard, but this was harder. Their hiding spot was just above the prime mover's rear wheels. With no insulation his ears were continuously assaulted by gear whine and tyre roar. On stretches of dirt road pebble showers added to the din, then there was the shaking and vibration. Despite the foam padding, after a few hours they were all covered in bruises.

At least Peter was true to his word about not letting them die. Their first stop was outside the small town of Timber Creek in a deserted truck stop by the side of the road. The town's lights glimmering in the distance were too far away to prevent almost complete darkness. Even the side lights along the trailers did little else but illuminate the ground below them. It was as if the darkness out here had more power than the light. With help from Peter's crew Najib and his men climbed out to relieve themselves.

'Don't wander into the bushes,' Peter snapped at a man who had entered a copse of tall shrubs, in search of privacy. 'I can't afford to lose you to snakes. And we're all men here.'

After a quick cup of tea and a small block of chocolate-covered sponge cake with coconut flakes on top, the men returned to their hiding spots and the journey resumed.

As the hours wore on, they made their way first east and then south. Najib tried to sleep, but he had been sitting too long and it was too noisy and uncomfortable. Dawn was breaking in the eastern sky at their next stop. He was groggy and disoriented and almost tripped and fell while climbing out of the shipping container.

'Take care. We can't afford injuries, brother,' Peter shouted.

Najib looked around; the world still moved even though he stood on firm ground. He had motion sickness from the bumpy ride, something he didn't get on the boat. 'The moon has more people.' He shook his head as he spoke. Till now they hadn't seen a single local inhabitant apart from Peter and their guides. He took the cup of tea but waved away the sandwich.

It was mid-morning at their next stop. The sun shone brightly in the deepest bluest sky he had ever seen. The earth was a rich rust colour sparsely dotted with grey-green grasses and dry knee-high shrubs. The two-lane road stretched as straight as an arrow towards the horizon.

'How far does it go like this for?' Najib asked Peter.

'Around two thousand kilometres more.' Peter smiled.

'How many of us will be alive by then?' Najib said. He was only half joking; he hadn't slept since the storm and was in a strange state between wakefulness and sleep. His body shook from exhaustion but nervous energy and a throbbing headache kept him from relaxing into sleep. His men were no better with most walking around like zombies. Haziq sat slumped on the ground, the cup of tea in his hand almost spilling over.

Peter handed out Valium pills after they were safely back in their hiding places. The drug worked wonders. Najib only realised he had fallen asleep when he was woken by a metallic banging sound from outside. Someone opened the hatch to reveal a night sky.

The sleep had freshened him and more importantly cured his headache, but he now felt sick from hunger.

He climbed out with his men. Like last time, they were parked in a lonely truck stop by the side of the road, far from civilisation.

Each of them was given half a loaf of bread and a full roast chicken. It was the first proper meal Najib had in two days. He gobbled it down and belched in satisfaction. 'Thank you. That was good. I needed it.' He took the can of Pepsi Peter offered him and gulped it down. 'Thank Allah,' He burped louder this time.

'I had a friend from Bahrain who used to burp like that,'

Peter said. 'He used to tell me it was his way of saying thank you.'

'Phew, I will just say thank you.' Najib smiled uneasily; he had eaten too fast and was finding it hard to keep the food down.

'You men should walk around the trucks for a bit and then we need to continue. We have only come halfway on our journey.'

PARALLEL PATHS

Lahore, Wednesday 10 January, 7:30 pm

Lieutenant General Bhatti's orders had a near-magical effect. Within an hour the rooftop of the famous four-storey Cuckoo Restaurant had been converted into a field office that overlooked both the old walled city and the Mughal era Badshahi Mosque. The ornately carved walnut chairs and tables had been pushed to one side. In their place were two large desks, communication equipment, large monitors and docking stations for laptops. A tarp covered the makeshift command centre and electric heaters blew warm air into the space.

'OK gentlemen, welcome to your new temporary office,' Major Amjad said. He was on his third double dose of codeine in as many hours and was testing the drug company's claims about it making people drowsy. 'My testicles are on the line so we need to get straight down to business.'

'I'm glad they are.' Sebastian stepped back from the edge of the roof where he'd been observing the army units as they searched the walled city. 'By the way, that's an impressive sight.'

'Our military always puts on a good show.' Major Amjad pulled up a chair and sat at the larger of the two desks. Ian and Sebastian joined him. 'Let's examine the facts.'

'Sure, let's…' Ian said.

'First, they came and left through the tunnels.'

'Yes—' Sebastian was interrupted by the shuffling of feet. He turned around.

Captain Usman had arrived carrying an armful of paper rolls. He put them down and saluted. 'Sorry I am late, sir.' He drew up a chair.

'Have you found the plans?' the major said.

'Yes sir, I just came from the municipal archives. Most of the tunnels were surveyed. The large printout I have here shows all the known tunnels. Can I show you?' He said as he rolled them out.

'Yes, go!'

'These blue lines are the old tunnels. They connect the fort to the walled city. These green... they are new tunnels that connect the walled city to the river and beyond. Any dotted lines like here and here, they ummm represent cave-ins. Everything is apparently open.'

'Bloody hell,' Sebastian pointed at a spot at the centre of the fort. 'Is this the Interrogation Centre?'

'Yes... Yes, it is.' Major Amjad looked embarrassed.

Sebastian shook his head. 'This is fucked... These tunnels are all open! Damn it man... we brought our highest value prisoner... to a place with the security of a... fucking public library.'

Major Amjad could feel the anger rising. As he sat back in his chair, his mind was in turmoil, trying to think of something with which to hit back but nothing came to mind. The problem was that the bastard American had a point.

'Wait, sir, look at this,' Captain Usman rolled out another printout with a flourish. It showed only the tunnels under the Fort. 'These maps from two years ago show the tunnels were blocked. Someone—'

'Fucking bastards,' the major stood. 'Wait till I get my hands on whoever did this.' The major clenched his fists as he stared at the map. He would bury them in the tunnels they had opened.

'Closing the gate after the horse has bolted,' Sebastian said.

'Captain, who opened the tunnels?' Major Amjad ignored Sebastian.

'Sir, I asked, but they were only clerks, they did not know.'

'We will deal with them later,' the major said. 'First, tell me where the foreigners went.'

'We brought in sniffer dogs and they led us to this clinic.' The captain jabbed a finger on the map. 'We also found a man wandering in the tunnel. He told us some foreigners paid him to cut steel grilles along the way.'

'It still sounds bizarre; how easily outsiders can just waltz in here…' Sebastian ground his teeth.

Ian cleared his throat. 'Is the location of the tunnels common knowledge?'

'The locals know there are tunnels, but believe they are sealed up.'

'Yeah, but these guys knew the tunnels went to your dungeon,' Ian said.

'Aah, yes,' the major sighed heavily as he wiped his brow with a tissue. 'I am afraid we have a traitor to blame for that. Captain Yousaf is working with them. He has been to the Interrogation Centre and would have seen the entrance to the tunnels from the lower level.'

'So was this planned beforehand?' Ian fired back.

'No, how… why do you say…?'

'It just seems too convenient,' Sebastian said. 'We bring Wafaa here on your request. Two days later these guys show up. They know where Wafaa is and how to get her out.' Sebastian shook his head and looked at Ian who cocked his eyebrows and grimaced. 'You know what our president thinks of your—?'

'If that is true, why would I bring the intelligence to Mike?' Amjad's neck was becoming as red as a plum yet he sounded pained. 'Believe me, gentlemen, we also can kidnap someone on foreign soil.'

'I believe Amjad,' Ian said steepling his hands. 'The ISI are incompetent and were outmatched by someone far more sophisticated… but let's stop bickering. We're wasting time.'

The major clenched his fists as he glowered at Ian. He said as he waved to an orderly standing to attention at the top of the stairs. 'Bring us all tea and something to eat… samosas and cake.'

'Let's just agree to be straight with each other from now on,' Ian said.

'I am straight,' Major Amjad said. 'But you tell me… What is an Australian spy doing in Pakistan?'

Ian took a deep breath and looked at the three men, 'I was

asked to keep an eye on Razane's, I mean, Wafaa's associates.'

'So did you learn anything?'

'Actually, yeah. We followed them to Waziristan. They stopped for a night at an army base—'

'What?' The major got up off his seat. A bolt of pain shot through his face making his head spin. He sat down and, with some effort, grabbed a bottle of water. He unscrewed the cap with shaking hands and took a few sips.

'Take it easy, man. Your stitches are oozing.' Sebastian grimaced at him.

'The army base, what army base?' The water had helped. His nausea was settling.

Ian pulled up a map on his phone and showed him.

'Shit,' the major said. 'That damn bastard, Yousaf. Wait till I...'

'Why don't you tell us about this Yousaf. Why is he working for the enemy?' Sebastian said, 'but... ummm... let Ian finish first.'

'That's all I have,' Ian said. 'I was told to return to Lahore.'

'Yeah, we got your report and checked reconnaissance aircraft footage. We didn't have to look hard. A small group including Sergei and Jane was observed heading from that army base through the Shawal valley into Afghanistan. A day later they retraced their steps. I'm curious what the fuck they were doing. Sebastian turned to look at the major. 'Any thoughts?'

'I think it is very obvious,' the major said. 'They were making contact with someone in their organisation.'

'Why there?'

'Afghanistan is like the UN for terror groups. Al Qaeda, Islamic State, the Taliban, Lashkar-e-Taiba all operate there.' The major said. 'New groups form all the time. Many only communicate in person. They have learnt the hard way that electronic signals emanating in a backward region always gets unwanted attention.'

Sebastian nodded. 'Yeah, well. It's plausible.'

'What I can't understand—' Ian began but stopped when

the major put up his hand.

The orderly had brought them their tea, which he set on the table. He began laying out the cups and saucers but stopped when Captain Usman put up his hand.

'Thank you. Leave it.' The captain got up to pour the tea himself.

Major Amjad waited for the orderly to retreat. 'Let us focus for a moment on the present. Our fugitives are somewhere in this cordon.' He swept his arm expansively to indicate the walled city below.

'Are you sure?'

'We had the whole walled city surrounded within fifteen minutes of hearing the gunshots in the dungeon. It was the first thing we did.'

'That's impressive for any army. Captain Usman, I'm impressed. How did you manage it?' Ian said.

'That was me,' Sebastian said. 'I called Langley, Langley called the president. He called your prime minister and so on…'

'Aaah, that explains things.' The major made a sour expression.

'So how do we keep them here?' Ian voiced what they all were thinking.

'They are only leaving here two ways, in chains or body bags,' the major said.

Ian shook his head. 'While it seems unlikely they'll escape, I wouldn't bet my house on it. They're resourceful buggers…' He stabbed his finger at one of the maps. 'Tell me, how are the new tunnels different from the old ones?'

'They were used in the sixties to smuggle alcohol and for people to escape police raids. The walled city was a hub of prostitution for the whole Punjab,' the major said.

'Shouldn't we consider them?' Ian said. 'I mean, if they used the tunnels to enter the fort why wouldn't they use 'em to escape?' Ian said.

Major Amjad leaned forward and studied the map. 'You have a point, but it is less likely. The old tunnels were built properly. They have historic significance so some conservation trust or heritage society is always talking about restoring and reopening them.' He took a breath; his pain medication was wearing off. 'The new tunnels were makeshift and so prone to collapsing that they undermined the city. Ever since they were dug there has been a push to fill them in. Many residents blocked the entrances to the new tunnels in their basements. They fill up with water every rainy season and would be muddy and most probably impassable.'

Sebastian sucked on a tooth. 'Still, let's not disregard it. All our asses are in a sling, if they get away.'

'Sir, I have just searched for tunnels through the news archives from the last five years,' Captain Usman said.

'Yes, and?'

'There is one entrance still open. It was found while they were digging to build a new shopping plaza.' The captain docked his laptop and duplicated his screen on a sixty-inch monitor that dwarfed the desk it sat on.

'Well done, Captain,' Sebastian got up and studied the grainy images on the screen. He walked over to the map table. 'Captain, can you show me where this is on this map.'

'There!' the captain pointed.

'That's on the main loop which leads out of the walled city,' Ian said.

'Good work, let's get some men down there.' The major picked up his phone and dialled a number.

* *

The absolute darkness gave the muffled sounds above them a menacing quality. The soldiers were taking far longer than was warranted by the size of the house. It meant they were searching every nook and cranny.

'They'll enter the basement, eventually.' The shrill note in Jane's voice telegraphed her fear. 'What do we do then?'

'What we can do?' Yousaf said.

'No way am I surrendering,' Jane said.

'If they have gas or flamethrowers?' Yousaf said.

'I agree with Jane,' Razane said softly. 'I'd rather die.'

'Yup, me too,' Sergei said. 'Yousaf you can give yourself up. Tell them we forced you.'

'No I stay. Major Amjad no believe. He will torture most badly.'

'Are we sure there's no way out of here?' Sergei said.

Yousaf flashed his torch around the space. 'You see way?'

'I wonder what this space was used for?' Jane flashed her torch around too.

'A good question,' Sergei adjusted his position so he could support Razane better.

'Thank you,' she whispered as she put her head against his shoulder.

Sergei stroked her hair and kissed her neck. 'Don't despair, we're not dead yet.'

Jane stood and began examining the walls. Sergei shone his torch to add to the light as he sat and watched Jane.

'Have you thought how fresh the air is for such a small space?' Sergei said.

'Hmmm, true.' Jane was examining the brick wall. 'They've used clay as mortar.' She used her knife to scratch some of it away. 'There are quite a few gaps in the brick; I can feel a breeze.'

'I wonder if we're actually in the tunnel,' Sergei said. 'It doesn't look like a tunnel because of this brick wall.'

Yousaf stood and looked closely at the mortar between the bricks. 'Yes is possible.'

'It would actually make more sense than a secret room in the basement.' Razane said.

'Smuggler tunnel very illegal. People make them hard to find.' Yousaf pointed at the tunnel they had crawled through.

'I don't follow.' Sergei looked at where Yousaf pointed.

'If you think about it, the narrow connecting tunnel we just crawled through was easy to hide inside the fireplace and a perfect way to hide the much bigger tunnel. That connecting tunnel would not prevent anyone pulling a crate of whisky from the tunnel into the basement.'

'Yeah OK then but why brick it up like this instead of simply blocking the small tunnel?'

'Maybe the owners were hedging their bets that they'd need the tunnel again and it's easier to break down a large brick partition wall than it is to re-excavate a narrow tunnel.'

'Hmmm, any ideas on how to break down this wall?' Sergei kicked at it repeatedly. Yousaf joined him, but even together their efforts had no effect.

'You'll hurt yourselves,' Jane said calmly. 'It'll come down easy with a little mind power.' Jane was smiling.

'Good we have an engineer… How?'

'Like this,' Jane worked the knife into the clay above the top course of bricks. The clay was wet and came away in chunks.

'You're a genius,' Sergei said. He took out his knife and joined her. Within a few minutes, they had created a gap above the brick wall along its length.

'Now let's try to loosen the top row,' Jane said.

'Let me do,' Yousaf said, taking the knife from her. Both he and Sergei scraped the mortar away. Sergei lifted a brick and lay it on the ground.

'*Ya Allah*,' Yousaf said as he did the same.

While Sergei worked on loosening the mortar along the second row, Yousaf piled the bricks on the ground.

'I'm gonna buy us some time,' Jane said as she pushed a brick lengthwise into the connecting tunnel as far as her arm could reach. She followed it with more, using handfuls of mud to fix them into place and close gaps around them.

'My love, that's so clever,' Razane whispered as she observed Jane. 'I wish I could help.'

'Don't worry, this is easy,' Jane said panting.

By the time she had finished she had laid three courses, end to end.

'I can make a wall faster than you two can break one,' Jane

smiled as she plugged mud into the remaining holes.

Sergei and Yousaf had pulled off six rows from the top, but the wall was still too high for them to climb over, especially for Razane.

A metallic sound startled them. Jane put her ear to the plug of bricks she had built. The sound came from the other end of the connecting tunnel. A gruff voice shouted something in Urdu. It was muffled but scarily close.

Yousaf put his hand to lips and switched off his torch. 'They find basement.'

With a quick look at her handiwork Jane switched her torch off. Sergei did too, plunging them into darkness.

Had she sealed it off convincingly enough? Would they be able to break through? Had she used enough mud? Her questions were answered as two tiny rays of light shone through small gaps in her newly constructed wall. She picked up two lumps of clay and plugged them, plunging their space into darkness again.

After what seemed like an eternity, the voices receded. Yousaf had his ear against Jane's freshly laid bricks. 'I think they gone.'

Sergei switched on his torch. 'OK, then let's keep working. Just quietly.'

'You hand me the bricks; I'll put them on the ground,' Jane said as she placed her torch in her pocket and turned it on. It provided enough light for them to see what they were doing. 'That way we'll be as quiet as possible.'

'I really wish I could help,' Razane whispered.

'You just rest sweetie.' Jane crouched beside her and kissed her forehead.

Sergei and Yousaf began working on the wall again. Jane took each brick and made a neat pile in front of the tunnel, placing the bricks as quietly as she was able. Each layer would make the job of any pursuers harder. She tried listening every so often but heard nothing more.

Sergei and Yousaf had progressed down to chest height. The remaining bricks were now loose and crumbly and easier to remove.

Within minutes they had removed enough to walk through. The dark tunnel stretched before them.

'You putting those bricks into the little tunnel is why we're walking out of here,' Sergei said as he gave Jane a squeeze.

'Yes, Jane Madam, full respect to you.' Yousaf shook his head in vigorous agreement.

Sergei crouched next to Razane. She was leaning against the wall, her breathing laboured. He put his arms around her and gently picked her up. 'My poor girl,' he whispered as he held her in his arms. Her hair covered part of his face. She was light as a feather but his arms had almost no strength left.

'Hey Serge, we can go faster if I walk.'

'Can you walk?'

'Let me try. I need to get my circulation going.'

Sergei put her down gently. 'Please tell if you can't manage.'

'Sure. Just help me through tight spots.' Razane stood unsteadily waiting for the dizziness to abate.

'Of course.' Sergei squeezed her gently.

DANK

Ian stepped up to the orange tape and stared into the tunnel entrance. Around him the pit the size of a tennis court and the depth of a three-storey building was buzzing with activity. According to the major it had been dug to lay the foundations for a shopping centre. Incorrect permits had stopped construction.

He curled his nose at the dank smell emanating from the tunnel and shivered as he watched his breath fog up. An army tech was setting up a floodlight to illuminate the tunnel entrance. Five labourers had formed a daisy chain and were busy removing the pile of soil and rocks that had partially blocked it. The team of eight soldiers were checking their gear and waiting for their orders.

According to the Captain Usman's map, the tunnel formed a crude semi-circle. The southern section passed through the middle of the walled city where it formed the main artery of a crisscross network that connected most houses. Its northern tip ended near River Ravi.

A lot of the crisscross grid was drawn with dotted lines. The only part relatively intact was the main loop. Even that had dotted sections, especially near the river. If the map was to be believed, the tunnels weren't a viable escape route. They still had to search them. If the fugitives didn't escape, they could use them to hide in.

The plan was for him and four soldiers to head towards the river and for Captain Zulfiqar and the other four to explore the southern section.

Another group of ten soldiers had been dispatched to look for the tunnel exit on the riverbank. Major Amjad was trying to get more soldiers from the barracks to guard all exits outside the walled city, even the ones that were supposed to have collapsed.

If their fugitives had taken the tunnels, they would be trapped.

'Ian Sir,' Second Lieutenant Saeed clicked his heels together and saluted. 'Tunnel is open. We go?'

Ian responded with an awkward salute. 'Yes, we should. Lead the way.' He took one last look at the map on his phone and turned his screen off. 'Let's find us some terrorists.'

* *

The tunnel had been crudely dug with hand tools and was neither straight nor of consistent size. The walls, floors and ceiling were mostly clay. In places, beams had been used to shore up the ceiling. The air inside was chilly and still with a wet, dank smell.

Water had collected in dips, turning the clay into a sticky and slippery mud that made it hard to walk. But there was worse to come; raw sewage had seeped into several places turning the tunnel walls black and putrid. The strong smell of rotten eggs signalled danger.

'We're smelling hydrogen sulphide.' Jane covered her nose. 'It can be deadly so we need to move fast and try to not breathe if possible.

It was easier said than done. When they had to take a breath, the stench was unbearable.

With Yousaf in the lead and Sergei taking up the rear they managed a steady pace even with Sergei needing to help Razane through the tighter bits.

After ten minutes the tunnel opened, the going became easier and the air fresher. They came to a T-junction.

'Which way?' Jane shone her torch in both directions. 'They look the same.'

Sergei consulted his phone. 'Left... no wait... right.'

'What's right?' Razane said looking at his screen.

'Not sure, but it looks like it's heading out of the walled city, towards the river. I'm hoping the fact that flood waters are still entering the city means the tunnels are open.'

'Water can seep through far smaller spaces than we can...'

Jane said.

'No more negative thoughts, please,' Razane sidled up to Jane who gave her a gentle squeeze. 'We're together. Compared to even a few hours ago you don't know how good that feels.'

Jane put her arms around Razane's neck. 'Yes, my darling. You're so right. I also feel alive again, even under this dirt.' She kissed Razane on the forehead. 'I love you,' she whispered. 'We'll get out of here... somehow.'

'How are your hands now?' Sergei said.

'I can feel them again but now they're throbbing like mad.'

'It probably means the blood is flowing again.' Sergei said. He had done a quick Google search and had read how constriction around limbs would stop blood flow in the extremities. It could cause nerve damage and in extreme cases limb loss. Hopefully, that wouldn't happen to Razane.

They turned right and walked on in silence, this time with Jane in the lead. They passed two smaller intersecting tunnels. The tunnel continued straight and level for another hundred metres before coming to an intersecting branch of the same size. Jane stopped and put up her hand. 'Shhh!' She put a finger to her lips and switched off her torch. Yousaf and Sergei did the same. 'I hear something.'

They all froze and listened intently. A faint light shone from the side branch. Men were shouting at each other.

'Stay here. I'll check,' Jane said as she slowly crawled into the small tunnel. As she followed it upwards and to the left, the voices became clearer. She heard people digging. The light became stronger, as if a floodlight had been aimed into the tunnel. As she got closer, she began to see men's shadows projected onto the tunnel wall. She stopped; she'd gotten close enough.

At the entrance, a cheer went up as the digging stopped. Men were speaking animatedly in Urdu and Punjabi. One man spoke in English; it was muffled to hear what he was saying, but it sounded like an Australian accent.

Someone barked an order. 'Attention.' The shadows formed into an orderly line. The same voice barked again. 'Follow me… quick march.'

Damn! They were coming towards her. Jane tried to control her rising panic as she turned around and crawled back.

She almost bumped into her companions waiting for her in the dark. 'Oh, here you are.' Her breath was coming in spurts. 'We need to move. We'll have company soon.'

'Shit,' Sergei said voicelessly.

'What about go back?' Yousaf said.

'No, we keep going,' Sergei said.

'If that's the way out of the city we should continue,' Razane whispered.

'I agree. Just hurry and keep quiet,' Jane whispered.

They now had no choice but to pick up their pace.

The tunnel curved gently towards the right. Sergei heaved a sigh of relief. Before when the tunnel was dead straight they had been sitting ducks.

Twenty minutes later the tunnel and after passing countless side branches the tunnel showed no sign of ending. Sergei kept checking his screen to confirm they were heading in the right direction.

'OK, we're now officially beyond the walled city.' Sergei whispered as he turned his screen off. As he did, he looked back. Was it his imagination or was there a faint light behind them?

'Razane is that light behind us?' He whispered in her ear.

Razane turned to see. 'Yes it is… and… it's coming closer.' Her voice was weak but calm.

'I can hear them,' Sergei whispered.

Jane and Yousaf heard and stopped in their tracks.

'Would they know we're here?' Sergei tried to sound calm but giant butterflies were brawling in his stomach.

'The ground feels hard. I don't think we're leaving footprints.' Razane said. 'But we should hurry.'

They set off again, their tiredness forgotten. Sergei kept looking back. The light behind was slowly growing stronger. At this rate their pursuers would catch up to them before they reached the river.

MA'SHALLAH

Lahore, Wednesday 10 January, 9:00 pm

The light behind became ever brighter as their pursuers narrowed the gap. They were now in a straight stretch and the soldiers were so close that if they had stopped and aimed their torches they would have spotted them.

Even though the river was still two kilometres away, the tunnel walls were wet to the touch. It did not bode well. The presence of water made a collapse more likely. What made it worse was that they had not seen an intersecting branch since the last ten minutes. At least, the floor was covered in gravel so they left no footprints.

'Damn,' Jane stopped abruptly. 'I was hoping not to see this.' She was breathing heavily.

'What?' Sergei tried to look past Razane who was bent over double, trying to catch her breath.

'The tunnel... ends.' Jane shone her light on a wall of clay.

'Could it be a cave-in?' Razane said straightening up, her brow knitted with worry.

They approached with sinking hearts. As they drew nearer, they saw a gap between the wall and the ceiling large enough for a person to crawl through.

Sergei lifted Jane up to have a better look.

'There's a passage.' Jane shone her torch into the gap. 'We can crawl through and...' She sighed with relief. 'It looks like it opens again.'

Sergei helped Jane climb up, then he clambered after her. With Yousaf's help, he hoisted Razane into the gap.

Sergei heard Jane jump down as he pulled Razane forward while holding her under her arms. Thankfully, they only had to crawl a few metres.

'I wish we could block this,' Razane whispered as Sergei

helped her down on the other side.

'If wishes had wings, sweetheart.' Sergei said.

Jane was already fifty paces away by the time the three caught up to her.

'I was wondering whether we should have taken a stand there?' Sergei said gasping for air.

'You mean pick them off as they show themselves?' Razane said with a raised eyebrow.

'Yes!'

'It wouldn't work. If they have grenades, we'd be toast. Or they could just sit there and call in reinforcements from the opposite end.' Razane said.

'Razane is correct,' Yousaf said. 'Tunnel defence very difficult.'

'Then we better hurry,' Sergei said as he flashed his beam. This section of tunnel was as straight and featureless as the previous one.

Their pursuers reached the collapse faster than they had expected. They had gone only fifty metres when Sergei looked back. The first soldier's head popped through, his silhouette outlined against the light coming from behind him. Thankfully he was too preoccupied, and they were too far ahead, for him to notice them.

'Turn your lights off,' Sergei whispered.

Razane passed on the message to Yousaf and Jane.

Darkness engulfed them as they pressed on. Their rate of progress slowed dramatically as Jane and Yousaf resorted to feeling their way forward.

Behind them, another soldier had squeezed through. Their large flashlight was being passed through the opening, its rays bouncing off the walls towards them.

Sergei was still looking back when he bumped into Razane. 'Ouch,' she said under her breath.

'I'm sorry, love. Why did you stop?'

Ahead Jane and Yousaf were examining the tunnel wall. Jane turned, her face reflecting the light from their pursuers, and pointed. It was an opening, possibly a side branch.

'We have no choice but to take it.' Razane's lips brushed his ear as she passed on Jane's message.

Sergei looked back. His heart leapt into his mouth. A large flamethrower was being carefully manoeuvred past the constriction.

'Shit, did you see that?' Sergei said.

'That's a classic weapon for tunnel warfare,' Razane said as she followed Jane and Yousaf into the side tunnel. 'Let's go… fast!'

With one last look, Sergei followed.

The side tunnel sloped sharply upwards. As it did, it narrowed, forcing them onto their hands and knees to squeeze through.

'Help me, please,' Razane said to Yousaf who was ahead of her.

'Turn around. I pull your arms.' Yousaf whispered.

'OK, wait.' Razane moved back from the constriction so she could turn. With Sergei pushing on the soles of her shoes, Yousaf pulled her out of the narrowed section.

The soldiers' footsteps reverberated in the narrow space. They were on the march again. His heart in his mouth, Sergei scrambled up the incline trying not to dislodge any debris as he forced himself through the gap. He was broader than Razane so he was glad to feel Yousaf reach down and grab him by the jacket collar.

'Thank you,' Sergei huffed as Yousaf pulled him up.

The soldiers reached the side entrance and stopped. Sergei could hear them discussing something. One of them shone their light into the side tunnel. The beam bounced between the walls and lit up their hiding space.

Sergei stiffened as he heard an Australian accent. Jane heard it too. It was the same voice she had heard before. She looked around. Above her, the narrow tunnel opened into a wider passage that ran parallel to the main tunnel the soldiers were in. She clambered up and touched Yousaf on the shoulder as she whispered. 'Tell them. We have to run.'

* *

Amjad grimaced as he swallowed four codeine tablets. Withdrawal would be hell, but he didn't care. He needed to concentrate. If their quarry escaped, his life wouldn't be worth living. The US would at the very least impose sanctions on key government officials. The retributions would reverberate through the corridors of power. Pakistan wouldn't be safe for him. The real Wafaa would see Razane's escape as a betrayal. She had a nasty reputation when it came to anyone who double crossed her. Leaving Pakistan wasn't a safe option either. The only way out involved tasting the business end of his own service revolver.

Sebastian sat next to him typing away. From the look, he was chatting with several people.

He had promised to get pressure exerted onto the army chiefs to deploy more soldiers at all tunnel exits.

To his right Captain Usman was monitoring communications and placing green markers on the walled city map to indicate houses that had been checked. The army had made great progress. They were at seventy-six percent; by midnight they'd be done.

If the fugitives escaped the walled city, they would be trapped inside Metropolitan Lahore. The army chiefs had agreed to cordon off the entire city and its surrounding suburbs and impose a curfew.

'*Ya Allah*, let it not come to that.' In one way the army had a better chance of sealing off the whole of Lahore than they did the walled city, but finding them in the larger area would take longer.

Sebastian took a samosa and a bottle of water and walked over to the parapet to gaze at the Badshahi Mosque.

'That's a beautiful sight,' he muttered as he munched the spicy parcel of potato.

'You seem surprised. You did not notice it before?' Amjad

took his eyes off the screen.

'To be honest, no. I was too caught up in—'

'They found the foreigners,' the captain's shout cut him off.

Sebastian and Amjad turned in his direction. The captain stood and pointed at the screen.

'Aaah, *Ma'shallah*... Wonderful news!' Amjad was beaming despite the pain in his face. 'Tell them we are on the way,' Amjad said as he stood, 'Sebastian, you can come with us.'

THE HOSPITAL

Lahore, Wednesday 10 January, 9:30 pm

The army floodlights fought a losing battle with the swirling smog that had rolled in over the last hour, covering everything in a semi-translucent mocha blanket. With it came the penetrating damp that found its way into everything.

Major Amjad tried unsuccessfully to suppress a shiver that made his face throb mercilessly. He was fighting his own losing battle against the pain. The painkillers were losing their efficacy. The only thing that propelled him forward was the fingernail-gnawing anticipation of putting an end to his quarry's bid for freedom.

A knot of soldiers around an armoured personnel carrier looked in a celebratory mood. An officer sat in the front passenger seat, one leg out on the ground, engrossed in a phone conversation.

Captain Usman pointed. 'Sir, that must be the prisoners.'

The major's heart beat faster as they approached. Mesh covered the APC's rear windows, but he could make out four people in the back. It was them.

'O Allah, I prostrate myself in front of your munificence,' he prayed under his breath and cast a glance skyward. Tomorrow he would feed a thousand homeless people to show his gratitude.

The throng of soldiers parted as he approached the vehicle. The inside was dark. He counted the bowed heads again. Four.

The captain pocketed his phone, stepped out of the driver's seat, and saluted. With an exaggerated air of triumph, he opened the rear door. 'Sir, we found them—'

Amjad charged into the vehicle, his fist raised as he grabbed a handful of hair.

'Hey, stop!' Sebastian locked his arm around Amjad's raised forearm.

Amjad froze as saw their faces. 'Dumb whores, motherfuckers…' he bellowed. A stitch popped in his face. They were the wrong people.

* *

The tunnel continued upwards at a steep incline before a ninety-degree turn to the left. A few paces later it levelled off before turning sharply right. It took a moment for them to register; it was a dead end. They were trapped.

Jane shone her torch at the bricks lining the walls and floor. 'Why is this part different?' Her tone betrayed her frustration.

Sergei took out his knife and prodded at the mortar. It was as hard as rock. 'We're not going to dig out of this one,' he mumbled.

Jane shone her torch at the ceiling. It was concrete with a rectangular opening in the middle also covered with concrete. She grunted as she pushed against it, unsuccessfully; it didn't budge.

'I don't get what this is.' Sergei shone his torch on the smaller slab of concrete. He pushed against it but wasn't able to move it either.

'Wait a second.' Jane walked back into the tunnel and returned with something in her hand. 'What does this look like?' she said as she placed the object in Sergei's hand.

Sergei frowned as he examined the object the length of his forefinger. 'It's a root of a tree or a shrub.'

'It means we're close to the surface. Most tree roots only grow around… half a metre underground. This could be a manhole cover,' Jane said.

'Or we could be in a grave?' Razane said.

'Oh!' Yousaf shivered. 'It is terrible thing… to be standing in grave.'

'Why would a grave open into a tunnel?' Sergei said.

'Muslims no make brick walls in graves. We bury dead people in earth.'

'It could be a crypt,' Jane said.

'What is crypt?' Yousaf said.

'An underground burial space. It might have been for a Christian or a Hindu,' Jane said.

'Don't Hindus burn their dead?' Sergei said.

'Actually, you're right. Anyway, if it's a crypt, we're close to the surface. If so… Maybe… we can move the upper slab if we all try.'

Sergei placed his palms on one end. Yousaf placed them on the other end. Jane stood in the middle.

'One, two, three,' Sergei said, 'push…'

All their efforts were in vain. The slab didn't move.

'Maybe we should all push in the same spot,' Jane said.

Yousaf and Jane moved closer to Sergei. Their fingers were now overlapping. They pushed. A shower of sand rained down on them, but the slab remained in place.

'Wait a sec… let's use our brains.' Jane blinked the grit out of her eyes. 'Let's try pushing sideways as we push up.'

'What're you thinking?' Sergei picked a small stone from Jane's hair.

'When we lift this end, the other end will pivot on an edge. An edge has low friction and should slide easily.'

'You sound like a physics professor, but it makes sense. Let's try.' Sergei braced his legs against the wall and positioned his hands on the end of the concrete slab. Yousaf and Jane did the same. Their hands were almost overlapping.

'One, two, three, push…'

The slab moved sideways ever so slightly. 'Push harder,' Sergei grunted. They tried again. The slab moved further. A blast of cool air hit Jane in the face. The sound of traffic flooded in. The dark grey pollution-laden Lahore night sky was a welcome sight.

'Hopefully no one up there's noticed,' Sergei said.

'We have no time to worry about that,' Jane said. Being able to get their hands in the gap helped them push sideways with more force. Jane could pull using her weight, while Sergei and Yousaf pushed. With a groaning sound, the slab moved sideways. The gap was now large enough for Jane to put her head through.

'Serge, hoist me up.'

With Sergei lifting her, Jane stuck her head through. The rough concrete was cold against her throat as she waited for her eyes to adjust to the dark.

Above them was a small triangular garden, enclosed on all three sides by walls. Above was the canopy of a giant tree. Beyond the wall to her right was a four-storey building. A few of its windows were brightly illuminated behind shades or curtains. The wall to her left was the tallest and topped with barbed wire. It separated the garden from the overpowering din of traffic on the other side.

'Let me down,' she whispered. There was no reaction. Sergei hadn't heard. With some difficulty, she angled her face downwards. 'Let me down,' she said louder. This time Sergei heard. Ever so gently, he eased her down from the tight gap.

'I think we're good. No one's out there and it's noisy as hell. Let's get out of here.'

It took two heaves to move the slab enough for them to squeeze through. Climbing out was easy.

It felt surreal being out in the open with no one pursuing them.

'Yousaf, what's this place?' Sergei looked up at the shadowy building as he waited for a GPS signal on his phone. He caught a whiff of disinfectant just as Yousaf replied.

'I think it is Lady Willingdon. It is baby hospital.'

The signal returned and with it, he saw Yousaf was right. According to Google it was the largest obstetrics centre in Punjab. The street outside the wall was the N5 arterial road.

'Are we outside the walled city?' Razane was barely audible.

'Yes, but very close. We need to get out of here and make sure no one sees our rifles.'

'Shouldn't we put the slab back? If those soldiers came through the side passage they'll be near.' Jane said.

'Yup, I agree.' Sergei helped Yousaf push the slab back, which was easier than it was to open.

'I wish we could put something heavy on top to make it harder,' Sergei looked around for something to use.

'We don't have time,' Razane said.

Jane was reading from the gravestone. 'Here lies Joseph Masih, who bravely gave his life to defend the new hospital from a violent mob. May he rest in peace. 1908 to 1934.'

'Someone must have moved his remains when they built the tunnel,' Sergei brushed the dirt from his hands.

'I'm glad he wasn't there,' Razane shivered.

'Me too sweetie,' Jane hugged her.

'I have a bad feeling though… we need to leave… please,' Razane said and pointed to a narrow path that led to the front of the hospital building.

The path and the gardens were deserted. A few hospital windows overlooked them, but they were covered in blinds. So as not to attract any unnecessary attention, Yousaf had wrapped their rifles in his jacket, carrying the bundle as if it was a sleeping child.

The path ran into a sweeping oval driveway that enclosed a treed garden at the front of the building. Cars were parked end-to-end along both sides.

Yousaf walked up to a beaten up Ford Transit van with the words "Ambulance" and "Patient Transport Vehicle" stencilled on the side. He flashed his badge at a man standing beside the driver's door. 'Are you driver?'

'Y-yes sir.' The man stammered as he took a long puff of his cigarette and stubbed it on the ground. He looked Yousaf up and down and then cast a glance towards the rest of the group.

'We have emergency. We take patient to Ganga Ram Hospital.' Yousaf pointed to Razane.

'Do you have gate pass?'

'This is my gate pass.' Yousaf showed his badge again, his voice hardening. 'You have problem?'

'N-no sir, sorry sir. Get in, please.'

Yousaf climbed into the front with the driver while the others climbed into the back through the rearward opening doors.

'Patient must lie down,' Yousaf turned around and pointed at the stretcher. 'She very sick.'

Razane lay on the stretcher. Jane covered her in a blanket. 'Make it convincing,' she whispered as she stroked Razane's hair.

As they approached the front gate, the solitary guard got up off his chair and motioned for them to stop. Yousaf waved him over to his side as he rolled out his window.

'She wife of General Akram. We take her Ganga Ram Hospital fast or she die. It is emergency.' He showed the guard his badge.

The man looked into the back at the woman moaning and thrashing about as two foreigners worked to make her comfortable.

'But I must get permission from inside.' The guard sounded apologetic.

'Fatafat karo,' Sergei said in an angry tone.

'If she dies you are accountable to General Sahib.' Yousaf said.

The guard hesitated momentarily, then with a shrug of his shoulders he walked to the gate and swung it open.

The large van lurched forward with a chirp of its tyres as it turned left and joined the traffic.

'Take the ring road and follow my directions,' Yousaf said. 'I know the fastest way.'

'Yousaf, do they have cameras in Lahore?' Sergei said.

'Oh yes,' Yousaf said, 'but no worry. They no work nighttime. Very foggy so camera no see.'

'You gotta love Pakistan.' Sergei shook his head. He meant it. They wouldn't have been able to do half the things they'd gotten away with anywhere else. Sometimes chaos had its uses.

Yousaf motioned for the driver to pull over at a bus stop. He took out his pistol and motioned for him to get out.

PLAN B

The hole was just big enough for a limber cat. The cave-in had happened years ago, and the fallen soil had become rock hard.

'It is blocked.' Second Lieutenant Saeed had a knack for stating the obvious.

'Yes it is, mate. Yes, it is.' Ian scratched the stubble on his chin. He felt deflated. His reasoning for leading a team into the tunnel was solid. Sergei and Jane had entered the dungeon through the tunnels so it made sense they would escape the same way, and they would have chosen the shortest route. Either they were still hiding somewhere inside the walled city or they had taken the longer route. The only other possibility was the side branch they had passed a short while ago. He should have trusted his instinct and sent a few men to explore it.

'Saeed, we have to go back and search that side branch you shone the torch into.'

'Yes, I was also thinking same. Soldiers... About turn! *fatafat!*' His booming voiced echoed in the tunnel.

* *

Sebastian and Amjad trudged silently back to their rooftop command centre. Sebastian had no desire to talk to Amjad. The man was insane. He would have killed the foreigners in the army truck, had he not restrained him. The sooner he ended their alliance the better. Next to Amjad, Mike had been a saint. His pocket vibrated. It was Ian.

'Yup, speak.' Sebastian regretted his brusque tone the moment he uttered it. Ian was one of the good guys and he'd need his help.

'Bad news, mate.' Ian's voice was uncharacteristically gloomy. 'I'm pretty sure they've escaped. We're looking for witnesses to confirm.'

'What do you mean?'

Ian told him how they had found the crypt in the grounds of a maternity hospital.

'OK, call me back when you're sure. I'll let Amjad know.'

* *

Ian looked out of the window at the vehicular bedlam around them. Lahore had the maddest traffic he'd ever seen. Wheezing sixty-year-old Bedford trucks, the latest model Toyotas and gleaming Mercedes and hordes of motorcycles and scooters all vied for road space in complete contempt of the supposedly immutable laws of physics.

'You never told me what you found at the hospital.' Sebastian said as he massaged his stiff neck muscles.

'Oh, yeah, we spoke to a few folk. An orderly saw four people matching our fugitives emerge from the garden at the rear of the hospital where the crypt is. Apart from that, nothing. We asked the gatekeeper, but he'd just come on duty and hadn't seen them.'

'These fuckers are more capable than they appear. That's not luck.'

'Too right.' Ian shook his head.

'We need a Plan B and fast,' Sebastian said.

Ian turned to look at his companion. Captain Usman had lent them an army Landcruiser so they wouldn't be stopped at the countless checkpoints. The government had declared a state of emergency and the army was putting Lahore into lock-down. Lahorites were in a mad rush to get home before the 11:00 pm curfew deadline. 'I agree, but I'd have a plan C and more.'

Sebastian nodded. 'I don't intend to sleep tonight.'

'You supply the coffee, I'm happy to nut out a plan with you.'

'We also need more info on these fuckers,' Sebastian said. 'Who are they? What are their motives? And... How the fuck did they stay under the radar all this time?'

'I got everything there's to know about them, their business dealings, financial info, Internet history, social media activities, even medical records,' Ian said.

'Good. It'll help.'

'Nah, don't get your hopes up. Nothing gels with anything. Sergei and Jane are your average empty-nesters with two adult sons. One's in Dubai and the other's a musician. Sergei dabbles in the stock market and runs a YouTube channel on investing. Jane's an engineer who owns a company that installs solar power in remote communities around the world. Wafaa's the more interesting of the three. She came to Australia as Razane Silan, claiming she was Iraqi Kurd. But get this, we couldn't find the background checks Immigration would've done on her. Somehow she slipped through the net. She's been running a security company helping businesses identify and deal with terrorist threats. Talk about the fox ruling the hen house... and... the strangest bit is the three are romantically involved.'

'With whom?'

'What you mean?'

'You stopped midway. Who are they romantically involved with?'

'Each other. They're polyamorous.'

'Oh! Yeah, I've heard of that. Funny thing. Do you think Sergei and Jane were drawn into Wafaa's nefarious activities because they're in love with her?' Sebastian said with a mirthless chuckle.

'It sounds bizarre, but anything's possible. How else do you explain it? None of them, even Wafaa, showed any signs of radicalisation.'

Sebastian stifled a yawn. 'You know something, man. I've long been of the view that we're collectively myopic on the whole Islamic terrorist threat. Much of it's not based on religion but politics. True, we've never caught a secular terrorist yet, but they're lurking out there. Wafaa might be one. Maybe that's how she hid so effectively.'

They turned onto Mall Road and slowed for the first army checkpoint. Ahead of them cars were being painstakingly searched, flashlights were shone into people's faces, their identity papers checked and boots, doors and bonnets were being opened. Their jeep was waved through.

'Talk about closing the barn door after the horse has bolted,' Sebastian gritted his teeth as he shook his head.

'Is it arrogance or incompetence?'

'You mean the Pakis' casual approach?'

'Yup.'

'I don't think either. Our fugitives have exceeded their expectations, that's all.'

'They've exceeded mine.'

'Our fucking president called the Pakistani prime minister and asked if he needed to run the country for them. Apparently, it didn't go down well.'

'They did put the checkpoints up.'

'I've got a feeling they were doing it anyway and not because he threatened to level the prime minister's residence with a cruise missile.'

'I think your president's a total nut job.'

'He's completely out of control, and he lacks a moral compass... But he's not the only one. So many more maniacs around the world have come to power recently. The loonies are running the asylum almost everywhere.' Sebastian sighed and yawned at the same time.

'I reckon the world's leaders are way more dangerous than all the terrorists put together.'

* *

The imposing mansion was a scaled-down replica of the White House in Washington. The only difference was that instead of being set in sprawling gardens, the front boundary wall was only two car lengths away from the house. By the looks of it, it was a popular design in the posh areas of Lahore and Karachi. Most were in white but Jane had seen a few pistachio-green and one in brick red.

The nouveau riche everywhere suffered from delusions of grandeur and poor taste in equal measure. But the absurdity of the building's architecture was farthest from Jane's mind. Her only thought, finding shelter to tend to Razane's injuries and take stock of their situation.

Yousaf pressed a series of buttons on a keypad on the thick pillar. The ornate spiked steel gate slid open. He walked up the driveway and used a similar keypad beside a garage door. As it swung upwards, he motioned to Sergei who drove the van inside. The gate and then the garage door closed behind them, plunging them into momentary darkness.

Tubelights turned on and illuminated the interior of the four-car garage, empty save for their van. Yousaf walked to a wooden door and pressed another keypad to unlock the door to the house.

'I usually have remote and key but Major Hamdani install number pads for emergency.'

'How safe is this place?' Sergei helped Razane from the stretcher.

'Is top secret… very safe. Every ISI major get budget for secret safe house. No one know.'

'You mean there's no record or paperwork?' Jane said. A frown on her face betrayed her incredulity.

'No.' Yousaf shook his head vigorously.

The wooden door opened into a medium sized lounge at the front of the house. Black leather settees were arranged in a square around the outside walls. Small wooden tables with identical lamps separated each settee and made it look like a doctor's waiting room.

They walked through the lounge into a large open-plan office space with monitors and docking stations on each desk. A double staircase at the back led upstairs.

'All bedroom up.' Yousaf pointed. 'Find good one. I make food for you.' He disappeared through a door to the left of the staircase.

Sergei and Jane helped Razane up the stairs.

The landing opened into a wide hallway. The two front rooms, one on each side, were marked private. Sergei opened the next door on the left while Jane tried the one on the right.

'This is nice and big,' Sergei said.

Jane walked over and peered in. 'OK, it's nicer than the other one.'

'Good, I really need to sleep.' Razane's voice was weak.

'I need to see your wrists first. I'm worried about your circulation.' Jane guided Razane to the bed and helped her sit. She kicked off her shoes and sat beside her.

Razane's hands were still many shades of purple. The indentations on her wrists had reduced but where the skin had been rubbed off, it was flaming red. Jane and Sergei exchanged worried looks.

'How does it feel now?' Sergei tried hard not to let his voice show worry. He moved Razane's hair from the side of her face and kissed her on the forehead, lingering as he did. She smelt of perspiration and fear. It was so unlike her.

'I stink,' Razane said and pulled away.

'You do.' He smiled a tired smile. 'But I'm so happy I can smell you.' He closed his eyes as he breathed her in. 'We were so afraid we'd lost you forever.' His voice choked up.

Jane put her arms around them both. For a while they sat in silence, feeling warm and together. As they relaxed into each other, the tension of the last few days began falling away, leaving only exhaustion.

Razane's face was wet with tears. 'I never gave up hope. You two kept me from going mad.' She smiled through her tears. 'They did terrible things...' her voice faltered. 'But they didn't break me.'

'What else did they do?' Jane was dreading the answer. The thought of someone torturing Razane was almost too much to bear.

'They beat me, put me in front of air conditioners, used a high-pressure hose on me. I might have been raped while I was unconscious.'

Jane smoothed her hair. 'I'll go downstairs and get some stuff to fix you up.'

'Don't worry about me. You two are my strength. You being close is the best medicine.'

'Sweetheart, we need to treat your hands, and you need antibiotics for any disease. You've got to get better. And then… we'll make them pay for every bit of pain… and humiliation they put you through… They will fucking pay.'

'Hey stop it! I love you both so so much… let's just focus on us. We're together again and it's all that matters.'

Jane sighed deeply. 'Just the thought of you in pain, while a monster treats you like a piece of meat, makes my blood boil.'

'I understand, my love.' Razane gazed deep in Jane's eyes. 'I'd tear up the earth looking for anyone who'd hurt you. But know this; revenge isn't the answer. Tell me, am I less to you because of what happened?'

'Of course not!' Sergei and Jane said in unison.

'How can you even say that?' Sergei said.

'Your love is the only thing that matters. It's why I breathe. If that hasn't been diminished then tell me… How have they diminished me? They only reduced their own dignity, not mine. Only I can do that to myself.'

'You know the man whose throat I cut in the dungeon. I'm glad I did it.'

Razane leaned over and kissed Jane. 'You're hopeless, my love.' She smiled. 'But I love you so, so much.'

While Razane rested her head on his shoulder Sergei searched the Internet for treatments for rope injuries. Jane went downstairs to ask Yousaf for a first aid kit.

Jane gave a gasp when Yousaf opened a nondescript door in the basement to reveal a mini operating theatre. Shelves on the walls were stocked with bandages, sutures, medicines, saline and glucose drips.

'That coolbox has plasma for emergency.' Yousaf pointed at a glass fridge.

'You have everything here but a doctor,' Jane said to herself.

Yousaf overheard. 'I find doctor but we need keep him here.'

Jane sucked in her breath. 'Oh no, I'd rather not kidnap… I just need something for Razane's hands.'

Yousaf walked over to a shelf and removed several items including compression bandages, pain medication, anti-inflammatory tablets and cream, a broad-spectrum antibiotic, antiseptic cream and saline solution. From the fridge he removed two icepacks. 'I no doctor but all Pakistani commando do first aid training.'

'Thanks, Yousaf, you're a good man.'

'Food ready soon. I bring up?'

'No, no, I'll come down or send Sergei.'

'OK.'

'Yousaf…' Jane turned around when she got to the door.

'What?'

'Thank you… for all your help. I really mean it. You've saved our lives many times.'

'No need thank. My mother tell me… save one life is like save humanity.'

'That's written in your Quran isn't it,' Jane said gently. Razane had told her the same thing.

'Quran not mine but belong all human being.'

'Yes, I suppose you're right. Anyway, it's a good saying. Your mother taught you well.'

When Jane got back to the room, Sergei was running the bath and helping Razane out of her clothes.

'Razane's wrists are sprained. There's definitely swelling… and according to a medical website she could have nerve damage. The pain could be from that. Thankfully the nerve most at risk is for feel, not movement. It also regenerates after a period. So touch wood, she'll be OK.'

'Sweetie, can you feel your fingers?' Jane was breathless from rushing up the stairs. She put the things on the bed and opened a box of tablets. She popped out two and handed them to Razane along with a bottle of water.

'Can you help me, please? My whole hand feels numb. I need my feeling back…'

'Of course.' Jane placed the tablets on Razane's tongue and offered the bottle to her lips.

Razane swallowed the tablets and coughed, wincing.

'Does swallowing hurt?' Jane examined Razane's bare chest. She gently touched a faint horizontal red mark just below her breasts. 'What happened?'

'They strapped me down really tight during water torture.'

'What?' Sergei stood, his mouth agape, his eyes wide with shock. Jane's lower lip trembled; her eyes blazed with fury.

Razane's eyes welled with tears. 'I'm OK. We're together…' Her voice faltered.

Jane and Sergei both put their arms around her. 'You should have seen the speed at which Jane killed that American who was with you… It was poetry in motion.'

Razane opened her eyes and smiled. 'My dear gentle Jane, I can't… picture it.'

'He wasn't the first.' Sergei told Razane about the two men in the dark courtyard of the steak restaurant.

'I'm awed by your strength, my love.'

'You said you can't believe it…' Jane said, a playful note entering her voice.

'No, I said I can't picture it but I do believe it… Anyone who can truly love can also kill.'

'Well, I'm guilty on both counts and strangely I feel no remorse.'

'You're amazing and… your Systema… well it proved useful.'

'Jane's Systema is crazy good.'

'I have a feeling there'll be more killing before we get to go home.' Razane tried moving her fingers.

'We'll fix you up, sweetie… and hopefully you'll get the feeling back fast.' Jane got up and walked to the bathroom to check the water. The temperature was nice and hot. The tub was halfway full, so she turned off the tap.

Sergei heard her and came in with Razane. They both helped her climb in. While Jane tended to her hands, Sergei gently massaged the rope marks on her ankles.

'She's fallen asleep,' Jane whispered after a while. Sergei looked. Razane's head was leaning against Jane in what seemed an uncomfortable position.

'Why don't you get in with her. I'll get the food,' Sergei said.

He held Razane while Jane undressed. Then he helped her climb in.

'Thanks darling. You're now almost as wet as me,' Jane said with a smile.

Sergei smiled as he looked at them. He felt truly happy. 'My two beautiful soul mates,' he whispered as he kissed them both.

* *

Sebastian waited till the waiter left before pouring more wine for himself. He took care not to disturb the white napkin wrapped around the bottle of Torres Mas La Plana. As a foreigner he was legally allowed to drink in Pakistan but the open serving of alcohol was frowned upon.

He took a sip and swirled it around his tongue. The locals didn't know what they were missing. The Spanish made great Cabernet Sauvignon. 'This wine's good.' He held the crystal cut goblet to the light and admired the deep red colour.

'The food was good too,' Ian said. 'I'm so glad they offer wine at these hotels.'

'It's only for foreigners and only if you ask nicely.'

Sebastian smiled.

'I don't get the Pakis we're dealing with,' Ian said. His mood changed. 'They're so hard to understand. Are they on our side or not?'

'Only while it's in their interest. They probably trust us as much as we trust them…'

'A mutual lack of respect…' Ian said.

'What do you expect when our president wants to bomb Islamabad?'

Ian shook his head. 'Your president has his crazy moments.'

'Crazy moments…? We're lucky when the fucker has lucid moments.' Sebastian said with a grimace.

'If the CIA could assassinate Kennedy…' Ian let the thought hang.

Sebastian coughed the wine out. 'Good heavens,' he laughed. 'Are all Aussies that forthright?'

'I forgot you boys don't admit to it,' Ian said with a smile.

'Shit, would you?' Sebastian took another sip. 'On a completely different topic… I've passed on the FATA army base coordinates to our military command. We're getting authorisation for a drone attack—'

'What! You really think they'll make it out of Lahore?'

'If they do and if they return to the army base or go on to Shawal, we'll be ready.'

'You think they'll head there again?' Ian said.

'Where else would they go? They can't return to Australia or go anywhere else. My guess is they've got contacts in Afghanistan. It's where they were probably headed before.'

'We'll see, but I've got a feeling they'll be caught in Lahore.'

'Let's hope so, but just in case… our drones are on standby. They can attack with thirty minutes notice.'

SHIT STORM

Lahore, Thursday 11 January, 8:00 am

Razane was the first to wake. She was on her side facing Sergei who was still fast asleep. She could feel Jane's warm body behind her. Jane had wrapped one arm protectively around her midriff. Sergei had his arm around them both.

Jane sensed Razane stir. She nuzzled her face in the dark tresses of her hair and sleepily kissed her neck. Sergei woke. His face lit up when he saw them both.

'How are your hands?' His voice was hoarse from sleep.

'The pain's less but I still can't feel them... Can you massage them for me, please?'

'Yeah, of course.' Sergei tried moving his arm out from under Razane and Jane. 'This bed's so tiny. My arm's fallen asleep.'

'You better not get nerve damage too.' Jane smiled sleepily.

'Nah. It's not that bad.' He smiled as he tried to move a limb he could no longer feel.

Jane lifted her head and tried to help him. 'Take your big fat arm back.' She smiled. 'Boy, it's heavy.'

'Hey, it's all muscle.'

'Yeah, of the grain-fed variety.' Jane giggled as Sergei reached over and tickled her with his free hand.

Razane lifted her head out of the way. 'You shouldn't sleep like that.'

'It's OK. I can feel the blood coming back...' He rubbed it vigorously. 'Being able to cuddle you two is worth all the pins and needles.'

'Well, I prefer my man to have two arms,' Razane said, her lips curling mischievously.

'Yes, true. We've only one man between the two of us. You

must have two arms.' Jane nudged him playfully in the ribs.

They lay there making small talk, saying silly nothings, luxuriating in the feeling of being together again. Then nature and hunger called.

* *

Yousaf was downstairs eating breakfast reading an online newspaper. 'Good morning.' He acknowledged them cheerfully.

Razane sat at the table with Yousaf while Jane and Sergei went to the kitchen to make breakfast.

'Will you have cup of tea?' Yousaf said getting up.

'Yes please.'

'How your hands today?'

'The pain's less but they feel numb.'

'Numb?'

Razane picked up a tea spoon. 'I can't feel this properly.'

'Oh, I am sorry. *Insha`Allah* it be OK?'

'Yes brother. Allah will do what's right.'

'Are you Muslim, sister?' Yousaf poured tea in a cup. 'How many sugar?'

'Half a teaspoon, please. Yes, I was born a Muslim.'

Yousaf handed Razane the cup and nodded as she thanked him.

He sat back in his chair suddenly at a loss for words. With an awkward cough, he resumed reading.

'Is there any news about us?' Razane said. She tried picking up the cup by its handle but gave up and instead used both her hands to lift it to her lips.

'News is you worse killer since bin Laden. Amreeki President say will attack Pakistan if no catch you.'

'He's an idiot but he can't attack Pakistan.'

'He can because he… idiot. Smart man first think. He no can think.'

Razane couldn't agree more. Whether the US president was a moron or playing to his voter base was almost not important. They were in the epicentre of the world's biggest shit-storm.

Jane and Sergei brought in bowls of hot porridge and French toast with a fresh pot of tea. For a while her worries were forgotten as they ate. Her appetite had returned, which had to be a good thing.

They spent the next two hours going over the news and their situation. They were the trending news on all social media and on every front page. Their photos were everywhere. The story of their escape was on continuous news loops on all news networks. Experts were talking about how a new breed of terrorists required a fresh approach from world governments. Curiously there was no mention of Yousaf.

'Why me not in news?' Yousaf said.

'I'd say an ISI captain helping terrorists is embarrassing,' Sergei said.

'It could help us,' Jane said.

'It's a tiny advantage but it won't solve our mess,' Razane said.

'Hey, we'll get through this,' Sergei said. The rest had done him good. 'When Jane was in jail facing the death penalty... we got her out. The situation was almost as bad.'

'C'mon, it was less complex,' Jane said. 'Now it seems hopeless.'

'Trust me, it felt the same,' Sergei said.

'Serge is right... and this time we have some advantages,' Razane said. Her face and voice were calm.

'Razane's right. We have a secret weapon in Yousaf,' Sergei said.

'And in the far corner we have the whole Pakistani army, the CIA, ISI, ASIS and goodness knows who else, all looking for us,' Jane said.

'Hmmm, yeah. But we had some bad fuckers after us the last time,' Sergei said, 'and for a long time we were unaware of them.'

'You're making me feel a bit better. I guess last time the

baddies followed no rules. Now the enemy all have to follow some protocol.'

'And all of us are together and stronger than last time,' Razane said.

'Yup, Jane's now a real killing machine,' Sergei said with a mischievous smile.

Jane flicked a bread crumb at Sergei. 'What else?'

'Well, we have no liabilities like Damon, our giant teddy bear who hasn't a single violent bone in his body.' Sergei said.

'Yup, bad parenting.' Jane said. 'Blame me.'

'Of course I blame you, sweetheart.' Sergei stroked Jane on the back and smiled at her.

'OK, now that we've pumped ourselves up does anyone actually have a plan?' Razane said.

DOORS

Lahore, Thursday 11 January, 10:00 am

Major Amjad stared at the map of Lahore as he tried to stop anxiety overwhelming his thoughts. Where in this sprawling metropolis of eleven-million people would they hide? Their names and faces were all over the media so they could not stay at any hotel or Airbnb. No private citizen would be brave or stupid enough to give them shelter, not with the army after them. That did not leave many places.

As the local, Yousaf would most likely guide them. What would he do? He had friends and family, but he would not risk their safety.

The major took a sip of water and sloshed it around in his mouth as he mulled over the possibilities. Yousaf would have access to Major Hamdani's safe-house. The location of safe-houses were carefully guarded secrets, known only to the majors in charge of them and their teams. The more he thought about it, the more plausible it seemed.

He swallowed reflexively as another thought occurred to him.

Like Yousaf, Fazal had been part of Major Hamdani's team. He would have visited the same safe-house. If so, it would show in his location history, stored in his personal Google account.

He picked up his phone and dialled.

'Yes sir,' Arif replied.

'Arif, you have another chance to show what a good hacker you are. I need to access my brother's Google account.'

* *

Sebastian and Ian waited while they connected to the online

meeting.

A beep indicated that Chip had joined the meeting. After a moment, his audio turned on. 'Hey guys,' he said in his booming voice.

'Good afternoon, sir.' Sebastian's voice trembled. Chip made him nervous, as did anyone higher than his direct manager.

'Chip, Stella.' Ian's greeting was far more relaxed.

'So what's new?' Stella said.

'The army are changing the search sequence.' Sebastian stammered. 'They believe our fugitives are likely hiding in sector-six because it's the most logical exit point if they're heading to Afghanistan.'

'That's good. The Pakis aren't dumb. Anything else?'

'The army are keeping the sector change under wraps. They don't want to broadcast it to the public.'

'I understand. We won't leak it.'

'Major Amjad believes the fugitives are in an ISI safe-house, and he's trying to break into a Google account to find it. I was wondering if we could help him?' Ian spoke.

'OK, I'll see what we can do… send us the account name. We'll get it done.'

'That's good, sir,' Sebastian said. 'That's all I have.'

'Good work guys. Keep it up. Talk to you soon.' The meeting ended.

* *

Jane felt her unease grow as she watched the TV. The news was grim. The government had placed the city under martial law and isolated it from the rest of the country with a ring of steel. The army had divided the metropolis into nine sectors. Further troops sealed each sector so no one could travel outside their own area. Two whole divisions were methodically searching every building, a sector at a time. While they searched, the sector was placed into a lock-down with a shoot-on-sight curfew. People in the rest of Lahore were advised to stock up on essentials to last the length of the search, expected to take four days.

If they stayed in Lahore, they would be found.

According to the TV announcer, the search began in the northeast, closest to the Indian border.

'Which is our sector?' Sergei said as soon as the news gave way to an ad break.

'We central west. Four sector from northeast.'

'They could search in any order. North to South could give us more time. If they go anti-clockwise we have maybe twenty-four to thirty hours.' Razane was staring at the map on Sergei's phone.

'Yousaf, any thoughts on how to escape from Lahore?' Jane said.

'No. Sorry.' Yousaf's voice was low, his expression glum.

'Do you know where the barricades will be?' Razane said.

'Yes,' Yousaf pointed at the map.

'How do you know?' Sergei said.

'Barricades always in same place. They leave barricade by side of road when no need.'

'He's right,' Jane said, 'we've seen the large wheeled barricades a few times.'

'Could we use an aircraft?' Sergei said.

'All plane grounded. Air Force will shoot.'

'What are these?' Razane pointed at a network of green lines heading out of Lahore.

'That is canal.'

'You mean like a water channel?' Sergei said.

'Yes for farmer,' Yousaf said.

'Can we use them?' Jane said.

'You mean with boat. Nobody use boat,' Yousaf said. 'And canal is next to road. Army and police see boat and shoot.'

'Damn it.' Sergei rubbed his forehead furiously.

'Wait, a second.' Jane sat upright. 'Isn't it foggy at night? And fog is densest over water...'

'Hey, yes...' Razane looked expectantly at Yousaf.

'Oh, yes. I forget. Canal very foggy in night,' Yousaf said.

'So you mean... use the fog to hide our escape?' Razane said, 'Jane, that's very clever...'

'If only we had a boat,' Sergei said, 'Yousaf, can you think of any?'

'No. No in Lahore.'

'We could always make one.' Jane had walked over to the kitchen door and was examining it. 'Do you have tools?'

'Yes,' Yousaf said, 'in torture room.'

Jane raised her eyebrows and shook her head. 'I think I might have an idea. Not sure if it's a good one, but at least I have one.'

'You are thinking of floating down the canal on doors, at night while it's foggy,' Sergei said, a faint smile on his face.

'So you think I'm being silly.'

'Hmmm!' His voice trailed away. 'It's definitely not silly...'

'It's daring and clever,' Razane said. 'Will those doors float with us on top?'

'I think so. I need to do some calculations,' Jane said.

'It's the best and only plan we have. But where would we enter the water? And, umm, how do we get to the canal without being caught?' Sergei said.

'And we need to steer and propel ourselves...' Razane said. 'I love the idea. If boating isn't big in Lahore, they won't expect us to use the canal.'

'I need to first confirm the doors are solid timber. Then I gotta calculate their buoyancy. It needs to be a light wood to work.'

'You mean like pine?' Sergei said.

'If you use door to make boat.' Yousaf was incredulous. 'Major Hamdani no happy. He want live in house when retire.'

'I thought it's an ISI house?' Jane said.

'This is Pakistan. No record of house so he take when retire.'

Sergei whistled in astonishment. 'A job with good benefits...'

'Yousaf, if we don't escape the major will retire in an Afghan jail,' Jane said.

'Yes, yes, I understand. I show tools. Take door if need.'

'Let me help,' Sergei said.

'OK, you two go. Yousaf and I will work on the rest of the plan.' Razane was looking intently at Google Maps.

'I put on big screen.' Yousaf said to Razane. 'But first I take Jane to torture room.'

'I don't like the sound of that.' Jane smiled. 'But I'll come.'

Razane looked up from her phone. 'Jane my love, it's an amazing plan, if we can pull it off.'

Jane kissed Razane on the lips and ran after Sergei and Yousaf.

* *

The torture room had every conceivable tool. Jane tried not to think how a nail gun or a circular saw was used on a prisoner. To her relief, they looked brand new. None had been used on a human. She picked up a tape measure and a drill with a hole-saw. 'That's so I can take a sample of the doors and check their buoyancy.'

'I'm a little concerned about balancing on the doors if we also have to paddle,' Sergei said as he watched Jane measure and then weigh a piece of wood to calculate its density.

'This wood is really light,' Jane said as she punched the numbers into her smartphone's calculator. She looked up at Sergei. 'Serge, darling, I wasn't planning on a door per person. We'll make a raft that fits us all. The canal is plenty wide.' She drew an outline of the raft she had in mind on the wall. It utilised seven doors in three layers.

'I'll bring you the doors,' Sergei said. 'How are we transporting this? Isn't it too big for the van?'

'We'll assemble it on site. It'll be easy, just eight bolts that go from the single door on the bottom to the four doors on top. Jane rummaged around and found eight thick bolts of the same size along with nuts and washers. Don't worry, we'll practice putting it together. Shouldn't take more than a minute.'

'You're a top engineer,' Sergei said as he walked off.

While Sergei unscrewed the doors from their frames, Jane busied herself, drilling bolt holes, rounding off the corners and chamfering edges. As Sergei brought more doors, she added two doors on top of the first followed by the final layer of four doors.

Two hours later their rudimentary, four-metre by two-metre raft was ready. Sergei climbed on board to get a feel for it. 'It's solid all right. I just hope it'll float.'

'It will,' Jane smiled.

'It's an honour to be in the presence of such engineering greatness,' Sergei said.

'You're getting carried away, darling.' She smiled. 'We still need to decide how to power it.'

'We could all lie on our stomachs and use paddles.'

'Or sit up. But whatever we do we should practise.'

After lunch, Jane put the finishing touches on the raft. Yousaf studied the canal for the start and end points. Sergei and Razane returned to their room. Sergei spent the next two hours massaging Razane's wrists, arms and lower legs before dressing her wrists. Razane fell asleep halfway. She still looked exhausted, but the colour had returned to her cheeks and she could use her hands without screaming in pain.

Sergei hugged her sleeping form and kissed her on the cheek as he tucked her in the blanket. He was about to get up when Razane reached over and grabbed him by the sleeve.

'Hold me, please. I need you to...' She was asleep again.

Sergei kicked off his shoes and climbed in beside her. She turned around and snuggled into his arms. At some point he too fell asleep, his face buried in her hair.

LOCATION HISTORY

Lahore, Thursday 11 January, 4:00 pm

Jane shook the sawdust from her clothes as she stood back to admire her handiwork. Paint fumes still hung thick in the air. Two doors, joined along their length, formed the top of the raft. A single door attached below held them together. Two more layers, each narrower than the one above, gave the bottom of the raft a shallow hull to aid in stability and manoeuvrability. She had sealed the timber with a thick coat of paint and added assembly marks to help them put it together.

Her stomach rumbled with hunger. She had forgotten lunch and apparently so had everyone else. Jane looked at her watch. The time had passed without her realising. She loved working with her hands and could get lost in her workshop at home. She even forgot she was using what were essentially tools of torture. While he helped her, Yousaf had explained the alternate use of most of the equipment; the spray cans were for eyes, drills were for shins and knee caps, pliers were for pulling tongues and the circular saw was to cut muscle and amputate limbs. Man's capacity for evil was seemingly limitless. She shuddered at the thought of what they would have done to Razane if they hadn't rescued her.

Jane removed her dust mask, goggles and earmuffs. The house was eerily quiet. Too quiet. Another sensation rumbled in her stomach, a nervous reaction to the sudden fear that gripped her. She grabbed a claw hammer and rushed out of the basement. Climbing two steps at a time, she reached the office area. Yousaf was nowhere in sight. Out of breath and with a painful stitch in her side, she ran up the stairs to the top floor. Her heart hammered in her chest as she opened the door to their bedroom.

* *

Sebastian checked his watch. Chip had asked for a meeting at 4:10 pm Pakistan Time. He clicked on the conference call link in the email.

'The network's so slow here,' Ian said. 'Ours connects within ten seconds in Australia.'

'Ours takes three,' Sebastian said. 'I hope they've managed to hack the account.'

Ian was about to reply when Chip came online. He cut in. 'A team of hackers are working on it. We'll have broken the password within the hour. You can then pass it on to Major Amjad.'

'Sir, that's awesome. Thanks for your support,' Sebastian said, flashing a nervous smile at Ian. 'With any luck we'll have them in custody by this evening.'

* *

Jane sat on the edge of the bed captivated by the sight of Razane fast asleep in Sergei's arms. She never grew tired of watching the two of them. How she loved them. She was tempted to dust off her clothes and climb in beside them, but something stopped her. An uneasy feeling in the pit of her stomach told her something was amiss, and it was the wrong time to let her guard down. She leaned over and kissed them both then went looking for Yousaf.

* *

Yousaf was stirring something on the stove. He turned as she entered. 'Dinner ready soon.'

'Oh, thanks.' Jane breathed a sigh of relief and sat on a stool at the kitchen bench. She was close to breaking down. Everything, even silence, unnerved her. 'Can I help with something?'

'Cut onion for salad,' Yousaf said without turning. 'Onion in fridge.'

Jane helped Yousaf finish preparing dinner, then she woke Sergei and Razane. They ate together in silence, savouring the tasty chicken curry with fluffy white rice.

'That was a yummy meal,' Razane said. 'You cook well, Yousaf.'

'Yes, your future wife will be a lucky woman,' Jane said smiling.

'Thank you.' Yousaf had grown red in the face.

When dinner was over Jane showed them the raft.

'Wow, it's looking good.' Razane said.

'I think we should all get on and work out how to position ourselves,' Jane said.

'Have you thought of paddles?' Sergei said.

'Here's two I prepared earlier.' Jane smiled as she retrieved two cricket bats from a cupboard. She handed one each to Sergei and Yousaf. 'I was thinking you and Yousaf could paddle, one on each side. I'll steer from the stern, while Razane can balance my weight at the bow and stop our weapons falling overboard.'

Over the next half an hour they practised assembling and sitting on the raft in their designated positions.

'Let's not forget to take the spanners with us,' Sergei said as he and Yousaf helped Jane carry the disassembled raft up the stairs and into the front hallway.

'If this works.' Sergei was huffing. 'They should make a movie on us.'

'Now who's saying if?' Jane smiled.

'You're right.'

* *

Amjad's phone rang. It was Sebastian. 'I'm sending through the password and the correct user name now. Your brother had two accounts with Google, both with the same password.'

'Thank you, Sebastian. Your team is even faster than my IT man.'

'We ended up approaching Google directly. They always

cooperate on national security issues.'

Amjad hung up and checked his inbox. Sebastian's mail was at the top. His heart beat a little faster as he logged into the first account. A twinge of sadness struck him at the thought of going through his dead brother's last movements. Fazal deserved privacy in his death. He clicked on Google Maps and then on "Your Timeline". A map opened on the screen showing today's date and the phone's location, which was his office.

Amjad went back to the day Fazal died. It showed the phone was outside Karachi in the Arabian Sea. He went back from there a day at a time. Predictably, Fazal had travelled between his home and the ISI offices and then to various places throughout the day.

Amjad made a list of all locations unknown to him. There were many. He called for a cup of tea and some food. It would be a long night.

By the time the orderly had brought him the refreshments he had gone back three months and had a list of twenty-one houses. Another hour later he was back to the time when Major Hamdani first hired him. His list of potential houses had grown to forty.

Amjad began cross checking his list against all of Fazal's friends. That reduced the number to twelve. Next he zoomed in to each location on Google Maps.

ISI safe-houses and the secrecy surrounding their locations were an essential part of the organisation. It allowed for autonomy and empowerment for all senior officers. It also provided plausible deniability for senior leadership. They couldn't be responsible for what they didn't know.

A safe-house was many things. It was a place of refuge for when an ISI officer's safety was compromised and an interrogation centre where detainees could be made to vanish. But their most important function was the reason they were funded so generously. They were part of a decentralised network to coordinate armed resistance in the event of an invasion. They were equipped with a high level of automation and were connected to ISI's Intranet through cellular data, satellite and fibre optic cable, a triple redundancy to ensure they could never be disconnected. They all contained a blast proof armoury and shielding to prevent electronic snooping.

To meet these requirements, the houses had to be large, double-storey buildings with a basement and surrounded by a reinforced boundary wall at least two metres from the house. They also needed a garage for at least four vehicles and sufficient roof space for antennae and a satellite dish.

This feature set helped him narrow the list of addresses to three, one each in Gulberg, Garden Town and Model Town.

There was another database he could check, the phone book. How foolish to not think of it earlier. He logged in and entered the three addresses and found the owners' names. Using another database, he looked them up. One was a factory owner and the other a retired judge. He couldn't find who owned the house in Model Town. It had to be the safe-house, and it was a short ten minutes drive away.

He sat back with a sigh and contemplated his next move. He needed to be careful. If he put out an alert, Yousaf might find out. Yousaf's login had been deactivated but he could have more user IDs. Even though he had never thought highly of Yousaf, he wouldn't make the mistake of underestimating anyone again.

The best way was to surround the safe-house with his own men and then call for reinforcements. That way they could cut off any attempts to escape.

He called Sebastian.

* *

Razane groaned as she woke. No, no, no. It couldn't be happening again. She was back in the dungeon, suspended from the ceiling. Her wrists, arms and shoulders were aflame.

The single bulb shone on Jane and Sergei's naked forms as they hung a metre away. Sergei's naked muscled body contrasted with Jane's slender form. Their eyes were closed.

She remembered the smell of the gas before the doors were kicked in. It must have been what had put them to sleep.

Razane strained to look into the dark. Yousaf wasn't there. Was he dead?

Footsteps sounded. It was the younger American, the pockmarked Pakistani and the perverted old man who had tormented her with his stick.

Her stomach dropped as she saw his small-sized chainsaw. As they came into the light, she saw they were all smiling.

'So Wafaa, we meet again.' The American righted the fallen chair and dragged it closer. 'You smell better. It was the only thing your escape achieved.' He fell into the chair with a sigh.

'You have made it worse for yourself. Now you will pay,' The ugly Pakistani said as he flicked lint off his army tunic. 'My man here will cut off your girlfriend's feet.'

'What? No, don't, please…' Razane screamed. Wild panic set in. She was hyperventilating. 'I'll do anything, be anything… please… just leave them alone.'

'Too late.' He looked bored as he signalled to the old man who started the motor. 'If you talk, I'll bandage her up so she does not bleed to death.' He had to shout over the noise of the motor.

'No, sto…' Razane could not get the words out. This wasn't happening to her darling Jane. 'No, please!'

The old man, his eyes glinting, moved closer to Jane. It was clear he was enjoying this. The chainsaw revved as he swung it, leaving behind an arc of thick smoke. It dug into Jane's flesh with a sickening sound. For a brief moment it threatened to stall then it continued, spraying blood. Jane's eyes opened wide in horror.

'No, no, no,' Razane screamed at the top of her lungs.

The pockmark-faced man turned to her, a sickening smile spread across his face.

* *

A bright light blinded her. Sergei was saying something. His voice sounded strange.

'Hey, it's OK.' He felt wet and clammy as he held her. But how? What was happening? The dungeon was gone. Sergei lay next to her, running his fingers through her hair.

'It's OK, sweetheart, everything's going to be OK.' He murmured in her ear.

How could he say that? 'Where's Jane?' Her voice was panicked. She looked around, past the bright light. They were back in the room in the safe-house.

'She's downstairs, making her boat.' Sergei wiped her forehead with a cloth. 'It's OK, you were having a bad dream.' He kissed her gently.

'Oh, thank God!' She held him tight. 'We can't let ourselves be captured. Those men… they're monsters.'

SAFE-HOUSE

Lahore, Thursday 11 January, 8:00 pm

'Let's load the raft in the van in the morning,' Jane said as they ate a light dinner of cheese sandwiches. 'I still think we should leave tomorrow.'

'OK, let's talk about it over breakfast.' Sergei took a sip of peppermint tea. 'Razane needs more time to recover. The journey to Afghanistan will be tough.'

'I see both sides,' Razane said, 'I don't want to stay here too long. But Sergei's right too. I'm no use without my hands.'

'Anyway, let's get some sleep,' Sergei stretched as he stood. 'Good night, Yousaf.'

'You have good night also.' Yousaf said.

* *

Amjad kept an eye on the security camera at the front gate as he absentmindedly adjusted his bullet-proof vest to stop a seam digging into his side. He had put on weight and it was chafing his stomach.

After some hurried phone calls, he had found replacements for Sibtain and Shakeel. Babur and Hussain were decorated commandos, the cream of the elite. Allah willing, they would not disgrace the regiments they had been seconded from. They were grim faced as they checked their equipment.

An army jeep stopped at the front gate. Major Amjad could see Sebastian and Ian in the back along with two other Pakistani civilians, their local contractors. He pressed a button to talk to the guardhouse. 'Tell Sebastian Sahib, we'll be out in a minute.' He looked at his watch; it was 8:15.

* *

Sergei pushed the large mattress in through the bedroom door. He had borrowed it from the adjacent bedroom. Jane helped him place it on the floor next to the one they'd removed from the bed. Razane spread the bedsheets.

'I can't wait for a comfortable sleep,' Jane said, 'and for us to be together... after so long.' She turned to Razane. 'You'll have both of us to help keep your nightmares away.'

'I'll be OK, my love.' Razane smiled. The colour was already returning to her cheeks.

'You really worked hard today...' Sergei said to Jane as he dropped the mattress to the ground.

'While both us lazy ones were sleeping.' Razane smiled.

'I enjoyed myself... but I'm totally stuffed. I shouldn't have taken a bath, it made me even sleepier.' Jane yawned and blinked away tears.

A knock on the door startled them. Sergei opened the door. It was Yousaf, worry writ large on his face. He held his laptop with the screen open in one hand.

'Big problem!' he said as he entered, uninvited.

'What is it?' Sergei stepped back to let him in.

'Army... They move to sector six.'

'Shit, that's our sector. How do you know?' All thoughts of a restful night's sleep were forgotten as Sergei's mind snapped to attention.

'Ladies, you better see this. Come, have a seat Yousaf.'

'I link to traffic camera network. Red light cameras work good.' Yousaf turned his laptop screen for them to see. The video feeds were grainy, but they showed columns of army trucks on the move. Each small camera window showed the location and the time. The massive army trucks were on Gulberg Boulevard and the time was 8:17. 'They come sector six. Make lockdown.'

'That means we need to leave now.' Jane let out an inaudible whistle. 'The raft. Let's get it into the van. We need our guns too.'

'How much time do we have?' Sergei said as he ran to pick

up their stash of weapons.

'Traffic heavy but maybe ten minute. Must quick hurry,' Yousaf said as he ran towards the stairs.

Jane helped Razane into one of the lined and hooded khaki coloured winter jackets that Yousaf had found in the basement.

They each slung a rifle over their shoulders and pocketed a pistol and rushed down the stairs to find Yousaf waiting. He was trying to move a section of the raft through the garage door. Jane and Sergei rushed to help.

'Razane sweetie, get the cricket bats and the spanners and pick up the bag of nuts,' Jane said as she lifted another section of the raft.

'We need to hurry,' Sergei grunted as he hoisted the last section into the back of the van. Jane was inside and helped guide it into place. 'We can't depend on traffic slowing the army trucks.'

Razane arrived with the cricket bats and the bag of heavy nuts, which she placed on the floor inside. Sergei took one last look at everything and closed the back doors.

'Where's Yousaf?' Sergei looked around. Yousaf was nowhere. 'Bloody hell, where is he?' Sergei ran back into the house. Jane followed.

'Yousaf, what's wrong?'

'Key… for van. I no find.'

* *

The fog was dense as Major Amjad along with Babur and Hussain drove out of the ISI complex. Following Google Maps, he turned left. Behind him, Sebastian and his team followed.

The dense fog slowed their progress, but they still reached their destination in nine and a half minutes.

Major Amjad parked three houses away under the branches of a giant banana tree. He killed the engine and the lights. Behind him, Sebastian did the same. The road was plunged back into darkness.

The house was an imposing double storey building with

tall columns supporting a portico. It was surrounded by a solid brick boundary wall lined with outwardly curved spikes as long as his forearm. He dialled a number.

'Yes.' It was Captain Usman.

'We are in position,' Major Amjad said.

'OK sir, the helicopter will be overhead in a minute. Our team will be on the roof twenty seconds after. Also two APVs are five minutes away.'

'Good job. Well done.' Amjad couldn't match Captain Usman's dispassionate delivery. He was too emotionally invested. It had always been his weakness. Today it wouldn't matter. He'd get his quarry and regain the trust of his superiors.

He cracked open his side window as they waited. The sounds of the outdoors rushed in. He ignored the stabbing pain as an ice-cold breeze wafted over his face. In the distance, the faint syncopated whirring of a helicopter was growing louder. Soon the inhabitants of the safe-house would hear it and attempt to escape.

'Get into position,' he said to Babur and Hussain as he climbed out and retrieved his M4 assault rifle from the back seat. He turned off the safety, put it into full automatic mode and waited. Babur and Hussain did the same. Further down the road, four dark shadows climbed out of Sebastian's car.

The helicopter was now overhead, the thrum of its rotor was deafening, its downdraft ferocious. Water droplets felt like tiny shards of ice as they blasted his face and neck. He turned his face down but not before catching sight of the dark shadows as they rappelled down ropes. He counted eight.

His quarry was trapped. The shadows landed on the roof and the helicopter ascended sharply. The men took positions, one on each corner and another halfway between them, weapons trained downwards. There was no escape.

Now for the armoured personnel carriers. They would complete the assault.

He called Captain Usman again. 'What is your position?'

'Sir, we are around the corner. Take cover as soon as we

enter the street. My men on the roof will blow the gate with an RPG.'

'You might need more than one. These gates are full military spec with armour steel plating. You should blow the corner of the boundary wall near the neighbouring house. It'll be weakest point. We can enter from there.'

'OK sir, understood.'

The drizzle turned to rain as Amjad took cover behind his car. He called Sebastian. 'Take cover behind your car. They'll blow a hole in the wall.'

* *

The drizzle turned to a torrent. For the briefest of moments, the curtain of rain seemed to shift sideways, the even pattern disrupting into chaos. Before their minds could register the strange phenomenon, the shock wave from the explosion passed them in the form of a sonic boom. A tremor went through the van. The traffic light suspended by twin chains swung in an arc.

Jane looked at the people in the other cars around them. They had all heard or felt it. People were looking around in alarm, their eyes wide in fear. Everyone was thinking the same thought; it was somewhere close by. The lights turned green, and the traffic took off like horses in a race. Wheels spun and horns tooted in a mad rush to escape.

'Was that connected to us?' Razane expressed what they were all thinking.

Yousaf pulled out his smartphone and turned on the screen. 'Oooh! They breach safe-house. Major Hamdani very angry with this.'

'Let's hope we reach him to convey the news,' Sergei said in a shaky voice.

'If we hadn't found the keys we'd be dead,' Jane said. 'I'm glad Razane thought of checking the ignition.'

'Always check obvious places first.' Razane's was the only calm voice. She betrayed no fear. She had always been able to maintain icy calm in such situations, at least at the beginning.

Jane patted Razane's leg and looked at her admiringly. Her strength was inspirational and comforting.

'This rain's bad… It'll wash away the fog.' Sergei looked up.

They passed a sign that read "Canal Bank Road - 5Km"

* *

Amjad stepped over the rubble as he followed Babur and Hussain through the jagged hole in the boundary wall. The grounds were dark. A solitary bulb illuminated the front porch. The solid timber double front door was surrounded by half a metre wide stainless steel frame. The door would have a core of armour-steel. An RPG wouldn't breach that.

Outside the boundary wall, a rumble signalled the armoured personnel carriers had arrived.

'Captain Usman, I need some cannon fire. Take out a window. We'll enter from there.'

'OK sir, take cover, there will be shrapnel. I'll go on ten.'

'OK, we are safe.'

The APV pulled up alongside the breach in the outer wall. Gears ground as its turret turned. The 30mm cannon erupted into hellacious gunfire as ten rounds pulverised the window surround into a cloud of dust that poured out into the front lawn, coating the waiting intelligence agents.

Amjad kept his eyes closed and lifted his sweater to cover his nose. Sebastian and Ian did the same. Babur and Hussain were the first to move. They approached the gaping hole, threw in smoke bombs and entered. Major Amjad shook his head. His new men were idiots. The dust cloud was enough to obscure all visibility. He removed his Glock from its holster, waited a moment longer and sprinted after them. Sebastian and Ian were panting as they tried to keep up. Their men followed closely behind.

When they reached the hole, Amjad stopped them. 'I

cannot allow you inside. Please wait here for me.' He paused to let Captain Usman and four commandos in full battle gear through. 'You will get full access to the prisoners.' With that, he strode through the breach.

The front office area was like the one in his own safe-house. Many things would be. Even though majors were given autonomy, they had to follow ISI guidelines to ensure the safe-houses maintained high operational capability. After construction, they were audited by a lieutenant-general of the ISI who was taken to the house, blindfolded.

'Give me infrared,' Captain Usman ordered as he crouched inside the opening.

'Thermal image feed is available now. I count eight.'

Captain Usman pressed a button on his goggles. A small screen showed a heat map of the house. It showed eight warm bodies. All were their own people.

Major Amjad patched into the video feed on his smartphone. It could mean only two things. They had escaped, or they were hiding from the infrared, either behind concrete or in aluminium lined space-suits. Safe-houses had both. So they would have to tread carefully.

'Get your men to fan out and check every corner,' Major Amjad said to the captain.

Hussain came into view. His face was covered in dust. 'Major Sahib, can I show you something in the basement?'

* *

The rain stopped as suddenly as it began. Yousaf indicated left as they approached the intersection at speed. Sergei braced himself as Yousaf took the turn without slowing. He gritted his teeth as the van skidded briefly on the wet road before it settled on its doughy springs.

Sergei exhaled, let go of the door handle and checked Google Maps. They were now on Canal Bank Road. The waterway, hidden by the dense fog, flowed to their right. The opposing lane of the road was on the other bank. 'Yousaf, did you find a place to launch the raft?'

'Yes, we there soon.'

Yousaf drove as fast as the dense traffic allowed, changing lanes to take advantage of every gap. They were getting harder to find as they came upon dense fog that slowed the traffic to a crawl.

'See there bridge... we go in water.' Yousaf pointed at something in the blanketing fog. Moments later a bridge appeared to their right.

Yousaf swung the wheel and cut sharply across two lanes of traffic. Behind them tyres screeched and horns blared as they turned onto the bridge that connected the two opposing lanes of Canal Bank Road. With a squeal of tyres, he stopped at the halfway point. 'We go here.'

Sergei opened the door and stepped out. Tendrils of fog floated over the road covering the surface. Jane and Razane got out beside him, shivering as the damp cold assailed them. Traffic on the bridge was light. A battered Suzuki hatchback passed them, honking at having to swerve. A few more cars and bicycles passed them, shrouded in the fog, but no one else showed any interest.

Sergei adjusted the hood of his jacket and looked towards where they had come from. The fog had turned car lights into mere pin-pricks. He walked to the railing. The fog was too dense to see the water. An eerie silence blanketed everything. He tried listening for flowing water.

'Can you hear the water?' he said as he put his arms around Jane and Razane.

Yousaf picked up a stone and dropped it over the railing. It splashed into the water with a plop. 'You hear?'

'How do we get down there?' Razane said as she tried to control her chattering teeth.

'Let's make sure we don't fall in. We'll freeze to death,' Sergei said.

'I think I see a way.' Jane walked to where the bridge

intersected Canal Bank Road. A narrow path led down an embankment. Holding on to the railing and then onto branches of a tree, she followed it down to the waterline, the fog growing thicker as she descended.

With almost a hundred percent humidity, the smell of the water was strong. It mixed with the toxic smog from the slow moving traffic just above her head. She had to fight the temptation to cough.

Below, in the almost complete darkness, waves slapped against the bank. She crouched down and turned on her smartphone torch. She was standing on a narrow footpath that ran alongside the water but a few centimetres above it. Thankfully she had stopped when she had. Another step to her right and she would have fallen in.

She bent down and touched the water. It was freezing. Sergei was right. They wouldn't survive if they fell in.

Sergei and Razane were anxiously waiting for when she emerged back onto the bridge.

'It's all good. We can get to the water from here.' Jane said, 'but be careful or you'll fall in.'

Yousaf had opened the van's rear doors. Sergei and Jane ran to help him. Together they lifted the sections of their raft and carried them to the beginning of the path that led to the water.

'We have a problem,' Jane said looking down. 'It's too dark down there to assemble and nowhere to stand.'

'Yes, but it's too bulky to carry down fully assembled,' Sergei said.

'Wait,' Yousaf stopped a man passing by on a bicycle. From his appearances he was a labourer returning home after a long day's work.

'Brother, do you want to earn five hundred rupees to help us for five minutes?'

'I would help you for no money but five hundred rupees will help me feed my children.' The man got off his bicycle, rubbing his hands to ward off the cold.

With the man's help and Jane's direction they assembled

the raft and carried it down to the water.

'I park van,' Yousaf said as he counted out the money for their helper. 'I meet you next bridge.' With no further explanation, he climbed into the van and drove off.

Sergei helped Razane onto the raft before climbing on himself. Jane sat on the left to balance the raft with Sergei to her right. They were about to find out if their idea would work.

What had seemed easy back at the safe-house became almost impossible. The hardest part was to get the raft to leave the bank without beginning to spin. Eventually they managed but smooth progress was harder than they had expected. Every little movement threatened to unbalance them and send one or all into the murky freezing waters.

'Let's lie flat,' Jane said as she lay on her stomach. Sergei and Razane did the same. It made a difference, but what they gained in stability they lost in paddling efficiency.

'Your paddling's not doing anything,' Razane said. 'I think the current's strong enough to move us as long as we stay far enough off the bank.'

Razane was right. As soon as Jane pushed them away from the water's edge, the raft picked up speed.

'We must keep the bank in sight, though,' Sergei said, 'or we may not see the bridge.'

It was easier said than done. The fog was almost pea soup thick. They could barely see the edge of the raft and the black of the water. The left bank was no longer visible.

'I'm going to slow us down till the next bridge,' Jane said as she put her cricket bat in the water. The raft hesitated for a moment and then turned towards the bank. Their speed dropped to a crawl.

'We're going in circles,' Sergei said.

'Well we need Yousaf, so let's go slow till the bridge,' Jane said.

They floated at a slow pace and in silence. Constant corrections made them bump into the bank a few times, but they accepted to ensure they didn't miss Yousaf.

The fog muted everything except the lapping waves and their breathing. Apart from the odd truck or motorcycle with a loud exhaust, the traffic on Canal Bank Road seemed distant.

They saw the bridge as they were passing under it. Sergei and Jane both paddled backwards, making the raft zig zag in the water.

'Careful or we'll spin,' Razane said.

Their efforts had slowed them but they were now past the bridge and the bank was nowhere in sight.

* *

'What am I looking at?' Amjad said as he examined the sawdust and wood shavings on the basement floor.

'They were making something,' Hussain said.

'What would I do without someone as clever as you.' Amjad regretted the sarcasm in his tone as soon as he spoke. Next time Hussain would be far more circumspect. 'You are right, son… but the question is what?' Amjad tried to sound kinder this time.

Hussain scratched his head and examined the tools.

'There are doors missing in many rooms.' Babur shouted from somewhere in the house.

'What is made of wood?' Amjad had crouched on the floor and was examining the offcuts.

'Cricket bats, doors, hockey sticks, chairs, donkey carts, rifle stocks, boats, crates…' Hussain was rattling off words.

'None of those make sense, unless…'

Babur had joined them. 'I think it is very obvious.'

'What?' The major scratched around the wounds on his face. It was sore but also itching like mad.

'They must have had carpenters in the house to replace the doors,' Babur said.

'Well… then why are they missing?' Amjad felt his phone ring in his pocket.

'Yes sir,' he listened to the colonel on the other end of the line. 'OK sir, I will do.' He pressed the off button and turned to Babur and Hussain.

'Put bedsheets over everything in the office area then invite the foreigners inside. We have been ordered to let them in.'

* *

They heard Yousaf's footsteps and his panting before the left bank came into sight. He was running along the narrow footpath. The raft slowed as it neared the water's edge.

Jane had her cricket bat in the water and could feel obstructions hit the bat. 'Hold on, we're going to hit tree roots,' she shouted. Her warning came too late. The raft came to a sudden stop, the force almost throwing Sergei forward into the water.

'Thank Allah, you stop,' Yousaf panted.

'We wouldn't leave you behind,' Jane said. 'Take care as you climb in… Stay low.' Jane shifted to the right and the rear as Razane shifted forward along the raft's centreline to make way for Yousaf.

The raft tilted alarmingly as Yousaf climbed in, but it righted itself when he lay down. Jane handed him the cricket bat.

Yousaf steadied his breathing before he used the bat to shove them away from the bank. The raft sped up. They were on their way.

'Yousaf, how far till the checkpoints?' Sergei whispered.

'Maybe two kilometre… near ummm, Thokar Niaz Baig flyover.'

'What's after that.'

'Lahore outer suburbs. Then farm and fields. But then big danger from Hudiara Drain.'

'What's that?' Sergei said.

'Canal go through big pipe when cross drain. Raft get stuck. We be drown.'

'That settles it,' Jane said, 'we need to get off before the drain.'

**

'Have you found any traces of them?' Sebastian said as he looked past Amjad down the stairs towards the basement.

'Yes, CCTV footage from inside the house shows they were here.' Amjad made no move to let Sebastian pass.

'We need to see everything including... the basement.' Ian was growing tired of Amjad's apparent shenanigans.

'You must understand there are things we cannot disclose.'

'OK, I'll have to talk to my bosses again.' Sebastian said in a tired voice.

'It will not matter. This is a military facility. I can, however...' Amjad hesitated before continuing. 'I can share images of the only thing out of place and also send you the CCTV images.'

'OK, now we're getting—' Sebastian said.

'But...' Amjad raised his hand. 'As long as you don't insist on going down there. Otherwise, be my guest and go back to your bosses. I warn you there is a line even my spineless leaders will not cross.' Either Amjad was telling the truth, or he was an excellent poker player.

It was Sebastian's turn to hesitate. He looked at Ian. 'Well... OK! Show us,' he said finally.

Amjad pulled out his phone and showed them what looked like a carpenter's workspace. Saw dust, wood shavings, and small pieces of timber lay scattered on the floor. 'We are trying to understand this. We are checking the CCTV footage for clues. Maybe builders are still working on the house. We do not know.'

'Are there any other signs of renovations?' Ian said.

'Some doors are missing throughout the house. Maybe they were getting new doors put in.' Amjad said.

'Can you let us see them?'

'OK, the rest of the house is open for you. Except anything

covered in sheets.'

'Why so secretive? What's this house?' Ian said.

'It is a military facility, but more I cannot say. Sorry!'

'When will you finish going through the CCTV?' Sebastian said.

'It is encrypted, so it takes longer to access. Men are going through it now. They gave me a file with the last few minutes before they left. Here let me show you.' Amjad turned his screen towards them.

The grainy images showed Yousaf, Sergei and Jane running through the house towards the garage and then back again before returning to the garage. The clock on the video showed it was twenty-seven minutes ago.

'That's gotta be a few minutes before we reached.' Ian exploded. 'How the bloody hell did they know we were coming.'

'They could not have—'

'But the—'

'They must have found out the army was imposing a curfew on this sector.'

'How?'

'I cannot explain... Trust me, there was no leak,' Amjad said.

'We'll deal with the trust thing later. Any thoughts on how we find them?'

'We are trying to read their vehicle's number plate to put out an alert. But the curfew is already in place so they cannot get far. They will be stopped.'

'We just got here. How can the army impose a curfew so fast without giving the people any warning?'

'They can. They announced it on the radio and in mosques. If you listen carefully, you will hear the mosque loudspeakers still broadcasting the message.'

Amjad was right. Sebastian had heard something being announced on mosque loudspeakers while they had waited outside the house. They hadn't paid it any attention. Pakistan was a noisy place at the best of times. Loudspeakers were used throughout the day for calls to prayers and for other announcements, but they were always in the local language. 'Could the announcements have been mistimed?'

Sebastian and Ian walked through the house taking photographs. Except for the mysterious off-limit areas, it looked like the opulent mansion of a rich businessman. They were getting nowhere. They were about to leave when Amjad called out to them. 'We have found the vehicle. It is an ambulance. They must have stolen it from the hospital.'

'Are you looking for it?' Sebastian said.

'Yes, not to worry. They cannot escape.'

Sebastian clenched his fists. He was tired of hearing the same empty reassurances.

CHECKPOINT

Lahore, Thursday 11 January, 10:11 pm

Sebastian was the last to pile into their Jeep.

'Sir, can we go?' Junaid, their driver looked in the rear-view mirror.

'Yes Junaid, back to the hotel, please,' Sebastian said. He took one last look at the safe-house. As he watched, a helicopter landed on the roof.

'Ordinary houses don't have helipads.' Ian let out a whistle.

'He did say it was a military facility. How odd.' Sebastian straightened and took out his phone. 'I'm calling Langley.'

'Uhu,' Ian muttered. He was studying a map on his smartphone. 'Can we... tell the driver to head out of town?'

'Sorry... I don't get... whadda mean?'

'Ask the driver how he'd leave Lahore if he was heading for... say, Dera Ismail Khan.'

'Sir, I can take you.' Junaid addressed Ian. 'I can take you to Dera Ismail Khan, but it is far...'

'We don't wanna go there,' Ian said. 'Not yet. But humour me. If you had to leave Lahore to head to Dera Ismail Khan where would you leave from?'

'Sir, the army has check posts in place to stop anyone leaving.'

'OK, take me to the check post they would try to get past.'

'OK sir,' Junaid said as he turned the jeep around.

Traffic in the narrow residential roads was almost non-existent but as soon as they hit the main road, they were ensnared in a long column of cars crawling at a walking pace. The curfew had caused panic and everyone had flooded the streets at the same time.

'Do you have a siren?' Sebastian said, growing impatient.

'Yes, sir.'

'Then use it for Christ's sake.' Sebastian restrained himself with difficulty. It wasn't Junaid's fault. He wasn't a mind reader.

With the siren and lights, Junaid still had to flash his high-beam and sit on the horn to get other cars to make way. They were now travelling faster than the rest of the traffic, but what should have been a fifteen-minute journey was taking far longer.

To make matters worse, the fog was getting thicker by the minute. It was a minute to ten o'clock when the check post came into view. Armed soldiers with flashlights walked between the column of vehicles. In each of the three lanes, soldiers corralled five vehicles at a time, opening all doors, boots and looking underneath with mirrors. They pulled on beards and hair, presumably looking for fakes. Women with face coverings were checked by female soldiers. A soldier with a camera was photographing them all.

The army wasn't leaving any stone unturned. Buses and trucks were diverted to a separate lane. Not a single shipping container was left unopened or a bale of straw left unprodded.

Sebastian and Ian got out and walked over to a uniformed officer in the driver's seat of a Land Rover. He looked up from his laptop screen as they approached. They identified themselves and asked for permission to observe.

'Yes you may,' the officer replied. 'By the way, I am Captain Shahab. If you see anything suspicious, please come to me straight away.'

'No one's getting past this,' Ian said as they walked down the column of cars back to their Jeep.

Sebastian nodded, lost in thought. The soldiers were as thorough as any checkpoint he'd ever seen. But he still felt uneasy. Their quarry were resourceful and cunning. They wouldn't bluff their way past the checkpoint. 'Something tells me they'll use another way.' He stopped in the middle of the road. The fog was growing ever denser. The footpath on either side was no longer easy to see from where they stood and anything beyond was completely shrouded. 'I wanna see what's in that foggy area. What if someone slips past there?'

'Yeah, good thinking,' Ian said. They turned right across the traffic onto the footpath. The ground, covered in grass, sloped sharply down to a service road running in front of a row of houses, all with tall brick walls and steel gates. The army had installed coils of barbed wire backed by angle iron frames right up to the front boundary wall of a house. Three armed soldiers stood guard along the makeshift fence. Others milled about. One of them rushed over and asked for their ID. No one would slip by here.

They crossed the road to check the other side. The footpath ran beside a row of tall trees growing on an embankment that dropped sharply downwards into opaque fog. Sebastian could feel his clothes damp from the moisture in the air. Ian took out his phone and turned on the torch. It was no use. The fog was like an impenetrable barrier. Unable to see well enough to climb down the slope, they decided against doing so.

'Man, this is giving me the creeps.' Sebastian was looking at Google Maps.

Ian was doing the same. He was the first to speak. 'It says Lahore Branch Canal.'

'A waterway?'

'It says so right here. It would explain why the fog's thicker.' Ian said. 'I'm gonna check it out.' Crouching, he grabbed a tree-trunk and lowered himself, feeling for something firm to stand on. When his feet hit solid ground, he let go of the tree. It was bone-chillingly cold and smelt dank and wet. The sounds of traffic were muted and seemed far away. He turned on his phone's torch. He was on a narrow bitumen path. To his right the ground dropped sharply into the canal. Waves lapped the bank. The water was less than a meter away. He approached slowly, bent his knees and dipped his hand in the water. The current was strong. Sebastian dropped to the footpath beside him.

'I think I know what those wood shavings were,' Ian said. 'The fuckers were making a boat.'

'Fuck!' Sebastian couldn't decide whether to laugh or cry.

In his haste to dial Major Amjad, he almost dropped his phone in the canal.

COILED BARBS

Lahore Outskirts, Friday 12 January, 12:30 pm

Sebastian's words acted like a hammer in the back of Major Amjad's head. The American bastard had discovered the escape route before him. 'Fuck this,' he smashed his palm on the table. It left his hand numb. He didn't hear Awan walk in.

'Sir, we have found something on the CCTV feed you should see.' Awan was still saluting.

'Wait… Let me guess. They made a boat.' He wanted to sound sarcastic but all he managed was bitterness.

Awan looked surprised. His mouth opened in amazement. He closed it again and swallowed heavily. 'Yes, sir… but it looks more like a raft.'

'OK, well done. Finish checking the rest of the footage. I want a full catalogue of all events on the feed with proper time stamps.'

Awan saluted and left. Major Amjad dialled the colonel. He explained the situation and suggested what should be done.

'OK, I will pass it on. Go to the checkpoint and monitor the operation. For your sake, they better not have slipped by.'

* *

Sebastian grabbed a tree trunk and pulled himself up to the road. Ian followed. Through the fog, he could see soldiers clearing a path between the cars. More came running, dragging a long coil of barbed wire. As he watched, two soldiers jumped into the water and pulled the coils behind them. More joined them and they began to pull the coils across the waterway.

'That was one of the quickest responses, I've ever seen.' Sebastian truly was amazed. 'Makes me feel cold just watching them.'

'They are fucking brave to jump in like that,' Ian said.

They walked back to their Jeep. More soldiers ran to the canal bank. Others piled into three pickup trucks and sped off down the road.

'I'm impressed,' Ian said. 'I usually need to beg on my knees for something to be done.'

The phone rang. It was Major Amjad, 'I am on my way but traffic is slowing me down. Are the soldiers doing anything?'

'You bet.' Sebastian described what was going on. As he spoke, more army pickup trucks drove off.

'Good,' the major said. 'The army will occupy all bridges and patrol the entire length of road along the canal to where it falls into the River Ravi. I tried getting helicopters but they cannot fly in the fog. If they are using the canal, we will catch them.' He hung up.

Sebastian thought about following one of the army pickup trucks but decided against it. In total six had sped off. It would be a wild goose chase if he tagged along with the wrong one.

At the checkpoint, the traffic was thinning, just in time for the curfew. The gates were closing after the horses had bolted.

* *

The impact threw them diagonally forward as a corner of the raft smashed into the bank. Sergei tried to get up but was thrown sideways as the raft rotated sharply. Fighting inertial forces, he reached out and grabbed a tree root that flashed by. It broke away in his hand. Yousaf grabbed another. The raft's rear corner smashed into the bank, got tangled in roots and tilted alarmingly as it came to a halt. Sergei reached out, grabbed a root with one hand and Jane's arm with the other.

'I'll hold while you three get off. Watch your step.' Sergei was gasping.

Half crouching, half standing, Jane and Razane crawled over Sergei's prone form onto the bank. The footpath was wider than where they got on. Jane's legs shook uncontrollably as she tried to sit up.

'It's OK my love, take a deep breath,' Razane said as she stroked Jane's back.

'I suddenly felt dizzy,' Jane said as she exhaled sharply and sucked air into her lungs. It seemed to help. The world righted itself. 'I'm better,' she said as she reached forward and grabbed the rifles from Yousaf.

Sergei was last off the raft. As he clambered up the bank with Yousaf's help it dislodged itself and with a few more rotations floated away into the gloomy mist.

They crouched on the footpath catching their breaths and listening for any threats. The road above them was strangely quiet. While they waited, two cars passed by.

'Where are we?' Razane said, looking at Jane's phone. Google Maps showed they were surrounded by fields.

Yousaf looked over her shoulder too. 'We outside Lahore. Up there is Mohlanwal Road.'

It explained why there was almost no traffic. Sergei was about to climb up the embankment onto the road when Yousaf stopped him. 'I go first. Must check is safe. Then you come.' With that, Yousaf clambered up the slope. He popped down a moment later. 'All empty, come fast.' He offered Jane a hand.

A few moments later they all stood on the upper footpath. The fog prevented them seeing the opposite verge of the road.

'Yousaf, how far is Mohlanwal out of Lahore?' Jane said.

'Not know. This very new housing estate. Many fields. Not many house.'

'So what now?' Sergei said.

'We find transport,' Yousaf said.

'OK, but how and where?' Sergei said, 'I hear nothing.'

'Come fast,' Yousaf said as he walked across the road. '*Fatafat*! Is not safe.'

* *

Nawaz Sharif shivered as he pulled the shawl closer. His stomach rumbled. His last meal had been twelve hours ago during his lunch break.

When he reached home after a hard day's work, Ruhina, his wife, was already in a foul mood. He should have quietly gone back out again, but he was tired and had decided to enter the kitchen for a glass of water. Somehow she had smelt the perfume Nayla had worn that day. He had tried telling her it was from a passenger he had picked up in his taxi, but Ruhina wouldn't listen. She began to hit him with the rolling pin she was using to make rotis.

'Get out of my house. Go to the whore you got this smell from,' she screamed at the top of her lungs, flecks of spittle filling the space between them.

He tried feigning indignation and put his hand up to motion her to stop. It only made her more irate.

'Who do you think you are? You two-bit taxi driver. You are not worthy of one woman. Why do you think you deserve two? You think just because you have the same name as the former prime minister you are somebody. You are nobody. You are a son of a dog. Get out of my house. You are not welcome here. Get out… get out, get out now…' Her stream of invective wasn't slowed by the blows she began raining on him.

At first he had tried standing his ground, using his height as an advantage and his open palms to cushion the blows but they too were hurting. His forearms were raw, his head rang from the blows that got through.

Meanwhile, his frustrated grimace only seemed to fuel her anger. In a move that would put Bruce Lee to shame, she switched the rolling pin to her left hand and slapped his face with her free hand. The force of the blow made him see stars. His anger boiled over and he roared in defiance. It was a big mistake. She turned to the stove and picked up a one handled saucepan full of boiling water.

Realising the danger, he made a dash for it. The sheet of boiling water flew after him. By the time it soaked him it had cooled somewhat but was still hot enough to scald the back of his neck as he ran from the kitchen. A plate missed him by inches.

'Leave and do not return,' she screamed as he grabbed his keys and wallet and ran out of the house.

For a brief second, he contemplated going to Nayla's house but her husband would be home. He was a policeman and would put a bullet in him.

It was a minute after nine and all the shops in Mohlanwal were closed for the day. He tried heading into Lahore but got caught in a traffic jam. When he heard of the curfew on the radio, he did a U-turn and returned to Mohlanwal. He found a place to park in the service lane that ran parallel to Canal Road, locked the doors, reclined the seat and wrapped his shawl around himself. He would wait until the morning for some food. Hopefully, by then his wife would have calmed down. If he froze to death overnight, it would serve her right. She would have to find work cleaning houses, the bitch.

He hated her. One day he would pluck up the courage and dominate her as a man should. If only she was less fierce, and he had bigger balls.

He closed his eyes and tried falling asleep. The pent up emotion was making it hard. The loud bang made his heart leap into his mouth.

BOGGIE PEHLWAN

Yousaf looked around and secretly whispered a prayer. 'Allah, I give you a million thanks.' The taxi parked on the roadside had seemed like a gift from heaven. But was it too good to be true? He half expected police cars or army jeeps to pop out of the mist.

The taxi driver had nearly jumped out of his skin when Sergei knocked on the glass like he had seen a ghost. A nasty bruise covered the left side of his face. A head wound bled onto his right ear and stained his collar a bright red. His movements were dazed and slow. Maybe he had been in an accident or had been robbed.

They piled in and before they had all closed their doors, the taxi was in motion. The driver was acting like he was in a dream.

'Go faster please, brother,' Yousaf said, unsure whether he should enquire about his condition. The driver hadn't even reset the old-style meter, which was strange.

Finally, the driver turned his head to look at him, his eyes were glazed over. 'Where do you wish to go, sir?' His words were slurred.

'Okara,' Yousaf said stealing a glance back at Sergei.

In the back seat Jane whispered to Sergei. 'He's telling the driver to go to Okara.'

Sergei looked at his phone. 'What place did you say?'

'O... ka... ra!'

'I've found it. It's the next town.' Sergei showed her his screen.

The thick fog prevented them from seeing anything beyond the edge of the road. The poor visibility was the least of their worries. The car was in a decrepit state, even worse than the driver. Its dull yellow headlamps barely pierced the fog. Each time they slowed the brakes groaned, and the tyres squealed.

Through thinner parts of the fog they could see a few houses. It was the housing estate Yousaf had mentioned. Apart from a few lit windows and the odd security guard, they saw no one.

A few minutes later the houses were replaced by empty fields.

'We're now beyond Lahore's outer suburb,' Sergei said, turning his screen off.

Yousaf was the most nervous. He had seen what their driver looked like. His movements were erratic, his reflexes dull. They were on a straight road with no traffic. If something came in their path would the driver be able to take evasive action?

'Brother, how much will you charge us?' Yousaf said trying to engage him in a conversation.

'Huh?' The driver turned his head slowly. Yousaf could see he was soaked in sweat. He wasn't well.

'Brother, stop here,' Yousaf said firmly. 'I will drive your taxi.'

It took a moment for the driver to register. Without saying a word, he pulled over.

Yousaf turned to Sergei. 'This man sick. I drive.'

Yousaf watched as the driver staggered around to the passenger side before he slid sideways into the driver's seat.

'Hey, he's bleeding,' Jane said noticing for the first time. 'That was a good call.'

They set off again. With Yousaf in control, they picked up speed. The driver wrapped himself in a shawl and promptly fell asleep.

'Yousaf, what are we doing in Okara?' Jane said.

'I know man there. He help us.'

'Yousaf, you are most resourceful,' Razane said.

'I Pakistani commando,' Yousaf said.

'Thanks for helping us,' Razane said.

Sergei smiled. 'You're very proud of Pakistan and the

army?' Sergei said.

'Yes very proud Pakistani. Pak Army my life. Very proud of Pak Army.'

'Yet you're still helping us?' Sergei said.

Yousaf looked at him with a blank expression, at first not understanding the question. 'Major Amjad very bad man. His friend, my enemy. His enemy, my friend. I help you so after you help me free Major Hamdani. He great man, very good Pakistani. Only he stop Major Amjad.'

'We need to free him too,' Jane said.

The fog thinned enough for Yousaf to speed up. The roads were mostly empty which made driving even more hazardous. Yousaf could feel himself nodding off to sleep. He turned on the radio and turned down the heater. He had to keep himself awake.

After a progression of small sleepy towns, they roared into the outskirts of Okara. A somnolent policeman by the side of the road, manning a checkpoint, glanced at the taxi then looked away. Yousaf slowed to drive over a speed hump in the road and turned left onto a nearly empty boulevard. He checked his watch. It was exactly an hour since they had set off.

He looked around for landmarks to jog his memory. He had never visited his contact in the night time. Boggie Pehlwan was the local *badmash*, the head of the local crime syndicate. He ran protection rackets, a counterfeiting ring, traded in drugs, alcohol and weapons in Okara and the surrounding towns and villages.

The man had helped Major Hamdani locate terrorists and Indian spies. In exchange, the major had given him protection against the police.

Boggie Pehlwan was a patriot and considered himself a principled and moral criminal. He prayed, gave alms to the poor, fasted during Ramzan and performed Hajj every year.

Hopefully, Boggie Pehlwan would help even without the major being present. Their lives depended on it. Yousaf recognised a tyre repair shop; it was the next right. They were in the older part of Okara. The streets narrowed with barely enough room for two cars to pass. The three and four-storey houses were vaguely reminiscent of those in Lahore's walled city except they were simpler.

He turned right into a dark alleyway that ended in a solid brick wall covered in faded tattered posters. He stopped and switched off the engine and the lights. They were plunged into darkness. 'Please wait in car till I back,' Yousaf said as he opened the door and stepped into the dark.

Somewhere outside a dog howled, setting off all the neighbourhood's dogs; the canine ruckus drowned out Yousaf's receding footsteps.

* *

Major Amjad looked at his watch. It was 3:45 in the morning. He took another sip of his Red Bull and shuddered. It tasted like cat piss, but it kept him awake. He noticed Captain Shahab leave his pickup and cross the grassy strip to his car.

'Sir, some developments... We found the raft - a patrol we sent ahead spotted it in the water. It was stuck under a bridge.'

'And the fugitives?'

'Sorry sir, no sign of them. I believe they escaped.'

'You believe? Why?'

'Well, sir. After my boys found the raft, they searched along the left bank. They found a guard outside a house. He had seen only six cars and one motorbike in the previous hour. One of them was full of people.'

'Oh! Did we get a description?'

'Yes, an old Suzuki Swift taxi.'

'Hmmm, good work, but captain... you do realise there are thousands of those?'

'It had green parking lamp bulbs and flew a Pakistani flag just like on a government official's car.'

'How odd, but that is good news. Well done, captain.'

'Thank you, sir.'

'And you can finish up here. The checkpoint is no longer

needed. In fact, the whole curfew can be called off.'

'OK, sir.' The captain saluted and walked off.

The major waited for the captain to leave and dialled the colonel.

'Sir, we need to put out a Kill Bulletin.'

'So you let them get away?' the colonel growled.

He was too tired to argue. 'Sir, I am requesting we ask the army and police to set up roadblocks to look for a Suzuki Swift taxi with green parking bulbs and a flag.'

'For how long?'

'Sir?'

'They found a way out of a curfew area cordoned off by our esteemed military. Do you actually think they will stay in the taxi?'

'Sir what do you suggest?' he said with a resigned voice.

'Use your intelligence man!' The colonel's tone was dripping with condescension but also sounded tired. 'You are supposed to have some. Come up with a plan that makes sense.'

'Sir, we have a few things in our favour. They do not know the country so they will stay together. So we are looking for a group of four people. Three foreigners and a Pakistani travelling together should be easy to spot.

'My plan is to mobilise as many roadblocks as possible but also engage our official and unofficial networks. If we offer a ten-million-rupee reward, every man with a gun will be out looking for them. But there is more sir. By tomorrow morning, with better visibility, we can use the National Camera Network. I propose we give the public temporary access to all the feeds by linking them on the Internet and announcing the same ten million rupee reward. Everyone with a computer will join the hunt. We should have thousands if not tens of thousands of eyeballs helping.'

'Hmmm, that is the first sign of brains I have heard all evening,' the colonel said. 'I authorise it all. Make it happen.' He hung up.

Hands trembling, Amjad logged into his network on his phone. He found the form needed to initiate the Kill Bulletin and began to fill it in. Thankfully most of it was ticking boxes. He attached his digital signature and forwarded it to the colonel for authorisation. The form froze. He checked it over. He had left out a reason without which the form wouldn't save and go to the next step. He typed in the reason and pressed Enter. The screen went black. He tapped the screen. It was unresponsive. Damn, the battery had died.

'Sebastian, Ian, do you have a charging cable for an Apple?' he called out.

'No man. Our phones use USB-C.'

'Captain Shahab, I need an Apple cable,' he shouted. The captain shook his head. In Pakistan, Apple phones weren't as common among the working class. What could he do? No shops would be open. He had to return to his office, and fast.

'Captain, call ahead to your checkpoints to let my car through.'

'Yes, sir.' The captain picked up his phone.

* *

The Mercedes had a musty old-car smell that reminded Sergei of his old classic Porsche back home. The interior was worn in places but its doors still closed with a solid thunk. Mechanically the car was sound. Its suspension soaked up the bumps with aplomb and the engine purred smoothly as Yousaf piloted it along the dark narrow undivided two-lane highway. The fog had cleared to a haze. It allowed Yousaf to wind the car up to two hundred kilometres per hour for brief periods till the inevitable ponderous truck or bus required a solid prod on the brakes. Mercifully the Mercedes stopped as well as it went.

They were now an hour and a half out of Okara and heading in a westerly direction. It was a relief to leave the sleeping taxi driver in his decrepit vehicle for something safer and quicker.

Yousaf's contact had given him two burkas for Jane and Razane and a long kameez, a turban and sunglasses for Sergei along with counterfeit plastic ID cards still warm from the printer. 'ID card for checkpoint,' Yousaf had said as he had handed them out.

Before they left the taxi, Sergei noticed Yousaf handing the driver a wad of cash and a piece of paper.

'What did you give the taxi driver?' Sergei said when they were safely in the Mercedes.

'I say he go to Bahawalpur and pick up my friend and bring him to Lahore.'

'What friend? Why?'

'If Major Amjad know about taxi, then I wish… no… I hope Major Amjad find him in Bahawalpur and think we go to south.' Yousaf took a right turn without slowing.

'Oh,' Sergei tried to work it out but his mental faculties had diminished from lack of sleep and Yousaf's maniacal driving.

'Yousaf, why do we need these stuffy burkas?' Jane said from the back.

'Every road have camera with face technology.'

'You said they don't work.'

'They no work in night. In day they work very good.'

Sergei had never been a good passenger. Yousaf was taking risks he never would have, but realised speed was of the essence. Any time now the authorities would clamp down with roadblocks. The farther they were from Lahore, the safer they would be.

'That is city of Jhang ahead,' Yousaf said.

'Are we going there?' Sergei said.

'No bypass.' As if to emphasise, Yousaf turned hard into a left-handed slip lane. The car's tyres squealed as they scrabbled for grip. Sergei held on to the door handle to stop himself falling onto Yousaf. Jane had to brace herself to hold on to Razane who had fallen asleep. She was about to say something but thought the better of it. Instead, she said a prayer under her breath.

'After Jhang it's only one more large city before we reach the tribal area,' Sergei said looking back. He smiled when he saw Razane asleep. He undid his belt and slipped out of his jacket.

'Darling, don't take your belt off! Please...' Jane's voice was tinged with fear. Yousaf was driving on the edge and she wasn't sure he was up to it.

Sergei clipped the belt buckle before he turned around and handed the jacket to Jane. 'Here use this to make yourselves comfortable.'

'Thanks, babe.' Jane accepted it gratefully and placed it over Razane and herself. Then she leaned against the side and fell asleep.

'Yousaf, drive carefully, please,' Sergei said when he had turned around again.

'No be worry. I do special driving course. I very good driver.'

'I can see that, but even good drivers can crash. Let me drive when you're tired.'

'Sergei. I take care. You like brother and Jane and Razane like sister. I no crash.'

'I drive after a while,' Sergei persisted.

'OK, we stop get food. Then you drive.'

THE KILL BULLETIN

The crimson rays of the morning sun on the sandy horizon behind them lit the inside of the Mercedes.

Yousaf screwed his eyes as he adjusted the rear-view mirror to avoid being blinded. Glare wasn't the only hazard. The encroaching sands of the Thal Desert had obliterated the edge of the road on both sides and reduced its width to a single lane. The wind had picked up and was tossing more loose sand and spindly unmoored shrubs onto the road, concealing potholes that peppered the bitumen.

The sand acted like tiny marbles reducing traction to near zero. The slightest misjudgement risked them sliding into a sand drift and rolling over.

To make matters worse, oncoming traffic had the sun in their eyes and the same narrow ribbon of bitumen to drive on. Evading oncoming traffic became a game of high-speed chicken. The reason they hadn't crashed was a combination of Yousaf's skill, the quality of their vehicle and sheer dumb luck.

The danger kept Yousaf on edge even though sleep was pressing on his senses. Sergei saw his predicament and willed himself to keep up a lighthearted conversation, but he himself was becoming less lucid by the minute.

Jane and Razane were fast asleep in the back. If he succumbed, Yousaf would too.

'That sun rising over the desert looks amazing.' Sergei looked through the back window at the vista.

'Huh.' Yousaf grunted.

Sergei turned back and looked at his phone to check their location. Damn, there was no reception. His best guess was they were somewhere in the middle of the desert.

'Sergei, bro. Mankera come soon. Stop have tea, food. Then

you drive.' Yousaf yawned and rubbed his eyes.

* *

Major Amjad checked his inbox. The only unread email was from the colonel officially approving the kill bulletin. He could now distribute it externally, including to the police and the paramilitary rangers. It authorised lethal force to apprehend the fugitives. Within the hour their faces would be on the news and with every law enforcement officer in the country.

He watched as Arif, the IT geek, tested the public-facing National Camera Network website.

'Sir, it is ready. You can see here how easily I can search for feeds and open as many windows, all with different cameras.' Arif pressed a button and turned his laptop to face the major.

The windows all showed views from cameras around the country. The resolution was decent. Even though many locations were still foggy, he could make out number-plates, the make and model of the vehicle, and see inside to count the number of occupants.

'Thank you, Arif,' Amjad said with a nod of his head. 'Now get on social media and let everyone know.'

'OK, sir.' Arif typed feverishly.

'Go do it in your office,' the major said, 'I have to finish something. Up! *Fatafat!*'

'Yes, sir.' Arif picked up his laptop and left.

Amjad yawned through a closed mouth. He was so tired he couldn't think straight. He had to do a few more things, but was struggling to remember what. He looked back at his laptop screen. The wound on his face throbbed mercilessly. His face burned and itched at the same time. He'd taken the last four codeine tablets half an hour ago, but they hadn't worked. On top of that, his hand still hurt from where he had slammed it on the table. He had become a wreck. He took a sip of water. It made him shiver. He pressed the back of his hand to his forehead. It was burning. He had a fever, which meant his wounds had become infected. The doctor had told him to take it easy for a few days. There was no time for that. He remembered what he still had to do; write a press release announcing the reward for information leading to the death or capture of the fugitives, and he had to send out the kill bulletin. He began to type.

* *

Hussain poked his head around the door. 'Major Sahib, can I come in.' He entered without waiting for an answer.

Amjad looked up. The head movement made him dizzy.

'Good news, sir. They found the taxi.'

'Allah be praised,' he said. His own voice sounded strange. 'Where?'

'Bahawalpur. They stopped him at a checkpoint.'

What...? His mind reeled. He had thought they were heading to Afghanistan. In a way, Karachi made more sense. After all, it was how they had escaped last time. What did they hope to get in Afghanistan, anyway? It could have been Major Hamdani? The foreigners had a history of breaking people out of custody, Jane from a police lockup and Razane from an ISI dungeon. Maybe they believed they could get Hamdani out as well. Maybe that had made more sense before they had broken Razane out. Now Karachi made more sense. Why linger where they could be caught? And besides, Afghanistan was far more dangerous than Pakistan.

He remembered Hussain was still standing in the doorway, waiting for an answer. To what...? He tried remembering... Oh, he had brought him the news of the taxi. 'OK, thank you.' His words were hollow, distant, feeble.

He picked up the receiver on his desk phone. He couldn't feel his hands as he pressed the fast dial button for Sebastian. The call went straight to voicemail. He mumbled his message telling Sebastian what he had just learnt and put the receiver on the desk without hanging up. The fog in his mind had made everything a greyish-white. He turned back to his laptop. The screen swam.

He had to send out the bulletin. He opened the app. The approved kill-bulletin sat in his inbox. He opened it and clicked on a tab marked "External Release". He began ticking boxes. The last set of boxes were to choose the geographical spread. Now that they had found the taxi in Bahawalpur he would be criticised if he made it country-wide for no reason. He ticked Punjab and Sindh but left off Khyber-Pakhtunkhwa and Baluchistan. In the last field, he wrote out his contact details.

The information he had entered would be formatted correctly before transmission. It would appear as a fax in every police station and army post, as a text message on every official mobile phone and as an email marked urgent to every member of those forces in the marked provinces.

Sightlessly he scanned the screen to check for errors, not registering what he read. He pressed the send button. It was 6:23 in the morning. A chasm opened, the room became a whirlpool sucking him downwards, his eyes went dark.

A faraway voice sounded. 'Are you OK, boss?'

He mumbled something as his forehead hit the keyboard.

THE RUSE

Hathala, Friday 12 January, 8:01 am

Sergei turned up the radio. There was only one station, and it was playing a slow ballad in Pashto, the language of Khyber Pakhtunkhwa province. They had left Punjab when they crossed the River Indus an hour ago. He understood Pashto even less than Urdu and Punjabi and the style of the music wasn't to his taste, but it was better than Yousaf's incessant snoring and the squeak from the door handle.

He slowed behind a tractor-trolley laden with hay and waited for a gap in traffic, before overtaking it.

The desert had ended at Bhakkar. The road was back to its full width, and the surface was smooth. Sergei was glad because traffic was heavy and most drivers showed a lackadaisical approach to safety. Either they were all suicidal, or they believed divine intervention would save them at the last moment.

Since Okara he had only seen five wrecks when there should have been hundreds. Maybe a higher power was at play. It had stepped in a few times on their behalf. Since Bhakkar he had been forced off the road four times by oncoming vehicles overtaking when they shouldn't have. The last time he had come to a full stop on the verge and their mirrors had still scraped. It didn't help that the road had no lane markings and no central divider.

With all his passengers asleep, Sergei decided to bypass Dera Ismail Khan, the last major town in the area, and press on. So far he hadn't seen roadblocks, but that didn't mean there wouldn't be people looking for them.

The signs to Hathala flashed by. For a moment, Sergei had a brain freeze. The name was familiar, but he forgot why. Then he remembered how Jane had saved him in the steakhouse.

A bump in the road made Yousaf stir. He shifted in his

seat, awoke, muttered something unintelligible, then fell asleep again. The snoring returned. In the back Jane and Razane, draped in their burkas, were awake. He knew because they were moving their heads about.

Razane caught Sergei looking at her and lifted her veil. 'I hate this garment,' she griped.

Razane was rarely flustered. Sergei smiled in empathy. 'I know sweetheart. It's only for the road-side cameras. We're so near, it would be terrible if…'

'I haven't seen roadside cameras. There aren't even street lights out here.'

She was mostly right. 'But I've seen poles whenever we pass a small settlement. I saw cameras on them.'

'You're right… I'm just in a bad mood, this thing's so itchy and closed-in—'

Jane lifted her veil and kissed her on her lips, cutting her off mid-sentence. Razane responded, throwing her arms around Jane and cradling her head from behind.

Sergei laughed. 'Hey, you're gonna make the cameras melt…'

Jane paused, 'Two burka women kissing in public would go viral on YouTube.' She smiled.

'We could make a fortune putting it on ourselves,' Sergei smiled.

Razane kissed Jane again and sat back, dropping the veil back over her face. 'Forget the money, it'd be funny to see how people react. Maybe we'd get a fatwa on us.'

Sergei smiled. 'You know, I was just thinking…'

'Hmmm?' Jane and Razane both said in unison.

'That steakhouse… we could stop by and show Razane the scene of the slaughter.'

'Ooh, I'd love to see, but just from the outside,' Razane said. 'It'd be too risky to go in.'

'No way, don't…' Jane said. 'You two are like kids…'

'It's coming up soon,' Sergei said.

* *

Sebastian woke with a start. He looked at his phone. It was 9.30 in the morning. The last conference call had ended at four in the morning; he had only gotten five hours of sleep. He massaged his neck muscles as he checked his messages.

The first was a voicemail from Major Amjad, his voice oddly slurred. 'The taxi with green lights was found in Bahawalpur.'

He sat up, all thoughts of sleep gone. It was an unexpected development. He looked for Bahawalpur on the map. It was halfway to Sindh.

What were they planning to do in Karachi? Maybe hide or escape by sea like they'd done before. Hiding was easier said than done, especially with the latest face-recognition cameras that could spot a single person in a football stadium. They were now so affordable that most governments were saturating their public spaces with them. The perceived threat of terrorism was the perfect excuse to spy on their citizenry. Together with advances in satellite photography and Internet-based surveillance, the only places left to hide were in dense jungle, forested valleys, caves and under water.

As for escaping, where would they go? They were international pariahs.

He had a quick shower and went downstairs for breakfast. Ian was sitting by himself at a table; Sebastian joined him.

'Morning. You sleep well?' Ian flicked the newspaper page on his iPad.

'Good morning to you.' Sebastian moved the chair forward. 'Yes, considering it wasn't long enough. Did you get Amjad's message?'

'Nah, what message?'

'They found the taxi in Bahawalpur.'

'Shit, that's halfway to…' Ian shook his head in disbelief. 'That fucking doesn't make sense!'

'Yeah, true.'

'Is it a ruse?'

'You think they're trying to outwit us?' Sebastian said.

'So far they're succeeding?' Ian's smile was more a grimace.

'Hmmm.' Sebastian shook his head. 'Then what do you think? Where are they heading?'

'Back to Afghanistan. Why? I don't know, but something made them go the first time.'

'Amjad seems convinced it's Karachi. Captain Usman forwarded me a copy of the KCB. It's a kill or capture bulletin for Punjab and Sindh only. That covers from here to Karachi.'

'How stupid to ignore other possibilities.'

'I don't understand the major's strategy. It seems stupid, but he's not entirely mad. There's a huge reward for their capture and the newspapers and morning news bulletins mentioned it prominently. The public's even been given access to the National Camera Network.'

'Oh, wow! I wasn't expecting that. He's so inconsistent. Sometimes he's as dumb as fuck, other times...' Ian shook his head.

The waiter came with pots of tea and coffee and took their order.

'I've organised to fly to FATA. The Pak army has been persuaded to lend us one of their Mi-17 choppers along with a pilot.'

'I'm impressed.'

'I was surprised how fast they responded. I didn't even have to go through Langley. I've a feeling they jumped at the opportunity. They're focusing on the route to Karachi and don't want us interfering.'

'Got any spare seats?'

'Yes, one with your name on it,' Sebastian smiled. 'My people have spoken to your people and you're coming along.'

'I could have saved your people the trouble. My people have already told me to accompany you.'

Their plates of thick cut French toast arrived with pitchers of maple syrup.

'So what's the plan?' Ian said as he drowned his plate in maple syrup.

'I expect they'll enter Afghanistan the same way as before. We'll head them off before they do. I have Drone Command standing by if we can get a lock on them. I also have a team of six Navy SEALs waiting at the Pakistan Air Force base for us to finish our breakfast. Let's discuss more on the flight.'

'Great,' Ian said as he took a sip of tea to wash down the French toast. 'Last time we spoke, we were going to get the Afghan Army to block their entry into Afghanistan--'

'Yeah, well it won't work. The border areas are in Taliban hands. Don't worry, we'll get them ourselves.'

EXERCISING CAUTION

Waziristan, Friday 12 January, 11:15 am

Jane ran her fingers through her hair as she braked to a stop next to the opening in the mud wall that led to the army compound. A few soldiers milled outside the gate, smoking and chatting. They took no notice. In the distance, an officer was shouting at his men while conducting a drill.

'You stay here, I talk with Captain Sherdil.' Yousaf closed the door noiselessly as he glanced at Sergei, who was fast asleep, his head on Razane's shoulder.

Jane was about to protest. Yousaf could be walking into a trap. Surely word of their escape would have reached them. But he had already walked through the gap in the mud wall. Yousaf's trust in Sherdil was discomfiting. He was foremost a soldier and thus beholden to his chain of command. Surely that counted for more than his friendship with Major Hamdani. It did not help that Yousaf had explained how the army was split into factions, religious hardliners versus moderates and that this sometimes overrode the normal command structure. It sounded bizarre and would make it hard for anyone to know where the next person stood.

If Yousaf had overestimated Captain Sherdil's loyalty to Major Hamdani, they were sitting ducks. They wouldn't stand a chance against the soldiers under Captain Sherdil's command.

She kneaded the knot in her neck. Driving on the narrow and windy roads had been tiring. Her earlier nap hadn't reduced her exhaustion, instead leaving her with an unpleasant neck-ache. Electricity surged through her as Razane leaned forward, her long slender fingers finding her sore spots within seconds. Jane stretched her neck side to side as Razane kneaded the pain away.

'Aah, that's beautiful.' Jane turned her head sideways and

kissed the inside of Razane's wrist. 'I could sit here for hours, but I need you to wake Sergei. I don't like this situation.'

Razane nodded. 'I agree.' She turned and ruffled Sergei's hair and kissed him on the forehead. 'Wake up, my love.'

Sergei stirred and was immediately awake. 'Where's Yousaf?'

'He's left us here to have a chat with Captain Sherdil. We're worried he might be—'

'Less hospitable than last time?' Sergei rubbed his eyes and yawned. 'Damn, I needed that sleep.'

'Yup.' Jane's expression was grim.

Razane looked around. 'Jane, can you reverse us back to the last bend in the road? It's higher up and protects us from an ambush. I'll get out and take cover behind this boulder.' Razane pointed at a rock the size of a tractor as she grabbed her rifle with the other hand.

'No way you're doing that,' Sergei said angrily. 'You're still hurt.'

'I'm much better.' Razane protested.

'They only have to lob a grenade at you and...'

Jane went ashen. 'Razane, you can't. We're dealing with the Pakistani Army, not amateurs.' Not waiting for a response, she started the car and began to reverse.

A shout stopped her. 'Hey,' Yousaf waved to them as he and Captain Sherdil came running up the path. Both men carried two rucksacks each. Jane braked. Sergei and Razane looked outside. There were no signs of an ambush. They placed the rifles back on the floor. Yousaf ran up to the window. 'Where you go?'

'Just looking at the scenery,' Jane said with a straight face. 'It's so beautiful here.'

Captain Sherdil opened Sergei's door. 'Welcome again.' His words belied his worried expression. He motioned for Sergei to move over. Yousaf climbed into the front seat.

'Jane, keep driving back.' Yousaf said as Sherdil closed his door quietly.

Jane reversed again. As they approached the bend in the

road. Yousaf said, 'keep going till no see army compound.'

'OK, that is enough. Please stop.' Sherdil said when Jane had fully rounded the bend. The army base was no longer in sight.

'What's going on?' Sergei said.

'This is for your safety. There is a kill bulletin with a reward of ten million rupees for your capture, dead or alive. I don't wish to test my men's loyalty. They may not all pass.'

'So what—?' Sergei said.

'Patience Sergei brother. I have a plan you must follow. I will get off here. You keep driving past the army base. In two kilometres you will see a village. The last house is a mechanic's garage. Inside are four motorbikes full of fuel; in their pannier bags you will find food and other supplies.'

'Sherdil. How did you know...?'

'I read in the newspaper that you escaped. I thought you might return here.'

'Phew...,' Jane was tearing up. 'How, how, can we ever repay you?'

'By staying alive and rescuing Major Hamdani.'

'Sherdil, I don't understand how you're doing what you're doing?' Razane said.

'You are Razane, also believed to be Wafaa Aal Zubeidi?'

'I'm only Razane, not Wafaa,' Razane said with a smile. 'Jane and Sergei told me how you helped them before.'

'I had the honour.'

'I don't understand. You're both army officers, sworn to serve your country and obey orders. You can get into serious trouble.'

'Yes, I can be court-martialled and shot. But first I am answerable to Allah,' Sherdil said looking up. 'I believe in doing what is right. Major Hamdani and Yousaf are my friends. I trust them like my own brothers. They have told me there are some bad anti-Pakistan elements in the ISI. I also am a good judge of character and you are not a terrorist. And if CIA catch you, then you will die in Guantanamo. That is no good for an innocent person.'

'You're a good man, Sherdil. There should be more people like you,' Razane said.

'I believe most people in the world are good,' Sherdil said. 'But not Major Amjad. I still cannot understand why—'

'Major Amjad blame death of brother on Razane and Major Hamdani,' Yousaf interrupted him.

'Who, the man I shot?' Razane said. 'On the boat in Karachi?' Her face was a mask of surprise.

'Yes, Fazal, he brother of Major Amjad.' Yousaf said.

'Oh!' Razane looked at Sergei and Jane.

'Yousaf told us in Lahore,' Sergei put a hand on Razane's shoulder.

'We should have told you, but it's been so crazy,' Jane said.

'Don't worry. I know now. It does explain things,' Razane said.

'It'll help to explain it to Hamdani,' Jane said.

'Major Amjad is not a good man.' Sherdil shook his head. 'He does not care about justice. I will go now,' Sherdil said as he stepped out. '*Allah Hafiz*, take care and watch for drones.' He closed the door, hopped over the mud wall and dropped out of sight.

'What did he mean by drones?' Jane said.

'Drone up in sky. American use drones for kill Taliban,' Yousaf said. 'Jane you drive now, *fatafat*.'

'If I was scared before, I'm petrified now.' Jane said. 'What are we mixed up in?'

'Yousaf since when have you known this?' Sergei said.

'What?'

'About why Major Amjad is after us.'

'I think after we go from safe-house. I remember Fazal is brother of Amjad. Anyway, we must go *fatafat*.'

'I still don't understand how we'll rescue Major Hamdani.' Razane said.

'I know not, too.' Yousaf said. 'We only know when reach to Afghanistan. Now we no talk, just *fatafat go*.'

THE TRAIL

Waziristan, Friday 12 January, 1:45 pm

The weak sunlight diffused by the hazy sky couldn't counter the stiff northwesterly breeze. Razane shivered in her winter jacket as she sat pillion behind Sergei. Up ahead dark clouds portended even worse weather.

As they left the green valley, the bitumen ended. The track became loose dirt that threw up choking dust clouds as they rode. Thankfully, it was wide enough for them to ride three abreast.

Sherdil had been true to his word. They had found the mechanic's shop closed, but the doors were unlocked. The four bikes, two large KTMs and two smaller Yamahas, looked in good shape. Razane decided her wrists were too sore to ride her own bike. They each carried a small backpack containing army ration packs, a thermos of hot water, a flashlight, a compass, binoculars, a first aid kit, a lightweight polyester blanket and a foil blanket along with a pair of padded gloves and woollen caps and scarves. They also carried the rifles they had taken from Major Hamdani's safe-house.

The path became narrower as they began to climb. Tyre tracks from four-wheel-drives had created a rounded central ridge in the surface that forced them into single-file again. Thankfully it was covered in coarse gravel, so they didn't have a problem with dust.

Progress became harder as they reached the snow line. Powdery snow covered the path, making it hard to follow the correct line. When they were not crashing into potholes they were sliding on icy sections where their winter tyres struggled for traction. At one bend, Yousaf almost slid over the edge into the valley below.

An hour later they stopped briefly for a light lunch. The food and hot tea gave them energy and woke them up. They needed the extra alertness. The track climbed a densely wooded slope. Exposed roots the same colour as the wet ground threatened to trip them up and skewer their spokes. By the time they emerged from the forest they were exhausted and wet from brushing past snow-covered foliage. But their troubles weren't over.

Yousaf was the first to hear the unmistakable sound of a helicopter. They were in a valley bounded by a gently sloping forest to their left and sheer cliffs to their right.

They looked around, but the helicopter was out of sight, which hopefully meant they hadn't yet been spotted. Wanting to keep it that way, they decided to leave the track and ride up the slope through the forest. The tradeoff was even slower progress through undergrowth so dense they had to lower their visors to prevent branches from flailing the skin off their faces. Humidity fogged their visors, forcing them to stop frequently to clean them.

After circling for what seemed like an hour, the helicopter headed off in a northerly direction. It was just in time as minutes later, fifty metres below the ridge, they ran out of tree cover. They had to dismount and push the bikes onto the stony path that ran along the spine of the mountain.

Yousaf was the first to make it. He consulted his compass and GPS while he caught his breath and waited for the others.

'We near Shawal.' Yousaf's teeth chattered as he turned to his companions who had stopped behind him.

Razane had never felt as cold in her life. By the looks of them, her companions felt the same. Icicles had formed on the vent holes of their helmets and along the edges of their visors and along the collars of their jackets.

They rode up the gently sloping ridge to the peak. As it levelled off into a plateau, Yousaf stopped and checked his GPS again. 'We go down there,' He pointed to a gently descending track.

'That helicopter worries me.' Razane said, her teeth chattering. 'Which direction did it go?'

'North like we.' Yousaf said.

'That means they could be waiting for us.' Razane's voice quivered from the cold.

* *

The helicopter was loud even over their headsets. The constant drone of the turbine and the sound of the rotors was beginning to be tiring. The Mi-17 was clearly not made for luxury travel, but it was fast. They had made good progress since leaving Lahore at a little past eleven in the morning.

The team of six Navy SEALs, led by Master Sergeant Andrei, were not a talkative lot. During the whole flight, they either remained silent or exchanged brief words with each other.

On the way, they had stopped once to refuel at the Mianwali Airbase, which took nearly an hour after the pilot was first refused permission to land then denied refuelling rights. Sebastian had to call Major Amjad to resolve the standoff.

By the time they were back in the air Sebastian was nearly foaming at the mouth and had to do breathing exercises to regain his composure.

It was 3:15 in the afternoon when they flew over the army base where Sergei and Jane had taken refuge. They had briefly discussed stopping and asking if anyone had seen their fugitives. Given the intense manhunt underway, the fugitives would do everything possible to leave Pakistani territory as fast as humanly possible. If the soldiers in the army base had given them shelter the first time, they might not be entirely reliable sources of information. So the decision was made to press on.

As they passed over dense forest, Sebastian asked the SEAL team to use their thermal imaging gear to search for the fugitives.

They spotted some musk deer and a few lone foxes. At one stage one of the team spotted what he thought were three or four people on motorcycles, but they lost them in the dense forest cover.

They debated dropping off a few men at that point, but

after finding no suitable landing spot they gave up on the idea and decided to continue to Shawal and prepare an ambush.

They reached their destination a short while later. The mid-afternoon sun shone over the little town nestled in a valley and halfway up a south-facing mountainside.

Their pilot, Khizar, landed the helicopter on a plateau above the peak in a spot that was hidden from the town.

They got out and walked over to the edge of the plateau. From their vantage point, they could see the whole of Shawal.

A thick layer of snow covered everything. Sebastian used his binoculars to scan for human footprints. Apart from hoof marks indicating deer, the town had no other living inhabitants.

He took out the satellite surveillance images and located the house Sergei and Jane had used last time. It was in a cluster of buildings along the northern edge of the valley floor.

'What's the plan?' Master Sergeant Andrei lowered his binoculars. Ian did the same.

'We confirm which building they stay in overnight. Then, kaboom, we blow it up.'

'We only have rifles, no rocket launchers.'

'No need for rockets. A Reaper drone is on standby in Khost airbase to deliver two Hellfires as soon as we give the go ahead. They've already locked in that house there.' Sebastian pointed. 'If they change their shelter, which they probably won't, we'll just send them the new coordinates.'

'So you don't need us, then?' Andrei sounded almost crestfallen.

'You can help us secure the scene while we sift through the rubble and identify the bodies.'

ARRIVAL

Melbourne, Friday 12 January, 8:00 pm

The truck braked to a stop. A bolt of pain surged through Najib's forehead as he struck the foam-covered bulkhead. He had fallen asleep a few minutes ago for the first time since the start of the journey, after exhaustion finally overcame his claustrophobia and discomfort.

He groaned as he massaged his scalp. He wouldn't last much longer locked in this space. How big could Australia be?

The truck turned right and began progressing up an uneven slope.

The chassis groaned as it flexed over undulations. Gravel crunched under the tyres and blasted the underside of the shipping container. Dust poured into the ventilation holes. The smells were fresh and aromatic, almost like lemon. They seemed to be in the countryside among trees. The truck levelled out and slowed to a crawl as it negotiated a left-hand bend.

With a gnashing of gears they began to climb again. The slope was steeper than before and the prime mover's diesel engine laboured under the strain. The path became rougher as they climbed. Every so often a wheel dropped into a large hole with an almighty thud. Not being able to see made it impossible to brace against the shocks. The pain in his head was now so intense he had to resist the urge to vomit.

According to Peter, they were on the last leg of their journey. Melbourne could not come soon enough. Forty-eight hours in a mobile torture chamber had tested him to his limits. God only knew how his men were faring. They would need a few days to recover from their ordeal.

It felt like the inside of an industrial washing machine. Maybe God was punishing him for being part of a terrible atrocity. He had been a coward and had watched as it unfolded.

The memory flooded back as the bile rose in his throat.

In the wrong place at the wrong time, he became an unwitting part of an Islamic State brigade that swept through the area. Had he not joined, he would have been killed.

He had marched into the Syrian town of Raqaa and was ordered to join a raiding party in two pickup trucks to scour the streets for enemy soldiers.

Instead of killing soldiers they had stood in the tray and had taken potshots at panicking civilians running for cover. At first they only shot at people in western attire. Then they included people who looked rich. Finally overcome by an insane blood-lust, they began killing anything that moved. After an hour of madness they halted outside a cluster of shops. All except a laundromat had already been looted and burned.

The proprietor stood outside his shop with two local men. All were armed with ancient bolt action rifles. Seeing the overwhelming numbers against them, they dropped their weapons and stood with their hands in the air as the Islamic State fighters began to ransack the laundromat.

They found the owner's wife and young daughter hiding in the apartment above the shop and dragged them outside. Seeing them, the proprietor fell to his knees and begged for them to be spared.

The leader of the IS group took out his pistol and shot the man's two companions, then he ordered his men to throw the little girl into one of the giant washing machines. The mother fainted, and the father became a blubbering mess as they closed the hatch and turned on the wash cycle.

The young girl struggled as the drum turned and the machine filled with water. She went around a few times till the hot soapy water filled her lungs. Then the crazed look on her face turned sleepy as she drowned.

Before they left, they decapitated the mother while her husband looked on. A bullet to the back of the head ended his life.

Najib was horrified out of his mind. Shooting westerners was one thing. Killing an innocent child in this horrible way just because her parents owned a business was pure evil. He escaped Raqaa that evening. The Islamic State was a level of monster he couldn't be.

He was in Syria to fight for the ascendancy of Islam, to bring back the glory days and to destroy western influences. He always understood that in a war innocents died. It was a price justified by the end goal.

Islamic State was different. Its vision was dark and evil. Its members killed for enjoyment and were even worse than the Russians or Americans.

In search of more noble companions he found his way to Eastern Ghouta, a rebel enclave on the outskirts of Damascus. It was lunchtime, and he was in a market square in search of a meal when the world exploded around him. He hadn't noticed the aircraft overhead and had not seen the bomb fall, but he felt the overwhelming force and the heat. He was flung to the ground. Everything went quiet except for a ringing in his ears. In shock he tried sitting up. A cart wheel still attached to its axle had pinned him to the ground. His rifle wrapped in a cloth bag had saved it from piercing his chest.

Chunks of masonry, splinters of wood and pieces of fruit intermingled with shreds of clothing, lumps of human flesh and globs of blood covered the scene of carnage. Bodies lay everywhere.

Wafaa's men found him, helped him up and gave him water to wash his face. Apart from bruised ribs and a cut on his head he was miraculously unhurt. Still dazed, he helped the men clear the square of debris and bodies. The bombardment had only been a precursor. The main event began as suddenly as the bombing. A tank rumbled into the square followed by a squad of Syrian soldiers. There was no time to think. He unwrapped his rifle and joined his rescuers in the firefight. After a desperate two days the government forces were pushed back. He was accepted as one of the victorious.

Allah had led him to Wafaa.

* *

With a furious expulsion of air, the pressure brakes pulled the truck to a halt. His inner gyroscope was still moving when someone opened the hatch and shone a light inside. With quivering legs, he climbed the ladder into the pleasantly fresh air. They had reached Melbourne.

AMBUSH

Shawal, Friday 12 January, 4:45 pm

Shadows were lengthening as they descended into the valley. It had snowed heavily since their last visit. The white powder had filled in the bomb craters and obliterated the charred ruins. Instead of a war-ravaged town it looked like a peaceful snowbound village in a winter repose. Only a few blackened walls, standing out like accusing fingers against the white backdrop, gave any indication of the horror that had befallen the people of Shawal.

The army rest-house they had stayed in before and half the town's houses were clustered at the bottom of the valley on both sides of a narrow street. A mosque and a shuttered grocery store indicated it might have been the town centre. The remaining houses were scattered up the northern slope. Like in the rest of Pakistan, Shawal houses each had their own compound surrounded by a brick boundary wall. Only a few were intact. The worst were piles of rubble.

The army rest-house was as they had left it. They found a room more weatherproof than the last time. A soft woollen rug covered most of the floor. They broke up a door and started a fire in the ornate fireplace. It was their first bit of warmth the whole day. Darkness descended as they ate a simple meal of day old naan and goat cheese, washed down with tea in front of the roaring fire.

Jane wiped the condensation from the window and stared into the dark night. 'Shouldn't we talk about Afghanistan before we sleep?'

'No make plan now… too early.' Yousaf yawned as he wrapped the blanket around himself and lay on the floor near the fire.

'I-I don't understand.' Jane joined Sergei and Razane on

the floor and snuggled into the blanket they had thrown over themselves. 'Last time you gave us a Taliban contact in Ghazni. What's changed?'

'Major Amjad also has contact with Taliban so now is more danger,' Yousaf said.

'You said without the Taliban we can't--'

'Oh yes is impossible. So we must find Taliban local commander and negotiate,' Yousaf said. Noticing their blank looks he continued, 'Taliban not one army. They is many many local army each with commander.'

'You mean like the Pakistan Army,' Sergei said.

Yousaf's eyes flashed with anger. 'No make joke of Pak Army, please, bro.' He sighed. 'We negotiate with Ghazni commander or no plan.'

'That's somewhat of a plan...' Razane said. 'I know what Yousaf means. We won't know more until we get there.'

An awkward silence descended as they made themselves comfortable. Razane lay between Jane and Sergei, who was on his side facing them both. He stroked Razane's hair out of her eyes. 'Goodnight.' He kissed her tenderly. Jane did too.

A log in the fireplace crackled and hissed. The flames flared up before decreasing to a small flutter. The room became darker. 'Yousaf sorry, if we make you uncomfortable,' Jane said after a while as she absentmindedly played with Razane's hair.

Yousaf had been drifting asleep. He took a while to respond. 'Why you think I uncomfortable?'

'Well, you're Muslim and what we're doing would be strange and *haram*.'

'Jane, you all very very strange...' he chuckled. 'But... also good. Allah love he who love others. Maybe is *haram* but... maybe Allah forgive.'

'That is very open-minded,' Sergei said.

'Pakistani not fanatic. We open-minded peoples,' Yousaf said in a defensive tone.

'Sorry, I didn't mean to offend you.' Sergei said.

Yousaf did not reply. Just when they thought he'd fallen

asleep he said in a voice barely above a whisper, 'I am also love… some lady.'

'Oh, Yousaf. That's lovely. Who's she?' Jane said.

'It is sad sad story.' Yousaf sounded crestfallen. 'She married to cruel man who beat her. I promise to her we marrying when I being major.'

'You shouldn't wait.'

'Her husband is squadron leader, is high rank from captain. He kill me if he find I talk with wife.' Yousaf sighed loudly. 'So I wait.'

'What's her name?' Razane said.

'Anum.' Yousaf sighed and rolled over.

* *

Sebastian looked through his night vision scope as he kneeled on the waterproof blanket. The house glowed brightly against a sea of black.

Sebastian brushed a snowflake off his smartwatch. It was eight in the evening. 'I think we can safely call the strike now.' He shivered inside his snow parka. The wind had picked up. The temperature was already below zero. They weren't going anywhere tonight. A part of him irrationally wanted to be in the warm house rather than acting as a ground support for a drone strike. The thought was silly because it wouldn't be a house for much longer.

He used his satellite phone to call Drone Central Command at Langley.

'The coordinates are unchanged. You can launch now.'

'Stay online please while we confirm launch.'

'Sure,' Sebastian said.

The other end went silent except for faint voices in the background. Five minutes later the man returned. 'I can confirm take off from Khost and handover to local control. You should see it in thirty-four minutes. Ensure there are no friendlies within at least one hundred metres. Cloud cover will prevent us from getting a really good visual so we'll need your eyes to keep a lookout. There's no appetite for collateral damage.'

'Yes, sure. There are no other humans apart from us and them within at least fifty miles.'

'Can you transmit visuals?'

'Sure,' Sebastian said as he checked the video camera to make sure it was fully charged.

* *

Razane watched the shadows from the open fire dance on the ceiling. The room was warm and toasty. Yousaf's snoring reverberated through the room, making it hard for her to drift off. Just as the sleep would envelop her, he'd emit a strangled chirp that made her think of a snake gobbling up a bird. His future wife would need to be deaf to sleep with him.

Sergei and Jane were deep asleep either side of her, which showed just how exhausted they were. Thankfully neither snored.

Normally she had no problems sleeping, even in rough conditions out in the open. But something bothered her.

Jane had committed the ultimate sin by killing an American. There was no way they'd give up hunting them. The helicopter they had heard on the way was undoubtedly looking for them. It could return or it may already be nearby. Their hunters could have anticipated them stopping in Shawal for the night. If that was the case, they might be under surveillance at that moment. They had thermal imaging that could pick out a rabbit in the dark, let alone a house with a fireplace. In the otherwise frozen and dead valley the heat signature from their fireplace would stick out like the proverbial.

The more she thought about it, the more it made sense. They wouldn't have to attack them. Sherdil had mentioned drones. It was the CIA's most effective weapon. The thought of a missile heading their way made her stomach turn.

She tried to listen to sounds outside the house but heard

nothing apart from the crackling of the fire and Yousaf's sonorous racket.

Fighting her terror, she got up and shook Sergei and Jane.

'Wake up!' She stood and began to wrap herself in the polyester blanket.

'What's wrong, sweetie?' Jane said, alarmed. Razane had a look of calm detachment she had seen each time they had faced a life and death situation.

'We need to get out of here, fast,' Razane's voice shook ever so slightly as she wrapped the foil blanket around herself.

'You look like you're going into outer space,' Sergei said with a tired smile.

'It's to stop prying eyes.' Razane finished wrapping the thin foil sheet around her till there was only a thin slit for her face. 'Someone showed me how this can fool thermal imaging night vision, at least temporarily.'

'What thermal vision?' Sergei was immediately alert.

'That helicopter we heard. I have a feeling it may still be out there,' Razane said, 'It sounded like a large machine. Big enough for a squad of soldiers.'

All signs of levity vanished from Sergei's expression as he bolted upright. 'OK, then let's leave,' He wrapped himself in the blanket and the foil. Jane followed suit.

Meanwhile Razane was shaking Yousaf by the shoulder. 'Get up Yousaf!'

Yousaf opened his eyes, his face was pinched with exhaustion. Seeing them all dressed in the metallised blankets shook him to wakefulness. At first he smirked at their appearance but when Razane explained he deftly followed their lead.

'Does this even work?' Sergei said as he picked up his rifle and handed Jane and Razane theirs.

'I hope so, but I wouldn't rely on it too much,' Razane was already at the door.

'I guess it sort of makes sense,' Jane said. 'In theory as long as the foil stays at the temperature of the surroundings and doesn't get warmed by our body heat, it should be OK. But doesn't night vision pick up everything, even our breath?'

'It depends on distance,' Razane was looking out of the large window next to the front door.

'Then we must try to stay out of sight,' Jane said.

'Of what?' Sergei said. 'We don't know where they are.'

'True. Follow me and stay down,' Razane said as she opened the front door.

The blast of cold air hit them like a sledgehammer. Jane had never experienced cold like this before. It was like the sun had taken every bit of warmth with it.

'You know, we could be walking into a hail of bullets,' Sergei said.

'Then let's stay low,' Razane said without turning.

* *

Sebastian looked through his night scope at the house below. In the distance it was the only thing visible. The whole countryside was a dark blue bordering on black. The house was a light yellow and the chimney a bright red.

It was too far to see through the walls but he was sure the targets were inside.

Overhead the sound of the Reaper was barely audible over the strong breeze. Drones had become quieter over the years and they could launch missiles from further away. Inside the house they wouldn't hear it at all.

'We have visual and have locked the coordinates and are ready to fire.' The voice came over the phone.

Sebastian looked at the darkness around them one last time.

'Do it.'

* *

Loud clicks preceded a flash of light made even brighter by the dark. They closed their eyes involuntarily as the ground shook and the world went crazy. Acting on instinct, they flung themselves onto the snow and shielded themselves as debris rained down from above. Then everything went quiet, so quiet that the sound of the blood coursing through the veins in their heads was deafening. The shock set in mixed with relief and irrational mind-numbing fear. Razane had predicted it, but what if she hadn't?

'Was that from a drone?' Jane couldn't hear herself whisper. The ringing in the ears was like thunder. Her head and chest throbbed.

'Yes,' Razane nodded. She looked dazed.

'Our motorcycles,' Jane pointed to the hut. 'How will we get to Afghanistan now?'

'We need to find shelter…' Sergei put his lips to Jane's ear. He shook as he held Jane's arm.

'We move uphill as far from here as possible.' Razane gestured as she spoke.

The ringing in her ears was subsiding; Jane could hear a bit better.

The army rest-house had collapsed into a burning heap. The blaze lit the valley floor and the lower part of both slopes.

Staying in the shadow of tall trees, they crunched through the snow up the northern slope towards a cluster of four houses. They had been built in the lee of a large boulder that rose vertically out of the hillside. The boulder appeared to be precariously balanced, but its lack of stability was only illusory. It had stood there for at least a few hundred years, as evidenced by the tall pine trees that ringed it.

'Let's try those houses. If the enemy is above us, they won't be able to see the houses because of that massive rock.' Razane said.

Jane had stopped and was listening, 'I think I hear a helicopter…'

'Yes, and that deep rumble…' Sergei said.

'That is avalanche, very common here,' Yousaf said. His voice sounded hollow.

'We must take cover,' Razane said, 'before they see us!'

Three of the four houses were roofless. One had a gaping hole in its boundary wall but its roof appeared intact. It was similar in size and construction to the rest-house.

Razane tried the door but it wouldn't budge. 'Serge, my love, you try… hurry.'

Sergei kicked the door but it wouldn't budge. Yousaf joined him and they kicked together. After two attempts the door swung open with a rending of timber.

The flames on the army rest-house were dying down, but there was enough light to see that the front room was empty except for rugs on the floor and curtains on the windows. A passage led to other rooms in the back. The house appeared weatherproof.

'We can't stay here. They may come looking for us if they don't find bodies. We left tracks in the snow.' Razane said.

'Then let's hope they don't look for bodies just yet,' Sergei said.

Yousaf mumbled. 'Razane you save my life. I owe to you.'

'Yousaf, you saved our lives so many times.' Sergei patted him on the back.

'Yousaf, we're friends. Friends don't have debts,' Razane said.

'You are my brother and sisters.'

'I am happy for you to be my brother,' Razane said. Her face was once again calm.

Outside the helicopter grew louder as it approached, its spotlight shining on the smouldering ruins.

'Please don't land,' Jane said.

'What if they do?' Sergei said.

'We have no choice but to confront them,' Razane said. 'The best time is as they land. Once we engage them, we can't let them get back in the helicopter. They'll call for reinforcements and hunt us down.'

'We kill them?'

'I see no other way,' Razane's voice was cold, emotionless.

'We can't hesitate when we engage them, so if you can't—,'

'You're my commander,' Jane said. 'I won't flinch. You can trust me.'

'My love, I'd also prefer not to kill them…' Razane said in a tired voice.

'Oh, please sweetie you don't have to justify yourself. I know you.' Jane gave Razane a quick peck on the cheek.

The helicopter continued to hover while they waited in nervous anticipation. Yousaf was reciting an Arabic verse. Jane had her fingers crossed. The helicopter rose, did a one eighty turn, and began to descend again.

'OK, here's what we need to do,' Razane said, a hint of steel in her voice.

CHECKMATE

Sergei used his hand to shield his face from the tiny shards of ice the helicopter sprayed as it hovered metres off the ground. Instead of landing it began to rotate, its spotlight sweeping across the valley.

The dark had swallowed Jane, Razane, and Yousaf as they made their way to the positions Razane had outlined in her hurried plan.

Jane was supposed to be a hundred metres across the slope to his left. Yousaf's position was one hundred metres to his right so he could approach the helicopter from behind once it landed. His job was to disarm the pilot and take him hostage. Razane was to climb up the slope behind the large boulder. The idea was for her to have a commanding view and be able to cover them. That was the fatal flaw. He realised with a sinking feeling that she'd be as blind as he was.

The helicopter stopped rotating and continued to hover two metres off the ground that was being illuminated by its landing lights. Two shadows jumped out and ran towards the opposite slope. As they passed in front of the main spotlight trained on the town centre, Sergei saw they were US Marines in full combat gear. They were followed by two more who ran towards the burning army rest-house. They disappeared among the cluster of houses that made up the town centre.

The last two who jumped out ran up the slope towards Sergei. He crouched lower behind a large snow drift, hoping the silver blanket wrapped over his jacket would blend him into the surroundings. Hopefully, Jane was doing the same.

The two soldiers nearing him split up. One headed towards Jane, the other stopped twenty metres downslope from him.

The helicopter finally touched down. The rotor slowed as the turbine began powering down.

Two men in civilian garb stepped out. Crouching low, they ran towards the smoking ruins.

Sergei's finger hovered over the trigger. They made good targets. If these were Razane's kidnappers, they deserved to die.

There was no way to be sure, so he lowered his rifle and looked away from the strong spotlight. He needed his eyes to adjust to the dark. Their real threat were the six Marines. From what he had glimpsed of them, he was certain they had night vision systems and would see them easily, metal foil blankets or not.

Meanwhile, the two civilians approached the blast site. A Marine came forward and spoke to them. After some nodding the three stepped through a gaping hole in the now roofless and still smoking rest-house. Flashlights came on. They were looking for bodies. Within moments they would discover them missing and tell their colleagues to search for them.

It was now or never. Sergei craned his neck to look for the Marine closest to him. A tiny flash caught his eye, but it vanished. He moved his head. There it was again. It was the man's night vision screen but in the dark it was impossible to judge the distance.

Fighting a sense of helplessness that threatened to overpower him, Sergei scooped two handfuls of snow and compressed it into a hard ball. Taking a deep breath, he threw it up and forward, hoping he had judged correctly. The hardened lump of ice landed in the bushes with a loud rustling sound. The screen moved as if the Marine had jumped. He began to walk cautiously down the slope away from him. His voice carried in the silence. He was speaking softly, 'Alpha Four here, something moved below me.' After a pause he continued. 'Something's in the bushes. I've no visuals on it.'

Even though walking through the soft snow was awkward, Sergei was grateful that it silenced his footsteps. As he crept closer, he hoped the sounds of his movement were being masked by those of the Marine's.

They were now so close that Sergei could have reached forward and touched the man's helmet. Without warning, the Marine stopped and bent forward to poke at something with a stick. Sergei had to crouch low to avoid bumping into the man.

Sergei held his breath as he decided what to do. The Marine was an arm's length away. Because of the slope his head was at the height of Sergei's stomach. He could hear the man breathe and his radio crackle as he spoke. 'I can't see anything. It must have been an animal.'

Sergei removed the knife from its pouch and hesitated for the briefest moment. He hated the thought of killing in cold blood. The man wasn't his enemy. He was just doing his job. He would have a family back home whose lives would be changed forever. But there was really no other option. These men were not here to talk. They had launched a drone attack against them and were here to finish the job. It was kill or be killed.

A shot rang out from the left. The bullet struck the slope behind him. Someone was shooting in his direction. There was no time to think further. Feeling numb, he grabbed the top of the Marine's helmet with his left hand just as the man began to turn his head sideways. As the Marine's head snapped back, Sergei sliced across his exposed throat. Blood seeped into Sergei's glove and covered his wrists as the Marine convulsed violently. Sergei let go of the helmet and clamped his hand onto the man's mouth. He needn't have bothered. A faint gurgling was the only sound as the Marine's life spurted out onto the snow below.

The smell of the blood was overpowering and made him nauseous. Sergei bent over and vomited, a vein pounding in his head as he struggled to breathe. He'd become a cold-blooded murderer, a butcher. He forced the thoughts from his mind. This wasn't the time. Regret would get him killed. He took a deep breath and tried to regain focus. The pounding subsided and his vision cleared. He propped the now lifeless body back against the snow, unhooked the man's helmet and placed it on his own head.

The valley came alive in one of his eyes as the night vision system pierced the dark. Sergei knelt in the snow and looked towards Jane. He could clearly see her crouched over what looked like another dead Marine. That would explain the shot that had narrowly missed him. The shot had come from Jane's direction. She had saved him by ambushing the soldier, just in time.

His headset crackled, startling him. 'Alpha Two, Alpha Four, report your status...' There was no reply. The voice sounded tense. 'Alpha Four, Alpha Two, this is Alpha One, stop fucking around.'

The two dead Marines were Alpha Two and Four. He briefly wondered which was which. Jane looked in his direction as put on the dead Marine's helmet. He gave her a thumbs up. She responded. Elation surged through him. They had reduced the odds against them.

Jane was trying to signal something. She pointed to her helmet and then towards Razane. He understood. He shook his head and signalled the same. He would take his helmet to Razane. She should cover him. He didn't wait for a response. Keeping in the shadows of trees, he raced up hill as fast as he could.

* *

Razane's heart sank when she saw the six Marines scatter and melt into the night. Her heart leapt as she saw two of them heading towards Sergei and Jane. Her makeshift plan had been too optimistic. US Marines were equipped with night vision systems and state-of-the-art communications built into their helmets. Against such an enemy the four of them were sitting ducks.

She tried looking for the enemy but it was no use. They had dissolved into the dark. She closed her eyes and tried listening. As she slowed her breathing, she heard a cacophony of sounds. The breeze rustled branches and whistled through crevices. She heard the faint sounds of footsteps and someone speaking in an American accent.

She heard more footsteps, and the voice sounded again. A

shot rang out that almost stopped her heart. As the reverberations died away, she could barely make out what sounded like grunting. Someone was struggling. Two separate struggles were going on.

Not being able to see was driving her mad. Hearing alone helped nothing. She opened her eyes. A crunch of snow and a snap of a twig alerted her to a presence close by. Someone was approaching.

A shot rang out from across the valley. It thudded into something near. A second shot reverberated. It had been fired from Jane's position, towards the opposite slope. What was going on? Gunfire erupted a few metres downslope from her. Whoever approached her was also firing across the valley. A volley of shots from the direction of the rest-house tore through the surrounding trees. The helicopter's spotlight went dark, plunging the already dark valley into an inky blackness. This was madness, and she was blind.

'Aah, fuck...' Sergei cried as he crashed through the undergrowth and dropped by her side. He was panting as he lay on the ground near her.

'Are you hurt, my love?' Razane moved towards his shadow, fearing the answer.

'Nah… I'm okay.' Sergei was trying to catch his breath. He coughed as he handed her something cold and round.

It was a helmet. She put it on. The screen in front of her left eye turned on. The ability to see came as a shock. The valley, the trees, the houses and Jane and Sergei were all clearly visible.

'Do your magic,' Sergei said, 'I'm going down to help Jane.' With that, he slid down the slope and was gone.

The visibility through the helmet was astonishing. She had used previous generation night vision systems, and the difference was like night and day.

She looked around for Yousaf. He was crouching behind the helicopter, motionless. Now that its spotlight had been shot out he would be blind.

Jane was hiding behind a pile of bricks, looking at the

valley below. On the opposite slope, a figure lay slumped behind a tree; he was motionless. Jane or Sergei must have hit him when they returned fire.

Another Marine lay motionless near Jane. The one Sergei had killed wasn't visible.

The surviving Marine on the opposite slope and the four men sheltering in the rest-house had all taken cover.

Razane looked back towards Jane. She was no longer there. In a panic, Razane searched for her. Jane was moving across the slope away from Sergei. She was out in the open and would be an easy target. With her night vision, Razane could see her clearly. It meant the metallised blankets were no longer effective. Maybe they never had been.

'What are you doing, my love?' Razane muttered as she frantically scanned for a threat. She had to locate them before they spotted Jane.

Then she noticed Sergei. He had moved to where Jane had been and was crouched over the dead Marine. What was he doing? Without a night vision system of his own, he was in an even more precarious situation than Jane. Their enemy on the opposite slope and the two Marines in the army rest-house had a choice of two targets. Razane began to sweat. She had to find the remaining Marines.

* *

Sergei could just make out the body, dark against the white snow. Sergei turned the dead Marine over and picked up his rifle embedded in the snow. Trying to stay low to the ground, Sergei removed the man's armoured vest and strapped it over his own jacket. He felt in the pockets and found four cannisters along with a spare magazine and a cylindrical object. He removed his gloves to feel what it was and realised it was a rifle scope. His fingers found a switch. It was a night scope. He looked through it. He could see. He should have thought of the rifle scopes before, but this was no time for self-recrimination.

The rifle was equipped with a grenade launcher. The cannisters he had found were grenades. Working by feel, he clicked the night scope onto the rifle's side rail and looked through it.

He had trained with M16s. This rifle was different but not too unfamiliar. It was probably the M16s replacement, the M4. He found the safety switch and turned it off.

Sitting back, he scanned for the remaining enemy Marines. Neither the one on the opposite slope nor those on the valley floor were visible. Even the civilians had taken cover. He looked towards Jane. She was running across the slope away from him. Damn, she was in danger. He had to do something, anything, to draw the enemy's attention away from her. Without a thought, he ran down the path towards the ruined rest- house.

* *

Brent Nugent shook his head to clear it. The morphine shot was taking effect. He had twisted his knee while diving for cover and it had taken all his willpower to not scream at the top of his lungs. But he was fine now. He would get the terrorist fuckers.

He was the sniper of the group. It was time for him to earn his keep. He unfolded the bipod and balanced his Heckler and Koch G28 on a rock. One of the fugitives was running across the slope. It was a woman. What in the name of Jesus was she doing? He made himself comfortable and took careful aim. She wouldn't feel a thing.

A disturbance caught his eye. The man was running down the slope towards the ruins. He carried an M4 with a grenade launcher. If he got within range of the town centre, he could inflict serious casualties. The woman could wait. He swivelled his rifle and aimed it at the man, his finger on the trigger. The man was running through a thicket of trees. 'Come to Brent,' he whispered as he waited for him to emerge from the tree cover.

The running man burst into the open, bingo! Brent's finger pressed the trigger. He never registered what happened next. A bullet had turned his brains to mush.

* *

Razane collapsed in a heap. Her hands shook violently. She had to pull herself together but that had been too close. She had spotted the fourth Marine, at the last minute, just as Sergei reached the valley floor. Her shot had been as much luck as skill. Breathing in, she focused her attention on the rest-house.

* *

Sergei heard Razane's shot reverberate through the narrow valley. She rarely missed, so it was a fair assumption the enemy on the opposite slope had been neutralised. It was time to finish this. His mouth set in grim determination, he crawled forward. He was now fifty metres from the still smouldering ruins. With fingers stiff from the cold, he loaded a grenade in the launcher, aimed it at the rest-house and fired. It landed harmlessly outside. Damn. He loaded and fired again. This time it found its target. The flash of the grenade lit up the inside.

Gunfire erupted from the cluster of houses behind the rest-house. He couldn't see anyone. Almost simultaneously, Razane and Jane opened fire. Yousaf fired from the helicopter. He must have overcome the pilot. Sergei loaded another grenade and fired. Again it hit its mark, landing inside the roofless rest-house.

There was no response. Sergei raised his hand, signalling for Jane and Razane to stop. 'Hey you,' he shouted at the men in the town centre. There was no response.

'Give yourself up. You're surrounded from all sides. We have your helicopter and have killed four of your men.'

There was still no answer.

'Listen, we prefer to talk,' Sergei shouted.

'What do you want?' a voice with an American accent shouted from inside.

'Lay down your weapons and come out. We won't harm

you… I give you my word.'

'The word of a terrorist means nothing.' The man inside shouted.

'We're not bloody terrorists,' Sergei shouted back, 'but I have a bloody short temper and I fucking hate kidnappers and torturers.'

He was met with silence.

'Look, I have a dozen grenades and that house has no roof. I could kill you now… if I wanted to. I don't need to see you to do it.'

He could hear men arguing. Finally, someone called out, 'OK… we're coming out.'

'Leave your weapons behind and put your hands in the air. We have three snipers. If you try anything, you're dead.'

To his right, the helicopter's headlight came on illuminating the four unarmed men as they stumbled out of the ruins.

UNCONVINCED

Shawal, Friday 12 January, 10:30 pm

Using tweezers from a medical kit, Razane removed the jagged metal shard from a Marine's shoulder before she dressed it. They had returned to the second house. Sergei had gotten a fire going, and the room was warm and toasty. Their captives, their hands bound behind their backs, sat on the carpeted floor in sullen silence.

Razane turned her attention to Sebastian. He was bleeding from his hairline. As she parted his hair, she could see a deep gash above his ear.

'How the worm turns,' Razane said softly as she examined the wound with a torch.

'You do know she's not a terrorist?' Sergei stabbed at the fire with a rusted poker that had seen better days.

Sebastian winced as Razane washed the wound with saline solution but pretended not to hear.

Sergei walked over, crouched down and looked him in the eyes. 'You fuckers kidnapped an innocent woman sleeping in her bed, based on what?'

Sebastian pursed his lips and turned his face away.

'Yeah, turn your fucking head. Keep pretending you're right.' Sergei said.

It was Sebastian's turn to stare. 'You just murdered four US Marines. You're holding the rest of us hostage. Whatever shit you were in before you've just multiplied it a million.'

'You're CIA or something, aren't you?' Sergei said with a shake of his head, 'You behaved like criminals. You broke the law. You kidnapped Razane, tortured her, claimed she was Wafaa something or other and then tried to fucking... kill us all. And you blame us for fighting back...'

The door burst open and Jane and Yousaf entered along

with a blast of frosty air.

'They're all dead.' Jane threw an armful of helmets and rifles onto the floor. She shivered as she shook the snow off her jacket. 'We've got their armour and their comms.' She pointed to the Kevlar flak jacket and communication device she had on. 'Oh, and the motorbikes... they're completely mangled.'

'Damn!' Sergei examined the rifles and helmets.

'Thanks for going and checking,' Razane said.

The second civilian turned to Sergei. 'Look mate.' His Australian accent took them by surprise. 'Surrender your weapons and come with us. We'll go back and investigate properly. If what you're saying—'

'Stop!' Sergei interrupted. 'What's your name?'

'Ian.'

'Well Ian...' Sergei ran his fingers through his hair. He was dizzy with exhaustion. 'Why the fuck should we believe you'll do anything of the sort if you haven't done so now? And what would you do with us while you investigate, check us into a fucking five-star hotel?'

'Serge, my love you're wasting your breath,' Razane said, 'they are convinced they're right.'

'We don't negotiate with terrorists,' Sebastian drew himself up as much as his bonds allowed.

'You stupid dick,' Jane practically spat in Sebastian's face. 'I should cut your fucking throat like I did the fat American...' She growled. 'The way you hung Razane from her wrists... You're a filthy animal.' She screamed the last words.

Razane stood up and put her arms around Jane in a warm embrace. 'It's OK, my love,' she whispered as she stroked Jane's hair. 'I'm OK. And we're together again,' she crooned softly.

Sergei put his head in his hands. Jane had just admitted to killing a CIA agent. It would be safer to kill their hostages, but doing so in the heat of a battle was one thing, killing helpless men was quite another.

He took a deep breath to stifle his anger but venom still dripped from his tone as he spoke. 'Gentlemen...' he paused.

'Razane was part of the Kurdish paramilitary most of her adult life. Since we met, we've not been apart a single day. There's no way she's working for the wrong side. If I were you, I'd start by checking with the Kurds. They'll identify her for sure.'

Sebastian stayed silent as Razane went back to tending his wound. She cleaned it and used superglue to close the skin, finishing it with disinfectant cream and a bandage. 'By the way, thank you for making your colleague go easier on me,' Razane said in a gentle voice. She had spoken absentmindedly and was momentarily taken aback at what had slipped out.

Sebastian was equally shocked. He looked at her, not sure he'd heard right. For a second he dropped his guard. 'You, you, mean with Mike?'

'I know you tried...' Razane said.

Sebastian's lips moved, but no sound came out. He shook his head. 'Lady, I wasn't being soft... I've no compassion for terrorists... I believe in following procedures.'

Razane sat back and let him speak. Her face calm and expressionless.

'I didn't want you dying in our custody without us learning the truth.' Sebastian concluded.

'I think there's good in you and you helped me... And... Sergei's telling the truth. I'm Razane and only Razane. You can check when you get back but we're not coming with you...'

'Guys, honestly,' Sergei turned around and faced Sebastian and Ian. 'You're supposed to be an intelligence agency. Think! If we're terrorists, we'd have killed you by now?'

He was met with stony silence.

'And you've gotta agree it's the easiest option.'

'I'm still tempted to shoot them all.' Jane locked Sebastian in a cold stare.

Sergei looked at Jane and whispered. 'You can't kill in cold blood either.'

'I'm not so sure any more,' Jane muttered.

'You're too beautiful a person to do that, my love,' Razane said to Jane. She turned to Sebastian, 'Do you know Major

Amjad?'

His reaction was enough of an answer.

'OK, then know this. Major Amjad had a brother, Fazal. Two years ago I shot him on a boat in Karachi to save these two,' Razane pointed to Jane and Sergei. 'And also Yousaf and his boss,' she nodded towards Yousaf who stood in a corner listening.

'Yes true. Fazal my colleague,' Yousaf said. 'He threaten they with gun... Razane save us.'

'You know Yousaf is ISI too,' Sergei sat cross-legged next to Sebastian. 'And his boss, Major Hamdani is in an Afghani jail... because of Major Amjad.'

Sebastian had resumed a look of cold indifference. Razane sat next to Sergei and took his hand in hers. 'The Times Square bombers will do it again. By focusing on the wrong person you're helping them.' Razane watched Sebastian for any signs she was getting through, but there were none.

'We'll leave them to think it over,' Sergei said. 'Yousaf please help me lock them in the basement.'

The basement was under the kitchen. A trapdoor in a corner of the kitchen was the only way in and out. Earlier, Sergei had used a rickety bamboo ladder to explore it. It smelt of dried fruit and spices. With no other doors or windows, it would make a safe temporary prison.

They cut the men's ropes and ordered them down the ladder. Then they pulled it up and closed the trapdoor, securing it with a heavy bolt.

'I really hope you guys think it over, seriously,' Sergei said through the cracks in the timber.

'I'm so sleepy.' Jane yawning as she watched Sergei slide the bolt home, 'Do you think they're secure?'

'Yup, positive. They might get frostbite, but they deserve it.'

Jane yawned again.

'Stop that,' Sergei said with a wry smile, 'or I'll fall asleep here and you'll have to drag me.' He wasn't joking. Now that the threat had abated, he'd almost lost the will to move.

'Come on my loves,' Razane said as she entered the kitchen, 'I'm not strong enough to drag the two of you.'

Back in the room with the fireplace, they lay on the carpeted floor, with their jackets as pillows.

Yousaf lay on the other side of the room. 'Good night,' he said and almost immediately began to snore.

'That's how a fire-breathing dragon would snore,' Razane yawned sleepily. She lay on her side, her head on Sergei's shoulder, his arm wrapped protectively around her. Jane lay on his other shoulder.

'With no motorbikes, how the hell are we gonna get to Afghanistan?' Sergei whispered.

Razane nuzzled against his throat. 'Stop it, my love. Do not worry if all the candles in the world flicker and die. We have the spark that starts the fire.'

'Rumi?' Sergei said as he kissed her closed eyelids.

'Yes, Rumi,' Razane smiled and nibbled his earlobe. Her atheist lover was becoming quite spiritual. 'We're all together, my love. Nothing else matters.'

'That was Metallica!' he smiled, suddenly feeling like a boy again, confident and strong. They'd find a way.

Razane giggled and blew warm air against his neck. He turned and kissed her on the lips and did the same to Jane.

'I love you both,' he said sleepily. He didn't hear their replies.

Razane took Jane's hand in hers, 'A bandsaw wouldn't stop me sleeping tonight,' she said and kissed Jane's hand. 'Goodnight my love.' The floor was hard and their jackets lumpy but they were together. She needed nothing else to feel warm and secure. Life at that moment was bliss. Within a minute she was fast asleep.

Jane lay lost in thought a moment longer. What if after everything, they reached Hamdani, and he refused to help them? She forced the thought away. Bridges would be crossed when they came to them. She yawned and snuggled closer and fell asleep.

Outside the snowbound valley was silent. Nothing moved, save for a wolf who approached the body of one of the slain men.

* *

Yousaf woke with a start. He lay awake and listened. The fire was nothing more than a pile of glowing embers, but it still gave out heat. His three friends were deep asleep. What strange people they were that they could sleep together and show so much intimacy in the presence of a stranger. Men often married more than one woman but they were supposed to meet them separately, not together in one bed.

But his new friends were good people at heart. They loved one another. It was a strange love, but they were not hurting anyone and who was he to judge? That was Allah's job. His mind stayed occupied thinking about the day's events till he forced them away by reciting verses from the Quran. It was the best way he knew to relax. Before long he was fast asleep again.

INSTRUCTIONS

Melbourne, Saturday 13 January, 5:00 am

Najib woke with a start. He stared at the ceiling in a daze. A dissonant noise had woken him. He was in the long shed he had fallen asleep in. Blinds covered the floor to ceiling windows, letting in only a sliver of light that leaked between the gap to the window frame. Outside dawn was breaking.

The noise sounded again, almost masked by the drone of snoring. It was a rooster outside his window. They were on a farm. He lifted his head and counted. All his men lay on their cots, fast asleep. He knew he should wake them. They had urgent work to do. He put his head back on the pillow to collect his thoughts and moments later he was asleep again.

The next time he woke the blinds were up. Light streamed into the room. It had warmed, and he was sweating under the blanket. He sat up feeling groggy.

* *

Najib doused himself with cold water from the washbasin in the small toilet. A dull headache pounded the inside of his skull. It would take many nights of good sleep to recover from the journey. Allah willing, he would not need to. He wiped his face with a towel and walked to the main farmhouse.

He entered through the kitchen door.

'Are you ready for breakfast, brother?'

'Yes, brother.' His voice was still hoarse.

'Then sit and I will bring it for you.' The cook pointed him to the dining hall next door.

Najib sat at a timber trestle table nearly as long as the dining hall. Within minutes the man brought out a steel tray full of food. Najib's stomach grumbled as the smells wafted up.

Najib ate the breakfast of scrambled eggs and tea with relish. His men trickled in just as he was finishing up.

'Sorry, we overslept,' Haziq said, an embarrassed look on his face.

'Not to worry, brother,' Najib said. 'Today it is excusable. I also overslept.' He excused himself and went in search of Peter. He was directed outside by one of Peter's men.

The property was in a heavily wooded valley. The house and the shed they had slept in were all under cover of trees. All buildings had roofs with a steep pitch and were a light brown colour that matched the surrounding soil. A reconnaissance plane would never spot them.

The two semi-trailers were parked behind a two-metre tall fence under a large dun coloured tarp strung between towering steel poles.

Najib spotted Peter and walked up to him. He looked rested and refreshed and was supervising his men as they unloaded the scuba cylinders and placed them in two neat rows on the concrete floor.

'Oh, there you are.' Peter smiled as he saw Najib. 'How was your sleep?'

'Good, brother. How was yours?' Najib bent down to inspect his tanks. They looked unharmed.

'I'm good.' Peter kneeled to examine the cylinders. 'Allah willing we'll learn today what our mission is and what you've brought these for.'

'You do not know?'

'No *Al-ukht-ul-akbari* doesn't share information before we need it. I have my duties and you yours.'

'Oh!' Najib kept his voice light to hide his disappointment.

'Cheer up. We'll call her after lunch,' Peter said.

'OK, till then we keep our secrets to ourselves.' Najib smiled and stood. 'Do you have a place to store these?'

'Yes, with your permission I was going to take them to our workshop. Is there anything I need to know? Like any hazards, dangers...?'

'No, just don't drop them.'

The workshop was a large structure cut into a hill. Its roof followed the original slope of the hill. Trees on the hill's summit and around the three sides of the structure blocked any views from the air.

Najib let out a whistle. 'Very well camouflaged, brother.'

Peter smiled. 'Thank you.'

'I am impressed.'

'Thank you. Let me show you inside.'

'How long have you had it?' Najib followed Peter in through the half-open roller shutter. When extended fully upwards, the doorway was tall enough to accommodate both semi-trailers. He looked around in awe. It was a fully equipped workshop complete with hoists, lathes, a five-axis milling machine, a welding station and a paint booth.

Four white Mercedes panel vans stood in the middle. A shower of sparks skittered out of the sliding door as two men used angle grinders in the load area of one of them.

'Nice arrangements.' Najib nodded in approval. Were the vans part of the mission?

'You're very kind.'

'Tell me, brother, what are my men to do in the meantime.'

'You can all join us in our drills. We do them every day... Wafaa's orders.'

'Sure brother. We did them daily in Malaysia too.'

* *

'OK brothers. You can rest now.' Najib wiped the sweat off his brow. The air was cool and fresh. The drill had been easier than in the Malaysian humidity. Maybe that was why people in cold countries were harder-working and more warrior-like than most who inhabited warm climates. By Allah's grace, his men had acquitted themselves very well. They had done their drill with the precision and ferocity that Wafaa had instilled in them and were as good if not better than Peter's men.

Peter had noticed too. 'Well done to you and your men,' he said with a smile. 'I was hoping to show you up, but you didn't let me.'

'Sorry brother.' Najib smiled too.

'Brothers, you've earned lunch after you clean up.' Peter shouted.

Najib wiped the mud splatter off his watch. Wafaa would call in exactly fifty-eight minutes. Allah willing, it would be a life-changing conversation.

* *

Peter's smartphone sat on the desk between them. They were in his private study with the doors and windows closed. Najib looked at his watch. One minute to go. Wafaa was a stickler for time and insisted all her men set their watches to an atomic clock on the Internet.

The phone vibrated before it rang. Wafaa was calling on the Kik app.

Najib swallowed as Peter answered. A large drop of sweat rolled off Peter's forehead and onto the carpet. For all his nonchalance, Peter was just as nervous.

'*Asalam aleikum, Al-ukht-ul-akbari.*' It wasn't a video call but Peter bent his head in deference. He turned on the speakerphone, his expression serious.

'*Asalam aleikum,*' Najib bowed his head as well such was the potent force of Wafaa's charisma. He was bowing even though it had seemed ridiculous when Peter had done it seconds ago.

'*Wa aleikum asalam,* my valiant brothers. Najib trust you had a good voyage.' her voice had a gentle intimate quality like she was speaking with a family member about how dinner was. Yet she conveyed absolute authority.

'Yes, *Al-ukht-ul-akbari.* Yes... and we're eager to be of service to you.'

'Not to me. The service is always to Allah.'

'Yes, yes, of course, of course... That is what I meant. Always to Allah, but you show us the way, always...'

That seemed to please Wafaa. Her voice became even gentler. 'Good. I have little time... So I will keep this brief. You can now share with each other the information I gave each of you. You will work together to combine what Najib brought to what Peter made. I expect it to take no more than two days to get everything ready. I will call you a day after tomorrow at the same time and tell you the next part of the plan.' She went silent. Najib bent over and looked at the phone's screen. She was still connected. What had Peter been working on? Was it the vans in his workshop? How would what he had brought fit what Peter had made? Could he risk asking her a question? Wafaa was very deliberate in the amount of information she shared over the phone even though Kik was considered safe. In reality, safety and secrecy were relative terms. The NSA could hack almost any system. Without any doubt, their conversation, in encrypted form, was being catalogued in an NSA computer. If it met a set of criteria, it would be de-encrypted. While Wafaa had taken steps to mask her voice and her IP address each time she called there was a chance, the enemy would find them.

Wafaa spoke again. 'I take it from your silence you understand what to do.'

Peter looked at Najib who nodded. 'Yes, we do.'

'Then I bid you farewell. *Asalam aleikum.*'

'*Wa aleikum asalam,*' Peter and Najib said in unison, but Wafaa had already disconnected.

**

Wafaa stood and stretched her arms above her head. Why did the slowest always think they were the best?

It was a risk for her to start in Australia but it was how Osama and she had agreed to do it. The great man had wanted each event to be on the evening news in each country. England would be next followed by the US. Victory was close.

CAPTIVES

Shawal, Saturday 13 January, 7:30 am

Sebastian heard footsteps above them. The trapdoor opened and light flooded into the basement. He tried to move, but the cold had rendered him stiff and immobile. He could no longer feel his hands and feet. His bladder was beyond bursting. In fact, he no longer felt it, which wasn't a good sign. The sound of the ladder, dropping onto the basement floor, woke his companions from their slumber.

Sergei stuck his head down. 'Time to go.'

Sebastian tried to stand but couldn't move. 'Hey man, I'm practically frozen here.' His voice was hoarse. The others looked even worse than he felt.

Sergei shone a flashlight on him. 'You look like shit.' He sounded sympathetic. 'Try climbing up.'

Sebastian stood unsteadily and waited for the dizziness to abate before he climbed the creaking ladder. 'I need to pee really bad.'

'Yousaf will go with you but don't try anything or...' Sergei left the threat hanging.

'What are you doing with us?' Sebastian said as Yousaf motioned him forward.

'We're going on a short flight,' Sergei said. 'And you're coming with us. All of you.'

* *

They offered their prisoners hot tea and biscuits before Yousaf and Sergei tied their hands and led them to the helicopter. All except Khizar, the pilot, were made to sit in the back; their hands and legs were secured to tie-down points on the floor.

Yousaf untied Khizar's hands and gave him a set of

coordinates. 'We go here.'

Khizar plotted them onto a map and nodded with a resigned shrug.

'Fly close to the ground and keep your radio off,' Sergei said.

'We could get shot down,' he said with a gruff voice as he started the helicopter.

'Yes we could, so make sure you fly under the radar,' Sergei said.

* *

The flight was the worst Sebastian had ever experienced. The floor was no place for passengers. Every vibration went straight through him. And it was freezing cold. Mercifully they landed after what seemed like fifteen minutes.

From his position on the floor, Sebastian couldn't see out. He guessed they were somewhere in Afghanistan, close to the border.

The wind was howling as the four escapees opened the doors to exit the aircraft. They tied Khizar's hands and marched him off without another word.

'What the fuck are they doing?' Sebastian said after a while. 'Are they gonna leave us here?'

'They're smart. Smarter than I'd have ever imagined,' Ian said. 'They'll probably release the pilot after some time. By the time he returns, they'll be long gone to wherever...'

He was correct. Khizar returned almost two hours later and spent another fifteen minutes untying Sebastian.

'Where are we?' Sebastian said as he rubbed his aching wrists.

'Near Urgun in Afghanistan,' Khizar said as he strained to untie Ian's bindings.

'You fly us back to Pakistan, I'll untie the rest,' Sebastian said. 'But please move fast. I don't want an international incident.'

* *

The fugitives had smashed the helicopter's radio and taken all their phones so they had to wait till the PAF airbase in Mianwali to contact Major Amjad. He didn't answer his phone, so they left a message with the operator. Sebastian looked at his watch. It was three in the afternoon.

* *

They followed a narrow forest path along a dried river bed at the bottom of a shallow valley. They kept Khizhar between them to make sure he could not escape. Apart from a white-bearded goat herd tending his flock, they saw no one. The old man eyed them curiously but then nodded without saying a word as they passed. They reached the outskirts of the little town of Urgun after a fifty-minute walk.

'Stay here.' Yousaf bade them to stay hidden in a copse of trees and walked into Urgun on his own. He returned a few moments later.

He took Sergei out of Khizar's earshot and whispered. 'Bus come ten minute.'

They cut Khizar loose as the ancient bus trundled into Urgun.

The bus was the ricketiest contraption any of them had ever sat in. It coughed and wheezed its way through the tortuously windy mountain roads for what seemed like an eternity. It picked up several passengers including a family with five young children. The woman was clad in a shuttlecock burka that completely covered her from head to toe. She made her children sit on two rows of seats ahead of her and every now and again would pass morsels of food to keep them occupied.

As they emerged onto the first section of straight road, Yousaf turned to them and spoke in a low voice. 'We near Ghazni.'

'Thank goodness.' Sergei's voice was hoarse. He was hungry, thirsty, and exhausted.

Yousaf stood up. 'We stop here.' He pointed to a dusty collection of mud huts built on the slope of a bare hill. 'Village elder my friend. I stay before.'

Yousaf signalled to the driver to stop and turned to Jane and Razane. 'Remember what I say,' he said in a low voice so that none of the other passengers could hear. 'Afghani woman only stay in house. No go outside without man. So please very careful. This Taliban country…'

Jane adjusted the rifle under her burka. She hated the Taliban. They didn't deserve to walk the earth. Hopefully, she'd get to teach a few of them a lesson. Her jaw clenched and her hands balled into fists as she imagined acts of violence.

'Coming, my love?' Razane got to her feet awkwardly as the bus swayed alarmingly. The rifle under her burka clunked against the seat frame. She looked around to see if anyone had heard. The family with five children had gotten off half an hour ago and a man carrying a net with five squawking chickens had taken their place. He had his hands full with his poultry and wasn't paying them any attention. Sergei had covered his hair and most of his face in a towel. Jane and Razane were concealed in their burkas. For all intents and purposes, they were locals going about their business.

Jane stretched her neck to relieve the tension and got up.

The bus creaked to a halt in a cloud of dust and diesel fumes that enveloped them as they stepped down onto the packed dirt.

'What's in this village?' Sergei coughed as he got a lungful of the foul air.

The bus belched more black smoke as it sped up reluctantly. Its spent shocks and limp springs were overwhelmed by the shoulder of the road as it climbed back onto the tarmac. For a moment it leaned alarmingly, threatening to spear into oncoming traffic before it righted itself with an ungainly wobble.

'They give shelter. We send message to Taliban from here.'

'OK,' Sergei grunted as he shifted the weight of his bundle to a more comfortable spot on his shoulders. The thought of dealing with the Taliban was unsettling. It would be a deal with the devil. So far, they had been wrongfully accused of being and consorting with terrorists. The irony of working with terrorists to prove they were innocent wasn't lost on him. But he was getting ahead of himself. There was no guarantee the Taliban would help them. They might even turn on them.

* *

The village was nothing like Jane had expected. She had lived for a month in Shakar Parian, a charming village in Punjab, while working on a solar energy project in Pakistan. It was green and shaded by tall leafy Banyan trees. Even though it had no modern amenities, its people were well nourished and happy and the village looked welcoming.

In contrast, this village was as bleak and forbidding as the surrounding hills. It was built on the side of a rocky slope and was surrounded by groves of deciduous trees. Their bare branches reminded Jane of a forest in a horror movie.

Thankfully the villagers were every bit as warm and hospitable as their Punjabi counterparts. Her travels had reinforced what she had always known to be inherently true. People were good everywhere. It was only a few greedy and power-hungry people who were responsible for all the evil in the world.

The villagers spoke to Yousaf and tried sign language with Sergei. Like they had expected, none of the men approached her or Razane. The women were nowhere to be seen.

'Women stay inside four walls. Only leave with husband,' Yousaf said when she asked of their whereabouts.

'They're more primitive than in Punjab,' Jane muttered.

The headman showed them to two vacant huts. One was for the three of them and the other for Yousaf.

Their hut was a rudimentary affair made of mud with a

single window and a door, both covered with heavy woollen drapes, rolled up, and tied above the two openings. The bed was a large embroidered cushion on a raised dais. The woollen rug on the floor was plush but had seen better days.

'For Afghanistan this very luxury,' Yousaf said as he examined their room. 'Chief gave you his home.'

'What?' Sergei was dumbfounded.

'I think this home of chief. He and family move to spare hut.'

'We can't take that,' Jane said turning to Yousaf.

'You no refuse. Big insult. Just take and say *shukria* to him. Send him gift.'

'We sure will.'

The headman was back an hour later with a basket of steaming chickpea stew and fresh flatbread. They sat cross-legged on the floor and ate the tasty meal.

'That really hit the spot.' Sergei swallowed a sip of tea as he leaned back against a cylindrical pillow.

'The tea's amazing as well.' Jane held the glass of steaming yellow-green liquid to the light as she examined the cinnamon bark and a cardamom pod floating on the surface.

'These people have hearts of gold?' Sergei shook his head.

'Yes. People from around here feed their guests before they eat themselves,' Razane said as she studied the map of Ghazni on Sergei's phone. He had saved the maps of Afghanistan and Pakistan on his phone the last time they had a good mobile connection. Razane was glad for it. Having someone understand technology made all the difference.

'Now that makes me feel bad,' Jane said as she drained the last of the sweet tea.

'Hospitality most important for Afghani,' Yousaf said and lifted the teapot to refill Jane's glass.

'Life isn't fair, is it?' Sergei said with a sad expression. 'They are the sweetest people. They deserve everything we have but look at them.'

'It's their corrupt rulers. They use religion to keep people down,' Razane said.

'Another reason I hate the Taliban,' Jane said as she waited for her glass to fill up.

'You and all of us.' Razane stroked Jane's shoulder.

* *

The wind howled through the crevices in the hillside as a blizzard drove snow horizontally into their faces. It built up on the lower part of their goggles and numbed their exposed cheeks and noses.

At least the heavy cloud cover had brought on dusk sooner for which Sergei was thankful. They could test their newfound equipment in a battle simulation and then go back into their huts before they froze to death.

The barren hills behind the village were strewn with large boulders, impossibly balanced as if a divine power had paused a movie of them rolling down the hill.

It had taken Sergei some time and his technology background to figure out how the Marines' communication equipment worked.

Basically, it was a local network based on GPS and radio technology that allowed them to see each other's positions to communicate. Sergei disabled the satellite uplink that would have allowed the US military to track them. He was glad he discovered the feature in Shawal, otherwise they would have risked another drone attack.

Their equipment enabled them to talk and even whisper to each other while protecting their ears from extremes of sound. It also had a sound enhancement feature that could be switched on to amplify the smallest sounds.

A separate screen attached to their forearms allowed them to see each other's locations and heart rates. They could work together as a unit.

'This shows why US Marines seem to have superhuman powers,' Sergei said as they rested in the lee of a large rocky outcrop.

'They can work as one and even help to keep each other calm,' Razane said.

'Let's go for another half an hour and then we go back. I can't feel my toes any more,' Jane said as she tried jumping up and down to keep warm.

They reached the end of their endurance before half an hour was up. The exercises had helped them understand how to operate their gear. But they were under no illusions. They weren't prepared for real combat.

'I'm never giving this stuff back,' Sergei said as they returned to their huts almost frozen to the core. The wind chill factor had made it feel like minus twenty degrees Centigrade.

'There are a lot of assumptions in that statement.' Jane rubbed her hands together as she tried to get circulation back in her fingers.

'We have to think positive,' Sergei said with a frozen smile. 'This stuff makes me feel a little more confident... it certainly improves our chances of getting the major out of jail.'

But Razane knew better. Professional soldiers spent thousands of hours practising drills. Even in the Kurdish Army they would practice a raid for days. Unless the Taliban cooperated, they had no chance.

THE MUD VILLAGE

Ghazni, Sunday 14 January, 7:00 am

They hadn't seen a soul for hours as they hiked through a remote corner of the Welsh countryside. The sun bathed the undulating hills in a gentle warmth, perfectly balancing the fresh breeze that swayed the tall grass around them. It was perfect. It was magical.

They spotted a narrow track that led up a grassy hill. They followed it to the summit where they found the perfect picnic spot. It had views for miles. They sat on a carpet of wildflowers under the spreading branches of an old oak tree.

After food, they lay on the soft ground and gazed up at the clouds. The sun was deliciously warm; the air smelt sweet, and they were together. Looking around, they realised the tall grass was the perfect screen from prying eyes. Before they knew it they had disrobed and were making tender, unhurried love.

In the afterglow, they lay spent in each other's arms, the warm air and the sun drying the sweat on their skin. Butterflies flitted overhead like the hands of a conductor playing peaceful country sounds that lulled them to sleep.

* *

The sound of the muezzin calling the faithful to prayer jarred Razane out of the dream. She tried holding on, but it slipped away. She dreamed it often. Their walking holiday in Wales was one of her most beautiful memories. But that was in another life.

Hopefully, they'd do it again. They would do it again. She had to be positive.

At least they were together. Jane lay on her left reading something on her smartphone. Sergei snored almost silently on the other side, sounding like a cat purring.

Outside the sounds were peaceful. The villagers had well and truly woken and were beginning their day.

Razane stretched, feeling the lactic acid from all their exertion drain away. She was feeling human again. Considering what she had gone through, it was surprising. But maybe it was not.

She recalled one of her favourite Rumi quotes. "Love is the cure, for your pain will keep giving birth to more pain until your eyes constantly exhale love as effortlessly as your body yields its scent."

She thought about it. Her mind, her consciousness, her whole being was steeped in love for Sergei and Jane. It left no room for pain. Her injuries were healing fast and her sensuous self was returning.

In two hours, the local Taliban leader would give them his answer. Thinking about it dissipated her sense of calm replacing it with anxiety. Would he help free Major Hamdani?

'Afghanistan no Pakistan,' Yousaf had said in the taxi as they had driven past the Afghani Security Forces building where he was imprisoned.

The building near the centre of Ghazni was a veritable fortress with watch towers on all four corners. In the dark it had looked evil and forbidding. It would require a large-scale military operation to breach its defences. It was not something they could manage on their own.

She took a deep breath to calm herself further. She wouldn't allow herself to succumb to fear. Panic made everything worse. Whatever came, they'd face it together.

* *

Major Amjad heard the blow ringing in his head before he felt the pain. He had expected his face to be aflame but the shock must have numbed it. Even so, a wave of nausea overcame him and he slumped loosely against his bonds.

'Sir,' he said weakly.

The colonel didn't turn around. Salim, the tall man in a black *shalwar kameez* and a plastic see-through apron, looked at the colonel as if seeking further instructions. On his right hand, he wore a knuckle duster, shiny with the major's blood.

'Sir!' Major Amjad tried again. The ringing in his ears muffled his own words. He would die today. The colonel would kill him and then blame it all on him. Not that it would matter after he was dead.

The colonel turned. 'It is too late Amjad, to beg for forgiveness. I can never forgive treason.' He shook his head. 'You jeopardised the service and made your country a laughingstock with your self-serving agenda.' He fished in his pocket, found a piece of lint and flicked it away in disgust. 'Don't bother making up any lies. Arif told us all. He has a pathetically low tolerance for pain.'

'Sir,' Amjad mumbled. Something warm and wet ran down his legs.

The colonel wrinkled his nose. 'The computer man did the same when we broke him.' He brought his face close to Amjad's, 'you misunderstood why you are given autonomy. It is not so you carry out your family vendetta…' He hocked and spat on Amjad's face.

Amjad didn't flinch as the globule dripped down his cheek. The shock had paralysed him. The only thing that still worked was his mind, racing at a million miles an hour.

The colonel didn't care about justice for Razane. He probably didn't even truly care about purging the ISI of moderates. His only priority was his own survival. If the Afghan forces captured the foreigners and handed them over to the CIA, the truth could come out. It would end the colonel's illustrious career. The problem would disappear if the foreigners died. But Hamdani had to die too. He was a loose end. It helped that the colonel hated Hamdani.

Through the pain and the shame, a plan crystallised in his mind. He knew what had to be done. He had gotten Sebastian's message that the foreigners had escaped to Afghanistan when he woke in the hospital. They were apparently somewhere in Urgun in Paktika district. That was Taliban country.

'Sir, I have the most marvellous plan if you only just hear me out.'

The colonel dismissed him with a contemptuous wave. He turned to the man with the apron, 'Salim, make him unrecognisable then throw him in one of the pits in the lowest level of the fort with no food or water.' He wiggled his legs and felt for the edge of his briefs where they had bunched up.

The colonel had become disgustingly flabby. Having to grovel to such a man with so little control over his own appetites was demeaning but somehow, he had to get through to him.

Another punch hit him below his left eye socket. 'Sir, I know what needs to be done,' Amjad croaked weakly. 'I, I promise I can rescue the situation.' His face was now on fire, a jackhammer was pounding his skull as a succession of blows rained on his face. Blood was dripping onto his shirt.

The colonel finished his trouser adjustments and walked to the door.

'Sir, I can make the problem go away completely.' Major Amjad blew blood bubbles as he spat his words out in haste. 'If we follow my plan, you will get all the credit. You will be the hero that you are, sir... but please allow me to help you. The newspapers will praise you...' Salim raised his fist to strike again but stopped when he saw the colonel's raised hand.

'Major Amjad, I give you twenty seconds to explain. Then I walk out and you will only see me in your nightmares.'

'Oh sir, thank you. Here is what we should do.'

As the colonel listened, his face broke into a smile. 'Major, I think a beating does your brains good. If this works, you will hand in your resignation and walk away. If it fails, Salim will continue reshaping your face. You will die of thirst in the dungeon under the fort.' The colonel motioned to Salim. 'Get a doctor here to stitch this *maddarchhod*'s face. Then bring him to my office.' He opened the door and walked out.

* *

It was his third visit to the hospital in as many days. The staff would be laughing at him behind his back, but he had more important things to worry about. Staying alive was one.

They pumped his face full of local anaesthetic and stitched him up. He couldn't feel his lips and drooled all the way back to the head office.

The colonel was drinking a cup of tea and reading a newspaper as Salim ushered the major into his office.

'We will call Abdul Ghanim and ask his help,' the colonel said as he folded the paper. Abdul Ghanim was the local Taliban commander of Paktika and Ghazni districts.

'Yes sir, that is a good idea,' Major Amjad swallowed with difficulty. He said a prayer under his breath as the colonel dialled. Hopefully, the Taliban leader would agree.

The major recognised Abdul Ghanim as he answered in a calm voice. 'Salam aleikum.'

'Wa aleikum asalam,' the colonel's manner was obsequious but behind it was steely authority. He didn't need to grovel. To the Afghan, he was one the most important men at the ISI. He supplied him with money and weapons and above all knowledge. At times he had allowed him and his men to take refuge inside the Pakistani border.

Abdul Ghanim waited in silence as if gathering his thoughts. The colonel did not call him often. After a while, he recovered. 'Colonel Sahib, may Allah be praised for bestowing such an honour on a humble man,' he said in halting Urdu.

'The honour is mine, brother.'

'How may this servant be of assistance?'

'Three Russian agents and a Pakistani traitor have crossed into Afghanistan.'

'Ya hawla wala quwwata illa billah,' Abdul Ghanim said almost automatically. 'Are you... are you referring to Captain Yousaf by any chance?'

'Yes, I am ashamed to say he is a traitor. I need you to

capture and kill them.'

'It is good you informed me. I was about to agree to help them.'

'Help with what?'

'They asked my help to release Major Hamdani.'

Major Amjad was glad he was seated. The bastards wanted to get to Hamdani to prove Razane was innocent. Hamdani would have no problem doing that. Hamdani knew the real Wafaa's identity as well as he himself did.

'Sir, Major Hamdani is a liability for us.' He whispered as the colonel put his phone on mute.

'Don't you think I know that,' the colonel said. 'He is a disruptive cunt and now he is also a dangerous one. He could know about the real Wafaa and tell the Americans. That is why the foreigners want to release him.'

'Is the major a traitor too?' Abdul Ghanim said on the other end of the line, 'Hello, are you there?'

'One-minute brother. Someone has just walked into my room. I will put you on hold.' The colonel pressed mute again.

'Sir, there is only one way to deal with this,' Major Amjad said.

The colonel nodded. 'Yes, I know,' he mouthed. He put his hand up to silence the major and resumed the call.

'I apologise brother. My visitor has now gone.' He took a deep breath before he continued. 'The answer to your question is yes, I am ashamed to say Major Hamdani has betrayed us.'

'Who knows what blackness is in the hearts of men? So what do you propose?'

'Brother, I have a request...' the colonel said.

The Afghan commander listened as the colonel spoke.

* *

Abdul Ghanim put the satellite phone back in his pocket, his mind in turmoil. He needed a tall glass of strong tea to clear his mind.

The colonel had been most specific in his request. They were to proceed with the raid then take the foreigners and the major to the Pakistani border and execute them using their M4 rifles. It was the strangest request he had ever received. M4s were used by Pakistani and American forces. The Taliban preferred the Kalashnikov AK47 because it was more reliable and ammunition was easy to make.

The last part of the request was easy to fulfil. By Allah's grace, he had a cache of M4s and two full magazines of the correct ammunition, the 5.56 NATO round. He had captured them from Afghan soldiers and was planning to sell them on the black market.

Raiding the prison to rescue Major Hamdani would be more difficult, but he had a plan. His forces had attacked Ghazni two months ago. After forty-eight hours American jets had turned the battle against them and they had to flee. He had lost nearly forty fighters, five mortars and a 2S3 artillery gun in the raid. He had found another heavy gun, but not the men. Experienced fighters were hard to come by.

Today the attack would be different. Instead of an all-out assault on the whole city, they would attack the well-off neighbourhoods in the north with mortars, shoulder mounted RPGs and machines guns. The northern enclave was where all the senior army officers and their families lived.

The attack would distract the army from the much smaller surgical strike to free the major.

But just in case he would keep an artillery gun in reserve in the city's west to repel any government forces attempting to stop them.

He also had an ancient anti-aircraft gun but did not expect he would use it. The last time the air force had sent jets two days after the operation had begun. If everything went according to plan, they would be out of there in two hours.

* *

Sebastian waited as the conference call connected. It would be a tough meeting. Their fugitives had escaped and four US Marines were dead. But that wasn't the part of the meeting he dreaded the most. He had to communicate his doubts about their suspect. How should he broach the subject?

His thoughts cleared as Chip's loud voice came online.

PREPARATIONS

Melbourne, Monday 15 January, 6:00 am

Najib woke early. He sat up and waited for the dizzy spell to abate before he stood. He was still exhausted. His sleep had been too restless to make much of a difference.

They had spent the last three days working till late at night trying to finish installing the machine guns. It had been a backbreaking and frustrating job.

The knowledge that Wafaa was disappointed in their progress had cast a pall over their whole operation. She had expected the job to take two hours, but it had stretched into three days.

Peter's men had done a remarkable job converting the Mercedes vans into Urban Assault Vehicles.

They had used armour plating and Kevlar sheets to protect all the vulnerable parts of the vehicle. The glass which was protected with 12mm polycarbonate shields, thick enough to stop police issue bullets. Ultra-high tensile strength bullbars at the front and rear gave them the ability to nudge traffic out of the way.

The armour plating had been smuggled into Australia with Wafaa's help. She had found a contact in Syria who stripped it off captured US military vehicles. It was welded inside a shipping container and sent to Turkey where the container was filled with agricultural machinery and sent to Australia.

The suspension was raised with off-road springs and shock absorbers. The tyres were run-flat, and the engines were upgraded to handle the extra weight and improve acceleration.

The roof had been subtly raised and split along its centre so it could open and close to accommodate machine gun turrets that could extend upwards. The workmanship on the roof was praiseworthy. With the turrets stowed, and the roof closed, the small join between the two halves of the roof were all but unnoticeable to a casual observer.

Najib's machine guns should have fit the turrets easily, and they did. The problem arose when they tried to lower them into the cavity. The roof opening was too short for the length of the barrels. It meant the machine guns couldn't be stowed.

To fix this they had to modify the roof and the lowering mechanism. Each day they had to explain to an increasingly frustrated Wafaa why they hadn't completed what was supposed to be a simple bolt-up job.

Last night they had finally put everything back together and had all worked smoothly.

* *

Peter greeted him as he shuffled into the breakfast room. 'Did you sleep well, brother?' he handed him a mug of steaming black coffee. 'Five spoons of sugar, just as you like it.'

'Thank you brother.' Najib took a sip. The smells and sounds of breakfast cheered him up. 'I was too tired to sleep well… but I am ready to begin the next phase of the mission.'

An hour later Najib split his men into four teams.

He embraced each of his men. 'May Allah give you the opportunity for martyrdom in this land of infidels. The next time we shall meet in heaven, *Insha`Allah.*'

'We hunger for martyrdom,' they all said. 'May Allah reward you for helping us.'

Teams Two, Three and Four were each given an address and told to report as soon as they arrived. He would stay with Team One at Peter's farm.

Najib watched his men drive off in the converted Mercedes vans, their machine guns safely stowed. The excitement of seeing his battle-ready troops begin their operation had obliterated his tiredness. He was raring to go.

Today all the teams would do a test run to measure the time taken between each stage and count the number of civilians they encountered.

If Wafaa was happy with the outcome, she would give permission for the real attack tomorrow.

Peter had organised a short-term rental for each team along one of the three main arterial highways that led to Melbourne's central business district. Team One would approach via the Hume and then the Tullamarine Freeway to enter Melbourne from the north. Team Two would enter from the west. Team Three from the east and Team Four from the South East.

Najib went inside. He had some time to kill, and he felt the urge to pray. Peter had already begun when he entered the prayer room. Removing his shoes, he performed ablutions in the small washroom. Suitably cleansed, he joined Peter on the prayer mat. He had a lot to ask of Allah.

TWISTS AND TURNS

Ghazni, Monday 15 January, 1:30 am

Snow covered Ghazni in a clean white funeral shroud as if to prepare it for the oncoming carnage. It muffled the already muted sounds of a city holding its collective breath waiting for the Taliban attack, the rumours of which had grown all evening. No one knew where and how it would unfold, but most of Ghazni's quarter of a million inhabitants were playing it safe. Those who were able, fled, the rest barricaded themselves inside their homes and covered their windows in heavy sheets.

The Taliban had spread the rumours themselves. It was one of their favourite tactics. About half the time nothing would eventuate but the city would still shut down and the Afghan army would expend valuable resources moving to battle readiness.

Sergei glanced at the four-storey monolith. With walls tapering to a domed roof and arrow-slit windows, it was a modern interpretation of Afghani architecture. It was lit from below by green floodlights. Even in the daytime, it would have dominated the street of mostly single and some double-storey buildings. In the darkened street its glowing green visage looked menacing.

Sergei shivered as he sized up the featureless brick perimeter wall. It was tall enough to hide the lower three levels from where he stood. A single heavy steel gate mounted on a track, controlled access. Guard towers on each of the four corners and a forest of security cameras and antennae left no doubt something important was being guarded.

A large steel sign announced the building as the Ghazni University of Islamic Studies. The board was lying. According to Yousaf, it was the regional office for RAAM or Riyast-i-Amoor-o-Amanat-i-Milliyah, the Afghani counterpart to the ISI.

The surrounds were Stygian by comparison. A solitary bulb illuminated a scratched Coca-Cola sign above a shuttered shop across the street. The next light was on a street pole in an intersection over a hundred metres away.

The street they were on ran parallel to the main thoroughfare through Ghazni. Sergei had seen no vehicles since they had arrived fifteen minutes ago, which was odd given the bedlam on the highways leading out of town. Maybe the Taliban had put up a roadblock.

Their proximity to the geographic centre of Ghazni made Sergei nervous. The narrow and icy streets would make it hard to get away from an advancing Afghan Army. Hopefully, Abdul Ghanim, the local Taliban commander, had secured their escape route back to the main highway that led in a southerly direction out of town.

Sergei pressed a button on the communications device on his shoulder. 'It's been snowing here,' he whispered as he watched his breath mist in the minus five degrees.

'Keep moving your fingers so they don't freeze. You'll need them,' Razane whispered. Her voice was calm as always.

'Sure, babe.' His voice trembled from the cold and the gnawing feeling in his stomach.

'I wish we were there with you.' Jane sounded annoyed. She had never been able to control her emotions in quite the same way as Razane.

'We'll be OK.' He tried to sound relaxed. He wished Jane and Razane were with him but he was also glad they weren't.

Yousaf had broached the subject, but Abdul Ghanim had insisted Sergei keep what he termed "his women" under lock and key. He had posted guards in the village to make sure they complied.

Razane was upset but Jane was livid. With that temper of hers, hopefully, she wouldn't do anything dangerous while they were away. The Taliban were barbarians and would show no mercy if they stepped out of line.

A snowflake caught Sergei's eye as it drifted on a current

of air. He held out a gloved hand and watched it disappear into the stretchy weave of the fabric.

He looked towards Yousaf's location. He was sheltering behind a brick wall across the road, no doubt praying.

Abdul Ghanim hadn't shared the battle strategy except telling them to follow Hashmat's orders. Hashmat was his lieutenant, a man with the nervous energy of an ice-addict and more scars on his face than skin. The guy didn't even speak English, so Sergei wondered how those orders would be conveyed. But that was the least of his worries.

What bothered him more was that they were at the mercy of a gang of thugs, on the wrong side in a war zone, hoping that Hamdani was inside the prison they were about to attack.

'How can you be sure?' he had asked Yousaf.

'It is from very good source,' Yousaf had replied.

'I hope so.'

'Relax Sergei, bro. We are in Allah's hands.'

He had wanted to retort that Allah might be a little busy - especially in this part of the world, to be relied upon, but he kept his peace. Yousaf had been good to them. But he was also deeply religious and there was no point in testing their friendship.

But it was gut-wrenching to think their futures hinged on the efficacy of the ISI's intelligence.

* *

Sergei's watch showed it was 1:35 in the morning. The attack was timed for 1:40. Waiting was torture and without Razane by his side, his bravado had already reached rock-bottom. She was amazing in a battle with a preternatural ability to transmit her calm to him. Without her he was like a boat adrift.

His breaths had become ragged and short. He closed his eyes and focused on inhaling, holding and exhaling like Razane had taught him. He had promised Jane and Razane he'd be back. He had to keep that promise. Inhale, hold, exhale, wait and repeat. After a while, his breathing slowed and deepened; his heartbeat returned to normal.

'Yousaf can you still hear me,' he whispered. He was calm now.

'Yes Sergei, bro. You be ready. One minute we go.'

'Razane, Jane, my sweethearts, we're forty-five seconds away,' he whispered.

'Take care, my love, keep the channel open,' Razane said. 'You did well to bring your heartbeat down.'

Sergei smiled. It felt good she was keeping an eye on him.

'Careful my darling,' Jane chimed in.

* *

The light from the kerosene lamp flickered as Razane tightened the wrist-strap on GPS tracker. It wasn't made for small-boned women.

The screen showed a faint map of Ghazni and three red dots representing Sergei, Jane and Yousaf. The fourth dot was blue and represented herself.

'They make these for big beefy American men, not Kurdish women.' Razane smiled as she tucked the sleeve of her jumper under the strap.

Jane tried smiling back, but it came out a frown. Sergei's life was in danger and they were sitting in this damned hut with the Taliban bastards guarding them like they were prize goats. She looked out of their small window across to the hut that contained the three guards. The guards were inside sheltering from the cold.

'I don't get why they're holding us prisoner. It's odd...' Razane said.

'I agree.' Jane turned to face Razane, her expression was pensive. 'Odd is putting it mildly.'

'Keeping us here is so important to them they're willing to spare three fighters to guard us. The question's why?'

'Yeah, true...' Jane said, 'why do you think?'

'I'm not sure but evil men have evil designs... Something

tells me we shouldn't allow ourselves to be at their mercy.'

Yousaf had told them in no uncertain terms that their guards would shoot them if they tried to escape. 'For Taliban woman life no have value. Woman same as cow and sheep,' he had said.

Jane turned to Razane. 'I've got the same bad feeling. We should be helping Sergei and Yousaf.'

'My love, sometimes one needs to take a step back to take a leap forward.' Razane tightened the strap by another notch. She was smiling.

'Darling, I don't understand…' Jane shook her head as she walked over to Razane. 'You're planning something, aren't you?' She gazed into Razane's beautiful dark eyes. Someone else smiling at a time like this would have infuriated Jane, but she could never bring herself to be annoyed with Razane.

Before Razane could reply, two red dots on their GPS screens moved. The raid had started.

'I can't stand this… Sergei's cold and in danger and… we're in a warm hut,' Jane said. 'It's driving me nuts.'

They could both hear Sergei's breathing become heavier. He was running.

Razane gently touched Jane on her cheek. 'My love, I need you to focus and be calm. We'll get out of here.'

'Oh shit… you do have a plan,' Jane gazed at Razane. 'I'm all ears, my supreme queen… lead me to battle…' The seriousness in Jane's voice belied her flippant comment.

'You are so silly sometimes,' Razane smiled as she stroked Jane's face.

Jane listened intently as Razane outlined a plan.

* *

The ground shook then it shook again. Corresponding shock-waves convulsed the air as all hell broke loose.

The battle had begun in the city's north. Within seconds the low cloud cover became a projector screen for the artillery bombardment as the Afghan army fought back against the second Taliban attack in as many months. They had lots of practice. Ghazni was the most active theatre of war in a country with a seemingly endless capacity for bloodshed. It had been under attack, off and on, since the middle of last year.

A thought occurred to Sergei. Yousaf hadn't told him how he had convinced the Taliban to help them. What would they expect in return? Scoundrels rarely had altruistic motives, and the Taliban were the worst of the worst.

But now wasn't the time to think. The noise from the northern battle intensified as it spread south. Small arms fire added to the raucous din.

An ancient Bedford truck, without its lights, barrelled up the street. As it passed the gate, it turned sharply right and smashed into the perimeter wall. The explosion was sharp and loud. A cloud of dust and smoke enveloped the building and poured out into the street. As the lights went out in the compound, the Taliban charged.

'We go,' Yousaf whispered.

Sergei's mouth was bitter and his legs were jelly but he willed himself to move. Like last night, running the first few metres with the night vision system was disconcerting, but he adjusted within a few strides.

A shadowy figure overtook Sergei and squeezed between the charred and mangled wreck and the jagged hole in the wall. It was Hashmat, the group leader. Within seconds he had vanished into the dark courtyard.

As Sergei followed, he glanced inside the crumpled cabin of the wrecked truck and instantly wished he hadn't. The driver's mangled corpse had been pushed into the foot-well between the seat and the pedals. His head had separated and was wedged between the shattered windscreen and the steering wheel. His arm lay on the ground outside. Inside the truck's floor was on fire and was slowly roasting the body.

Yousaf put his hand on his shoulder, shaking him out of the shock. 'Bro no look at dead man in battle!'

Trying not to inhale the smell of burning flesh, Sergei squeezed through the hole and emerged into the dark courtyard teeming with Taliban fighters. Above him the building stood dark and silent, brooding.

The ground shook as a shoulder mounted missile struck the front of the building and punched a gaping hole where the entrance had been.

Sergei covered his face as billowing clouds of dust rolled into the courtyard.

For a moment there was silence as the world was shrouded in dust. As it cleared, he could see that the windows above were dark with no sign of movement within. Had the defenders given up or were they lulling them into a false sense of security?

Sergei and Yousaf ran to a parked van. Its windows had been blown out in the blast. They waited as more Taliban fighters squeezed through the breach and assembled in the courtyard.

Like a conductor, Hashmat silently arranged them into two formations on either side of the entrance.

'Wait till Taliban enter building,' Yousaf whispered. 'But when you running also look up,' he whispered. 'Must look every place.'

Sergei remembered the Super-Normal-Hearing switch on his headset. The compound came alive as he turned it on. Somewhere above him a glass broke. He looked up just in time to spot a figure at a window three floors up. The barrel of a gun poked through. Shit! Sergei swung his rifle up, remembering to turn off the safety catch. He aimed and fired. The barrel disappeared. A Taliban fighter joined him, spraying the front of the building with bullets before Hashmat shouted at him to stop.

Floodlights mounted on the building's roof came on, momentarily blinding him before the night vision system adjusted. The compound was awash with light. Several objects flew out of top windows.

'Oh, no. Grenades. We go now,' Yousaf was sprinting towards the building.

For the second time that evening the world went mad.

Sergei followed as bullets and bits of masonry filled the air.

A grenade exploded to his right. Sergei felt the blast and heard the ping as fragments glanced off his helmet. Thankfully he felt nothing else but overwhelming relief as he passed through the gaping hole into the shelter of the building.

Hashmat and the rest of the Taliban were already inside.

'They're brave fuckers,' he said to no one in particular as he followed them deeper inside, his night vision system instantly adjusting to the dark.

They were in a small lobby, empty except for Yousaf and Hashmat who was talking on his radio. Passages led in all three directions. Flashes from gunfire in the building's interior bounced off the lobby's dark walls, making him jump.

Yousaf waited for Hashmat to get off the radio before he pointed to a staircase and asked him something.

Hashmat shook his head.

'Prisoner in basement,' Yousaf whispered to Sergei.

'Have you been here before?' Sergei said to Yousaf between gunshots. Somewhere a grenade went off. Fighting seemed to have intensified. The defenders were putting up a good fight.

'No, I see from photos. ISI have good intelligence.'

'Most impressive.' Sergei followed Yousaf down the flight of stairs, keeping close to the wall. Remembering, he again pressed the Super-Normal-Hearing switch on his shoulder. He heard the scuff of a shoe and heavy breathing. Someone was at the foot of the stairs, waiting.

'There is at least one person,' Sergei whispered into the mic. At the same time as he tapped Yousaf's shoulder to make sure he was listening.

Motioning for Sergei to take cover, Yousaf pulled a grenade from his belt, flicked off the pin and lobbed it down the stairs.

It bounced on the last few steps before reaching the bottom where it rolled for half a second and then exploded.

Sergei turned just in time as the whoosh of air up the stairs peppered him with debris.

Recovering, Sergei turned on Super-Normal-Hearing again. He could hear whimpering and moaning and uneven raspy breathing. Someone in the basement had been hit. What if he had inadvertently hit the major? After all, he didn't know where he was.

'Damn,' he muttered to himself. Throwing a grenade blindly down the stairs could turn out to be their undoing.

'What wrong?' Yousaf said coming up alongside him.

'We could have hurt the major with the grenade,'

'Allah protects,' Yousaf said.

'Let's go,' Sergei shook his head and began to tiptoe down the stairs, senses on alert. His throat stung from the acrid smoke and dust that hung in the air. Three figures were sprawled on the ground, their limbs askew. Only one was twitching. Sergei picked up their rifles and tossed them to one side. He couldn't take any chances.

A survivor sat next to a pillar holding his stomach. Sergei was about to crouch down to check on him when the Taliban who had followed them down the stairs shoved him aside. In shock, Sergei could only watch as the Taliban plunged a knife into the injured man's throat.

The victim made a gurgling sound as he fell forward, the smell of blood filling the basement.

A groan escaped Sergei's lips as he saw a flashback of the Marine he had killed in Shawal. The memory of the man's warm blood made him wipe his hand on his jacket. He fought the twin urge to throw up and smash his rifle into the Taliban's head.

Yousaf grabbed him by his left arm and propelled him forward.

'No stop or think in battle,' he chided Sergei. 'Soft soldier is dead soldier... Come find major.'

Sergei took a deep breath to calm his nerves. It only made him want to throw up more. With an effort, he focused his attention on his surroundings. They were in a narrow dimly lit passageway lined with solid steel doors with grates at eye level.

'You go left. I go right,' Yousaf said.

Sergei walked to the end, looking through each grate, trying to make out the shapes within. 'Major Hamdani,' he whispered into each as he walked along.

'I find,' Yousaf said excitedly into his earpiece. 'Major Sahib stand back.'

Sergei turned around. His path was blocked by the Taliban fighter who was conversing with a man inside a cell. Before Sergei could stop him, he placed the barrel of his rifle centimetres from the lock and pressed the trigger. The sound was deafening as the steel rang to the impact of the bullet. It was followed by the sound of several ricochets. The door didn't open.

'Fucking idiot,' Sergei muttered, glad the bullet hadn't hit him. He walked back to the bottom of the staircase and noticed a small anteroom with a bank of switches in a console. 'Is there a number for the door?' he said to Yousaf.

'Yes, five number.'

Sergei pressed the switch marked five and heard a remote click and the sound of Yousaf pushing the door open.

A sharp pain in his side made him gasp. The Taliban had elbowed him in his side. He was trying to get at the controls to release other prisoners.

Reacting instinctively, Sergei smashed his fist into the side of the man's face. 'Fuck you!'

The punch would have felled a horse but the man merely grunted in surprise, managing to keep his footing. He shook his head as if to clear it as a murderous look appeared in his eyes.

Striking the man had been a mistake, possibly fatal. Sergei had no time to contemplate. With a single movement, he removed the knife from the sheath on his belt, pivoted his wrist and plunged the blade into the man's chest. As the Taliban slumped to the ground something clattered from his hand. It was the blood-stained knife he had used on the injured man.

Yousaf was right. There was no time to think in a battle. Sergei shuddered at how he'd nearly become the Taliban's second victim.

Yousaf appeared supporting a weak and disoriented major. Compared to when they'd last seen him on the superyacht in Karachi waters, he looked like a broken man.

'Major Hamdani, what a relief.' Sergei said.

'Mr Markoff, what are you…?' The major's voice trembled as his last words were lost in a wheezy cough.

'Let's get you to safety…' Sergei flinched as several explosions rocked the building.

'That is music to my—' the major coughed again.

'We have the major and are preparing to leave the basement,' Sergei said to Razane.

'Good work, my love… keep up your guard.' Razane's words were punctuated by a huge explosion. The ground shook. A body tumbled down the stairwell.

* *

Jane slowly pushed open the rickety door with one hand as she held the kerosene lantern in the other. A flurry of snowflakes flitted past on a gust of wind, bright white spots contrasting against the black night.

A faint light shone from the hut commandeered by their Taliban guards.

'Slow and steady,' Razane whispered in her earpiece.

Feeling vulnerable without a rifle, Jane inched forward into the night. With a clang, the door to the guard's hut opened and one of them looked out, his rifle at the ready.

'He's coming out,' Jane's voice shook.

'I have him in my sights. If I see anyone raise their weapon, I'll shoot.' Razane had cracked open their window. The barrel of her rifle rested on the window-sill.

'Pani,' Jane shouted. It meant water in Urdu. Hopefully, it was a similar word in whatever language these men spoke.

A man shouted from the right. Jane looked in his direction.

'There are two more guards in a hut at three o'clock.' Jane's voice shook in dismay.

'Are they outside?'

'One' outside each hut. The rest I see through the windows… No wait, they're all coming out.' Jane's whisper increased in intensity.

'Give me some shadow,' Razane whispered. 'I don't want them to see my rifle.'

'Pani,' Jane repeated loudly as she held the lantern away from her body.

The men in both huts swarmed outside, buttoning up their jackets and shouting at Jane as they waved her back in.

'Pani,' Jane shouted. 'I need—'

Her words were interrupted by one of the Taliban shouting as he ran towards her, the butt of his rifle raised in preparation to strike. The rest followed.

Jane threw the lantern at the man closest to her and turned towards the door of her hut. She wasn't quick enough. One of them grabbed her by the wrist.

Instinctively, she dropped and kicked rearwards.

The man let go as he fell heavily to her right.

Jane grabbed under the burka for her knife.

The Taliban were too fast for her. Three pairs of arms clamped on her and lifted her into a standing position.

She screamed furiously as her hand was trapped halfway under the black enveloping garb, her hand just touching the shaft of her knife.

She winced as the butt of a rifle flashed towards her, but there was no contact. The man crumpled to the ground where he stood. Jane had registered a silenced shot moments before. Another violent ping and the smell of blood filled her nostrils. A man holding her from the left slumped against her. The other two relaxed their grip as they let go of Jane and grabbed their rifles.

She stood in the direct line of fire and Razane was seconds from death. Jane's fingers closed over her knife. She pulled it free and with a scream, plunged it into the neck of a man to her right. As she did, she pushed him hard into the others.

One enemy remained on her left. Pivoting on the ball of

her foot, Jane grabbed him by the hair as she half stabbed half sliced his throat. The man collapsed into the open door of their hut, his hands unable to stop his lifeblood spurting onto the ground.

She turned towards the remaining man, her mind in a murderous frenzy, but he lay on the ground, twitching.

'It's over,' Razane's calm voice whispered in her ear as she came out of the hut and took her in her arms. 'Are you OK, my love?'

Jane surveyed the scene in a daze. Five bodies lay on the ground, their blood seeping into the snow. Instinctively, she looked around for more threats. A few villagers were peering out of their huts. None carried weapons.

'Fucking hell, yes, I am,' Jane was breathing heavily. 'How the fuck did you shoot them so fast, you're insanely good.'

'I'd say your knife skills are...' Razane smoothed the hair from Jane face. 'Incredible, almost superhuman.'

'I'm only trying to live up to your standards.' Jane's knees felt wobbly. The adrenaline was kicking in. She desperately wanted to kiss Razane on the mouth and sink into her, but the villagers were staring at them.

'You're my fierce tigress,' Razane's voice was husky. 'I want to make love to you now, I am so turned on.'

'Oh, my goodness, me too, my darling,' Jane's voice shook.

The moment didn't last. The villagers surrounded them, all talking at once. Someone pointed down the hill.

A small band of armed men were headed up the narrow path towards the village.

'Shit, what now?' Jane said, her panic rose like a wave that threatened to engulf her.

MEAT GRINDER

Ghazni, Monday 15 January, 3:30 am

Sergei covered his nose and turned his face away from the swirling cloud of dust that poured down the stairwell. An acrid smell of burnt gunpowder, singed hair and flesh overpowered his nostrils.

'Stay back,' he shouted at Hamdani who had collapsed into a crouching position and had covered his face with his arms.

The malodorous stench intensified as a cloud of methane from a ruptured pipe permeated the building.

'We need to get out,' Sergei said. 'This place can blow any minute.'

The battle above them raged on unabated. Their choices were stark; both were potentially fatal.

Sergei crept up the stairs followed by Yousaf who was helping Hamdani.

The sounds of gunfire and running footsteps grew more intense as they neared the top. A spent casing tumbled down towards Sergei.

A Taliban came into view. With his back to them he stood at the top of the stairs and fired at someone.

Keeping his weapon on the ready Sergei climbed higher, stopping when his head was level with the top step. Using his phone as a mirror, he scanned for signs of danger.

Yousaf shouted something to the Taliban who looked down at them and beckoned for them to hurry.

Another two fighters, one with blood dripping from a head wound, came running from the left passage as Sergei, Yousaf and Hamdani made it to the entrance.

Sergei turned on his night vision goggles and looked outside. Two Taliban crouched beside the wreck of the truck were exchanging gunfire with someone in the upper storeys of the building. The courtyard was littered with bodies and chunks of masonry.

As Sergei watched, a third Taliban stepped through the breech, an RPG launcher on his shoulder. His body jerked as he was hit by several rounds. Somehow, he took aim and fired.

The rocket hit the top floor with an earth-shaking explosion that jarred Sergei. Reacting by instinct Sergei leapt back from the entrance just as a man-sized chunk of concrete fell where he had been standing, demolishing the concrete awning above the doorway. A counter shock wave from inside the building pushed them out into the courtyard.

Sergei barely kept his footing as he was propelled forward. Small pieces of mortar still rained from above, pinging off his helmet. A piece of burning timber glanced off his shoulder.

Behind him, Yousaf and Hamdani were less lucky. Both stumbled and fell.

A Taliban fighter ran past them towards the breach in the outer wall. He pivoted and trained his rifle at the upper floors of the building.

Sergei stopped and helped the major to his feet.

'We better hurry,' Sergei said as he glanced up. The rocket had blown a gaping hole into the top two floors and had knocked out all but a solitary floodlight. A large beam suspended by a single steel bar dangled precariously above them.

They ran as they could. As they reached the breach in the outer wall, a large concrete section of the front facade collapsed onto the ground.

'Sergei, my love, what's happening?' Razane's equanimity made him realise his heart was beating a million miles an hour. He took a deep breath and focused.

'I… we… just left the building. We have the major.'

'That's great news. Are you clear to leave the compound?'

The two Taliban who had covered them ran out in the street. The man in the lead was hit with a volley of bullets that spun him around as he fell. The other ran back towards them.

Keeping behind the smouldering truck, Sergei tried to

work out the direction of the gunfire. He looked towards the top of the building. There was no one there. Puzzled, he looked towards the intersection in the distance and froze. Two armoured personnel carriers stood in a V-formation on the far-side of the intersection. Both were equipped with turret mounted machine guns.

'We're pinned inside,' Sergei whispered to Razane as he tried not to gag at the smell of the body still roasting inside the truck.

* *

'Sergei's in trouble,' Razane said. Her voice was calm but her face showed the strain.

Jane looked back at the column of Taliban advancing on the village. 'We can't engage those fuckers or we won't be able to help him.' Her eyes were wide with fear.

Razane knew Jane was right. They had taken the Taliban by surprise and Jane's combat skills had been extraordinarily effective at close quarters, but the new arrivals were too many for them to defeat. Even if they could, they'd be held up and too late to help Sergei and Yousaf.

None of the villagers spoke English, but they appeared to understand their predicament. An old man pointed up the slope and beckoned them to follow him.

They raced into the hut to scoop up their gear and ran to catch up to their saviour whose pace belied his age. Keeping in the shadows, they threaded their way between the huts to the back of the village.

'I hope he doesn't lead us into a trap,' Razane whispered.

'He doesn't look a bad sort,' Jane said.

The village ended in a chest high fence made of piled up stones. Beyond that the slope steepened as it climbed. The old man opened a rickety gate and turned right. They were in a shadowy gully that curved away from the village as it dropped.

As they descended, it became almost pitch black. Jane and

Razane put their helmets on and used the night vision system to avoid tripping over the rough terrain and marvelled at the old man's abilities to navigate by memory.

'He's agile like a mountain goat,' Jane whispered.

'He must know every millimetre.' Razane held on to a rocky outcrop as she lowered herself down a sharp incline. 'Take care here.'

'I see it,' Jane grunted.

After a short walk, the gully opened into a plateau. To their north, Ghazni lay shrouded in smoky darkness punctuated by flashes of light that accompanied the thump, thump, thump of heavy guns.

'That's an artillery barrage. The Afghan army are fighting back,' Razane whispered.

The old man had stopped and was pointing at the foot of the hill and the main road they had arrived on. It was chock full of traffic heading out of Ghazni and none going the other way.

'Salam aleikum,' the old man said as he turned on his heels.

'I think we're on our own,' Jane said as she nodded at the old man. 'Shukria, thank you. *Wa aleikum asalam*,' Jane called after him. The man appeared not to hear. He rounded a corner and was gone.

Razane and Jane made their way down the winding path to the road, hoping their burkas and the darkness of the night made them invisible.

'I think I know where I can find us a vehicle,' Razane said as they reached the road. She had to shout above the din of the traffic.

'Where?'

'Those Taliban didn't walk here,' Razane said.

They found two old four-wheel-drives, a Mitsubishi Pajero and a Toyota Landcruiser parked at the end of a narrow track, fifty metres away. 'Let's take the Toyota. It looks newer,' Razane said.

'What about a key?'

'They wouldn't use keys in case the driver gets killed…?'

'Oh… so?'

'They would have a switch somewhere.'

'I keep forgetting you were in a militia like this. I-I mean—
'

'Except we weren't a bunch of murderous thugs…' Razane sounded pained.

'Of course not, my darling. You know that's not what I meant.' Jane touched Razane on the arm.

'Sorry, I was getting too sensitive…'

Jane looked up the path towards the village. The Taliban were nowhere to be seen. 'They're probably roughing up the villagers, the bastards!'

Like Razane had predicted, they found the ignition switch below the steering column near the driver's door. Jane pressed it and the diesel engine clattered into life, Razane looked up towards the village. No one seemed to have heard.

Jane pressed the stiff clutch and engaged first gear with a loud crunch. 'This is heavy,' she said as the Toyota lurched forward in a cloud of smoke. Its wheezy engine groaned as they sped up. 'It's got no power steering.'

Razane looked around the inside. The old Toyota was in a decrepit state with stained seats and torn headlining. Its tired suspension banged into every pot hole. The scratched and pitted windscreen became almost opaque in the glare of oncoming headlights.

Razane grabbed the overhead handle to steady herself as she pushed the button to talk on her comms. 'Sergei, we're about six to ten minutes away, if we get a clear run.'

'No, no, no… don't! You can't come,' Sergei pleaded. 'Head the other way and we'll catch up.'

'Shut the fuck up.' Jane scolded him.

'I saw Afghan army units with heavy weapons.'

'Sergei my love, would you run in the opposite direction, if it was us?' Razane said.

Sergei didn't reply.

'Tell me honestly.' Razane's tone was gentle.

'Of course not.' Sergei let out a long sigh. 'But you can't... damn it, it's too dangerous.'

'Serge, darling we'll be careful,' Jane said. 'We have night vision too, and we've Razane.'

'You make me sound like a weapon,' Razane said with a chuckle. 'Let's get close and we'll work out what to do. Keep your head down till then.' Razane looked at the traffic heading towards them. They were the only fools heading into Ghazni.

'I feel bad for the villagers,' Jane said. 'We left those dead bodies and they'll cop it.'

'If they're smart, they'll blame us.'

'The Taliban won't believe women could do that. I mean even while they were fighting us they kind of looked unbelieving.' Jane said. 'They'll have quite a story to tell their thousand virgins.'

'They only get seventy two,' Razane said.

'Yeah, whatever. I pity the virgins!' Jane said.

'If there's any justice they'll go to hell and spare the virgins,' Razane smiled.

Jane glanced at her. Her ability to remain calm and even joke was amazing. From the peaceful expression on her face, Razane could have been going to the movies.

The road began its descent towards the shallow valley and the sprawl of Ghazni. Apart from a few streetlights and the traffic leaving the city everywhere else was dark.

'That's quite a battle.' Razane looked towards the flashes lighting up the sky in the city's north.

'It's almost like a thunderstorm.' Jane nodded.

The road levelled out as they reached the outskirts. All shops were shuttered and houses dark.

'My love, do you think you can drive with only your night vision?'

'Good idea. I can try,' Jane slowed to a crawl and switched off the headlights. They were plunged into momentary darkness as their night vision system kicked in.

Razane rolled down the window, 'We need to hear.'

Jane did the same.

Smoke and the sound of explosions and gunfire filled the cabin as they picked up speed, a dark shadow moving through a dark city.

Jane slowed to turn left onto the main road running into Ghazni. Here the road was wider. Oncoming traffic thinned out as they passed stragglers.

The sounds of machine gun fire grew louder. Not being able to see the source made the noises even more frightening.

'We're heading into a meat grinder.' Jane's voice was laced with fear.

Razane studied the GPS tracker. They were just over a kilometre from Sergei and Yousaf.

'Let's try to make it to the street parallel to theirs. Go left here.' Razane said.

Jane followed her direction. They were now driving down a narrow street between darkened houses.

'Serge, my love, tell us as much as possible. What direction is the enemy fire from?'

* *

'There's been no shooting for a few minutes,' Sergei said as he peered through the gap between the brick wall and the wrecked truck. The armoured personnel carriers hadn't moved from the intersection. The machine guns were still trained in his direction.

Yousaf had done a quick walk around the compound. The only exits were through the heavy steel gates and the hole in the wall. The army machine guns covered both.

Hashmat and they were trapped in the courtyard while a gun battle still raged inside the building.

'Yousaf, how many Taliban are inside?'

'No idea,' Yousaf said.

'My love, give us your position,' Razane whispered.

'I hope we get reinforcements soon.' Sergei's words were

drowned out by a helicopter gunship flying low along the road just above roof height of the buildings that lined the road. From their left a rocket zoomed towards the helicopter. It let out a string of flares and ascended rapidly. The rocket veered off course and struck a building across the road. Large chunks of masonry blew into the road as the building exploded.

Two rockets flew in the opposite direction. A massive explosion shook the ground and night became day. The two pickup trucks, they had arrived in, were mangled balls of fire. Two men with their clothes and hair alight jumped out of one of the pickups and ran a few steps in his direction. They tumbled over and lay still, their bodies continuing to burn.

Sergei shook the horror from his mind and remembered Razane's question. 'I'm ten metres north of the main gate,' he whispered. 'A machine gun nest a hundred metres north west has pinned us down and a helicopter gunship is flying overhead. Be extremely careful.'

'We can see the chopper. It's around half a kay away,' Jane said.

'We'll try to get closer,' Razane said.

'Careful, they'll have night vision too,' Sergei said.

A rocket flew out of the side streets and struck the helicopter in the middle of the tail section. It spun as it dropped. Its tail smashed into a building causing the front to collapse. With its rotors flicking up concrete, the large machine tilted sideways and disappeared into the building, its tail rotor continued flicking up large chunks of mortar before it seized up.

Sergei braced himself for an explosion, but to his relief it didn't happen.

'Did the chopper just go down?' Razane said.

'I hope the pilot's OK,' Jane said.

'Yup.'

'We're less than two hundred metres from your position,' Razane whispered. 'We're looking for a way to the roof of this building.'

A pickup with a machine gun stopped to his left. A Taliban

fired towards the intersection. Sergei ducked back into the compound as the two APCs returned fire. Theirs was distinguished by tracers.

Another machine gun erupted. It wasn't clear who it belonged to, but the APCs stopped firing, leaving absolute silence.

To his left two pickup trucks loaded with Taliban zoomed into view. Hashmat saw them and dashed out into the street. Sergei stole a glance towards the intersection. The APCs had been over-run by a crowd of Taliban. The other machine gun he had heard must have ambushed them.

The speeding pickup trucks braked heavily and stopped in the middle of the road. The men in the back jumped out and ran towards Hashmat who said something to them as he pointed back at the compound.

Five Taliban headed towards them, guns on the ready. Another five headed towards the intersection.

'I think they're here for us,' Major Hamdani said standing up.

'Razane and Jane are near,' Sergei said.

'We no wait for them,' Yousaf said. 'Say to them… go back, we now okay.' Yousaf helped the major stand. Sergei stood too. The five Taliban were fifty meters away.

'It seems we're going with the Taliban,' Sergei whispered.

'No. I don't like it,' Razane said.

'Don't, it's a trap,' Jane said. 'We had a fight with our guards in the village and they sent many more to get us. I think they wanted to kill us,' Jane said.

'What? Why would they do that?' Sergei said as he turned and looked at Yousaf.

Yousaf turned to the major. 'Sir, what you think? Can Taliban harm us?'

'They're more dangerous than snakes but I do not think so.'

Yousaf glanced at his phone and stiffened. He was on Twitter.

'How are you still getting reception?' Sergei said.

'Ghazni is falling to the Taliban,' Yousaf said in a hollow voice, ignoring Sergei's question.

'Oh dear Allah, that's bad,' the major said.

'You guys confuse me. I thought you support the Taliban.'

'I will explain later,' the major said, 'just know that Ghazni falling to the Taliban is the worst possible outcome. We're trying to negotiate and end to hostilities. If they win an important town like this…'

'Ghazni cut Kabul from Kandahar,' Yousaf said helpfully.

'Fuck!' Sergei said. 'We've helped these monsters capture a town.'

'Mr Markoff, you overestimate yourself greatly,' the major said. 'The Taliban have been fighting on and off here for months.'

'Sergei, we're on the roof of a building in the next street,' Razane was breathing heavily. 'I can see the five men heading towards you but can't see much else of the street.'

'The place is teeming with the buggers. Another group of five are walking north towards the next intersection, which is also crawling with them.'

'First things first. I'm going for the five men heading towards you,' Razane said, 'You're in the line of fire. Step back from the opening.'

'I agree, but we're choosing the losing side,' Sergei said.

'You're not listening. The Taliban won't let us leave alive,' Jane whispered.

'Razane we try kill men you not see,' Yousaf said as he ran towards the main gate to the left of the breach. 'Sergei bro shoot pickup drivers.'

'OK,' Sergei said. Adrenaline was coursing through his veins as he stepped sideways. Glancing back, the major had sat down again behind the truck's steel bumper. 'Sweetheart, we're safe.'

'I ready… in position,' Yousaf said, breathing heavily from the sprint.

**

Razane adjusted her rifle sight as she crouched down on the roof top. 'Jane, you take the two on the left, I'll take the two on the right. Whoever wins does the one in the middle.' She fired without waiting for a response. Her target pitched forward.

Jane hit her first target a fraction of a second later, propelling him to the ground.

Razane got her second shot as the remaining three Taliban were turning. Her second victim was hit in the side of the head and fell backwards. Jane missed her second shot. The two survivors bravely stood their ground, lifted their rifles and fired blindly shooting out windows across the street.

Yousaf fired off two rounds at the group of five Taliban nearing the intersection. They were crouching near the ground trying to work out the direction of the gunfire.

Razane fired again, almost at the same time as Jane did. Both men dropped. 'Sergei, they're all down. You're good to go.'

**

Sergei stepped out from behind the truck just in time to see Hashmat and the two pickup drivers leave their vehicles and take cover behind them. Sergei glanced towards the intersection. Yousaf had killed one of the five Taliban. The rest were nearly at the intersection.

Sergei made his choice. He fired at the farthest man. He dropped. It was a lucky shot. A running man was a difficult target. Yousaf fired a short burst. Two fell, two were left.

The running Taliban stopped and turned. Yousaf fired another short burst. Both fell in a heap.

'Good shooting, bro,' Sergei whispered as he turned his attention to Hashmat and the Taliban drivers hiding behind the pickups. One of them had his leg sticking out the side. Sergei took aim and fired. The man let out a scream and fell back. It was one of the drivers.

Yousaf saw him roll and the ground and fired. The prone Taliban convulsed briefly and was still.

The second driver stood and began running towards the south. As he did, he half turned and fired a burst in their direction. Sergei winced as bullets pinged into the surrounding brickwork. One clanged into the truck. The damn bastards were accurate even when fleeing. Yousaf fired a burst. Sergei fired too. The man pitched forward and fell.

Hashmat was nowhere to be seen. Sergei spent a second looking, then he turned his attention towards the intersection. The Taliban were engaged in a firefight with someone beyond the intersection, out of Sergei's sight.

'See anyone else,' he said to Yousaf.

'No.' Yousaf sounded annoyed.

'Same for me.'

'If it's safe you should leave now,' Razane whispered.

'I agree. But one man got away. He'll be calling for reinforcements,' Sergei said.

'Sergei cross road with Major Sahib,' Yousaf whispered. 'I cover. You doing same for me.'

'OK Yousaf. Razane we'll try to come to you,' Sergei said in a whisper.

'No see enemy,' Yousaf whispered. 'Go fast.'

Sergei helped the major squeeze through the hole in the brick wall and past the truck. They were out in the street. The gun battle at the intersection had gone quiet. If the Taliban had won and had taken control of the APC mounted machine guns, they were in trouble. Nothing stirred as they crossed. The knowledge that things could go crazy any second was unnerving. It made him feel vulnerable, almost naked.

The temperature had dropped a few degrees since they had launched their attack on the RAAM building, the road surface felt even more slippery than before.

'I will walk by myself,' the major said. 'Lead the way. If I get hit, just keep going.'

Sergei left the major and stepped off the footpath, onto the road, the snow on the road's edge crunching underfoot. The sound of the battles raging in the distance made the stillness on their street almost otherworldly.

Sergei pressed a button to engage Super-Normal-Hearing. He heard running feet, men shouting commands, a diesel engine, squeaky tracks and a heavy rumble. Any minute and they would be outgunned.

'Sergei can you run?' Yousaf whispered. 'I hear tank.' He too had engaged Super-Normal-Hearing.

'Oh shit,' the word made Sergei's blood freeze. 'Wh, what about the major—?' he stammered

'You help major more if you go fast to other side. Try enter big white building.'

'Sergei, we have a group of Taliban in our street, parallel to yours.' Razane said.

'Damn,' Sergei huffed as he picked up his pace. The tension had given him a massive stitch in his side. Trying to push the pain aside, he looked at the double-storey building on the opposite side of the street.

'I'm entering what looks like an abandoned hotel. It's the only double-storey structure. Tell me if any Taliban enter it from the rear.' Sergei said.

'Sure. I can only see the major... not you,' Razane whispered. 'That building extends all the way to our street. Take care—'

Her words were drowned out by two gun shots. Sergei felt the punch to his chest. His legs were no longer under him. He dropped his weapon and braced with his hands as the ground rushed towards him. His helmet's peak took the brunt of the force to his head. The snow cushioned the impact to his face. Behind him, someone was moaning. The major had fallen.

The force of the impact had knocked his breath out. His mouth stung from the impact with the ground. His head hurt from where the rim of the helmet had struck his forehead. His neck burned from where the helmet straps had pulled on his neck.

'Sergei, talk to me, my love.' Razane was no longer calm.

'Serge, darling…' Jane was just as frantic.

'I no see gunman,' Yousaf warned just as the crack of another gunshot reverberated between the buildings.

Sergei could feel the bullet rip through the air millimetres above him. He thanked whatever impulse had made him try to catch his breath and not stand up.

'Yousaf, can you see him?' Razane's voice was hard edged.

Sergei felt beneath him for his rifle as he spat out the snow.

'Gunman is behind pickup. I no see him.' Yousaf said.

'I think I'm OK.' Sergei groaned as his M4 scraped along the snow. Trying to stay as low to the ground as possible, he carefully slid his rifle forward and took hold of the stock. His finger found the trigger. He moved his head sideways and cleared the snow from his night vision screen; amazingly it still worked.

'Your biometrics are good,' Razane said. 'You haven't been hit.' Her voice had regained its icy calm.

'This body armour's amazing,' Sergei grunted. 'But I think the major's hurt.'

He tried to use his night vision with his right cheek in contact with the freezing ground, but it was an impossible angle. He couldn't see his assailant. 'I need help, I can't see the man.'

'Wait, I fire grenade. If he move, you shoot.' Yousaf said as he clicked a grenade into the launcher tube. 'Head down!' Yousaf whispered sharply.

Sergei instinctively closed his eyes as the grenade landed a few meters from the Taliban. He forced them open to see Hashmat rolling on the ground, trying to get away. Sergei fired two shots. The first missed, the second found its mark. Hashmat cried in agony as he fell forward, convulsing in pain.

The major crawled towards Sergei who heard him and turned his head. The major waved him on.

'Don't go back for the major,' Razane said.

'We need him,' Sergei whispered.

'Yes, but it helps nothing if you're dead,' Jane said.

'Sergei leave major, I help.' Yousaf shouted.

Half crouching, Sergei ran the remaining distance to the abandoned hotel. Once there, he dropped to the ground and scanned the street. 'Yousaf, it's clear. Hurry!'

Yousaf left the gate and sprinted across the compound towards the breach in the wall. Without stopping, he squeezed past the truck and ran towards the major who had shakily gotten to his feet.

Sergei frantically scanned both sides of the street for any signs of trouble. Something was approaching from the south.

'Hostiles to the south,' he whispered loudly. 'Hurry Yousaf!'

'I see three or more vehicles on your street,' Jane said. 'They look like Taliban.'

'You have twenty seconds to get off the street.' Razane warned. 'I'll try to slow them.'

Yousaf ran across the road, stopping briefly to help the major. Sergei took careful aim and fired three rounds at the approaching vehicles.

* *

'Jane, help me try and hit them,' Razane said.

Jane looked through her gun sight. Three or four fast moving pickup trucks were racing towards Sergei and Yousaf's position.

She could only see glimpses through gaps in the buildings that lined the street as they flitted in and out of sight.

She pointed her gun further north through a gap from where she could see down to the surface of the road. A second later the trucks crossed the gap. She fired. The trucks passed out of sight. She moved further north looking for another gap and found an even smaller one just as the lead truck crossed the narrow gap. Both Razane and Jane squeezed off a few rounds. Two more trucks followed and disappeared.

'This is hopeless,' she said in an annoyed tone.

'We hit one,' Razane said breathlessly into the mic.

She ducked as a bullet whizzed past her followed by two more. Someone from the street below was shooting at them.

'Shit!' Jane said.

A crowd of around twenty-five fighters had gathered and were looking up at them. Some were pointing their rifles. Even though they had used suppressors, someone must have heard them.

'Oh, no,' Razane whispered to Jane, 'see what that man has on his shoulder?'

'Oh fuck,' Jane went pale. It was a shoulder mounted RPG launcher.

BATTLE FOR GHAZNI

Ghazni, Monday 15 January, 4:15 am

The four Taliban pickup trucks had stopped five hundred metres away. A crowd of fighters piled out and dissolved into the darkness, wrecked cars and other debris providing them with the perfect cover.

'The trucks have stopped,' Sergei said as Yousaf and the major dropped beside him.

Yousaf looked up the street. 'Bro, very good shooting.' Yousaf was breathing heavily from the sprint.

'We have not stopped them.' The major shook his head, looking worried. 'When they get here, we are in trouble.'

'Agree. And we don't have enough ammo to fight them off,' Sergei said. 'Our only hope is to get to the next street. Razane and Jane have a car to get us out.' He climbed a flight of marble steps to the front door of the white building. 'Cover me.' Without stopping, he kicked in the middle of the double door. 'Ouch.' The shock jarred his shins, but the doors wouldn't budge.

Limping, he turned his attention to the boarded-up windows. He grabbed one of the thick wooden planks and yanked. Rusty nails squealed as the board yielded.

'Help me, Yousaf,' he grunted.

Yousaf ran to help. The major also approached, but more slowly. The fall in the street had twisted his knee, and he was limping painfully. Thankfully, he otherwise appeared uninjured.

With their combined effort, the boards came away easily. Soon they had enough room to walk through sideways. The glass behind was riddled with bullet holes. It might have explained why the boards had been necessary. Sergei used the butt of his rifle to remove the rest of the glass. He took extra care with the jagged edges.

'Do you have a spare weapon?' the major said as he

glanced at the approaching Taliban running towards them.

Sergei gave him his pistol and squeezed through the opening.

The interior of the building looked like it had been hit by a hurricane. Furniture was toppled over, chandeliers were askew, a pane of glass was smashed. The floor was littered with masonry and broken objects. Paper was strewn throughout the spacious lobby. At the back, a shrivelled plant in a man-sized pot stood next to the splintered remains of the reception desk.

Behind him, glass crunched as Yousaf and the major followed. Muffled gunfire sounded from the back of the hotel.

'We're inside the white double-storey building. It definitely was a hotel.' Sergei said into the mouthpiece. He was answered by a muffled explosion.

'We are under attack by two dozen Taliban,' Razane said after a pause. 'They have an RPG launcher. Jane just dropped the man carrying it but another is picking it up. Our viewing angles are terrible. We could use help.'

The sound of gunfire continued. An RPG launcher was bad news. They had to do something. Sergei ran through the large lobby, past a desk marked "Valet" and into a wide and long corridor. He paused outside two double doors at the end of the corridor to catch his breath as he waited for Yousaf and the major to catch up.

The doors were slightly ajar. Sergei glanced into a spacious hall. Rows of chairs, many toppled over, faced a stage with a dais on the left. The back wall was covered in floor to ceiling windows. Outside he could see several tall buildings. His heart beat faster as he realised Razane and Jane would be atop one.

'I can see the windows at the back of the hotel,' Sergei spoke into the mic as he stood aside to let Yousaf and the major enter the hall.

'Careful, the windows are only half a storey above the street. And it's full of Taliban,' Razane whispered.

Senses on high alert, Sergei hurried to the windows and looked down. Yousaf joined him.

A crowd of Taliban were milling around, pushing and shoving each other and gesticulating frantically. They seemed to be having an argument. As he watched, two men took potshots at the top of a modern four-storey building.

His blood froze as he spied a Taliban hoisting an RPG onto his shoulder. There was no time to consider options. Sergei punched a hole through the windowpane with his barrel, flicked the M4 into full-auto and pressed the trigger as he swept the crowd.

The man with the RPG and several others fell. The rest ran helter-skelter. In the chaos, two men on the opposite side of the road turned, crouched down and lifted their rifles.

Sergei saw them just in time and ducked as bullets tore into the room. Sheets of falling glass brushed his jacket as he fell back.

Yousaf wasn't so lucky. His head whipped back as a bullet found its target. His hands flew to his face, and he staggered backwards and fell.

'Shit, Yousaf's hit,' Sergei said in a panicked voice. 'The RPG is on the ground. Can you stop them grabbing it?'

'Jane, use your grenades,' Razane said.

'Get down. Here it comes,' Jane said moments before a grenade fell and exploded, followed by another.

The blast knocked the few remaining panes of glass from the window frame.

Sergei lifted his head above the window sill. The Taliban had lost all cohesion and were running for cover. 'Let's get as many while we can,' Sergei said as he flicked his rifle back to single-fire mode.

Jane and Razane must have had the same thought. Bullets rained onto the street.

Within thirty seconds the Taliban had dissolved into the shadows leaving behind eleven bodies. Sergei counted. 'I wonder how many got away,' he said.

'They'll be back,' Jane said. 'How's Yousaf? Can you make it across the street?'

Sergei turned and looked at Yousaf who lay groaning on the floor. The major was cradling his head. 'I'm checking him now.'

'I can see an elevated heartbeat and low blood pressure,' Razane said, 'he must be wounded.'

'Major, please cover for me.' Sergei said and crawled over to Yousaf. 'I can see blood but no entry wound.'

A loud detonation made his chest reverberate. The double doors to the hall burst open and slammed closed again as the room filled with dust. The hotel was under attack from the front.

The major teetered as he picked up his fallen rifle.

'Major, you help Yousaf,' Sergei whispered and ran to the entry doors to the hall and looked out. A cloud of dust filled the lobby and the corridor and smelt of burnt metal.

Sergei activated Super-Normal-Hearing. Men were whispering nearby.

'They're inside the building,' Sergei said in a low tone, his voice barely louder than the thumping of his heart. Fear roiled his stomach, constricted his breathing and turned his legs to jelly. They were caught between an enemy out in the street and an unknown number inside the building. With Yousaf injured and the major barely able to walk properly, he was running out of options.

'Sergei, you can make it?' Razane whispered in a calm voice. She could sense his fear. 'Do you have any grenades left?'

'Y-y-yes…' He stammered.

'There's a ledge outside the large windows. From there it's a small jump to street level. First, use your grenades to stun the enemy. Then get the major to cover you while you carry Yousaf out of the building. Then cover the major. Once you're outside, we'll cover you while you cross the street. Now go my love, fast.'

Sergei felt his tension ebb as he listened to Razane's calm voice. 'Major, cover me,' he shouted as he opened one door and lobbed a grenade into the hallway. His legs felt leaden as he ran towards Yousaf and the major.

The grenade burst and the shock wave blew the doors

open again, propelling him forward like a giant hand had shoved him.

It took a momentous effort to keep his footing and sidestep the major who was crouched beside Yousaf.

'Get up, son,' the major was saying as he tried to help Yousaf up.

'I'll carry him,' Sergei said. 'Just cover me.' He stood on Yousaf's foot as he crouched down. With his left hand, he used a fireman's carry to lift Yousaf onto his shoulders.

'Oh shit, you're heavy,' Sergei grunted as he tried to stand upright. He was out of practice and Yousaf was one of the burliest men he'd ever hoisted onto his shoulders.

Glancing back at the doors, Sergei stumbled to the window. Outside the Taliban hadn't yet regrouped. The reprieve wouldn't last. They were persistent and brave. They would be back. Feeling vulnerable, he clumsily clambered out onto the ledge.

Behind him, the major had reached the window. Sergei turned and fixed his gun sight on the hall's entrance doors as the older man clambered out onto the ledge beside him. His grenade must have hit the mark. No one was following them yet.

With trembling legs, Sergei eased himself off the ledge. Even though it was barely more than the height of two steps, his legs almost gave way from Yousaf's weight. It took all the strength he could muster to straighten himself up.

Just in time he noticed movement in a doorway across the street. 'Look out,' he shouted at no one. Glad his rifle was already aimed in that direction, he pulled the trigger.

The man in the shadows fell forward.

Behind him, the major grunted as he eased himself off the ledge and followed him, limping across the street.

They had crossed halfway when Razane cried out. 'Hostiles behind you in the hotel.' She opened fire. Jane joined in. Sergei turned to see bullets shatter the large panes of glass and shadows scurrying inside the hotel.

'Shit.' He tried to pick up his pace but his legs were ready to give in. A deep sub-sonic rumble cut through the fog of exhaustion. He felt his stomach drop when he realised what the sound was. He hoped it was not too near.

'Hurry Sergei,' Jane whispered, her fear palpable. 'There's a massive battle tank heading our way.'

'Oh, shit,' Sergei said. The thought of the tank sent shivers down his spine. They'd be caught in the crossfire.

As if Jane had read his mind. 'Serge darling, you have less than a minute before it rounds the corner.'

'Sergei, my love, diagonally to your left is a narrow covered-laneway. It runs alongside our building. It's in complete shadow and can be defended. Get there and try to hold it. I'll come down and help.'

'Sure,' Sergei grunted as he adjusted Yousaf's weight on his shoulder. He hadn't told Razane that he had only one round left in his magazine.

His legs and shoulder on fire, Sergei continued his glacial pace across the street.

'Do you need help to carry Yousaf?' the major said as he caught up to him.

'I'm fine, major. Thanks.' Sergei grunted.

Across the street, in the shadows, a bearded man watched Sergei and the major as he sat up. He felt around for his fallen rifle.

* *

Razane wiped the sweat from her brow. Her ears and her hands and feet were freezing cold but her body was wet from perspiration as she fought to maintain concentration.

When Sergei had emerged from the abandoned hotel, she had almost broken down with relief. Her heart swelled with love and pride when she saw him carrying Yousaf on his shoulders. Sergei could never leave anyone behind, whatever the cost to him. But now he was slow and vulnerable. She didn't want to lose the only man she had ever truly loved. Yet she could also not ask him to do something that went against his nature. She just had to pray and hope for the best and do her bit, which was to cover him.

It was easier said than done. Their night vision system gave them an enormous advantage, but the enemy had hundreds of nooks and crannies to hide in. They also were fearless. Suppressing fire provided a far smaller window than with any other adversary she'd ever encountered except for Islamic State fighters in Syria. It was well known that Islamic State used crystal methamphetamine to induce fearlessness. The Taliban disavowed drugs. Their courage came from having nothing to live for and a fanatic belief in the rewards of martyrdom.

Razane glanced over at Jane who was alternating between the night vision scope on her rifle and the screen mounted to her helmet to watch her side of the street.

It was amazing how far Jane had progressed, driven purely by love and her iron-will.

When Jane had announced her intention to learn to fight so she could protect them, they both had just smiled. It was inconceivable that their gentle Jane could ever develop an aggressive bone in her body. It was also hard to imagine them being in another combat situation. But fate had a funny way of rearranging lives.

'Jane, I'm heading down. Hold the fort for a while.'

'Sure,' Jane whispered back, her voice trembling with the cold.

Razane heard Jane gasp. The tank had swung around the corner. Marching behind, using it as cover, was a unit of Afghan Infantry. The tank's searchlight swung in an arc as it brightened the street. Sergei, Yousaf and the major were lit up like fireflies.

'Razane, what do we do?' Jane squeaked, 'I've one grenade left.'

'Don't—' Razane's reply was cut off by the staccato of machine-gun fire. 'Oh no,' The blood drained from Razane's face as she spun around. Her heart stopped then started again as she saw Sergei still standing, carrying Yousaf.

The government troops had fired at someone else.

Sergei's face was turned towards the advancing Afghan troops as he stepped over a small concrete divider in the middle of the road. He lifted his rifle and waved at the tank as if saluting them. The major waved too. As Razane and Jane watched with disbelieving eyes, they calmly continued crossing the road as the tank rumbled closer.

'W-w-what... what just happened?' Jane's voice had a faraway quality. She couldn't believe her eyes.

'No idea... but I think Sergei's safe from them. Let's focus so we can get out of here.' Razane said, unable to control her trembling.

Sergei, Yousaf and the major had reached the footpath on their side of the street and were out of sight. Razane stood at the top of the staircase and took a deep breath. The temperature had dropped further, making deep breaths painful. Something made her look at the northern sky. It had gone quieter. She could no longer see any flashes. The artillery bombardment had stopped. That Taliban attack had fizzled out. It explained the tank. The Afghan Army was sweeping south and would soon close off the southern approaches to Ghazni. The window to leave the city was rapidly closing.

The steps were icy and Razane's limbs still trembled as she began her descent.

'Jane, my love focus on the south side... and be ready to come down when I say and... please... mind these icy steps,' Razane gasped as her foot slipped on the third step. A pain shot through her wrist as she grabbed the icy cold banister. Her heart almost fluttered out of her chest as she held on for dear life. That was too close. Her head was spinning, and she wanted to sit down but she forced herself on. She had to get to the bottom fast.

'Focus, focus, focus,' she whispered to herself as she kept one hand on the railing as she moved her other hand to the successive treads above her as the staircase wound down to the small courtyard below.

Sergei was neither in the narrow passage along the side of

the building nor in the connected courtyard. Willing her legs to move, she ran towards the front of the building.

'I think I can see the passage entrance you mentioned,' Sergei whispered

'I'm nearly at the front. I should see you in seconds,' Razane said. 'Tell the major it's me.'

She heard low voices and turned on Super-Normal-Hearing. Sergei was talking to the major. As she reached the mouth of the passage. Sergei was less than ten metres away and the tank was almost level with the building. Its spotlight made her night vision system redundant.

'Are you OK with Yousaf?' Razane said.

'No, he's built like a bear,' Sergei was straining to speak.

'There's a sheltered courtyard twenty metres that way.' Razane pointed as she led them back into the dark passage. 'Major, please keep an eye on the rear. Jane, my love, come down but take great care. I really mean it. The stairs are icier than when we climbed them.'

'Sure.'

'I really mean it. I slipped and almost fell.'

'I'll take care, my darling.'

They reached the courtyard. Sergei put Yousaf down and felt for a pulse. Dry blood caked Yousaf's face.

'He has a pulse,' Razane showed Sergei her telemetry screen.

Jane entered the courtyard. 'Aah, thank goodness. I never thought we'd see the end of that,' she said as she knelt beside Yousaf, 'how is he?'

Sergei removed Yousaf's helmet and handed it to the major who examined it as Sergei shone a flashlight on Yousaf's face.

The front of his forehead was matted with blood.

'This explains it.' The major stuck a finger through a hole in the helmet. 'He was shot.'

'The bullet's not in him so hopefully… It's only a surface wound.'

'He's unconscious. The bullet would have knocked him out, even just by grazing him,' Razane said looking worriedly towards the front of the building. 'Let's get out of here so we can fix him up.'

Sergei hoisted Yousaf onto his shoulders again and they set off down the passage towards the road at the back of the building. Jane led the way and Razane took up the rear.

Jane squeezed through the small gap between the parked Landcruiser and the building wall. Crouching near the front bumper, she scanned the road. Apart from their building and a mosque directly across the road, all others were single storey with a narrow frontage. Many were shops all with their shutters drawn. The street was deserted.

'We're all clear,' Jane whispered.

Razane opened the tailgate and Sergei placed Yousaf in the back. Then he clambered over the second-row seats into the front.

'Am I driving?' he said.

'You can,' Razane said, 'the rest of us will watch for threats.'

'How do I start...?' Sergei was feeling for something. 'Is it this switch?'

'Yes,' Razane's reply was drowned out by gunfire. The street they had left had just erupted into a battle zone. The sound of jets overhead propelled Sergei into action. He pressed the switch. The starter motor churned reluctantly before the engine wheezed into life.

TRIAL RUN

Melbourne, Monday 15 January, 10:55 am

Najib climbed into the front passenger seat of the Mercedes van and glanced at his watch. It was five to eleven. Four of his men sat in the back. Salamat, one of the truck drivers who had transported them south climbed into the driver's seat beside him.

'Salamat will be your driver, today and tomorrow, *Insha`Allah*.' Peter said coming to his window.

Najib nodded, '*Insha`Allah*.'

'God be with you,' Peter said as Salamat started the engine.

'It's eleven, now.' Peter said, checking his watch. 'Time to go.' He stepped back as Salamat put the transmission in Drive and depressed the throttle. With a chirp of tyres and a spray of coarse stone chips, they were off.

Najib used a pencil to make the first tick on the turn-by-turn directions list on his clipboard next to the word "Start". In a box on the right, he recorded the time.

Wafaa would use Google Maps to track the progress of all the teams but sometimes Google Maps lagged. His job was to make sure they recorded the exact times.

At exactly eleven minutes and two seconds, Salamat turned right onto Plenty Road. It was warm and sunny and the traffic was light. They passed a row of shops and a McDonald's fast-food restaurant. After two roundabouts the speed limit increased to eighty and then one hundred. They were now driving past farms. A tractor pulling a reel-mower was cutting a path through tall grass on his left. People were few and far between, most were in cars or working in the fields. The population density was too low to make an attack in that area worthwhile. The people here would be the lucky ones.

They continued past more farms. At eleven-fifteen and thirty-seven seconds Salamat slowed to take a right-handed turn at a roundabout. More countryside flashed past them.

At eleven-twenty-six and forty-one seconds they turned left onto the Hume Freeway. Here the traffic density was much higher. At eleven-thirty and thirty-one seconds, they took the off ramp for Craigieburn.

The housing suburb lay to their right as the road descended a small hill. It was the first urban area along their route. Its population density made it an ideal target.

At precisely eleven-thirty-two they turned off the main road and entered the housing estate. Najib turned on his GoPro video camera. In the evening they would analyse the footage and count the number of people. That would be their casualty target for the next day when they would use machine guns instead of cameras.

They drove in silence down the quiet streets, past the rows of neat brick-veneer houses, most with small well-tended gardens. The .50 calibre NATO rounds would penetrate brick with ease. Even the houses in the row behind were not safe.

The residential section ended in a park full of children, young mothers and older people. A shopping mall followed, full of mainly women of all nationalities.

As Salamat turned back onto the main road, the clock showed eleven-forty-seven and three seconds.

At eleven-forty-eight and fifty-nine seconds they turned right onto the Hume Highway. Traffic was free flowing all the way to Somerton Road. From here the businesses lining the road became smaller and traffic was heavier.

At the eleven-fifty-nine they passed a cemetery on their right. After tomorrow Melbourne would need a few more. The traffic was now dense. Every lane was full of cars.

A short while later they passed a pub, a car dealership and a tram, disgorging passengers, all great targets, *Insha`Allah*.

At twelve-oh-five and fifteen seconds they passed the busy Bell Street intersection and entered Sydney Road. They were headed straight for the heart of Melbourne. Sydney Road was crowded with pedestrians going about their shopping. The speed limit dropped to forty and cars were driving even slower. Here two of their men, armed with automatic rifles, would walk alongside on the footpath, killing anyone the machine gun did not.

The slaughter would be a glorious chapter in Islamic history. It would be the biggest honour to die a martyr and be remembered by believers and infidels for the next thousand years.

* *

Peter watched on Google Maps as the four vans made their way to Melbourne via their assigned routes. They were all supposed to reach at precisely the same time. It was his job to coordinate the drivers and adjust for any holdups.

The vans were to be a diversion to sow confusion and to distract the police and counter-terrorism responders.

The main attack would begin in the city from machine-gun nests atop three high-rise towers. He understood now why he had bought those penthouse apartments for Wafaa.

From their three vantage points tomorrow, they would unleash a rain of death onto an unsuspecting populace.

After tomorrow no one in the western world would ever sleep easy again. They would understand the plight of Muslims in countries like Palestine, Libya, and Iraq who lived in constant fear for their lives. Tomorrow the war between the Christian west and true Islam would go global.

* *

Wafaa scanned the video feeds from each van and from each of the shoulder cameras worn by her men. Her second monitor displayed their progress on Google Maps.

The four teams had done better than she had expected. They each arrived at the centre of Melbourne within a twenty second window.

Tomorrow would be harder. It always was when the killing began. But her men were battle-hardened and had proven themselves in the most dangerous theatre of war. Compared to Syria, Melbourne would be like taking candy from a baby.

For the first time she was sure of success. Tonight, she would sit in prayer and contemplation. Tomorrow she would unleash Allah's wrath.

BLACK ICE

Ghazni, Monday 15 January, 5:50 am

Heavy clouds over Ghazni were keeping dawn at bay. In the icy darkness, a lone dog foraged in a rubbish-heap by the roadside. It was the only sign of life. Everyone who had decided to flee had already left, the rest hid in their homes, many no doubt regretting their decision as the sounds of war drew ever closer.

No one spoke as Sergei drove the decrepit Landcruiser as fast as he dared. A thin dusting of snow covered treacherous black ice that threatened to send them careening off the road at the slightest hint of a curve. Sergei was a skilful driver but his exhaustion and the conditions were testing him to the limit.

In the front passenger seat, Major Hamdani used his calmest voice to guide Sergei. His white-knuckled grip on the overhead handle was the only sign of his nervousness.

Jane and Razane kept watch in the back. The knowledge that death could be around any corner kept them on the edge and compounded their fatigue.

Artillery fire had restarted. Shells and rockets howled overhead as the Afghan army pounded Taliban positions on the southern outskirts. The Taliban response was sporadic. Every so often a wayward shell exploded nearby, making them jump.

'Where are we going?' Sergei voiced everyone's thoughts.

'As far from Ghazni as possible. I have a small hut near Orgun in the hills. We use it as a base away from home while we work here.'

'You mean like another safe-house,' Sergei said.

'Hmmm, I take you have seen a safe-house?' When Sergei nodded, the major continued. 'I supposed you can call it that. It has medical supplies and other useful things. We can help Yousaf there.'

'I hope he'll be OK,' Razane said.

'We must all pray,' the major said. 'He is a good man.'

'We all agree. He's great.' Jane said.

'Let us get to safety then you can tell why you rescued me. I am keen to know.'

'We can tell you—' Jane began.

The major put up his hand to silence her. 'Please not now; we must focus.'

Jane took a deep breath. Yousaf had a satellite phone the major could use to put things right, that's if he had the power to do so. She held her peace. After an agonising twelve days a few hours wouldn't matter. A lack of focus could kill them.

Sergei slowed to take a right-hand turn onto a narrow street lined with large old bungalows. The old Toyota fishtailed as it skittered sideways, its tyres scrabbling for grip.

'Take the next left.' The major's voice shook with the strain.

At the next turn, Sergei slowed even more to avoid a repeat of the skid. Two roundabouts later they spied columns of vehicles choking the single highway out of Ghazni.

'Turn left and merge with the traffic,' the major said. 'We will be safer in the crowd.'

Much to their surprise, the traffic parted to let them merge. They were now crawling at walking pace. A general sense of hysteria pervaded the scene. Drivers honked impatiently as they jostled for position, flashing their high beams and revving engines at every sign of a slow-down. Smoke from hundreds of exhaust pipes mixed with the fog to create a pea-soup smog that turned headlights into light sabres. Periodically the scene was lit by a flash from an exploding shell.

'More people are going right,' Sergei observed as they approached a Y-junction.

'They are going to Kandahar. We must go left, towards the Pakistan border.'

It soon became obvious that the road they turned onto was in the government's control. Soldiers were directing traffic with megaphones and spot lights directed from a tank parked on the roadside.

To their right a skirmish was underway. An army helicopter hovered over a village built on a hill, similar to the one where they had stayed. Its searchlight followed a group of men running towards two parked vehicles. As they ran, one of them turned and fired in the air. The helicopters fired two rockets in response. One hit the ground in the middle of the group. The other struck one of their two vehicles. Huge explosions shook the ground, sending fire and plumes of smoke skyward. The helicopter ascended rapidly to avoid the thick plume of black smoke. More gunfire followed. The running men were firing up the hill at two Humvees that raced down towards them. One man made it to his vehicle under a hail of machine gun fire from one of the Humvees. Somehow, he started his vehicle and made it twenty metres before another salvo brought it to a halt for the final time.

'The army isn't taking prisoners,' Sergei said.

'The Afghans have had enough,' Major Hamdani said tersely. 'Too many times the Taliban agreed to a ceasefire and then broke it.'

'Then why do the Pakistani military support the Taliban?' Jane said leaning forward.

'We have not supported them for a long time but it has been difficult to separate entirely,' the major said. When no one replied, he continued. 'I was here to bring the Taliban factions together one last time and offer them a deal. I thought they had agreed, but...'

'Is that when you were arrested?' Razane said.

'Yes I was—'

Yousaf groaned loudly. Razane and Jane turned and looked. Yousaf's eyes were open as he stared blankly at Razane. His head wound was oozing. He moved his lips as if to speak.

Razane put down her rifle and clambered over her seat back into the luggage area. She rummaged around for a fentanyl lollipop in her first aid kit and placed it in Yousaf's mouth. 'This will take the pain away,' she said as she stroked his hand. She waited for the drug to take effect before returning to her seat.

'Yousaf has saved our lives many times,' Jane looked back. Yousaf was fast asleep.

As they rounded a bend in the road, they saw a squad of soldiers clearing a scene of carnage.

A mangled and blackened truck was on its side. Charred bodies lay everywhere. Soldiers were carrying them to the side of the road and covering them in blankets.

Other soldiers were directing traffic around the choke point.

'It's too gruesome, best not to look,' Sergei said, feeling a hollowness in the pit of his stomach that made him want to retch. 'I'll have nightmares after tonight.' Sergei was looking queasy as a strong smell of burnt flesh entered the cabin. He tried focusing on the road but it was hard to unsee and unsmell something like that. 'You two better not look.'

'We won't.' Jane shivered as she looked away.

'Major, why did that tank not shoot at you and Sergei?' Razane said, trying to change the subject.

'Oh, yes I was surprised too… I can only imagine because of Sergei and Yousaf's uniforms,' the major said.

'Uniforms…?' Jane repeated as it too dawned on her. 'Oh, they thought you were US Marines?'

'It must be. I almost had a heart attack when I saw Sergei waving at them,' Razane said.

'I had one,' Jane said. She took Razane's hand in hers. 'How's your wrists?'

'Still tender but they don't feel broken any more.'

The traffic sped up as they cleared the bottleneck. They passed several pickup trucks covered in bullet holes with drivers slumped at the wheel and bodies of mainly young men in civilian clothes. Many buildings had been reduced to rubble.

They followed a stream of cars as they turned right onto Ghazni-Sharan Road. Sergei slowed for a checkpoint manned by soldiers and a tank. The soldiers were using flashlights to look into passing cars.

'We are crossing out of the Afghan army-controlled zone,' the major said. 'Just stay calm. They are looking for Taliban.'

Traffic picked up after the checkpoint. As they headed out of the city limits, the road surface deteriorated markedly. Even though Sergei tried, he couldn't avoid all the potholes. The Landcruiser was taking a beating, crashing and banging, threatening to shake to bits.

Razane and Jane kept glancing back at Yousaf to make sure his head didn't move too much.

'Sorry,' Sergei said after they hit a hard-edged pothole that made the vehicle shudder. 'These headlights are so bad I can't see the road surface.'

'Just do your best,' the major said.

They drove on in silence following a bus laden with people and their luggage. Sergei was able to predict bumps from what was happening to the bus in front.

'Are we headed in the right direction?' Sergei said, 'I've completely lost my bearings.'

'Yes, it goes east towards the Pakistan border. My hideout near Orgun is about twenty kilometres from the border.'

The sky was lightening as daylight began winning over the clouds and the night.

'I'm worried about Yousaf. If he has a fracture, these bumps will only make it worse.' Razane said.

'Yousaf is in Allah's hands. If he wills it, Yousaf will be OK,' the major said.

'Well let's hope for the best,' Sergei said diplomatically.

'How far to Orgun?'

'About 100km but the road is very bumpy and narrow and it is mountainous so drive carefully. It normally takes two hours.'

'Two hours. Isn't that too long for Yousaf?' Razane said.

'Yes, I agree,' the major said turning around. 'But we cannot stop here. Soon we enter Taliban country. If they catch us, they will kill us on the spot.'

Sergei lowered his window a fraction to let in some air, which was noticeably fresher than it was closer to Ghazni. He yawned and shook his head to clear the tiredness. He had to stay awake.

* *

Abdul Ghanim ground his teeth as he lowered his night vision binoculars. He fished in the pocket of his khaki puffer jacket for his satellite phone. It had been ringing constantly for the last two minutes and he had been trying to ignore it. He was in no mood to talk to anyone.

Their unit needed to retreat without losing more men. His casualties were already double the last time. Agreeing to rescue the major had been a mistake. Most of his losses were from the raid on the RAAM building and the fight with the foreigners. According to his men and the villagers, the women had done most of the damage. It sounded incredible, but he had heard some western women were strange, almost like men. These even walked like men.

He took a deep breath to calm himself before answering the call.

'Asalam Aleikum, Akhoond Ghanim.' The voice on the other end was distant but familiar. He took a second to recognise Major Amjad, the colonel's vile underling. He would have preferred executing him instead of Major Hamdani.

The ISI knew everything the Taliban did in real time. Major Amjad should know better than to call him now unless to offer reinforcements.

He took another breath to calm himself further. 'Major Amjad, now is not a good time but how may I be of assistance?'

'By sharing the news of your success.'

'No success today, brother. We retreat.'

'Did you capture the major and the farangi?'

'No. They in Ghazni somewhere. Also, we lose women.'

'How is it that… a most esteemed commander cannot hold on to simple civilians?'

Abdul Ghanim could feel his face go red. 'Brother, how is

that… you did not tell us the truth about these… simple civilians.' His voice was low and brittle.

The major went quiet. Abdul Ghanim hung up. The ISI would have known how dangerous the foreigners were. It had been dishonest of them not to warn him. In fact, it was intolerable. He would discuss this with the *Amir-ul-Momineen* at the next gathering of the Taliban elders, the *Loya Jirga*.

* *

Major Amjad stared unseeing at his computer monitor. His heart raced uncomfortably as the bile rose in his throat, his fingers buzzed and his wrists hurt. His blood pressure had peaked. If he continued like this, he would have a heart attack. There was no use asking Abdul Ghanim to go after the foreigners. He would not listen and they could be anywhere.

The fucking foreigners had outsmarted him again. He had to seriously consider leaving Pakistan or the colonel would carry out his dreadful threat.

Yet there was someone outside Pakistan who was even more dangerous than the colonel. Wafaa was not known to forgive people who reneged on their promises.

ORGUN

Orgun, Monday 15 January, 10:50 am

The morning was bleak and featureless and biting cold. The low cloud cover blended with fog to erase the distinction between the ground and the sky. Four hours of crawling in refugee columns had sapped any strength they had left.

Their hopes of stopping in the next town of Sharan were dashed when they saw hordes of Taliban fighters patrolling the streets in their pickup trucks. Turning their faces away to avoid being spotted, they drove straight through the town without stopping. After leaving Sharan, the road began to climb.

As the road climbed it became narrower and its surface worsened. The big Toyota pitched and yawed as its wheels thumped into an unending succession of potholes. To their relief, nothing broke or fell off. As the mercury plummeted, the road became icy, making the off-camber hairpin bends treacherous in the extreme.

Ominous towering black clouds, the colour of the sheer cliffs above them, portended a storm. They didn't have to wait long. Intermittent rain followed by hail soon overwhelmed the jerky windscreen wipers and made visibility almost non-existent. Sergei kept his headlights on and drove as slowly as he was able.

By now he was beginning to see double and his neck and shoulders were a sea of pain. He moved his jaw to ease the tension and blinked several times to clear his vision.

Major Hamdani shifted in his seat and cleared his throat, startling him. 'Up ahead is an old Soviet era tank. Take the next left just after it. But... be very careful. It is very narrow and bumpy.'

'How can it be worse than this?' Sergei yawned as he spotted the derelict structure, covered in rust and missing its turret and track.

The major's characterisation of the track had been overly optimistic. Width-wise, it was little more than a goat track. By the looks it had been carved by the forces of nature over millions of years. Sergei came to a complete stop as he neared the turn to assess the correct approach.

He looked at the major as if to say, 'Are you sure?' before he turned the steering wheel.

The Landcruiser's engine laboured as it began the slow climb. Sergei kept a watchful eye for sharp stones protruding from the track. Even if they had a spare wheel, it was too steep to change it.

'Have you ever driven up here?' Sergei said as they slowly rounded a sharp bend. Sharp rocky outcrops gouged deep grooves in the bodywork as the track narrowed.

'Yes. I have been coming here since a long time... first helping the Mujahideen against the Soviets and then the Taliban... but I should not be telling you classified information.'

'Everyone knows the CIA, and the ISI created the Taliban,' Razane said.

'Public knowledge is a euphemism for unsubstantiated rumours. Without official sources... to confirm...' The major paused to choose his words.

'Official sources? Isn't that just carefully fabricated lies?' Sergei countered.

'Hmmm, yes I suppose... reality is sometimes fabricated.' The major smiled. 'Intelligence agencies deal in both information and misinformation. They hand out both in measured amounts to the appropriate people at the right time.'

'Isn't that something out of a John Le Carre novel?' Sergei said with a tired smile.

'No, but it could be. Have you read any of his books?'

'Yeah, most of them. Tinker Tailor Soldier Spy is my favourite.'

'It was nicely written,' the major said.

'OK! So... are his books accurate?'

'Aaah... yes, sadly. The world is very twisted.' The major

straightened in his seat as the road levelled off.

They had now been driving on the track for half an hour. Sergei's arms were tiring from continuously fighting the steering wheel.

They crossed a shallow stream flowing across the track. As they emerged, the back-left wheel crashed into an unseen dip. The Landcruiser lurched sharply to the left, almost toppling them on to their side. Somehow their momentum carried them forward.

'Bloody hell,' Sergei muttered.

'You are doing fine,' Major Hamdani said. 'Just keep moving.'

That was easier said than done. While the path had straightened it also became steeper and the comforting cliff face to their right dropped away to a yawning chasm.

'How much longer does this go on?' Sergei craned his neck to see. The sight of the drop to his right gave him goosebumps. 'I'm not very good at off-roading.'

'We are about half way there... it is quite high,' the major said. 'Do not worry, you are driving fine.' His tight grip on the overhead handle belied his nonchalance. 'Whatever happens do not stop.'

'What happens if we have to...' Sergei said as the rear wheels spun, moving them sideways towards the edge.

Fighting panic, Sergei brought the big four-wheel-drive to a halt. His heart thumped as he moved the drive mode lever to Low-Range.

'That will not work.' The major said. 'On these old cars, you need to lock the hubs... at the wheels.'

Feeling rather stupid, Sergei pulled the handbrake as hard as he could.

'Hey, we'll do it,' Jane said before Sergei could open his door.

'Be careful,' he said as Jane and Razane climbed out and walked to the front wheels.

'I almost couldn't watch you.' Sergei said once they were

safely back inside.

'It looks worse from the driver's seat,' Jane said breezily.

With low range engaged, the big Landcruiser stalled a few times before Sergei could finally get them moving again.

'I can see why you didn't want me to stop,' Sergei said as he wiped his sweaty hands.

'You are doing fine,' the major said. 'This is a challenge for anyone. The road stays steep for only a little while longer. Just go slowly.'

'Is there anything else up this mountain?' Sergei said.

'No, just our hut,' the major said as the track turned and began to follow a ridge along the spine of the mountain. Instead of the drop off being on only one side, it was now on both. Sergei looked down and wished he hadn't. They were above the clouds. A river flowing between trees in the valley below looked toy like. One false move and there would be nothing to break their fall.

'Be careful here. Keep your wheels in the big ruts. It is very easy to drive off the ridge,' the major said.

Sergei's heart beat louder than the engine, the creaking suspension and the howling wind combined. He tried keeping the Landcruiser along driving along the ridge, but the wheel fought back as the tyres followed every groove and rut along the path.

'We are very close now,' the major said. 'The worst is now behind us.'

It couldn't have happened too soon. Sergei heaved an audible sigh of relief as they drove onto a treeless snow-covered plateau that ended in tall cliffs. 'I don't want to do that again soon.'

'So where's your hideout?' Jane said as she kneaded Sergei's neck. His skin was drenched in sweat.

'Only five more minutes more.' The major pointed to a gap in the rocks. 'Just follow this stone track through that cutting.'

Following the major's directions, Sergei guided the Landcruiser up a short but steep slope into a narrow gorge lined on both sides with near vertical cliffs.

'I don't see it anywhere,' Sergei said.

'You will. Be patient. It is not a safe-house if you find it easily.'

The cliffs ended in a circular depression, the shape of a soup bowl and the size of four football fields. It was deep enough to hide their Landcruiser. The ground within was dotted with man-sized boulders that looked like advancing infantry.

'Down there?' Sergei stopped the Landcruiser and looked at the major.

'Yes carefully, the ground is often soft. You don't want to slide into one of those rocks.'

Using a light throttle, Sergei drove down the narrow track into the bowl. The path zigzagged between the boulders before climbing out the other side.

'That is the hut.' The major said as they reached the top. He pointed to what looked like a giant-sized boulder perched on the edge of a precipice.

As they drew nearer, they could see it was a man-made structure of stone with a corrugated iron roof.

'When was this hut made?' Jane said.

'In the early nineties.' The major turned to face her. 'We flew in stonemasons by helicopter. I oversaw the construction. If I had known how many days I would spend here, I would have added more luxury features.'

'It's impressive!' Sergei rolled down the window to let in some air.

'Those mountains are in Pakistan.' The major pointed to a row of snow-covered peaks in the distance. 'As the crow flies, it is only twenty kilometres away.'

'Wow!' Jane stifled a yawn.

'The hut looks scary sitting on the edge like that.' Razane opened the Toyota's door and jumped out, 'Can we go and look?'

'Yes, but give me a minute. I need to unlock it and disarm the security.'

The major returned after two minutes. 'Sergei, help me with Yousaf. Ladies make yourselves at home. There is food in the kitchen.'

While Sergei and the major carried Yousaf inside, Razane inspected the outside. She had learnt from bitter experience how important it was to know the terrain in any battle. They were still in Taliban country. But hopefully Abdul Ghanim was too preoccupied to come after them.

The building was considerably larger than a hut. The outer walls were of stone as thick as the length of her forearm. Letterbox windows set above the height of an adult were designed to shoot out of. Whoever designed it had made defence a priority.

Unless the Taliban were skilled mountaineers or had helicopters, they would need to approach from the west the same way they had come.

Razane walked to the edge of the escarpment that ran in an almost straight line along a north-south alignment for a few hundred metres in either direction before dropping out of sight.

As she looked down, the strong updraft took her by surprise. It was as if the wind was trying to push her away from the edge.

A metre below was a ledge wide enough to walk on. It was invisible from anywhere except where she stood and ran below the eastern wall of the hut and for a few metres either side. It looked too straight to be natural. Maybe it was cut out of the rock face to aid the hut's construction.

Beyond the ledge was an almost vertical drop to the mist covered valley. If someone fell, they would have a long time to contemplate their fate before hitting the valley floor. She shivered. Normally she didn't fear heights, but this gave her vertigo.

Steeling herself, she lowered herself onto the ledge, grateful for wind pressing her against the rock face. After a short pause to steady herself, she walked sideways. The hut was now directly above her. She shuffled sideways a bit more till she was below a large window.

Making sure her weight was well forward, she stood on tiptoes to look inside. Jane was in the kitchen getting something from a cupboard.

Razane tapped on the window gently so as not to startle her. It didn't work. Jane nearly bumped her head against an open door.

'What are you doing out there, sweetie?' Jane said as she slid the large plate-glass window sideways. 'Oh, for God's sake. Get inside, please.' Jane had a hard time looking down as she grabbed Razane firmly by the arm.

'Take my rifle. I'll manage,' Razane said as she grabbed the window frame.

'Sweetheart, we've got a perfectly good front door,' Sergei said as he rushed over to help Razane.

'Call it paranoia but I was just checking the escape route.' Razane dusted her clothes and looked around the wood-lined interior. 'Just in case we're attacked.'

'The walls are solid and these windows are decent.' Sergei led her into the main living area. 'They remind me of arrow loops in castles… they just don't point downwards.'

'Let's hope the Taliban leave us alone,' Razane said. Something told her it was a forlorn hope.

'It's so cosy,' Jane said from the kitchen. 'It's less a hut and more a chalet, really.'

While Jane boiled water for tea, Sergei found some dry wood and before long they had a roaring fire.

* *

Major Amjad's phone vibrated. A red LED blinked. He had a new notification from an app that monitored one of a dozen motion sensors he was keeping an eye on.

He clicked on the notification. The app opened showing a green triangle flashing on a map. He zoomed out. He took a few seconds to register its significance.

'*Ya Allah*,' he shouted as he got out of his chair with more enthusiasm than he had felt in days. He looked skyward, 'Please let this be who I think it is.'

Major Hamdani was one of the few people with access to the Orgun safe-house. It had to be him. It was an authorised entry otherwise it would have shown as a red triangle.

He tried looking for a video feed from the location but found none. The site comms hadn't been upgraded. The remoteness and a lack of high bandwidth mobile broadband services would be why. Transmitting video feed over satellite required specialised equipment and was harder to get when budgets were tight.

He smiled as he dialled the colonel's number.

THE TRAP

Sharan, Monday 15 January, 12:30 pm

Abdul Ghanim stared at the black tea leaves circling in his cup as he took a sip of the sweet frothy brew. It was his first cup in sixteen hours and felt good. A black dog with a missing ear skulked nearby hoping for some crumbs from one of the patrons of the outdoor tea stall. Abdul Ghanim threw it a piece of buttered naan. It missed its mark and fell into a shallow drain. In a move that would have delighted a fisherman, the dog dipped its snout in the ice-cold water and fished it out before the current swept it away.

Abdul Ghanim sighed as he looked around the streets of Sharan. His mood was as black as the dog. The defeat at Ghazni was hard to bear, especially because he could have won. If he had not been forced to attack the RAAM building, he would be drinking tea in the governor's house in Ghazni instead of in Sharan.

The defeat cost him dearly in men and equipment, forcing him to withdraw to his stronghold in Sharan. Over the last two years around fifty men loyal to him had infiltrated Ghazni and lived there like normal citizens. All of them had joined the fight. The ones not killed had fled to Sharan with him.

In time, he could get more weapons but fighters were in an increasingly short supply. The Islamic State was becoming active and drawing an increasing number of young Afghans. It would be many months before he could try again. In the meantime, the Afghan Army might grow bold enough to venture into Paktika Province.

His phone rang. He ignored it and studied the passing traffic. More than half had Ghazni number-plates. His phone went silent but then almost immediately rang again. If it was the major again, he would not be so cordial. He sighed and answered.

'*Asalam Aleikum,*' he said gruffly. He stiffened when he heard the colonel's voice.

'*Wa Aleikum Asalam,*' the colonel said. 'Brother, I heard they escaped?'

'Yes, we suffered a defeat and had to run,' he said.

'Oh!'

'Those Russian agents were not spies but highly trained soldiers. They killed many men and turned the battle against us.'

'I swear I did not know, else I would have mentioned it,' the colonel said. 'But... I do know where they are right now. Grab a pen and I will give you the coordinates.'

Abdul Ghanim asked the waiter for a pen and wrote on the back of his hand. 'Thank you brother, for giving us another opportunity. That place is very close... And... this time it is personal.'

'I wish you best of luck,' the colonel said and hung up.

Abdul Ghanim entered the coordinates into his GPS. The terrain looked familiar. He had never been to the summit of that mountain but he could see it was a dead end.

It would take him ninety minutes to reach but he had some men in Orgun, halfway there. He would call them to block the road so the enemy could not get away.

* *

Razane checked Yousaf's pulse. He was barely conscious. The bullet had cleaved his forehead from above his left eye socket to a point above his right temple, exposing the bone and detaching his scalp. Razane tried to stitch the gash to stem the bleeding but was only partially successful. The bullet's rifling action had made a mess of the tissue. He needed proper medical care. While she bandaged his head, the major set up a glucose drip with a strong antibiotic to stave off infection.

'Thank God for your medical supplies,' Razane said as they washed up.

Sergei and Jane had prepared a meal of flatbread, tinned

cheese and hot tea sweetened with condensed milk.

'How's Yousaf?' Jane said as she carried the tray to the front room.

'Not good. We need to get him to a hospital,' Razane said.

'I will try to organise a rescue squad, but the Pak Air Force will not want to fly a helicopter into Afghani air space. We might have to take him on land,' the major said.

'I don't like the sound of that,' Jane said.

The major retrieved Yousaf's satellite phone. It was dead. 'Ah, it has run out of battery.' He went to look for a charger.

Even though they were starving, they ate with little enthusiasm. Exhaustion and worry had taken their appetite.

The major returned and joined them. 'Eat more my friends,' he said. The colour had returned to his cheeks. 'You will need the energy. Now tell me why you rescued me. I am dying to know.'

'Razane was kidnapped by the CIA.'

'What?' Major Hamdani almost fell off his chair. He frowned as he looked at Razane.

'We found out and came to Pakistan—' Jane said.

The major raised his hand. 'But why here...?'

Sergei looked at Jane and continued. 'Well, we discovered that someone in the ISI told the CIA Razane was Wafaa.'

The major screwed up his face in surprise. 'Wafaa...? Huh?'

'We thought, um you could help us—' Jane said.

'Are you saying they... you mean Wafaa Aal Zubeidi?' The major sat back in his seat. 'They linked her with... Razane?'

'Yes, that's right. Someone here showed the CIA false evidence that Wafaa was Razane or... rather Razane was Wafaa,' Jane said.

'And so how is Razane here?' The major looked puzzled. 'Don't tell me—'

'We got her out. Yousaf helped. Then we came to rescue you...'

'You rescued Razane? From where?'

'The Lahore Fort… look, it's a long story…' Sergei said.

'What? The CIA does not bring prisoners to Pakistan.'

'They did. Major Amjad was—' Jane said.

'Major Amjad? But he knows Wafaa. I mean the real Wafaa. We both do.'

'You know the real Wafaa?' Sergei's expression darkened.

'Why is she free if you know?' Jane voiced what they were thinking.

'It is complicated but… Anyway, Major Amjad knows the truth, why would he let Razane be brought here as a prisoner?'

'Major Amjad took part in torturing me in a dungeon in the Lahore Fort,' Razane said in a calm voice.

'I don't know what your relationship is with Major Amjad but he's not who you think,' Jane said leaning forward. 'Yousaf told us he betrayed you to the Afghans.'

The major looked at them one by one. Then he shook his head. 'No. It does not make sense. We have our differences but we go back a long way. And why fabricate—?'

'He knows I killed his brother,' Razane cut in.

'Oh!' The major's startled expression spoke volumes. He turned to Razane. 'B-but, we kept that detail out of the reports.'

'Well, he found out,' Sergei said. 'And I think he betrayed you to get you out of the way.'

'Major Amjad has always been a reasonable man. Sometimes he broke the rules, but then we all do…' His voice trailed off.

He slapped his leg, startling them. 'Oh no! What have I done?' He grabbed a handful of his own hair, his face ashen.

'What happened?' Sergei looked at Jane and Razane who both looked at the major with their mouths open.

'I need to make a phone call.' The major stood and went back to fetch the satellite phone.

Sergei went with him. 'Major. What happened? What did you do?' He put his hand out to stop the major.

'All our safe-houses send a signal to the head office whenever someone enters them. Major Amjad would know we are here.'

'Oh fuck!' Sergei said. His drowsiness dropped away. 'The Taliban… How soon before they can get here?'

'Depends where they were. They could be outside.' the major indicated with his hand. He picked up the satellite phone and dialled a number.

'Who are you calling?' Jane had joined them.

'I need to find my CIA contact.'

Sergei and Jane exchanged glances as a faint voice came from the phone's speaker. They could just make out. 'US Embassy Islamabad, how can I connect you?'

'It's the moment of truth,' Jane said. Razane had joined them. She squeezed Jane and Sergei's hands.

Something hard struck the front door and bounced on the rocky ground below. The air was sucked from the room as a loud thump shook the ground and everything in the hut.

THE SAFE-HUT

Islamabad, Monday 15 January, 3:10 pm

The view to the Margala Hills was shrouded in a rain band that moved with the wind and gave the impression of grey curtains swirling in the breeze. Sebastian was glad to be indoors.

He waited as the printer spat out Wafaa Aal Zubeidi's dossier followed by Razane Silan's. He preferred reading large documents on paper than on a screen. It helped him concentrate and make notes.

Since he had first created Wafaa's dossier, he'd spent at least a thousand hours sifting through information from multiple sources, trying to add to it. It was hard and frustrating work. Wafaa was, without doubt, the most careful terrorist he had ever encountered. It was the secret of her survival. So why had she become careless? What series of events had led to her unmasking?

According to the Pakistanis, a captured Islamic State fighter had identified her in an interview. He claimed he had met her and seen her face. But something felt wrong about that.

Wafaa was a legend in jihadi circles and secrecy was her trademark. If someone had seen her face, it would have been the news of the decade. Over time, it would have shown up in jihadi Internet chatter. He had last checked with the NSA last July. There had been nothing significant that he could have added to her file. It meant that the purported contact with the captured IS fighter would have happened in the last six months. This was implausible. Islamic State and Al Qaeda were bitter rivals. The former was a spent force in Iraq and Syria. Meanwhile a resurgent Al Qaeda had rebranded and reestablished itself in both countries. One of its offshoots, The White Helmets, had become a darling of the western media. Wafaa would have nothing to gain from Islamic State.

Whatever the truth, there was now sufficient cause to

doubt the veracity of Major Amjad's source and maybe even the major himself.

Sebastian now turned his attention to Razane's file. It immediately struck him as odd that several parts had been erased. According to US law, it was illegal to delete data from intelligence files. The same was true for Australia and the other Five Eyes countries, Canada, Britain and New Zealand. Intelligence data proven to be incorrect would be marked as superseded with a simple double line drawn through it. If something had to be kept hidden, it was redacted. The redacted parts were readable only on an authorised computer terminal by someone with the correct security clearance. Data still went missing occasionally, but only because of an input or a storage error. These errors were usually in the form of a missing letter and sometimes a word. In Razane's file, whole data fields were wiped out. The pages were blank. The data wasn't unreadable, it was missing.

He had checked the record's metadata. This was information on when and by whom the file was created, read or edited. It had originated in Australia. The missing bit was an ASIS report, titled "Department of Immigration Assessment, July 2017". So why was it missing?

Razane was born in Iraq and had emigrated to Australia. That could not have happened without clearance from the immigration department. If a mistake had been made in her assessment, surely her records would have been updated.

Ian was probably still in Pakistan. Maybe he could shed some light on the curious development. Sebastian was about to pick up his smartphone to call him when his desk phone rang. It was the switchboard.

'Sir, there's a Major Hamdani calling you on a satellite phone. He says it's urgent.'

The name rang a bell. Major Hamdani was the second of the two Pakistani liaison officers the CIA normally dealt with. His absence during last week's events was most peculiar. Major Amjad hadn't mentioned him once.

Sebastian sighed and put his smartphone down. 'OK, please put him through.'

'Yes, sir.' There was a momentary silence on the line before a buzz told him he had been connected.

'Hello, hello, can you hear me,' a man with a Pakistani accent said.

'Yes, I can. Is this Major Hamdani?'

'Yes, Major Hamdani here. Who am I speaking to?'

'I'm Sebastian Corder. Acting Station Chief for the next two days.'

'Oh, where's Mike…? Never mind, I need to get in touch with Stella Katsis, urgently!'

'Let me check… It says she's offline… in transit and not contactable. Is there something I can help with?'

'If she is on a flight somewhere, then surely I can reach her.'

'No, she's on personal leave.'

'I have information on one of your top fugitives, Wafaa Aal Zubeidi. She will want to know.'

Sebastian was stunned. Was the missing puzzle about to fall in his lap? 'Major, tell me and I'll make sure it's passed on.'

'Mr Corder… Sebastian. The Taliban are outside our door. We are under attack. If we die, so does the information.'

'Whadda you mean under attack…? And who's we? What's the information?'

'We are in Afghanistan with little ammunition and an injured soldier. We need help only you can provide…'

'So what's the information?'

'Her identity and location.'

'Tell me I'll pass it on,' Sebastian said.

'Sorry, I need someone in authority who trusts me and can give us something in exchange. There's no time. Please contact Stella and call back on this number. Tell me when you have a paper and pencil.'

The unmistakable sound of gunfire crackled through the phone's speaker as Sebastian reached for a ballpoint pen. 'OK, I'm ready.'

* *

Major Amjad waited for both Major Hamdani and Sebastian to hang up before he too disconnected. He removed the headphones and rubbed his throbbing temples. The situation was rapidly deteriorating. He needed to warn Wafaa about the risk. But how? The Americans could have him under surveillance.

The bastard Hamdani was resourceful but Allah willing, Abdul Ghanim would reach him before Sebastian found Stella Katsis. Abdul Ghanim had promised a speedy end to the foreigners and the major.

He dialled the colonel's number. 'Sir Hamdani has contacted the CIA.'

'What?' the tiny speaker tizzed with the colonel's anger.

'Sir, he wanted to speak to Stella Katsis. He didn't tell Sebastian anything.'

'So?'

'So Sir, we have a small window before Stella calls him back. We can still stop them.'

'I told you that!' the colonel snapped back. 'We are stopping them. Abdul Ghanim and his men should be there any time.'

'I know sir and they are already there sir…, in fact, I could hear gunfire in the background.'

'So the problem is fixed…? Or am I missing something?'

'Sir, I do not think the foreigners can get away but I want to make sure, one hundred… no a thousand percent sure.'

The phone went silent before the colonel spoke again. 'What do you want?'

'I want to launch an air strike, sir. I want to send in the air force.'

'Huh, what? Major Amjad, are you mad? Of course, we cannot,' the colonel barked. 'What am I, the fucking Prime Minister?'

'No sir, but—'

'But I agree we must leave no stone unturned. If you had been this conscientious all along, you would not be in this mess. So… take the Embraer jet to Mianwali and from there an Mi17. I'll call ahead to have it armed with Ataka anti-tank missiles. That will destroy that stone hut. A team of commandos will accompany you. If you hurry, you can be in Orgun in under three hours.'

Major Amjad smiled. He knew what Ataka missiles could do. 'Thank you, sir. I have a good feeling this time.'

'Bring back proof of death or the commandos will have orders to arrest you. Dis… missed!'

* *

Another grenade landed, this time further away. Compared to the movies it sounded more like a firecracker. A succession of bullets struck the hut like a violent hailstorm, making Jane wince.

Major Hamdani hung up the phone and shrugged his shoulders. 'I have tried my best. The rest is in Allah's hands. I…'

The rest of his words were drowned out in another barrage that struck the hut. A couple punched through a window and smacked into the back wall, snapping them into action. Razane, Jane and the major threw themselves to the ground.

Sergei was slower. Before he could react, a grenade flew through a window and showered them all with glass. It bounced off a leather chair and landed in the middle of the floor, rotating before coming to a stop.

Frozen to the spot, Sergei watched its trajectory in horror. They were seconds from death. With a furious roar, he lifted the heavy wooden table by its legs and upended it onto the grenade.

The muffled explosion lifted it, with Sergei on top, half a metre off the ground.

Too far away to help, Razane and Jane covered their heads. Dazed, with their ears ringing, they stumbled to their feet and ran to Sergei's side. He lay slumped face down on the upside-down table.

'Help me,' Jane said as they both turned him around.

Sergei's mouth was open as he struggled to breathe. Jane held him as she stroked his face. He groaned and clutched his chest.

Razane crouched beside him and took his hand away. 'Are you hurt, my love?' Her voice broke with emotion.

'I hit the bloody table leg,' Sergei could hardly get the words out. 'I might have cracked a rib. Aah… fuck!'

Razane unzipped his jacket and lifted his sweater out of the way. A black bruise covered his chest. 'That'll hurt!' Razane winced as she spoke.

A grenade bounced off the outside wall and exploded, sending slivers of stone flying through their hut. 'We have to fight back,' Sergei said as he tried to get up.

Jane glanced madly around for their rifles. They were propped up against the pillar near the door. Crouching low, she ran and picked one up.

Another volley hit the hut. 'Why are they wasting ammo?' Sergei said through gritted teeth as he and Razane each picked up a rifle.

'Here are more magazines,' Major Hamdani threw one to Jane who caught it deftly.

Razane was first at the window. 'It's suppressing fire. They're preparing to storm the place. We must fight back or it's over.' As if to reinforce her point another grenade struck the outside of the hut and exploded.

**

Major Amjad felt the G-forces push him into the seat as the Embraer jet took off from the air force runway. A message from the Colonel popped up on his phone.

'Abdul Ghanim's forces have them surrounded. And… try to spare the hut.'

'I will try, sir. One way or another we close this today.'

'Remember the proof of death.'

Major Amjad sat back in his seat and allowed himself to smile. The jet had levelled off. He undid the safety belt and reached for the can of Coke in the chilled compartment next to his seat. He could understand why the colonel did not want the hut destroyed. That part of Afghanistan had been in Taliban hands since their inception and was a perfectly safe holiday retreat for the many ISI officers who used it as a place to unwind and recharge.

* *

'Major, do you have rope?' Razane shouted above the bedlam as she fired off three rounds at nothing. The enemy were attacking from the safety of the hollow and hadn't yet shown themselves.

'Yes, I'll bring what I have,' he said and disappeared.

'What are you thinking?' Sergei clicked in a new magazine.

'A plan to fight back,' Razane said. 'Are our comms still working?'

'Mine was when I switched it off last night,' Jane said.

Sergei nodded. 'Yeah, mine too.'

'Good, then here's what we do,' Razane said. Her voice as calm as if they were discussing dinner arrangements.

The major returned with three coils of thick rope. Razane took one and tested it. 'Help me.' she threw two at Jane and Sergei. 'Tie one end of each around this pillar.' Razane pointed to the thick wooden pole the size of a tree trunk in the middle of the hut.

While Jane and Sergei got to work, Razane smashed the large glass on the eastern wall taking care to remove sharp remnants at the bottom. 'I hope you're a good shot, major,' she said.

'I won a few trophies in my day,' the major said, 'but that was a long time ago. I am out of practice.'

'A few things you never forget,' Razane said. 'Get your comms gear on. It's time to go.'

'I have none,' the major said. 'Yousaf's is in the back of the Landcruiser.'

'OK, then Jane you signal to him,' Razane said. 'But remember, wait for me.'

Keeping low, Razane and Sergei walked over to the large window on the eastern wall. 'OK, help me now,' Razane lifted her arms as Sergei cut a four-metre section from the rope and made it into a Swiss seat harness around Razane's waist and thighs. They both knew the rope technique well, having used it while mountaineering together. Today they would use it as a safety harness to take the strain off Razane's wrists.

Sergei tied the end of one tether to Razane's harness, then he helped her climb out of the window onto the narrow ledge below. He handed Razane her rifle before he joined her on the ledge.

'OK. Can you both hear me?' Razane said into her mic.

'Yes,' Sergei and Jane said in unison.

'Let's make this happen. Sergei be careful, my love, this ledge isn't very wide,' Razane said. 'And let me get the first shot.' Jane took up the slack in the rope as Razane inched towards the north-east corner of the hut. Then she did the same for Sergei as he moved to the other corner.

'Careful, you two, I'm going to my position,' Jane said over the noise of Taliban gunfire. Keeping low, she made her way to a window on the opposite wall where the major was waiting.

'Razane, we're both in position.' Jane said.

'I'm in position too,' Sergei said as he cut the rope.

'OK, stand by.' Razane cautiously looked over the edge, her rifle on the ready. She could see along the north wall to where the Landcruiser was parked. To her shock, she saw two pairs of feet behind the far side wheels. The Taliban didn't waste time. As she watched, the two fighters each took turns to fire a burst at their front door.

'Sergei, can you see anyone?' she whispered.

'Eight men just climbed out of the bowl,' Sergei's voice was hurried. 'More are behind them.'

'Can you see the Landcruiser?'

'Nope. It's outside my view.'

'Jane, when I say two, you and the major fire three rounds in the direction of the bowl, but without exposing yourselves.'

'OK,' Jane whispered.

'Here goes,' Razane said as she took careful aim at the feet of the Taliban furthest from her and squeezed the trigger. With a cry, the man fell sideways. Razane fired again, catching him in the chest. He jerked violently and was still. The second man stood up, as if in shock and looked through the Landcruiser's glass towards Razane. She was ready for him. The bullet hit him in the centre of his forehead. He fell against the side door leaving a red smear on the glass. 'Two!'

From inside the hut, Jane and the Major opened fire.

'Sergei, go now,' Razane said as she took out her knife and cut her tether.

From his position on the ledge Sergei fired single shots in rapid succession. 'Got one,' he grunted. 'Make it two. A third is hit but crawling… they're retreating.'

Ignoring the pain that shot through her wrists, Razane hoisted herself up to ground level and crept along the northern wall.

'Jane, both of you join in. Your targets are at eleven o'clock.' Sergei said.

Razane made it to the north-west corner just as the last Taliban fell face forward into the bowl. Six bodies lay on the ground. On her screen, Razane saw Sergei move forward.

'Sergei be careful, I can't confirm all sightlines are clear,' Razane shouted.

'We have to get to the top of the bowl,' Sergei said. 'It's a perfect hiding spot for the buggers.'

He was right. The enemy had a perfect spot to amass for an assault or to harass them from. But Sergei hadn't thought it through. The Taliban were the toughest fighters she'd ever encountered. They were not easily intimidated or traumatised. She was almost certain they'd recover and attack Sergei before he got there, while he was exposed out in the open.

'Sergei, return now!' Razane shouted. Fear gripped her.

The panic in Razane's voice made Sergei freeze. He had never heard her lose her cool.

'Sergei get back, please,' Jane was pleading. The change in Razane's demeanour frightened her too.

In a panic, Razane ran towards the Toyota, propped the rifle on the bonnet and scanned the edge of the bowl.

Meanwhile, Sergei had stopped and was retracing his steps. A flash caught her eye, a hand holding an AK47 emerged from the bowl. Bullets tore through the air as Sergei threw himself to the ground. Several thudded into the hut and the Landcruiser.

Razane pivoted her rifle and squeezed the trigger. She was too late. Someone from the hut had fired first. The hand that gripped the AK47 exploded into a bloody mess. The man's pitiful screams were painful to hear.

Razane looked towards Sergei, her heart beating fast. Please don't be hit! 'Sergei, get up, please. Run!' Razane shouted. She heaved a sigh of relief as Sergei got to his feet. But instead of running back, he crossed the front of the hut to join her behind the Toyota. In the bowl, men were arguing angrily.

'That was close,' Sergei was breathing heavily as he took up a position beside her.

'Serge my love, we need to be spread out,' Razane said as she kept her eyes on the enemy position, her finger on the trigger.

'I thought of moving the Landcruiser to shield the hut's door,' Sergei said. 'Cover me.' He climbed in and started the engine.

'Good idea but next time, more communication.' Razane walked alongside the Toyota as Sergei slowly backed it up.

'Yes, my commander. I'm sorry.' Sergei said in a contrite voice.

'You're forgiven this time,' Razane said as she scanned for threats. The argument in the bowl was still going on. 'Leave a gap to the door so we aren't trapped.'

* *

Abdul Ghanim was furious. He had just begun the climb to the peak when he got a call from Muhammad Azzam, the leader of the group he had sent to stop the foreigners escaping.

The stupid faggot was complaining because he had lost nine men after their assault was beaten back. The shit-eater had not obeyed orders to wait. Now that they had lost the element of surprise, the farangi would be harder to kill with only light weapons. He would have to wait for his artillery and rocket launchers that were still in Sharan. He had hoped not to have to drag them up the mountain. Reluctantly he took out his phone and dialled a number.

* *

'That was an amazing shot. Who was it?' Razane said as soon as they were back in the hut.

'Your student… me,' Jane said as she continued watching through the window.

'You'll soon be the teacher,' Razane said as she leaned against Sergei. 'I'd have struggled with that shot.'

'Did you teach her to shoot?' the major said as he too kept a watch.

'Razane taught us both.' Sergei put his rifle down and pulled Razane close. She was trembling like a leaf. 'It's gonna be OK,' he whispered into her hair, damp with sweat. 'Wow, your hair's so wet.' He helped her into a lounge chair. 'I'll fetch you some water.'

Sergei sat with Razane while she drank. After a while, the colour returned to her cheeks. 'The smell of blood on the Landcruiser made me all woozy.' She handed him the glass.

'Poor baby.' Sergei stroked her face as he held her. Gradually her breathing returned to normal.

'Thank you, my love.' She turned and kissed him on the lips. 'We need another plan. If they bring any heavy weapons, we're vulnerable.' Razane squeezed Sergei's hand before she stood up. 'Major, any news from your CIA contact?'

Major Hamdani shook his head. 'No. She may not get back in time. You three should go to Pakistan. I will hold them off as long as possible.'

'We can't leave you and Yousaf,' Jane said. 'Anyway, we'd be walking from the frying pan into the fire.'

'Jane's right,' Sergei said. 'Can't you call someone else?'

'Yes, someone higher-up... whom you trust,' Razane said.

'I was thinking of calling the colonel, my boss but... he could be in with Amjad? I...,' the major shrugged his shoulders. 'I do not know who to trust anymore.'

'Can you negotiate with the Taliban? I thought they know you.' Razane said.

'They have chosen their side. Nothing I say will change that.'

There was a moment's silence while they all contemplated their choices.

'Well, until we think of something, we should take turns to keep watch,' Sergei said. 'Major... unless you have a better idea.'

'Your night vision systems worked well in Ghazni. Wait till dark. You will have the edge. Maybe enough to clear that bowl and push the enemy further back.'

'That's true. We could hunt them off the mountain,' Sergei said.

'With only three of us and goodness knows how many of them? I don't like our chances in this terrain but...' Razane said. 'It's better than to wait for death.'

'I need new batteries. They are all low on power,' Sergei said.

'I have fresh ones of all types in the back room,' the major said. 'On the way back can you please fetch me a glass of water and some aspirin.'

'Sergei, can I have some water too?' Jane said. 'This is thirsty work.'

* *

Razane and Sergei had a small snack before swapping places with Jane and the major. Outside the wind had picked up. Without glass in the windows, it howled through the drafty hut making the fire in the fireplace flare dangerously. Clouds were darkening the sky. A snowstorm was brewing. Razane was glad she had wrapped herself in a woollen blanket as she scanned for attackers.

The major checked on Yousaf while Jane prepared a quick meal.

'How is he?' Jane said as he joined her in the kitchen. It was too dark to see the major's expression but by his walk, he seemed dejected.

'He's now unconscious and his pulse is faint. We could lose him if we don't get help soon.'

At the front of the hut, Sergei and Razane were finding it increasingly hard to keep watch. The wind was blowing straight at them and outside it was becoming dark.

'We'll need our night vision soon.' Sergei was shivering.

Jane poured two cups of tea and brought them over to Sergei and Razane.

'I can't drink and watch,' Sergei said after he tried taking a sip. 'The steam takes away any remaining visibility.'

* *

Major Amjad scanned the ground looking for the hut. A blizzard had blanketed the mountain blotting out its features.

'Sir, I have a heat signature,' Captain Iqbal said over the intercom 'It's on that ridge.'

The major followed his finger and smiled. 'You have eagle eyes, Captain. I need you to fire a missile on the hut.'

'OK sir. I will try.'

The major watched impatiently as the pilot tried in vain to

lock on to the target. The wind was too strong.

'Sir, it is too choppy to fire from here. We need to climb above this storm.'

'How long will it take?'

'Max five minutes, then I can destroy whatever you wish.'

'OK, be quick about it.'

THE STINGER

The storm front momentarily weakened to a lull as the old Toyota Hilux made it up onto the plateau. Mateen braked to a halt and breathed a sigh of relief, glad to be on level ground. He muttered a prayer. 'Thanks be to almighty Allah'. He looked back at his load of mortars, RPGs, a Stinger in its crate and a heavy calibre machine gun. They had not shifted.

He sat for a moment to catch his breath and calm his nerves. He had almost not made it. Halfway up he had hit an ice patch. Even with four-wheel-drive and low-range he still needed eight men with ropes to stop him sliding over the edge and falling to the valley below.

Ghazni had been a bad loss. Why then was Abdul Ghanim risking his remaining men and weapons climbing a deserted mountain? Was it a sign they needed a new leader?

He was about to move forward when Gulru and Khadim came running out of the dark.

'What is keeping you?' Gulru came to the window. 'The commander is furious.'

'With whom? Me? I have been going as—'

'He is angry with us all for taking so long and attacking too soon.'

'He has gone mad. How is it possible to be too slow and too quick?' Mateen shook his head.

'Never mind. He is the commander.' Khadim came to the window. 'We came to tell you to drive into that large depression so we can unload the weapons.'

'Where is it?'

'Just drive. You will see it,' Khadim banged on his door to hurry him along.

'Who are we fighting?'

'Some white-faces… the Russian agents from Ghazni, now move.' Khadim waved to him as he ran ahead.

A Russian bomb had killed his aged parents. It was why he gave up teaching and first joined the Mujahideen, then the Taliban. Allah willing, he would kill some Russians today. He selected first gear and followed Khadim.

* *

No one spoke as they donned their armour and their gear, their minds on the dangerous task ahead. They were about to attack an enemy they knew nothing of, except their almost otherworldly persistence. The equipment they had taken off the US Marines, their only edge.

Major Hamdani tried calling Sebastian again, but to no avail. Like the last five times, it went straight to voicemail. He shook his head and muttered. 'I told him how serious it was.'

Jane handed him a rifle scope and showed him how to turn it on.

The major looked through it. '*Ya Allah*, this… this is amazing,' he said as adjusted his grip on the rifle stock.

'Remember how we planned this,' Razane said. 'The major covers us from inside. Jane and I take up our positions at the edge of the bowl. From there we decide if and when Sergei can proceed with his move. Sergei, your silencer isn't on. Please do it now.'

Grim-faced, Sergei screwed on his suppressor while he and Jane listened intently. In situations like this, Razane was their natural leader.

Razane held her arms out. The three came together in an embrace made awkward by their body armour and helmets. They ached to be closer and for longer. They all knew the risks involved. This could be the last time they were together. But alas, there was no time.

'Good luck,' the major said, trying to sound cheerful.

Sergei gave him the thumbs up. 'We don't need luck,' he forced a nervous grin. He was right. They needed a miracle. Pity he didn't believe in them. Anyway, it was the wrong thing to dwell on. He followed Jane out of the door, keeping low and in the Landcruiser's shadow. Razane lay on her stomach near the front wheels and scanned the ground between their hut and the bowl.

'Anything?' Sergei whispered as he crawled beside her.

'No. I tried using Super-Normal-Hearing but got lots of jumbled voices...' she sighed. 'The wind is making it harder. It sounds like men arguing. Lots of them. You can see a few have flashlights. They are planning something.'

Sergei turned on Super-Normal-Hearing. The wind and the raised voices sounded like a murderous cult in a horror movie. It made his skin crawl. It was the sound of hate.

'Let's hit the fuckers hard.' Sergei clenched his jaw.

'No emotion, my love. We're just doing a job. Rise above your feelings...'

Sergei looked at her and nodded. She was right.

'Jane get into position. I'll cover you.' Razane said.

Jane kept low as she ran towards the left edge of the bowl. Her gait athletic and graceful but precise. 'Stop there and crawl the rest of the way,' Razane said.

Jane dropped and crawled the last few meters to her appointed spot between a cliff face that bordered the depression and a large boulder that hid her from the Taliban.

From her position, she could see the entire bowl. Six pickup trucks were parked, nose to tail, near the other end. One was near the centre. It was hard to count the men because of the boulders, but she was sure there were at least twenty-five. Four stood around the bonnet of the lead pickup. They had their backs towards Jane. A group was unloading something from the trucks while the rest congregated in two groups arguing animatedly. She slowly scanned the rest of the depression and the steep cliffs rising behind but saw no more men. Thankfully, none had attempted to scale the cliffs. If they had, they would be able to take pot shots at them without fear of retaliation.

Jane described the scene. 'I think I see something that looks like RPGs being unloaded. And there's something in a large crate.'

Razane let out a low whistle. They had been right not to underestimate their foe. They were preparing for an all-out assault. It was consistent with what they had seen all along. The Taliban never gave up. No wonder they had been so devastatingly successful. 'My love, I am moving into position now. Cover me.' Razane said as she ran towards the right-hand edge of the bowl. Like Jane had done, when she got near she dropped and crawled the rest of the way.

'I'm here now,' Razane whispered.

Jane could see her. 'Sweetie, you need to take cover. You're too exposed.' Jane watched as Razane crept sideways behind a rock barely higher than her helmet. 'Better, but not enough.'

'It'll have to do,' Razane's voice was firm. 'Sergei get ready.'

Sergei climbed into the Landcruiser and started the engine. As it clattered into life, Jane watched for a reaction. There was nothing. The men were too busy arguing, and the wind was too loud.

'Serge, you're good to go. They can't hear you. Be careful.' Jane said.

'We'll get out of this alive. I promise...' His words trailed off as he put the transmission into low range four-wheel-drive mode and pressed the accelerator.

The old Toyota bounced and bucked over the uneven ground as Sergei tried to maintain a fast walking pace. He used his night vision system to follow the tracks they had made when they arrived.

The ground climbed as he approached the edge. In the dark the bowl looked black, the path leading into it, invisible. For their plan to have any effect the Landcruiser needed to reach far enough inside to create a diversion and bring the enemy forward, but to be safe he had to remain outside the depression. Timing was everything.

The Landcruiser crashed into an unseen pothole,

causing Sergei to strike his head on the roof. He cried in pain as the helmet crunched down onto his ears. For the briefest moment, he glimpsed the shadows of the enemy congregated near the middle of the bowl. That's what he had to aim for.

He cracked open the door to prepare to jump. Just a little further. Another bounce and the Toyota's front wheels were momentarily airborne before its nose dipped sharply as it careened down into the depression.

Sergei swung open the door and tried to jump clear. But his inertia pushed his body forward causing his foot to jam onto the accelerator and his rifle to catch on the door frame. He managed to break free, but his jump wasn't what he had envisaged. Instead of a clean, forceful exit, he tumbled out, arms flailing. Somehow, he kept his legs clear of the spinning wheels. The ground rushed up and thumped the wind out of him and he slid down the loose-gravel slope in the Toyota's wake.

'No,' shouted Jane. 'Sergei's fallen… in the wrong place.'

'Hold your fire unless someone spots him,' Razane's voice was ice cold. 'He's still shielded by the Landcruiser.'

'Not for long!' Jane whispered furiously.

**

Mateen shone the torch as Abdul Ghanim loaded a rocket into the RPG7 launcher. He removed the plastic safety cap off the rocket and handed it to Hamza.

'You are a soldier of Allah. May you achieve martyrdom.'

Hamza shouldered the RPG launcher and turned. A Toyota Landcruiser loomed out of the dark barrelling straight at him. His mind not comprehending, he acted on instinct. With a great power of will, he sidestepped it but two other men were not so lucky. The Toyota hit them hard. They flew face down into the snow moments before the tyres crushed their bones into the rocky ground.

Abdul Ghanim watched, his mouth agape. He had more time to react but only just as the Landcruiser punched into the back of the pickup truck he was unloading.

Someone fired at the Toyota. Then more men joined in. They were wasting bullets. He put his hand up to stop them but it was dark.

Something warm splashed on his face. He knew before he had touched his cheek what it was. The smell of blood was unmistakable. His mind in turmoil, he looked around for the source. Something soft on the ground made him look down. He shone his torch. It was Mateen with half his face missing.

'Stop!' He let out an almighty roar. 'Stop firing!' He aimed his AK47 above his head and pressed the trigger. His men stopped and looked at him. 'We are under attack. Take cover.' As he spoke two more men fell where they stood.

* *

'Keep firing and make it count.' Razane said as she squeezed the trigger. Another Taliban fell. 'Sergei, my love. Are you OK?'

'I'm fine,' Sergei grunted. He had stopped sliding and had crawled to the right of the path behind a low boulder barely big enough to hide him. 'It's just another cracked rib or two.'

'Find a bigger rock for cover, this'll get messy.'

Two enemy fighters came running, carrying RPGs on their shoulders. 'Jane take the left one.' Razane took her time to aim at the one on the right before she pulled the trigger. The rocket exploded in the launcher with a mighty bang. A deafening silence ended in a shower of pebbles and droplets of blood.

'Yuck,' Jane shivered as she tried shielding herself. She couldn't afford to be squeamish. She looked just in time to see the second man get hit. His head whipped back as he fell, first onto his knees and then face forward. The RPG dropped from his hand and clattered onto the rocks. 'Sorry, that was my one,' she whispered into her mic. Another Taliban fighter emerged from behind a rock and headed towards the fallen RPG launcher. She adjusted her sight and fired. The man spun as he fell. This was getting crazy.

'Sergei I can't see you.' Razane said.

'I'm behind a big fat rock along the outer circle. I'll try to engage the fuckers from the side.'

'Careful, my love,' Razane said as she searched for more targets. The Taliban had fallen back and had taken cover behind the pickup trucks.

'If I move forward, I think I can try to outflank them,' Sergei said as he ran to the next boulder along the outer circle.

'Sergei don't...' Razane said. 'You're putting yourself in—' a loud metallic scream rent the night followed by an earthshaking tremor that convulsed her surrounds. The ground beneath her disappeared, and she was flung forward into the bowl. In a total daze, she landed on the slope and slid the rest of the way to the bottom.

Jane, too, was propelled forward. She hit the boulder she was hiding behind and fell sideways, stunned and out of breath. She gasped at the sharp stabbing pain in her neck. Looking back she saw the hut on fire, its front wall was a pile of rocks on the ground exposing the burning insides. 'Oh, oh, no,' she cried in despair.

'What the fuck just happened?' Sergei's voice was tinged with alarm.

'I don't understand. The hut blew up,' Jane said in a weak voice. Her ears were still ringing. But there was another sound, mechanical and familiar. She looked up. The heat from the helicopter bloomed on her night vision screen. What was it doing here?

'Major, are you OK?' Sergei whispered.

'The hut's a pile of rocks,' Jane was crying. She looked around for Razane. 'Sweetie, where are you?'

'In the bowl. I fell,' Razane said as she felt herself for injuries. 'I'm OK, just shaken. Can you see the helicopter?'

'I can,' Sergei said, 'Bloody hell. I think it fired at the hut.'

'Yes, I heard the missile just before the bang.' Razane said. She glanced at her screen. 'Serge, you have gone too far forward. You are nearly in Jane's line of fire.'

'I can see the bastards behind their pickups.'

'How many?'

'Fifteen, sixteen, give or take but they're all low down and hard to distinguish. I can just see their halos.'

'What's a halo?' Razane said.

'Oh, I found it when I turned the night vision to the max. You can see the air around the person, especially above. So even if they're hidden you can see where they are. The only problem, it buggers up the resolution.'

'Do you have something to hide behind?'

'Yes, I am moving to that large pear-shaped rock near me.'

'Listen, I need to get to the RPG,' Razane said. 'It's around twenty metres from me, next to the Landcruiser's back wheel.'

'If you stay low and behind the Landcruiser they won't see you.'

Razane got up and ran. Sergei's assessment was good enough for her. In battle, opportunities never came twice. She reached the back of the Landcruiser and crouched low. So far so good. 'My loves can you see me?' Razane said.

'I can see you,' Jane said. 'But they can't. I'll cover you.'

'I am covering you too,' Sergei said.

Staying low, Razane reached forward and pulled the RPG towards her. She had used the same type before. It was an RPG7 with a live round. It appeared undamaged but its safety cap had been removed. It was heavy and cumbersome but she crawled with it back to the boulder taking extra care not to bump the tip of the grenade.

'Serge, can you still see the enemy?'

'Yes.'

'When I fire this RPG at the helicopter, the Taliban will see my location. Coordinate your shots to confuse them.'

'We're ready,' they both said.

Razane raised the rocket towards the sky. The helicopter was a faint dance of dots on her night vision screen. She aimed as best as she could. The RPG7 was a Soviet-era weapon mainly used for ground assaults. It had a maximum accurate range of two hundred metres. The helicopter was at least five times that distance. But she wasn't looking for a direct hit. The RPG7 had a safety feature. It blew itself up if it reached nine hundred and fifty metres. She hoped the shock wave would at the very least destabilise the helicopter and make the pilot have second thoughts about coming closer.

She said a little prayer and squeezed the trigger. The projectile popped out of the launcher tube and for a brief moment appeared to head downwards, before its main thrusters lit up. Its trajectory snapped straight as it accelerated upwards. It was out her hands now. She forced her eyes away and turned her attention to the gunfight.

Overhead the RPG exploded, turning that section of sky into day. She stole a quick glance. The helicopter was nowhere to be seen.

The Taliban did as Razane had predicted.

Jane watched as they stood up en masse and opened fire on Razane's position. 'Sergei I see one,' Jane whispered frantically.

'Wait, they're moving forward,' Sergei whispered. 'Let more come into the open. They don't yet have Razane in their sights. Razane don't move.'

'I can't,' Razane said, 'some bullets came really close.'

More Taliban moved forward, firing as they went.

'OK, that's them all,' Sergei said. 'Let's start from the back. Mine are the odd numbers. Ready.'

'Yup,' Jane replied, her finger itching.

'Go.'

They both fired in sequence, their silenced rounds masked by the continuous sounds of gunfire as the rest of the Taliban advanced towards Razane. Before the men at the front realised the danger five of their comrades in the rear lay dead.

By the time they turned, four more lay dead.

'Razane you're clear,' Sergei whispered.

Razane rolled out from behind her boulder. She could see the backs of two men. She fired. The men fell where they stood.

The rest ran back to the safety of their pickups, while Jane and Sergei continued to pick them off one by one.

Only one Taliban made it back.

'Bloody hell. It's like shooting fish in a barrel,' Sergei's voice shook.

'Fuck yes.' Jane's voice was equally shaky. 'This American gear's amazing!'

'Stop it!' Razane's rebuke was sharp. 'It's not over. Can anyone see the last man?'

'I can see his halo, very faintly,' Sergei said, 'he's down between the two trucks at the back.'

'I can't see anything. He's completely hidden,' Jane said.

Above them, the helicopter was getting closer.

'I think I know a way,' Sergei said suddenly.

'What?' Razane was looking up at the chopper.

'Jane you do it. Turn up your vision systems to the maximum. See if you spot him.'

'Hey this works,' Jane said. 'I can see the halo.'

'OK, Jane tell us if the image moves.' Razane said. 'Sergei cover me.' She ran to the Landcruiser. 'If he stands, I've got him. Sergei can you get behind the pickups.'

'Yes. Wait.' Sergei began to move from boulder to boulder. He was now level with the last row of pickup trucks. 'I'm nearly there.'

'The halo is getting more defined,' Jane whispered.

Suddenly the man stood and ran towards the back. Razane and Sergei both fired. He fell. 'Got him.' Sergei let out a deep sigh.

'Everyone, check the wounded,' Razane said. 'We don't want surprises.' She moved forward to inspect the bodies.

'Holy shit!' Sergei was examining something on the ground. 'Look what they were doing.'

Razane ran towards him. A partially assembled machine gun lay on its side in the snow.

'Phew, if they had put this together...' Razane left the rest unsaid.

'Hey the helicopter is getting closer,' Jane said.

They all glanced up. It sounded oddly familiar.

'Help me with this machine gun,' Razane said.

'Wait. There's something better.' Sergei opened a crate on the ground. 'Do you know what this is?'

'Of course. It's a Stinger.' Razane said with a triumphant note in her voice. 'Forget the machine gun.'

'What is it?' Jane ran over.

'A Stinger,' Razane repeated. 'Help me with it.'

'You found an anti-aircraft missile?' Jane whispered. 'Is it loaded?'

'Sergei, do you know how to use it?' Razane said.

'Yes, I trained with it, a long time ago,' Sergei said.

The helicopter shone a strong spotlight on the hut as it hovered above.

'Sergei, we need to move fast.'

'Help me then!' He hoisted the weapon onto his shoulder. 'I need the battery coolant unit. It looks like a car's oil filter.'

Jane looked in the box. 'I found three.'

'Hand me one.' Sergei said as he looked over the controls, hoping he remembered correctly. He took the device from Jane and inserted it into its receptacle and twisted it to the lock position.

Pressing the ON switch on the grip stock, he sighted the helicopter whose spotlight was moving in their direction.

His training came rushing back. He could see the helicopter in the rear reticle. He pressed the UNCAGE lever at the front of the launcher, all the while keeping the helicopter in the sight grooves. 'Here goes,' he said as he squeezed the trigger, keeping the launcher pointed at the chopper.

The missile shot out of the tube. At first, it appeared to stall, but it recovered as the main two-stage solid-fuel rocket engine ignited, straightened and accelerated towards its target at a breathtaking speed.

'Take cover.' Sergei pushed Razane and Jane to the ground next to the Landcruiser. 'Get underneath,' he shouted.

As they scrambled below the Landcruiser, a loud

explosion tore through the sky. It was many times brighter than the RPG. Night became day. The Stinger had found its target. Sergei stuck his head out. The helicopter had disintegrated into four large pieces and countless smaller ones, some were on fire. The rotor separated and plummeted into the valley beyond the hut. Debris rained down into the bowl. Sergei squeezed next to Razane and Jane. Something large thudded into the ground nearby, something small but fast struck the Landcruiser with a deafening bang.

The silence, when it came, was almost as extreme as the chaotic bedlam that preceded it.

They almost didn't hear the unmistakable throbbing of another helicopter. By the time Sergei squeezed out from under the Toyota it had begun landing and men were rappelling down ropes. A second helicopter appeared behind them, bathing the bowl in a strong spotlight.

'Fuck. Who are they?' Jane said.

'US Marines,' Sergei muttered angrily.

'Damn. What do we do?' Jane said.

'Nothing just yet,' Razane whispered. 'Leave the weapons on the ground.' She stood slowly, hands in the air.

'But they'll arrest you,' Jane said. 'We can't let that happen.'

'My love, we're surrounded and outgunned. Just put down your weapons.'

Sergei left his rifle on the ground and stood. Every fibre of his being wanted to hold on to his gun but Razane was right, they were outnumbered and outgunned. Jane too stood with her hands visible.

A PAINFUL CUT

Sergei removed his helmet. With the floodlights his night vision system was useless. There was no point anyway. They were surrounded by eight armed US Marines.

The second helicopter landed. Sebastian jumped out followed by Master Sergeant Andrei.

'We need to check on our friends in the hut,' Sergei stepped from behind the Landcruiser as the pair approached.

The blow hit him square in the jaw and reverberated through his skull. The world went dark as he fell against the Toyota's door.

Sergeant Andrei stood over him glowering. 'That's for what you did to my men.' He said as he aimed his pistol at Sergei. 'I should shoot you—'

The sergeant never registered the pop of metal as Jane pivoted on the Landcruiser's bonnet. By the time he heard her furious yell and turned to face her, all he saw was the studded pattern of her sole smashing into his face. It was too late. The crunch as his nose broke was the last sound he heard before he lost consciousness and he too slumped to the ground.

'For what you did to my man,' Jane said, not bothering to look down. Before anyone could recover, she had somersaulted behind Sebastian. She sprung upright, chopped her left arm up and outwards and forced his head into a choke-hold. Her other hand pressed her knife at his throat.

Jane's speed caught everyone by surprise. The two closest Marines ran forward and grabbed Jane from behind. Razane, who hadn't yet emerged from behind the Landcruiser, dropped to the ground and retrieved her rifle. As she stood, she fired two rounds in the air.

'Leave her alone,' Razane trained her rifle on the Marine

who had grabbed Jane's knife hand.

Jane tightened her grip around Sebastian's neck and dug the blade in harder. A few droplets of blood trickled down the sharp steel. Sebastian jerked and tried putting his arms up. 'Don't move,' Jane growled in his ear as she began to twist his neck

'No, stop!' Sebastian howled.

Jane struggled to maintain complete control over Sebastian but was losing the battle against the two Marines trying to free him.

She fought back with fierceness, channelling all her love for Sergei and Razane and all the anger towards those who wanted to take them away. Her muscles and tendons were ablaze. She didn't want to hurt Sebastian, but she would cut his head off before they pried the knife from her fingers. 'Tell your men to back off and drop their rifles... or you die.' Jane was breathing heavily.

Razane fired. One of the Marines holding onto Jane fell to the ground, blood oozing from his boot.

The crack of the bullet jolted Sergei into consciousness. His face was numb. His neck felt broken. A surge of anger energised him. He was not going down without a fight. No one was watching him. Trying to steady his hand, he grabbed the pistol from Sergeant Andrei's limp fingers. A Marine stepped forward and shouted. 'Freeze!' His rifle's muzzle inches from Sergei's face.

'You fucking freeze,' Sergei pivoted the pistol upwards.

His ears ringing, Sebastian yelled out. 'Stop!'

The remaining Marines now swarmed forward, weapons trained on the three. 'Stop Goddammit. It's a fuckin' order!' Sebastian was beside himself.

The Marine facing Sergei relaxed the grip on his rifle. The Marine fighting Jane let go of her arm and stepped back.

'You too, Razane and Sergei,' Sebastian said in a milder voice.

'First you!' Razane wasn't sure she had heard Sebastian properly. What had he called her?

'Put them down,' Sebastian shouted to his men. 'Put the

bloody weapons down.'

Razane exhaled as the Marines obeyed. She tried to make sense of the turn of events. She could see the ambivalence in the Marines' faces. She looked at Sergei who was trying to maintain his balance as he stood upright. He still held his pistol, but it was pointed to the ground.

'Everyone, ten steps back then we disarm,' Razane said.

'Do it,' Sebastian screamed. Jane had been steadily increasing the pressure on the knife. The cut on his throat burned red hot. Blood trickled down his sternum. He hated blood, especially his own.

The Marines stepped back.

'Now let me go… please.' Sebastian said to Jane. 'Fuck, it's hurting.'

'My love, let the man go,' Razane whispered in Jane's headset.

Jane couldn't do as Razane asked. Sebastian was the only leverage they had. If she let go, they were dead. She shook her head.

'Razane is no longer a person-of-interest,' Sebastian said, trying hard not to cry out in pain.

'Oh, how come?' Jane sounded unconvinced.

'We heard from our Kurdish contact an hour ago. Razane checks out.' He spoke fast.

'Fucking hell,' Sergei said. 'All this shit…'

'We could have told you from day one,' Jane said.

'My love, please let the man go.' Razane stepped forward.

Jane looked at Sergei, who nodded.

'OK,' Jane relaxed her grip and the pressure on the knife.

Sebastian heaved a sigh of relief and stepped away. He took out a tissue from his pocket and placed it on the cut.

'Sebastian, we need help with our friends,' Sergei said looking back. The smoke was drifting in their direction. 'They're in the hut.' Talking hurt his face. He touched his jaw. It felt puffed up and raw.

Sebastian had seen the burning hut as he landed. 'Who's

in there?'

'Major Hamdani and Captain Yousaf. Both ISI.' Sergei said as he tried to relieve the pressure in his neck. He noticed Jane and Razane's expressions. Their emotions mirrored his own. Now that the immediate danger was over, they dreaded what they would find.

Sebastian motioned to his men.

* *

The missile had struck the hut from above and had blown out the front wall which had collapsed the roof. A Marine used a fire extinguisher to douse the flames. The timber girders were piled on the floor.

They found Major Hamdani under one, dead, still holding his rifle. His head had been staved in. Sergei felt like throwing up. The major was a decent man. He didn't deserve to die like this. He put his arm around Jane who looked pale.

'I'm OK,' she said. 'Let's find Yousaf.'

'Shit yes,' Sergei said as he joined Razane and the rest trying to gain access to the rear of the hut. They found Yousaf, barely breathing, caught in a tiny space between the back wall and a fallen beam. His steel camp bed was twisted into an unrecognisable shape.

It took all their combined effort to free him.

'Take him, Sergeant Andrei and Chuck to the army hospital in Mianwali,' Sebastian said to one of the Marines. 'I'll call ahead for permission to fly into Pakistani Airspace.'

'You can't do that,' Jane said. 'Yousaf is wanted by the Pakistani authorities. Without Major Hamdani's protection, they'll court-martial him.'

'Not any more. The Pakistani army and ISI just arrested several ISI personnel including a colonel and several of their computer division. They're being charged with conspiracy to overthrow the government and treason.'

'What the fuck?' Jane said.

'You three come with me,' Sebastian said.

'We're not going anywhere except home.' Sergei said.

'Where do you want to take us?' Razane said.

'We're going to Kabul and then getting you on a flight back to Australia.'

'And that's it. You prance into our home, kidnap one of us, brutalise her and just wipe your hands clean,' Sergei said.

'Well, consider yourself fortunate. You're going home. We had an alternative plan.'

'Yeah, what?' Jane's brow furrowed in anger.

'The Middle East chief argued strongly for it. It can still be put into operation if you don't sign a confidentiality agreement and a legal waiver that you won't seek compensation.' Sebastian's voice hardened.

'Well, fuck you then. I was gonna give you Wafaa's address but probably won't. You arrogant shits...' Jane was beside herself with fury.

'What do you mean, the real...? How do you have that?' Sebastian raised his voice in a shout.

'The major told me before we left the hut. He went all strange and said he'd probably not make it back to Pakistan. I don't know why he said that, but he asked me to memorise it.'

'Jane, we need it. We have good intelligence Wafaa is planning a high casualty event,' Sebastian said. 'Do you want that on your conscience?'

'I don't trust the CIA or any intelligence agency. Get us back on a plane to Australia. You can have the address when we reach Melbourne,' Jane said.

Sebastian shook his head. 'We can't wait another twenty-four hours.'

'My love, can we please talk?' Razane stepped forward and placed a hand on Jane's shoulder. 'You too, my dearest,' she looked at Sergei.

Sebastian nodded at her and walked towards the helicopter.

Seeing him, the pilot spun up the turbine. 'What's the

story, chief?' he said as Sebastian climbed on board.

'They're having a conference. We wait for them.'

* *

Razane unbuckled Jane's helmet, then she took off her own. Their faces were frozen with fatigue and covered with grime.

Jane pulled her close. Then she reached out for Sergei. She was shaking her head, tears were running down her face. 'I can't forgive these bastards,' she moaned, 'for what they did to you.'

'My love,' Razane gently moved Jane's sweat-soaked hair out of her eyes. 'My love,' she touched Sergei tenderly on his swollen cheek. 'We're together again. We can go home and clean ourselves up and help each other heal. Let go of anger and hate towards them. While you're angry, you can't feel love.'

'But I do love you both, madly and deeply,' Jane kissed Razane on the lips. 'Of course, more than the anger and hate I feel towards them.' She smiled through her tears and kissed Sergei. Razane's logic was impossible to argue with. Suddenly the world shifted. The pain and grief was still there, but it felt bearable.

'So my love, what's your decision?' Razane kissed Jane's swollen eyes.

'You're right. You always are.' Jane smiled. 'I'll give him the address. I couldn't stand it if an innocent person dies because of me.'

'OK, now you can prepare for takeoff,' Sebastian said as he watched Jane flanked by Sergei and Razane walk towards the helicopter. She was stunning when she smiled. He fingered the cut on his throat and remembered what she'd done to Sergeant Andrei. He hadn't stood a chance. How could someone who looked so innocent, even angelic, be so lethal?

The pilot guessed his thoughts and grinned. 'Hell hath no fury, chief.'

'I think you should shut the fuck up,' Sebastian said, fingering the cut on his throat. He watched the three strap themselves in as the pilot engaged the rotor.

ISTANBUL

It was dark outside. Wafaa looked at the row of clocks on her wall. It would be 6:00 am in Melbourne. It was soon time to call Peter and to bring her jihad, begun so many years ago, to its glorious conclusion. Today would go down in history.

She got up from the table, grimacing at the pain in her lower back. Her kidney cancer had metastasised to her spine. She would soon be paralysed. This would be her final attack on the enemies of Islam. And she would die fighting like the storied Muslim *mujahideen* through the pages of history.

Her Apple Wallet contained her boarding pass for a flight to O'Hare Airport in Chicago. She would leave for the airport as soon as she had supervised the attack in Melbourne. The flight would take nearly twelve hours. She had enough time to drive from O'Hare Airport to Banff Tower in downtown Chicago and join her US team in their final stand. By then the world, reeling from the attacks in Melbourne and Birmingham, would have changed irrevocably.

The western way of life was on death's door. Like Osama had predicted, the remaining token freedoms enjoyed by much of the world would be curtailed. Citizens would be closely monitored with the concept of privacy and identity extinguished.

But, she was getting carried away, dreaming instead of doing. The attacks would not happen without her initiating and then guiding them.

She carried the dishes to the sink and poured herself a glass of tepid water. It was time for her pills, the worst part of cancer. She poured out the ten tablets and capsules in different sizes and colours. A laugh escaped her lips. How futile when she would not live to see another day? She let them fall into the swirling water and watched as they fell one by one into the drain.

It felt good to see them disappear.

Feeling lighter, she walked to the corner and sat on her prayer mat to organise her thoughts while she still could.

For the umpteenth time, she thought through the sequence of events in Melbourne. She would be the eye in the sky with Google Maps and the webcams that had views of the freeways into the central business district. Peter would be in one of the three penthouse apartments in downtown Melbourne. He would relay her orders to the teams and they would cut a swathe through Melbourne's suburbs. Peter would wait for them to reach the city centre before launching the final assault from his machine-gun nests atop the three towers.

She had built in sufficient redundancy to ensure that nothing could stop the carnage. The only variable was the death count. Even if a link failed, the rest were instructed to continue independently and kill till they themselves were killed.

The three chosen targets, Melbourne, Birmingham and Chicago were regional cities full of smug people who never thought the global war could reach them. They would find there was no place to hide from Allah's wrath.

* *

The white high roofed Ford Transit van had its hand brake pulled on tight as it sat parked on the steep incline outside 109 Esref Effendi Sokak. Eight men clad in bulletproof vests sat in the back studying the building layout on their Apple iPads.

'Memorise them,' Tom Hewitt, their team leader said. 'Team Alpha will deploy in exactly five minutes.' He looked at his watch. 'Team Beta is already in position. Remember ESCE time is seven minutes. And no shots to the head. We need a clear photo for the media.'

The men each nodded silently. ESCE stood for Enter, Secure, Capture and Exit. The target was an unarmed female. The job sounded easy and routine, but the critical goal was not. They had to ensure she transmitted nothing.

'One last time,' Tom ignored their groans as he moved the pointer. 'We enter here and here. Guillaume places the charge on the target's door. We wait for Team B to jam the wireless comms and deploy stun grenades. As soon as her door blows, we go.'

'I still don't get why we can't cut all comms to the apartment?' Armin spoke up. He was a big burly man with a bushy beard. He never spoke unless important questions were left unanswered.

'As I said before,' Tom sighed as he shook his head. 'The grown-ups tried, but the Turks wouldn't budge. Americans ain't flavour of the month in Turkey. Questions?'

In some countries, they would have used nerve gas to disable the target with little regard for collateral damage, but Langley hadn't been brave enough to try it in Turkey. Hopefully, they'd manage without it.

They had to prevent her from alerting her associates. It would be the speed of his men against her ability to press a button on her phone.

* *

A movement caught Wafaa's eye. Her computer screen had just turned on. It showed an image of the street below. A young couple strolled by arm-in-arm. A poodle on a leash strained as it sniffed the ground. It stopped in front of a large white van and lifted its hind legs.

'What a dirty animal,' she muttered as she pondered the Ford van. It bore no signage and hadn't moved for the last half an hour which was odd. She had never seen it on the street before and it was past the time for deliveries. So what was it doing there?

She got up from the floor and walked to her computer. Maximising the security camera feed window, she studied the van carefully. It looked like a tradesman's van but had no lettering on the side. Nothing on it showed its purpose. There was something odd about the way it moved, rocking ever so slightly on its suspension. Was someone inside? The front cabin was empty, which meant someone was in the back. The realisation smacked her in the gut. She was under surveillance. What irony, the enemy had tracked her down during her final hours on this earth.

She rapidly went over last week's events. Major Amjad had called a few times. Maybe he was under surveillance. It meant she had to work fast. She opened WhatsApp on her smartphone. It wasn't working. She checked her WiFi signal. It had zero bars. She opened her connections app on the phone. Normally she could see between eight and ten wireless networks, hers and those of her neighbours. There were none. She double-checked to make sure her phone's WiFi was turned on. It was. She walked over to her router. It was connected to the Internet which made sense because her PC which was connected with a cable was receiving a signal. That was how she saw the camera feed. But the router wasn't sending a WiFi signal or maybe her phone was not receiving it.

Back at her computer, she saw shadowy figures emerge from the van. She clicked her other camera feeds. A second van on the opposite side of the street disgorged a group of similarly attired men.

They were after her. It was the moment of truth.

Fighting rising panic, she turned off WiFi on her phone hoping it would connect to Turkcell, Turkey's largest mobile phone network. It had never not worked but now nothing showed. She scanned for other mobile networks. Nothing. With shaking hands, she restarted her phone. The screen went dead as it began the reboot process.

The phone screen was coming to life. Samsung and Turkcell logos followed each other. It was the latest model, the world's fastest phone but her time had slowed and it felt almost interminably slow. It seemed ages by the time her home screen appeared. Her apps arranged themselves. It took another long second to confirm there was no mobile coverage.

As she fought through the haze she remembered, she also had WhatsApp on her PC. How stupid to forget.

The sound of breaking glass was followed by a loud compressive poof that hurt her temples. Her ears were ringing.

Shaking all over, she sat at the keyboard and clicked on WhatsApp. Peter's name was at the top. The world had shrunk to her screen. Everything else had gone a greyish-black. She pressed on Peter's name and typed. 'Begin now!' She pressed ENTER. She moved the mouse to the top of the screen and clicked on the phone symbol.

Hands grabbed her arm. Another pulled her away from the screen.

'The PC is secure,' a baby-faced man triumphantly held up a blue LAN cable he had ripped out of the back.

Wafaa was on the floor. Someone kneeled on her chest. A gun was pressed against her forehead. Had she pressed ENTER before baby-face ripped the cable? Not knowing made it hard for her to breathe.

* *

Alpha team's work was done. Forensics moved in. They were fortunate the suspect's smartphone and laptop were unlocked. It made their job easy. They didn't stop with those devices. Everything, including the router, external hard drives, thumb drives and optical disks were bagged.

Before Forensics had completed their job, Wafaa had been handcuffed, gagged and hooded and transported in the back of the van to a waiting C-130 Hercules bound for the United States.

EPILOGUE

Sergei reached over and turned off the alarm. He'd fallen asleep only an hour ago. It was their first night together in a safe place and they had to make the best of it. They'd made love into the small hours and had fallen asleep spent and exhausted but happy beyond measure. Razane's black hair was fanned out across her pillow as she lay nestled in his arms, her wrists still bruised and black were folded against his chest. Jane's feet were on the pillow next to Razane's head. She had got a pedicure and her red nail polish glinted in the early morning sun. They both embodied the perfect human, empathy, love and grace juxtaposed with strength of will and character. He had so much to live up to and live for. The desire to remain worthy of them would keep him sharp.

His eyes opened. It was later but still early. The sun was shining in the room making it warm. They had forgotten to lower the blinds. A strong pulsating sound reverberated through the house. It was what had woken him. Sleep vanished. Helicopters? Was he still dreaming? He couldn't be. Everything seemed too real. The sun too warm, Razane and Jane too soft.

He jumped out of bed and rushed outside just in time to see a trio of three army Blackhawks disappear behind the hill north of their property. He smiled as he heaved a sigh of relief. They had enough excitement to last a lifetime. He didn't want to see another military helicopter or a gun as long as he lived.

Someone slipped an arm around his waist. He turned his head to the left. It was Jane. She stood on the deck in her bare feet, dressed only in a white cotton T-shirt. He smiled. 'The sound of helicopters set my pulse racing.'

'Mine too,' she said. 'I wonder what they're here for. I've never ever seen three together.'

Razane came out yawning. 'Did I hear helicopters or was I dreaming?' She leaned against Sergei and yawned again.

Sergei opened his arms and pulled them both closer. They waited a while but saw and heard nothing further.

While they were preparing brunch, they heard gunshots in the distance. It wasn't an unusual sound out in the country among farms. But there was something odd about them. Hearing them so soon after the helicopters made them wonder. Were the helicopters and gunshots linked? All three were exhausted and traumatised. Guns and helicopters were the last thing they wanted to talk about. Thankfully, the episode soon dropped from their minds.

* *

Thick cumulonimbus clouds and a southerly wind change had brought a welcome cool change. Razane lay on the settee out on their deck and watched the dark clouds roll in as she sipped the cool peach kombucha. The smells of the sizzling roast on the barbecue were making her hungry.

'Another hour to go.' Sergei guessed her thoughts. The bruise on his face made him look ever more dashing than normal. 'I should have put it on earlier but we woke so late.'

'It's OK,' she said as she rolled over and kissed him on the chest. 'I can wait. How's the book?'

Sergei put down his e-reader and kissed her forehead. 'I don't know.' His lips found hers. 'The plot's a bit unrealistic,' he said as they came up for air.

'What just happened to us sounds like an unrealistic plot,' Razane said. 'No one would ever believe it if we told them.'

Sergei stroked her hair. He looked at Jane, who lay beside Razane. 'Poor sweetheart's still asleep.' He leaned over Razane and kissed Jane gently.

A large raindrop submerged his eye. It felt pleasant, like a kiss from the heavens. He blinked it away. Thunder rumbled in the distance. Lightning forked into a faraway paddock. The rain felt cool. Within seconds it became a downpour.

They ran inside, laughing. The six o'clock news had just started. Razane turned up the volume and froze.

'Police raided several properties on Melbourne's outskirts as part of a terror investigation,' the newsreader said. 'Sources say they uncovered a large cache of prohibited weapons. Investigators believe they were in advanced stages of planning and their operation was imminent.'

Sergei and Jane sat beside her, dumbfounded.

Jane was the first to speak. 'That must be what those helicopters and the shooting were about. That's near us somewhere. Do you think...?'

'You mean linked to Wafaa. No!' Sergei said. 'Now that... would be totally bizarre.'

'It would make our story sound even more unrealistic,' Razane said as she pulled the two people who mattered the most to her closer. 'I'm the luckiest person... in the world.'

'We all are.'

"I want to see you.
Know your voice.
Recognise you when you
first come 'round the corner.

Sense your scent when I come
into a room you've just left.

Know the lift of your heel,
the glide of your foot.

Become familiar with the way
you purse your lips
then let them part,

just the slightest bit,
when I lean in to your space
and kiss you.

I want to know the joy
of how you whisper
"more."

— Rumi

GLOSSARY

Akhoond: Imam, religious leader

Al-ukht-ul-akbari: Bigger sister

Amir-ul-Momineen: Supreme leader

Amreeka: America / USA

Amreeki: American

Asalam Aleikum: Peace be with you

Bahin Chodd: Sister fucker

Bahut: A lot of

Baji: Elder sister. Term of respect for an older woman

Baju Seluar: Malay for shirt and pants

Beita: Child or son, depending on context

Degwalah: A cook who uses a deg, a large cauldron

Fatafat: Quickly or hurry

Gandu: Literally it means a person receptive to anal sex; but it is often used as banter between friends

Haram Khor: Corrupt person

Haramzada: Illegitimate Child, bastard

Insha`Allah: God willing

Jannah: Heaven (in Arabic)

Karo: Do

Loya Jirga: Gathering of Afghani elders to decide important legal matters

Maddarchhod: Motherfucker

Maghreb: Sunset

Ma'shallah: God has willed it, used in a positive sense.

Maulana: Muslim priest

Mujahideen: Holy warrior

Roshandan: Rectangular windows high up on a wall, usually near the ceiling

Selamat pagi: Good morning

Shaheed: Martyr

Shalwar Kameez: A loose shirt worn over baggy pants held up with a drawstring

Shukria: Thanks

Tuan: Lord, sir

Yaar: Friend or lover, depending on context

Ya Allah: Oh God

Ya hawla wala quwwata illa billah: There is no power nor strength except by Allah

www.ingramcontent.com/pod-product-compliance
Lightning Source LLC
Chambersburg PA
CBHW020537120726
47903CB00001B/15